This is a story of love, and commitment, and life and family

GIFTS NO BOWS

IN LOVING MEMORY of KENNY HENNINGER

VIETNAM 1969

D1565564

1

Mid 1990's

The jet hit the runway as though fixed to tunnel into the ground. My thoughts cleared to hear the flight attendant announce our landing, "We have landed at Cleveland Hopkin's International Airport. Local Cleveland, Ohio time is I:45 p.m."

I was fairly certain most of us had figured the landing part out! I was back home for the first time in over twenty years. After retrieving my luggage, I settled into a cab, and asked my cab driver, "Could we avoid freeways as we head to Bay Village? The higher fare will be fine."

"Sure can. Don't worry, no fare change. You said the Holsten Inn, Bay Village, right?"

"That's right. Thanks." When Bette Stein called about Kate O'Malley's death, she informed me I'd have a reservation at this old inn she and her husband own. Looking out the cab window I thought, *I've known Bette since we were young children. Back then she was called MaryElizabeth, MaryElizabeth Lotis, and we were friends but not close friends. Karen Fry and Lindsey O'Malley were and always will be my dearest friends, my sisters. I haven't seen them for so long. When she called, Bette said neither one will be at the funeral. It was a good decision, a few months ago, making sure Bette had my unlisted number. I told her not to give it to anyone.*

I smiled a bit as we drove passed the drive-in movie theater where our family used to go and where we double dated with our boyfriends. Only the arched entrance was left with a sign posting the property for sale. Driving further and looking where Brice and Frank Fry's, Karen's dad and uncle's, furniture store used to be I saw a bookstore and coffee shop. Minutes later we passed where I thought Art O'Malley's, Lindsey's dad's, office had ar business here, and it looked like more stores would be built soon. I realized if I was blind folded and dropped off here, I wouldn't know where I was. I wondered if many people wouldn't recognize towns where they grew up.

I'd been lost in rambling thoughts when I glanced in the rearview mirror and saw my cab driver smiling as we moved onto Detroit Road in Westlake. Whatever I'd been thinking about vanished as I noticed that most of the

2

spacious yards and small houses that used to be along here were gone, replaced by office buildings, apartments, condo's, and nursing homes. Then a familiar site caught my eyes, a sign that had been in place forever, "White Oaks Restaurant established 1928." We turned down Cahoon Road and slowed down a bit to navigate the curves leading toward the White Oaks. As we passed I saw cars still filling the parking lot.

We crossed the old Nickel Plate Railroad Tracks and entered Bay Village, the village where Karen, Lindsey, and I, and Bette grew up. Immediately turning toward Dover Center Rd, I remembered the old one lane bridge and expected my cab to either stop or speed up. We kept the same pace as the old bridge over Cahoon Creek was gone, replaced with a wider road. We passed Zipp Manufacturing next to the tracks and turned onto Dover Center. I saw a new ice cream store replacing Sell's Ice Cream and Candy Shop. I didn't see Rozie's Pizza, Keever's Delicatessen, or Hap's Gas Station.

Calling out to my driver I asked, "Could you please turn left on Wolf Road passed the shopping center, and the high school?" I remembered that Kate told me our high school is now a middle school. "Well, I guess it's the middle school, now. I'll pay the extra fare." I saw Ernie Olchon's Gas Station as I asked, and it had a new name. Bay City Hall still looked majestic.

"Certainly we can. I'm enjoying this. It's nice not to be in a rush. It's beautiful here with all of these big trees. The leaves still have color." He turned into the shopping center parking lot. The names of a lot of the stores from the 1950's and '60's entered my mind as I noticed that Avellone's, Grebe's Delicatessen, Nichol's 5 &10, Larry's Beauty Salon, James Hardware, Houk's and Barth's Meat Market, Kroger's, and Hough Bakery were no longer there. I did see Bay Barber Shop, Andy's Shoe Repair, Bay Lanes Bowling Alley, and the shoe store survived. We passed a drug store and a hardware store having new names, and I noticed a new hair salon. Several stores were new to me, but the shopping center still looked the same.

Leaving the parking lot, I saw the Bayway Cabin quickly remembering girl scout meetings, dances, and the

3

fun we had inside. Stopping for a red light at Cahoon Road, there stood our old high school, now Bay Middle School, anchoring the entire southwest block. My heart lightened as I watched youngsters walking out of their middle school and crossing the street. Many were talking, some were laughing, and some were just in a hurry to get home. I smiled for a second remembering the excitement of being released from school's confinement into open-air freedom.

Just before the light turned green, I called out, again, "Hello, again. Could we turn right toward the lake and then left toward Huntington Park, please? Then you can drop me off at the inn, I promise!" He grinned as he made the turn. First thing, I noticed the snow fence in place where the ice skating ponds soon would be filled. Seeing the old fire station and the Bay Village Community House across the street, old images that decades had blurred, focused clearly. I pictured Lindsey with Bobby, Karen with Jeff, and Jimmy with me walking across the grass on our way to dance inside the old Community House. Looking back at the ice skating ponds, I thought about the night Bobby and Jeff gave my best friends their I D bracelets.

The lake was calm as we turned toward the park passed the site of the Bay Gun Club onto the bridge over Porter Creek where the creek's water neared the lake. We turned into the park. Glancing at the Huntington Playhouse, we drove down the hill that used to close for sledding when huge lake effect snow falls turned Bay Village into a winter wonderland. I looked at the giant trees that were everywhere and saw yellow, red, and gold leaves falling like a snowfall. We drove very slowly. In his rear view window I caught another glimpse of my smiling driver. He parked on the side of the street and put the front windows down. Turning to look at me, he asked if stopping for a minute was ok and added, "If you're cold, I'll put the windows right up. I love the smell of burning leaves in the fall. Brings my old dad to mind."

"No, I'm fine. It's wonderful," I replied while thinking, *It brings my dad to mind, too.* We both enjoyed peaceful moments watching the colorful leaves float silently to the ground while noticing the faint aroma of burnt leaves.

4

Gazing at this sight, it looked the same as it had 40-45 years ago. Momentarily all of those years vanished.

Too soon he closed the windows and in seconds we were passing old Glenview Elementary School heading down Wolf Road. We passed our old high school, the shopping center, again, and turned on Dover Center Road toward the lake. Moving passed the front of City Hall, then the tennis courts, and baseball fields; we turned right onto Lake Road nearing the Holsten Inn. Driving closer, it looked beautiful. The new addition blended right in. The hotel was still painted white with dark blue shutters at each window. Flower boxes beneath the windows in front held mums as in all past autumns. My driver stopped his cab near the inn's front doors, turned to me and said, "No extra fare. Welcome home."

For a second I wondered how he knew and quickly thought, *It's obvious.* "Thank you." I smiled and paid him with a huge tip. Smiling back, he thanked me very much and added, "Enjoyed it."

A bell hop quickly opened my door and reached for my hand. He carried my suitcases up the eight, wide, curved steps leading to the lobby doors. I followed him seeing large flower pots holding more mums realizing in a few days the mums would be replaced with Christmas flowers. Walking past the rocking chairs on the veranda through the large doors into the lobby, my blue eyes captured the overstuffed chairs and the crackling flames in the large fireplace. I looked at beautiful flower arrangements on buffets along with tea sandwiches, pastries, fruit plates, vegetable plates, cheese plates, tea and coffee carafes, and an assortment of wines and beers. I heard soft conversation along with soft music, and I saw relaxed faces.

The doors into the dinning room were open. Standing still for a moment, memories of past celebrations and quiet memorials held inside this room rolled through my mind, and long gone faces filled my eyes. I stood for a while. Then someone handed me my room key and told me my suitcases were already in my room. I asked if Bette Stein was at the inn and was told she just left for the day.

My room was perfect. Everything was arranged with comfort in mind. I had a beautiful view of Lake Erie through doors that led to a balcony. Looking at the lake and settling into the most comfortable chair ever, I thought, *Bette, you sure know what you're doing. You've made the Holsten Inn even better.*I needed to shower and change clothes for the evening's visitation at the funeral home. *I'll just sit here for five minutes, and then I'll get moving,* I reasoned. Snuggling into the feather down cushions, thoughts of Kate filled my mind, *God Bless you, Kate. I'm so grateful for you. I'm sorry I let you down these many years. How could I not have come home, even once, in all of these years? You were always here for me. I love you. I'm glad you came to stay with me ten years ago, gosh, ten years.*

My last thought before falling asleep. Damn chair.

Father Tom Brown stood ready to say Kate's Funeral Mass in the small stone chapel located on the side of St. Joseph's Church. I loved this chapel when we were growing up. On this morning the twenty filled pews made the chapel the perfect place for Kate. Standing in my pew I turned to see Father Tom as the arched wood doors closed, our singing began, and he followed behind her casket. Singing "Here I Am Lord," I remembered Kate loved this hymn. We finished singing, and bright sunshine lit the stained glass windows. A warm glow filled the chapel while we remained standing, and Father began the opening prayers. In California and now in Portland my family and I attended an Episcopal Church. But "once a Catholic always a Catholic," the prayers for Kate's Mass came to my lips.

His homily was sweet and personal. He reminisced about the day he met her. Thanking God, he spoke of her loving friendship that had blessed him all of the years he's been at St. Joseph Parish. "I can't imagine this Thanksgiving arriving so soon without Kate. God Bless all of us missing loved ones during the holiday's." Father paused several seconds finally saying Kate's full name, "Emily Katelyn O'Malley. Not many of you sitting here knew her first name was Emily. She told me she was named after her own mother. Her mom called her Kate and that was that." Father Tom continued by mentioning a few of the many kind deeds she'd done throughout her life. Mostly he reminisced how much she loved her family. With a smile he told us about the wonderful weeks Kate, Lindsey, and Karen shared here just months ago. He let us know that Lindsey and Karen understood she did not want them traveling back for her funeral stating that her Mass was being recorded for them. He looked directly at me and said, "Most of you here today know how much Kate will always love her daughters, Lindsey, Samantha, and Karen. Along with Art, they filled her life."

Father Tom concluded her Mass. While the Chapel bells rang, we were handed a rose as we followed her casket and walked to St. Joseph Cemetery located behind the large Church. We breathed in the chilly late autumn

7

air, and I noticed the faintest scent of burnt leaves as final prayers were said. Everyone passed by Kate and placed a rose on her casket. As I placed mine, Father's face lit up, "Samantha, I was so relieved when I saw you at Mass. I was worried when I didn't see you at the funeral home last night." We hugged.

I thought about that damn chair. "I'm sorry I wasn't there. I've missed you and Kate so much." Tears spilled from my eyes.

"You know she wouldn't want tears, Sammy. Her life was full. She loved you, Karen, and Lindsey forever. Karen and two of her grandchildren stayed with Kate just two weeks ago. They had a wonderful time. I'll see you in a few minutes at the luncheon." Then he excitedly added, "Let's have dinner later. I want to hear how you're doing, fill you in on Lindsey and Karen, and tell you about Kate. We'll be able to relax at dinner."

You don't want to hear how I'm doing, I thought. I did want to know about Lindsey, Karen, and him, and certainly about Kate. "Father Tom, I would love that. I'm going to stay here for a few minutes. Call me at the Holsten Inn later to tell me when you can go. I'd love to have dinner at the White Oaks, if you would like that." I smiled at him having no intention of attending the luncheon taking place in the Church Hall.

He looked at me with that same, *I know what's going on in that brain of yours*, expression he used when we were growing up. "Try to come to the luncheon. Otherwise, I'll call you at the inn later to let you know the time. The White Oaks sounds great."

"Thanks. See you soon." We hugged, again. A man greeted him, and they left for the luncheon.

Alone now, feeling slightly tired and a tad dizzy, I sat down on the grass near Kate. *That's better,* I thought. I stared at all of the flowers. *I bet you want me to take a few flowers to my parents' graves, and Grand's, and -* I heard the school bell.

A distance away St. Joseph School's noon recess bell echoed giving way to the sound of youthful energy. I smiled at the sounds and, again, noticed a hint of smoky autumn air. A place in my heart that had been still for years stirred as I looked toward the school. *Bobby, Jeff,*

Jimmy, Lindsey, Karen, and I, and Bette played on this playground. How many years ago? Fifty? Lord, yes, almost fifty. The schedule and rhythm of those days repeated through those years as though nothing would ever be different. We wanted to grow up, but somehow the familiar pattern of those days: get up, go to school, play at recess, go home, chores, play, eat dinner, homework, go to bed; get up, go to school, play at recess; fall, winter, spring; fall, winter, spring. It seemed this part of our lives had been going on and would go on forever.

Thoughts and memories filled a locked place in my heart, and words that were a tad late spilled from my lips, "Kate, you are the very best thing that ever happened to me. You still fill my heart. I thought I'd always have you here." I searched my pocket for a Kleenex as I sat and cried.

Finally getting myself under a little control, I slowly stood up. It took a few seconds. The cold ground was damp and straightening my legs and back hurt a bit. I moved a few slow steps to touch her casket. Softly I said, "I'm sorry I let you down. You were always here for me, for all of us, and I left you alone these years. When we needed, you took over for our parents, who couldn't figure out their own lives. You did it easily, gracefully, lovingly. How could I let all of these years pass by without you?"

"Everything in my life is a mess, Kate. I should have confided in you." My tears kept coming. "I wish I could hug you and feel your arms keep me safe. I need you."

I stopped talking, got another Kleenex, resolutely wiped my eyes and nose, then said, "What am I doing feeling sorry for myself? I should be thinking about you, how you feel. Gosh, you're in Heaven now. I believe there's Heaven, and Linds absolutely believes. I bet Art is so happy you're with him. Have you seen my mom and dad? Are you all together, you, Grand, Brice, and Frank? Maybe you found" Suddenly I heard a voice behind me.

"I hope they're together, too. Although, maybe you shouldn't be talking with Kate as though you're expecting an answer!"

Startled for a second, I still recognized his voice. I turned and saw Jim's face looking gentle, not so indifferent. I took a wobbly step toward him, and his arms

9

saved me from stumbling. Then I cried in his arms until his sweater got soggy. The kind of crying where what was coming out of my eyes and nose got all mixed up.

I heard, "It's ok. Let it all out. Don't give a thought about my wool sweater shrinking."

Thinking what he said was a little funny, I got it under control and looked at him.

With a horrified expression he responded, "Oh Lord, you're a mess." He handed me a tissue from his pocket.

I couldn't answer. I felt dizzy and sick, a feeling that had become much too familiar. I felt air escaping my lungs, and I knew there wasn't another breath coming. I thought, *I can't breathe.* Then everything was gone.

"Hey, Samantha, what's wrong? Hey, are you all right? Oh Lord!" Jim hurriedly spoke as he realized her legs were buckling, and he held her from falling. Leaning her back to get a look at her face and seeing her eyes were closed he thought, *She's passed out.* He laid her down on the ground to make sure she was breathing and felt for a pulse. She had one. "Ok, you're breathing, and you're not choking, and I don't have my stupid cellular phone with me." He picked her up and started running toward the rectory. "I've been running about five miles, five times a week, Sammy. This should be a piece of cake." He took some breaths and continued talking to her, "You know, the air is a little smoky. Maybe it got to you." He stopped running and walked. "A cool towel on your face and a little water will fix you up." He inhaled and exhaled a few times and sounded winded. "We're almost there. You know, I should start carrying some weights when I run." He instantly knew that was a dumb thing to say. "You're light, Sam, I'm not implying anything. Ok, we're here," catching his breath, struggling a little, and adding, "I just need to kick this door a few times. Someone will hear and open it."

Father Tom was about to go out the side door, back to Kate's Luncheon, when he heard the commotion at the front door. "I'm coming. Hold on a second." *The child who's kicking my freshly painted door is in big trouble,* he thought. Opening the door, he was pushed out of the way.

Jim rushed in and laid Samantha on the sofa. "Get a damp cloth and a glass of water. And call 911." A throw was on the sofa, and he covered her.

Father Tom immediately got the cloth and water. "What's happened to her? I'll call for an ambulance." He heard her speak and stopped just as he turned toward the rectory kitchen to use the phone.

"No! No ambulance," she said while looking around the room. Her mind suggested, *Think, just think.* She saw them watching her. "Where are we?"

"We were talking, and you fainted or something while at the cemetery. We're in the rectory," Jim answered.

11

"Oh," Still looking all around she added, "it looks different. It's hot in here."

"I don't know why I covered you. You've got your coat on. We need to get your coat off. Here, let me help you."

Moving slowly, she sat up and with help got her coat off. She drank some water and tried to put in order the space of time between Kate's Mass and sitting here in the rectory. The silence became awkward, and she noticed them staring at her.

My God, no wonder I was able to run while carrying her. There's nothing to her. She's way too thin. "Sam, what's going on?"

Indignantly she answered, "There's nothing going on. Why are you staring at me?" She looked down and then remembered the crying and her nose. She touched her face. *I must look awful.* Her expression softened. "Jimmy, I'm sorry. I need to use the bathroom." She looked around, again. "This is the same rectory from when we were kids, right?"

Father Tom smiled while looking at them. "It's the same place, just remodeled."

"Is the bathroom in the same place?"

Jim answered, "No, it's all different. I'll show you. It's this way. Are you sure you're all right? I can get Gina, the parish secretary, to help you. She's here in the office."

Arriving at the bathroom door she answered, "I'm fine, Jimmy, really, I'm good."

Back in the rectory living room Jim said to his closest friend, "Something's going on with her. She's way too thin. God, I hope she doesn't have cancer. My Liz lost so much weight, remember?"

"Now hold on. You don't need to go there. You're putting the 'horse in front of the cart."

"That's not right," Jim's attention turned to the incorrect wording of the idiom.

"Well, of course it isn't! You can't make such quick assumptions about Sam's health."

Jim irritatedly answered, "No, I mean what you just said. The horse should be in front of the cart. You should have said, 'The cart in front of, never mind." He resumed talking about Samantha. "She passed out or fainted at the cemetery less than fifteen minutes ago. That isn't normal. We can see her weight isn't a healthy weight."

"The last time Kate and I had dinner together, she mentioned she was worried about Sammy." He looked out the window as mentioning Kate changed his thoughts. "I already miss her. She's been part of my life since the beginning of my priesthood. Somehow she always understood what everyone needed. If she were here right now, she'd be helping her Sammy."

He looked at Jim and got back to the present situation. "Samantha must be fine. Her family wouldn't have let her travel alone if anything was wrong. We've met her husband, Rob. He definitely 'makes the shots' in their family. He wouldn't have let her come all this way if she were ill."

Oh God, Jim thought. "You mean he 'calls the shots' in their family. I guess you're right. He wouldn't let her travel alone if she were ill."

Father Tom turned away to smile and then looked back at Jim. They both flinched as they heard a loud thud. They rushed to the bathroom and found Samantha on the floor. Jim called 911. She was still unconscious when the paramedics arrived. Tom and Jim hadn't moved her. Jim made sure that she was breathing, but he'd been afraid to move her. She had a large bump on her forehead.

Only a few minutes passed when everyone in the rectory knew Samantha was conscious, again. She repeatedly yelled, "Leave me alone. Stop! I do not need any help. Please stop, I'm fine. No hospital!"

At first the paramedics tried to calm her. When that didn't work, they ignored her demands. They continued to help her, strapped her onto a gurney, and wheeled her out into the ambulance.

Father Tom and Jim walked beside the gurney and told her they would meet her in the hospital.

13

Standing at the curb in front of his rectory, Tom inhaled as he opened the passenger door to Jim's car and got in saying, "What a week this has been. One minute I'm stepping into Kate's kitchen ready to enjoy one of her delicious dinners, and the next minute I'm giving her Funeral Mass. And now, after not seeing Samantha in so many years, we're following an ambulance holding her inside."

Jim quietly said, "I just can't get over how thin she is. I should have realized something was wrong. I was actually able to run while carrying her. I used to carry Liz when she became so sick, and Liz hardly weighed a hundred pounds. Carrying Samantha, it was the same."

"I told you not to go there. Just hold on. We're on our way to the hospital. Let the doctors sort this out. We'll stay with her. When we know what's happened to her, we'll call her family. Do you remember her daughter's name?"

"I can't remember it right now. It'll come to me." They arrived at the emergency parking lot, parked, and hurried through the emergency room doors.

Sandy, the nurse on duty, recognized Father Tom and happily greeted him. "Hi Father, they told me you were coming. You're here for Samantha Green. She's conscious, and Dr. Jameson is examining her." She looked at her chart. "I just have a few questions I hope you can answer, then I'll take you to Mrs. Green."

He thanked her and offered, "We've known her for over fifty years. We're as close as family. Jim went to grade school at St. Joseph's and was in her class way over fifty years ago. They were dear friends all through high school and college."

He looked at Jim and Sandy. "I'm sorry, Sandy. This is Jim Peterson. Sandy, I've forgotten your last name."

"It's Jones."

"Jim, meet Sandy Jones."

"I'm glad to meet you, Sandy," he smiled and glanced at Tom, "and it's not fifty years, yet."

She asked her questions, and quickly realized neither one knew much about Mrs. Green. They didn't know her address, phone number, anything about her health, let alone her medical history. "Well, you two are a bundle of information. Not to worry. Dr. Jameson will get her medical history directly from her. Tell me what happened earlier today to Mrs. Green."

Jim explained as Sandy led them down the hall in front of Samantha's examination room. She told them the doctor would be finished soon and returned down the hall.

While they waited Father Tom attempted to apologize, "Hey Jim, that way over fifty years comment, I only meant to show how long we've known Sam. You and I seem like contemporaries. You've been principal at St. Joseph's for over fifteen years. I don't remember how many years you taught at St. Joe's after graduating from college, and you were vice principal at another school in-between. But when we met, you were just a kid in third or fourth grade, and I was in my first years of priesthood. It seems a long time ago, now. Soon I'll be hearing about my jubilee celebration."

"For sure you will, and it was fourth grade. Lindsey, Kate, and Art had just moved here."

"Yes, I was about eighteen months into my priesthood when I was assigned to St. Joseph's. I'd been here a little over a year when Kate and Art moved in. That terrible murder had occurred. Bay Village became very well known. It was so tragic. Well, we definitely weren't contemporaries then. Father Aurther was about to retire. Gosh, he was eighty-two. I'm getting darn close to that age. Yikes! Anyhow, I was 'yellow behind the ears' as they say, preparing to become the new Pastor. Kate welcomed me into her family all of those years ago. She's been the dearest friend ever since."

Another slaughtered idiom Jim thought and said, "It's wet behind the ears.' And you're right, I am considerably younger than you even if it is hard to tell at this point. You don't seem to age at all. It was Marilyn Sheppard who was murdered and almost everyone thought her husband, Dr. Sam Sheppard, killed her."

With a slight smile Tom thought, *messing up those old sayings always gets his mind off troubling things. Although, I really thought it was "green behind the ears."*

15

Oh, well, "Yes, Jim, 'wet behind the ears' and I didn't forget their names."

"My parents never thought Dr. Sheppard was guilty. A lot of people thought he wasn't. Anyway, Sammy, Bette, Jeff, Karen, Lindsey, Bobby, and I were just kids. I'm sure attending school at St. Joe's shielded us a bit from everything that was happening." Jim added, "I haven't thought about our childhood for a long time. I mean really thought about Bobby and Lindsey, Jeff and Karen, and Sammy and," he didn't finish. "Remember Jeff? I wonder how he's doing. Once out of high school, I never saw him again. We'd been close friends. He's never come back. He could be dead!"

"Let's try to be a little optimistic."

The door to Samantha's examination room opened wide. A doctor holding a chart walked directly to Father Tom and Jim. "Hello, Father. I'm a member of St. Joe's Parish."

"Yes, I recognize you. You're Dr. Jameson." They shook hands.

Jim also shook hands and introduced himself to the doctor, "Jim Peterson."

Dr. Jameson said, "Mr. Peterson, I understand you were with Mrs. Green when she fainted."

"The first time, when she fainted at the cemetery, I was with her. I carried her to the rectory."

"Ok, now I understand. Then she passed out, again, while in the bathroom at the rectory. Truthfully, she hasn't been forthcoming about what happened today or about her medical history."

From her bed in the examination room, Samantha heard Dr. Jameson and made a face. She'd overheard Jim mention their childhood together, too.

"How are you related to her? She said you're family," the doctor continued.

Father Tom answered, "We've known her since she was a child. While she was growing up, I was very close with her mother and father. Along with two other families, Samantha, her parents, and I became one family. We had dinner together once a week, spent many holidays together, and had celebrations together. We were as important to one and other and as close as family." He

16

looked at Jim a moment, "She left Bay Village after her college graduation, moved to the West Coast, and has lived there with her husband and daughter ever since. It's been years since we've spent time together. She returned here yesterday to attend her mother's funeral."

Jim glanced at Tom. In her room, Samantha's expression softened.

Dr. Jameson looked surprised. "I misunderstood. I didn't realize it was her mother's funeral. Her husband and daughter didn't attend?" He didn't give Tom or Jim the chance to respond. "Families can be difficult at times." He kept talking, "Could you contact her husband? Mrs. Green is very pleasant but evasive about her health. While I was examining her, she passed out again. I don't want her discharged from the hospital yet." He seemed slightly annoyed and added, "She won't sign the consent forms. She doesn't remember her home phone number. She's not sure about her insurance. She doesn't have her purse here, and she really wants to leave. Can you talk with her and convince her to consent? Here's my card. I'll be in the hospital another hour. The consent for treatment form is on the stand beside her bed."

Samantha heard everything and thought, *Of course I want out of here. I'm not signing anything.*

Jim looked at the doctor and said, "She'll sign." He walked into her room with Father Tom right behind.

She was sitting up in bed with a smile plastered on her face, *If you think I'm signing a consent form, you've got another thought coming.* "Hi," she said.

"Why, look at you! You look ready to get the heck out of here," Jim said while thinking, *She looks like hell. Something awful must be going on.* "You've got to be exhausted after traveling all the way from Portland yesterday. Being so darn tired can cause all kinds of problems. It's probably the reason you've passed out three or four times in the last few hours, but you do look great."

She kept her smile going, although not quite as confidently, and she shifted in her bed just a tad.

Father Tom thought, *Ok, we all look ducky. How is this conversation ever going to get to signing a consent form?*

Jim continued, "Sammy, I know losing Kate is a heartache. Do you remember when you met her? So many years have flown by. You haven't been back home, back here, in many years. I bet you wish you could have been with her just one more time. She loved you."

Samantha's smile slipped away.

"If Kate was sitting here with you right now, she'd be worried about you. You know, because of this fainting three or four times thing. You may not realize that you have a bit of a bump on your forehead. She would want you to get that bump checked out. We could be out of here in an hour if you would just sign this consent form. Let them check the bump on your head, Sam."

Father Tom smiled, *He did it.* He said, "I've got our dinner reservation at the White Oaks. Get the bump checked. Then we'll take you back to the Holsten Inn to change clothes. We'll be having dinner together and reminiscing in no time."

Feeling positively awful, she touched her forehead and noticed the swelling. *Of course Kate would want me to stay,* she thought. Tears filled her eyes.

Jim handed her the clip board holding the consent form and pen. In the next second she signed. "Thank you." He took the clip board and headed for the nurses station.

A small smile crossed Father Tom's face. Her tears and expression reminded him of when she was a child and had finally chosen to do the right thing. "That's the ticket, Sammy, everything will be fine," Father Tom said and patted her hand. Then tears flooded her face. Her hand was weightless as he held it and took in how very thin she was. "It's ok, honey. How about we ask Jim to join us for dinner? We'll be together, again, almost like old times."

Her tears dropped on Father's hand and on the sheets. She slid her hand from his and hid her face with both hands. Suddenly, she slouched over and began shaking.

"Samantha, what's wrong? God help us." He couldn't find the nurse call button on her bed or night stand and pressed the emergency call button then put his arms around her. "We need help in here," he yelled.

Two nurses rushed in and each went to a side of her bed. One nurse told him to wait in the hall. Dr. Jameson hurried in.

Standing in the hall, Father Tom watched Jim run toward him.

"What happened?" Jim looked pale as he asked.

"I think she's having a seizure. I don't know. She was ok, and then she wasn't."

About twenty minutes later, one of the nurses came out and confirmed it was a seizure. "She's breathing on her own, but she's unconscious. We'll be moving her to a room on the third floor in the intensive care wing. Dr. Jameson has ordered a brain scan to be done, now. He's scheduled other tests for tomorrow. Sister Veronica will take you to Mrs. Green's room after the scan. Why don't you go to the cafeteria? Sister will find you there."

"That's where we'll be," Tom answered. They got sandwiches and cokes. Neither one had eaten at Kate's luncheon. For a few minutes they talked about Samantha. There was no doubt they were worried, but they knew there wasn't anything more to say until after the scan. Soon they were discussing school matters, pastor and principal, best friends as well.

Almost two hours later Sister Veronica found Tom and Jim. She pleasantly walked with them telling them how wonderful it is that Sacred Heart Hospital has such great technology available. She led them into Samantha's room adding, "Mrs. Green has not regained consciousness. The doctor will be here soon." She left.

"I hate hospitals," Jim announced.

Father Tom started to challenge the statement. He changed his mind remembering everything Jim watched Liz go through in the hospital. He simply gave Jim a pat on his shoulder and said, "Samantha looks comfortable, Jim. Thank God you were with her at the cemetery." Talking quietly as the heart and blood pressure monitor repeated it's monotonous beat, they waited for the doctor.

After an hour or so, Dr. Jameson came into the room. "I can tell you that her scan is clean, no bleeding or other difficulties. You should go home for the night. Mrs. Green is in good hands." Without missing a beat he added, "I really must talk with Mr. Green. I need his wife's medical

19

history. Actually, if their daughter is an adult, I could speak with her. Here's my card with my phone numbers. I have a new cellular phone. That number is listed, too. I'll talk with either, husband or daughter, no matter the time." Looking at their tired faces he said, "Come on, follow me. I'll show you the short cut out of here."

Father Tom turned toward Samantha and kissed her forehead. Out loud, he said a short prayer. All three men blessed themselves and left.

In the car on their way back to St. Joseph's not much was said. Jim broke the silence, "I hope I still have Sam's and Rob's phone number. I'm sure I do. I'll call him as soon as I get home." A few seconds later he said, "Tom, in the morning I'll head to school, take care of matters, and then go to the Holsten Inn. I'll fill Bette in on Sam's situation. She can help me gather a few things Sam might need. I hope to be at the hospital before noon. Look for her purse in the rectory. Let me know if you find it. Otherwise in the morning, I'll look by Kate's grave. I don't remember seeing a purse near the grave, but a lot was happening."

"Sounds like a plan." Father Tom opened the car door as Jim drove in front of the rectory. As he got out he said, "She'll be fine, Jim. Get some sleep. I may go back to the hospital later tonight."

~~~~~~~~~~~~

Jim walked into his den after grabbing a beer from the refrigerator. He sat down at his desk and opened the personal phone book finding Rob's and Sam's address and phone number also noticing their Christmas card from last year. Setting the card aside he dialed their number. Immediately he heard a recording stating that the number dialed was not a working number, and he tried it again with the same result. He hung up thinking, *Ok, in the morning I'll go to the Holsten Inn, first, and find out what number Bette has. I know she called Samantha about Kate.* He got up to get another beer. One more thing occurred to him. He sat back down and opened the Christmas card the Greens sent last December looking to see if their daughter's name was included. It wasn't. He noticed that the professional printing in the card's Merry Christmas message matched the printing of Rob's and Samantha's names. It also matched the address printing on the envelope. He decided against another beer, turned off the lights, and went to bed.

The next morning he drove to the Inn. The wind chill from Lake Erie's gray churning waves encouraged his jogging toward a bellboy who greeted him, hurried with him up the eight steps, and held open the lobby door. Jim passed by the breakfast pastries and fruit on one of the buffets and warmed himself near the fireplace. Looking around and seeing Bette at the front desk, he took a deep breath. Bette and he had a long friendship, but there were things about her that annoyed him. He thought, *I hope Ron's here. He seems to calm her.* He walked toward her seeing she was working on a Christmas wreath.

She looked up and then back down, "Jim, how are you? Can't believe Christmas is around the corner already. I just need to tie this."

"Hi Bette. Go ahead and finish it. I understand Samantha Green is staying here. I need"

"She sure is, although, I haven't seen her this morning. Did you have a chance to see her at Kate's funeral? I couldn't go yesterday." She put the wreath down. "Ron and I went to the funeral home the night before. I guess we missed you. I did see her for a minute yesterday when she was leaving for church. I just can't get over how thin she is. Have you seen her? You know, she's checking out tomorrow morning."

He tried answering, "I need your"

"I bet she doesn't weigh a hundred pounds. She's way too thin. The floor maid told me Samantha didn't touch the dinner I sent up to her room the other night. And yesterday morning, this maid told me she hardly touched her breakfast. Why isn't she eating, Jim? I just don't get it. She"

"Bette, stop!" In a softer voice he said, "Samantha's in Sacred Heart Hospital. I need to pick up some things for her. Can you help me?"

She stood there silently.

"Can we go to her room? You would know better than I what things she would want."

"Sure, of course I'll help you. What happened?" She got a key card from the lobby desk.

"Well, she passed out several times yesterday. The first time at the cemetery." He decided not to tell her everything. "Right now, she's resting in her hospital room. I meant to ask you right away, do you have a new phone number for Samantha? The doctor needs to talk with Rob or their daughter. I can't remember their daughter's name. Do you?" He watched her shake her head slightly back and forth. "Anyway, he needs to talk with either one of them."

She looked at him remembering that Sam didn't want her phone number given out. "Let me check when we finish getting her things." She decided it was necessary for him to have it and quickly added, "I think I have a new number. She had her first phone number in Portland changed. I have the new one. It's a private listing."

"Do you know if she has a cellular phone?"

"I don't know. Let me check her information when we're done. I might have a cell phone number. I'm not sure about that."

They finished getting Samantha's things and Bette went to the front desk. She wrote down the new phone number and said, "I don't have a cellular number for Sam. She might not have a cell phone. Let me ask if anyone has seen her using one. I'll let you know either way. I only have this one phone number. Do you have her new address in Portland?"

"No."

She wrote that down, too.

"Thanks, Bette. I'll keep you informed." He asked how Ron, her husband, was doing.

"He left to go on a golf trip this morning. He'll be home in a few days. I'd appreciate knowing how Samantha's doing. I'll keep her room for her, no charge. Please let me know if I can visit her in the hospital."

Jim jogged back to his car and drove to St. Joe's. Once in his office he dialed the number Bette gave him. He heard the phone ring eight times, and then he heard Samantha's voice telling him that they weren't able to answer the phone and to please leave a message. "Rob, this is Jim Peterson from Bay Village. Samantha is in Sacred Heart Hospital. She's resting comfortably," he added not wanting to scare him or their daughter. He continued, "She collapsed while attending Kate's funeral." He looked down at the card Dr. Jameson had handed him, "The doctor who admitted her is Dr. David Jameson. You can reach him at: 713 555 5006 extension 515." He gave Rob two more numbers from the card, including the cellular number. "Call me if" the answering machine beeped because his message time was up. He called back and continued, "It's Jim, again. Call me if I can help you in any way. These are my phone numbers." He left his home phone, school office, and his new cellular number and hung up. Then he sat straight in his chair looking up the hospital phone number. He called Rob back. "Sorry, it's me again. Here's the hospital number. I can pick you up at the airport."

He took care of the things on his desk needing immediate attention then left for the hospital.

Jim arrived in Sam's hospital room finding his best friend staring out the window and Samantha lying in bed with her eyes still closed.

"No change," Tom turned his head with a minimal smile. "Dr. Jameson mentioned a few minutes ago that Samantha could be suffering form anorexia. He really needs to speak with Rob."

"Glad you said that. Bette just told me a maid at the inn said the dinner and breakfast trays in Sam's room were left untouched. Why would she do this?"

They looked at each other for a second. Father Tom said, "I talked with her at the cemetery. We really didn't have much of a conversation. I thought she looked tired. She asked if we could go to the White Oaks Restaurant when we talked about having dinner. I just never considered that she might have an eating issue. I mean I noticed her weight at the rectory. My first thought was cancer."

"What?" Jim raised his voice, "You told me not to go there. Now you're telling me that you agreed with me?"

"Oh, don't get your 'shirt in a twist."

"It's shorts, not shirt."

"Whatever! I didn't want you to be miserable, again. Liz's battle with cancer was so tough on you, too. You're reasonably happy, now. I didn't want you thinking about all of that. Apparently, I was right!"

"Did you find her purse?"

"Yes, I found a small purse in her coat pocket. The other pocket was empty. A call from a parishioner got me busy on another situation, and I forgot it. It's on the kitchen counter."

"Ok, after school, I'll go back to the rectory and see if there's a phone in it. Rob's and their daughter's numbers should be listed in her contact list. Bette gave me Sam's new phone number and new address in Portland. The number I tried last night is disconnected. Bette doesn't have any additional phone numbers. She's going to check if anyone saw Sam using a cell phone. We didn't see one in her room." He looked at Samantha. "I'll head back now."

24

Driving to St. Joseph's school Jim thought about how much Liz wanted to live. *She fought so hard. She had so many things planned for us. Good health is precious.* He looked at the road ahead thinking how much he missed his wife, Liz.

Some anger emerged within him. *Why would Sam hurt herself like this? Why would anyone wreck their health?* For a second, he pictured Sammy from decades ago. The emotion he felt seeing her at the cemetery took hold. He immediately shut the feeling down. He gazed straight ahead. Out loud he said, "I guess I never really understood you, Sammy." He thought, *One thing's for sure, I need to get your husband to call Dr. Jameson. I hope you have a cell phone.*

In the hospital, Dr. Jameson walked into Samantha's room. "Father, we're noticing a change in Mrs. Green. I've ordered another scan. They'll be taking her in a few minutes. Don't worry. I'll get back to you as soon as the scan's done."

"Can I be with her," Tom asked and then remembered what Bette told Jim. "Jim just told me that Samantha hasn't eaten very much in the last few days. She's left food untouched in her hotel room."

"Thank you, knowing that helps. This scan won't take long. Why not wait here or go get a cup of coffee? She'll be back here soon."

Tom moved beside Sam's bed. He held her hand and gently rubbed her fingers as he blessed her. He stepped aside as she was effortlessly lifted onto a transport bed and wheeled away. He decided to get a coke at the cafeteria.

She was in the middle of her scan when everything went wrong. With a press of a button, Samantha moved feet first out.

The wait in her hospital room stretched into two hours, nearing three hours. Tom expected the scan to take longer than the doctor said. His concern was mounting when Sam's transport bed hitting the door jam announced her return. He stood up as they moved her back into her bed. The flurry of activity that followed surprised him. Nurses quickly connected Sam to several monitors. Dr.

Jameson walked in, checked everything and said, "She gave us a bit of a scare during her scan. She's doing fine now. There is slight bleeding in her brain. We're giving her medication to keep her sleeping and prevent swelling in her brain. This is just until the bleeding subsides. She's in the best place, here, in intensive care. Have you reached her family?"

Tom couldn't think for a moment. "Um, no, I don't think so. I mean, no. Jim's getting her purse right now. We're looking for her cellular phone, if she has one, hoping to find more phone numbers. I'm not sure if he's spoken with Rob. I'll call him right now."

"Listen, she needs this resting. The bleeding is from the bump she suffered when she fell in the bathroom, and I think it will subside soon. Indications are she's suffering with severe anorexia. She's very weak because of that. We're addressing it the best we can. Her medical information will help. She's resting now."

"I'm going to the lobby. Will you be on this floor awhile? I'll find out if Jim's talked with him. I'll be right back."

He got his phone out of his pocket thinking, *Thank goodness I remembered to bring this darn thing with me.* "He found Jim's name and pressed the number. "Hello Jim. Did you speak"

"Tom, you're breaking up. I'm here getting in the elevator. I'll see you in a second." Jim flipped his phone shut and put it in his pocket.

The elevator door opened on floor three with Father Tom standing in front of it holding his cell phone to his ear as though he was still using it. He lowered his phone and said, "She had a problem during her brain scan. She has slight bleeding in her brain. Dr. Jameson wants to keep her resting, sleeping until the bleeding stops. Did you find her phone and talk with Rob?" He closed his phone and held it as they walked toward her room.

"She had another brain scan? Is she ok, now?" He ignored the phone question and couldn't believe so much had happened.

"Yes, she's comfortable and back in her bed in intensive care. She's being closely monitored. Dr. Jameson is in her room right now."

"This really is unbelievable." His mind changed gears and returned to the problem of getting in touch with Rob. "She couldn't have a phone in that purse. It's too small to hold her phone with the things she has in it. I'm certain Rob would have a cellular phone, and he'd make sure Samantha had one, too. He and his father have their own law firm, and he certainly can afford these phones." Jim thought, *Why haven't I thought of reaching him there?* "Do you know the name of Rob's law firm?"

"No."

"I don't either. Bette might know. Anyway, I bet Sam has one, too. He'd love having the ability to call her anytime or anyplace. That's the impression he gave me the one or two times I had the honor of being in his company a very long time ago. He was an arrogant ass, and I doubt he's changed!"

Father Tom looked at him and said, "Now, Jim, stop."

"You're right. I'm sorry. I just think Rob would make sure his family had them. At the rectory I searched all over the sofa and in the bathroom. You found her purse in her coat pocket, and I realized her phone might have been in the other pocket. I went back to Kate's grave and looked all around to see if it fell out. I looked where I carried her to the rectory, too. I checked with Gina, and no one has turned in a cellular phone to the school or church offices. Maybe she left it in her room at the Holsten Inn, maybe in a larger purse. I'll call Bette and ask her to check Samantha's room for another purse, and maybe she knows the name of Rob's law firm, too."

"Ok, in the mean time we'll just keep trying the home phone. Dr. Jameson really needs her medical information."

They entered Sam's room and the doctor was there. Jim said, "I've left a message on Samantha's home phone. We don't know for sure if she has a mobile phone. I'll keep calling her home phone."

Dr. Jameson looked at both men thinking, *They look tired.* He said, "I could use a cup of coffee. Join me."

After they bought their coffee and sat down in the cafeteria the doctor told them, "She's suffering from anorexia. Everything indicates it. She's had this illness, and it is an illness, for quite some time. She weighs under one hundred pounds. Her ideal weight is at least twenty to twenty-five more pounds. It's possible her head injury caused her to lose consciousness when she arrived here. The earlier episodes were caused by the anorexia, most likely. She hadn't bumped her head when she passed out at the cemetery. As soon as the bleeding stops we'll reduce the medication. Do you have any questions?"

Jim looked at the doctor, "What should we do to help her?"

"You can stay with Mrs. Green as much as you'd like. I'll arrange for you to have continuous visiting hours. You can hold her hand. I want her to rest, however. Do not turn on the T.V. Keep things calm."

"Can we talk to her," Tom asked.

"Let her know that you're with her. Hold her hand for a few minutes. Talk with her about things she loves. She needs good rest. Just talk a little while. Her body is using everything it has left to support her. She hasn't been doing the correct things to nourish her body. She's depleted her reserves. Let's do this for the next twenty-four hours or so, until the bleeding stops. One more thing, when you enter or leave Mrs. Green's room, wash your hands thoroughly." He stood up and added, "Get hold of her family, please." Dr. Jameson walked out.

As Jim and Father Tom silently walked back into Samantha's room, an idea struck Father Tom. *We can't reach her present family, but we can reach out to her childhood family.*

Entering her room, they washed their hands. Tom pushed the best chair in her room close to her bed. Sitting down, holding Samantha's hand, and rubbing his thumb across her knuckles he softly said, "Sammy, I've been thinking about everyone we loved while you kids were growing up: your mom, dad, Brice, Frank, Grand, Art, and our Kate. I can see their faces so clearly."

Jim stood near the bed for a minute and said, "Tom, I'm heading home, and maybe I'll stop back at the Inn. I'll call you later."

"Ok, I'll be here."

Father Tom gently held her hand, "Kate and Art moved here when you and Karen were about nine years old. I was fairly new to Bay Village, too. Our wonderful, wonderful Kate made everything just right. Can you see her, honey? I can picture her in her slacks. Most ladies wore dresses in those days but not Kate. She wore slacks most days, remember?" He sat quietly, now, just holding her hand.

~~~~~~~~~~~~~

"I can see you, Kate. I'm back, I'm home. I feel so peaceful here. I can see you! I can see everyone, all of your dear faces."

Smiling faces from long ago filled her mind. Precious faces dangling gentle respite from everything else in her life. Long ago faces of loving family cheering on dreamy memories, beckoning her to let them stay. They seemed to be making her a beautiful promise. Giving in to those sweet faces was no contest. "Stay. Stay with me."

She could feel Kate's arms wrapping around her in a safe hug. "I remember the day I met you, Kate. My dad was finished raking leaves to the ditch by the street. My dear dad, FBI agent Jack Cole, was home with me for the afternoon. He was standing guard near the burning leaves. I'd made it through my first day of fourth grade with Sister Gladiola, and now I was playing outside in the smoky autumn air with my dad near. I watched you, our new neighbor, walk across the street toward him. After talking a minute, my dad called me over, 'Samantha, this is Mrs. O'Malley, our new neighbor. Mrs. O'Malley wants to speak with you."

"Those words changed everything in my life, Kate."

"Samantha, I'm happy to meet you," Kate O'Malley smiled and said. "You and your friend, Karen, are the biggest reason Mr. O'Malley and I decided to buy a house on your street."

Surprised at that, I asked, "We are?"

"Yes, you are. While we were looking at our new house, we noticed you two playing. Mr. O'Malley and I especially enjoyed watching you two and some other children playing baseball. You and Karen are really good."

I gazed at her blue-green eyes and immediately saw the kindness they held.

"Hey Samantha," my dad said, "Mrs. O'Malley just gave you and Karen a nice compliment. Say"

"Thank you," I said looking from my dad back to Kate.

"We have a daughter who's the same age as you and Karen."

"You do? I haven't seen her."

"She's been staying with her grandmother while we've been getting things moved into our house. Her name is Lindsey. She'll be in Sister Gladiola's classroom with you. She's just like you. She loves playing baseball, games, and dolls. I've seen you carrying your Tiny Tears doll. Lindsey has a Tiny Tears doll with hair."

"Karen's has real hair, too."

Kate smiled, "I want you and Karen to meet Lindsey. Her dad and I are picking her up from her grandmothers on Sunday. I'd like for you and Karen to come to our house for a tea party on Monday after school. Lindsey won't begin school until Wednesday. She's a little worried about not knowing anyone in her class. Your mom is coming, and so are Karen and her grandmother. I asked your mom if I could invite you. Will you come?"

I felt so special being invited to a tea party. "Yes, I'll come!" I glanced at my dad and added, "Thank you!"

I began stepping away because I couldn't wait to talk to Karen about it. "I'm going over to Karen's, Daddy. Ok?"

"Sure."

I ran across the street, passed the O'Malley's house, and opened the side door a little at the house next door. I hollered, "Oh Kar-en!"

Grand came around the corner in her kitchen and opened the door wider. "Hi Sammy," she said and gave me a hug. "She's in her room."

I hurried through the first floor, up the steps, and bounced into her room talking, "Hi!Have you heard about the new girl? I didn't know the new neighbors had kids. She likes all of the things we like. She likes to play baseball, and her mom said she's good. Wait until Jeff, Bobby, Jimmy, and the rest of those jerks find out there's another girl. They'll be so mad. And Karen, we've been invited to a tea party! Isn't that neat?"

"We haven't ever had tea before. I tasted some coffee once, and it was awful. What if we hate tea? This party is all about tea. It's a tea party," Karen answered looking nun too happy.

Grand finished putting folded towels into the linen closet upstairs and walked into Karen's room. She said, "Now, what's your problem? You aren't still worried about the tea party, are you?"

"Grand, what if we hate the tea," Karen asked looking terrified.

"Oh for Pete's sake, get down to the kitchen the both of you. Sammy, call your mom and ask if you can have supper here. Tell her we'll be having ourselves a cup of tea as well. It'll just be the three of us. Karen's dad is working late at the store, and Uncle Frank is out of town."

My very best friend's family was different. Grand was more like a mom to Karen than a grandmother. Karen's mom was a singer and an actress, and she was almost famous. She lived in New York City. Every once in a while Karen's mom came home to see her and to see her husband. Frank, Karen's uncle, moved back home after his wife died. So her family was her grandmother, dad, and Uncle Frank. She hardly ever saw her mom.

Everything Grand cooked always tasted so good. We sat down to warm baked ham, scalloped potatoes, string beans, and buttermilk dinner rolls. We found out we loved hot tea with milk and sugar. We talked about lots of things including our teacher, Sister Gladiola. Grand reminded us to treat everyone with kindness, no matter what.

I ended up staying over night at Karen's that night. We had our baths, and I borrowed one of her nightgowns.

My mom came over later and brought my school uniform. We heard my mom and Grand in the kitchen talking and laughing while Karen and I laid in bed whispering about the new girl and the tea party.

SLEEPING MEMORIES 1954

It seemed forever for Friday and the weekend to pass.
Finally it was Monday, the day to meet the new girl.
"Samantha, wake up. Time to get up." My mom hollered
into my room. "I'm making scrambled eggs and toast.
Your underwear, slip, blouse, and jumper are on your
chair."

I stretched while listening to my mom walk back into
the kitchen. I loved her vacation weeks. *She'll be home
this week just like the other kids' moms. When I get home
from school, no lonely house because she'll be here.*

I slid out of bed and walked a few steps into the
hallway to our bathroom. My happy mood vanished as
thoughts of Sister Gladiola filled my mind. My stomach
ache revved up. Her face floated into view. I thought, *she
never looks glad. She looks old, nasty, and mad. Most of
the kids call her Sister Madiola.* I smiled a second.

When we had dinner with Grand the other night, she
reminded us that we had to be kind and good for Sister.
She told us that Sister was the oldest teaching nun at St.
Joseph's. We'd managed to figure that much out for
ourselves. Sister Gladiola's face, what we could see of it,
was all wrinkles. She used her cane with every step she
took, and when she walked she almost disappeared in her
habit. Her voice was strong, though. It was loud and
screechy. Sister didn't like to repeat herself, but it sure
seemed like she did. She loudly repeated that sentence
several times each day.

My mom was happy. We quickly had breakfast
together, and I loved that. She told me she loved me with
all of her heart as I walked outside. While we hardly ever
had breakfast together, every morning she told me she
loved me with all of her heart. I walked down our
driveway, and Karen was waiting at the end of hers.

She waved and announced, "It's Tea Party Day!"

"I know. I can't wait to meet Lindsey. I still haven't
seen her."

We chatted while we walked the three blocks to
school. The air filled our senses as we passed the neat
yards the dad's maintained and the two, three, and four

34

bedroom houses the moms kept comfortable. As near to our houses as these houses were, they felt distant to us.

We turned the corner to St. Joe's School hearing the warning bell. We quickly hurried past St. Joseph Church with its magnificent stone walls, ten foot tall arched wooden doors, and glorious stained glass windows. Then we hurried up the walk leading to the school, which mirrored the church minus the stained glass windows. We stood very still in line. When the next bell rang the arched wooden school doors opened. Within three minutes we walked into Sister's room, hung up our jackets, put our homework on her desk, and with folded hands sat silently at our desks. While waiting a few seconds to hear the tardy bell, we looked around our classroom at maps of the world, the United States, Europe, and Canada. We looked at posters of past presidents, the planets, and Jesus; not one of us even whispering. Once the tardy bell rang, we began our day the same way we had for the last three years. We stood up and blessed our selves, bowed our heads, folded our hands, and recited "Our Father" and "Hail Mary." Next all of us put our hands on our hearts and said the "Pledge of Allegiance." My stomach ached as I wondered how long I would last before Sister Gladiola let me have it. She didn't like me one bit.

I didn't last long. Sitting at my desk at the end of the row in between Bobby and Karen, I apparently didn't follow Sister's seating chart instructions. I was sure she said that the last person in each row should take the chart and write their name at the top. So when Bobby handed it to me, I wrote my name at the top. I handed it to Jeff sitting in front of me and the chart went on it's merry way. Karen told me, later, that Sister actually said that the last person in each row should take the chart to the first person in the next row to write their name at the top, and she said Bobby made the mistake.

Sister was facing the blackboard when she looked at her seating chart and called on me. She turned and didn't see me sitting in the front seat. "Samantha Cole, where are you? Raise your hand."

Uh oh, I thought while raising my hand and sinking in my seat. The next second she came hobbling toward me so fast I thought she would trip. She didn't trip. She smacked the top of my head twice and said, "How can you be so stupid? You're not sitting in the first seat of this row. You ruined my seating chart! Move your things to the baby desk next to mine."

I remember trying so hard not to cry. Our classroom was still and silent while I moved my supplies into my new desk. When I put my last pencil in she said, "Now, put your head down and pray for some brains." I was glad I could put my head down and hide my face. I felt sick and afraid. Tears spilled from my eyes, and I squeezed them shut. Sister resumed teaching.

After what seemed a very long time, the lunch bell rang. I was told I could sit up. She excused our class row by row. I was the last one excused. I could hear the kids in the cafeteria as I walked as fast as I could down the hallway to the fresh air outside. Running in the hallway wasn't allowed.

Karen was waiting. "Sammy, are you ok? Bobby made the mistake."

I didn't answer thinking, *I still think she said that the last person should put their name at the top.* We didn't talk the rest of the way home, but Bobby was waiting on his bike when we turned the corner to our street. "I'm sorry, Sammy," he said and quickly rode away.

My mom was sitting on our stoop when I got home. "Hi, our lunch is ready." Then she looked at me from top to bottom and asked, "Are you ok?"

I decided not to tell her what happened.

"Samantha, were you crying?"

"No, my eyes got itchy."

She looked at me a second longer, hugged me, and said, "Come on, lets have lunch." I felt so safe wrapped in her hug.

That afternoon with Sister Gladiola presented two of three images of her that have remained sharp and clear in my mind. Excitement caused by an emergency alarm, which sounded much different from our normal school bell, set up the first unsettling spectacle. As the alarm blasted, the obnoxious noise startled all of us. Immediately our class got out of our seats, got under our desks, and covered our heads. I peaked at Sister and saw that she hadn't moved from her chair. I thought for sure she might die. However a few minutes later, our normal bell sounded three short rings signaling we'd all survived the possible atomic bombing. We could safely return to our chairs. When I looked at Sister Gladiola, again, I was surprised to see her laughing as she said, "All of you, and she looked right at me, too, were excellent Bert the Turtles." For several seconds she couldn't stop laughing, and she covered her face with her hands. When she finally picked up her book, her face looked normal.

Forever that image of her laughing has stayed with me. Years later I figured out she was likely laughing about the absurdity of using a desk for protection against an atomic bomb. But her laughing face as well as the opposite image I saw after we were dismissed that day, have held a place in my mind.

The school day ended, and Karen and I were walking toward the sidewalk when I realized I didn't have my sweater. "Karen, I need to go back for a minute. I don't have my sweater. I'll hurry and find it."

"Ok, but don't bother Sister Gladiola. I'll wait for you."

I didn't see it in the hallway. Our classroom door was closed, and I slowly opened it just a little. Sister was still sitting at her desk staring out the window. I looked at my desk and saw my dumb sweater on the floor beside my chair. She hadn't noticed me. I held my breath, took one step into the room, and froze as I heard her raised voice.

1954

For Sister Gladiola, the first days of another school year were over. She sat alone looking toward the window. Her bones ached. *I'm so tired of these stupid children,* she thought. Staring at the window she suddenly saw her dead mother's face and said, "Oh wonderful, what are you doing here? This day has been bad enough with that dimwit, Samantha Cole, never following directions. Let alone this morning, I got the great news they've added another student to my classroom giving me thirty-eight, nine and ten year olds. Damn baby-boomers!"

"I'm so sick of these brats. Every bone in my body throbs, but we must be obedient, right? Now you've shown up. Stop looking at me like that! Why are you here?" She began crying, "Don't give me that, 'Poor, poor Papa routine.' It simply doesn't matter anymore. Just get out of here. Leave me alone. Get out!" She slammed her cane against her desk. "Good, you're gone." Crying, she put her head in her hands.

I heard, "What are you doing here?" I thought for sure I was in more trouble. When I opened my eyes and looked at Sister, she was still looking out the window. I stood still for a minute looking at my sweater near her desk. She kept talking. She called me a dimwit while looking out the window. I finally realized that she didn't know I was there. I made my move and grabbed my sweater. She began to cry.

As I made it back into the hallway, Sister yelled, "Get out," and smacked something. Disobeying a rule, I ran down the hallway, opened the large wooden door, and ran outside to the sidewalk. I looked back to make sure she wasn't coming after me.

Karen was walking slowly nearing the corner of our street. I didn't call out to her. Seeing Sister Gladiola alone in her classroom, yelling as she looked at the window, and then crying; stirred unfamiliar emotion.

Karen looked back at me and hollered, "Hurry up!"

~~~~~~~~~~~~

Father Tom and Jim sat in Samantha's hospital room. For the last few days one of them or Bette had stayed with her. Nothing had changed. Her husband, Rob, hadn't called the doctor, and her cell phone was still missing.

Things were about to improve. A smiling Dr. Jameson pushed open the door to her room. He washed his hands, checked the chart hanging at the foot of her bed, looked at the monitors, and washed his hands again. "Well, the result of yesterday's scan shows the bleeding has stopped. We've begun reducing the medication. I think she'll wake soon, maybe today. She'll be moved out of ICU back to floor two. The nurse will give you her room number. Talk to Samantha and encourage her to wake. I'll see you this afternoon on the second floor. He hurried out.

Neither Jim or Tom moved for a few seconds. Father Tom said a short prayer, "In the name of the Father, and of the Son, and of the Holy Spirit, Amen. Thank you for answering our prayers. Please keep Samantha safe as she returns to us. Please help us reach Rob. And, if she has one, help us find her cellular phone, Amen."

Catching up with Karen, I heard, "You found your sweater. What took you so long?"

I didn't like Sister Gladiola one bit, but I actually felt sorry for her. I decided not to tell Karen what I just watched. "I didn't see it right away. Let's race home."

As soon as I walked into our side door and saw my mom waiting to hug me, I forgot all about Sister Gladiola. "Sammy, wash your face and hands and change into the clothes on your bed. Hurry, it's time to meet Lindsey at her tea party."

A few minutes later, I walked into our living room wearing my favorite green pedal pushers, white blouse, and pink and green sweater. My mom brushed my hair into a pony tail and added a green ribbon. Then she said a very good thing, "Honey, please remember how important it is not to hurt people. I mean, just remember the important thing about a person is that their heart is kind. Let's go meet Lindsey and have a good time."

For a second I wondered if she knew that I'd watched Sister Gladiola. The part about the 'kind heart' didn't fit.

"I almost forgot. This is a little present for Lindsey." She took a small gift wrapped box out of a bag. "Let's leave it here for now. If you decide you'd like to give Lindsey a gift, you can come back for it. Actually there are two more wrapped boxes in this bag, one for Karen and one for you. Later, you decide if you want to get them."

My mom stood up with a huge grin, "Come on," she held out her hand, "let's go to the tea party."

Walking out our front door, we saw that Karen and Grand were almost there. They waved to us, and we walked directly across the street to Kate's front yard and joined them. I saw Art stepping down his front steps to greet us. Kate and Lindsey walked out next, and they had the biggest smiles on their faces.

Lindsey's arms were behind her back. The sun was shining just behind her making her gold-blond curls sparkle with light. I whispered too loudly, "Mommy, she looks like a princess. She's beautiful."

41

Everyone laughed a nervous laugh. Art walked to my mom and Grand, "Thank you. We're so happy you're doing this."

While Art spoke, Karen and I walked closer to Lindsey. Slowly she moved her arms from behind her back. We stopped walking. We just weren't prepared for what we saw. No one had told us or warned us. Lindsey's arms and hands didn't match. Her one arm and hand were way smaller, not right at all. Karen and I hadn't ever seen anything like this. We didn't even know something like this could happen. Seconds passed. Lindsey cleared her throat, and her beautiful bright blue eyes and sparkling golden hair regained our attention. In that same instant Kate had her arms around our shoulders, "Let's all go inside and meet each other."

Art held the screen door open as everyone stepped into the living room. He said, "Please, everyone sit down, and I'll get refreshments."

The three of us nine year olds were stuck in silence. Karen and I sat down on the couch with my mom and Grand. We sat facing the living room window and looked out avoiding everything and everyone inside, especially, the arm! Although the volume was low, we could hear Eddie Fisher singing "Oh! My PaPa." Kate made a start at ending these awkward seconds. "Lindsey, these are our new neighbors." She looked at Grand, then Karen. "This is Mrs. Fry and her granddaughter, Karen."

Grand happily continued the conversation, "Lindsey, I'm so glad to meet you. I hope you'll call me, Grand." She looked at Karen and me, "That's what these two precious ones call me."

Kate smiled and continued the introductions. "And this is Mrs. Cole and her daughter, Samantha."

Lindsey looked at Karen first and answered, "Hi, Karen. Thank you for coming over."

Karen replied, "Hi."

Softly Lindsey said, "Hi, Samantha."

It was my turn to speak. "Call me Sammy. Only teachers or people mad at me call me Samantha."

More nervous laughter sounded as my mom jumped in keeping this conversation alive, "Hi, Lindsey. We're all so happy you moved here. I hope you'll be allowed to call me Joan instead of Mrs. Cole." She looked at Kate.

"I think that's a grand idea. Everyone laughed, especially Grand. "And we would love for the girls to call Lindsey's dad, Art, and me, Kate."

Then we heard Art call out from Kate's kitchen, "I think it would be easier if you came in here for your drinks."

Kate answered back, "We'll be right there."

She looked at Karen and me and explained Lindsey's small arm. "Lindsey was born with one of her arms being smaller than the other. We were very surprised this happened. While both of her arms have grown since she was born, they are always going to be different from one and other. This is new for most people to see. Lindsey, her dad, and I have often said that sometimes people really have to look hard at new things. That's all right. We understand. New or unusual isn't bad. It's just different, and sometimes people really look at things that are different."

Karen and I sure were looking. But then, we were just looking at Lindsey and Kate.

Kate smiled. It was silent except for Perry Como singing "Try to Remember." She said, "Well Linds, what do you think?"

She had the biggest grin, "I think my dad is eating all of the cakes."

"Well, we better get moving!" Kate led us the few steps through the dinning room into her yellow kitchen. In both rooms Karen and I saw the prettiest tables we'd ever seen. Several glass vases filled with pink flowers surrounded everything on a white lace table cloth. A silver platter cradled chicken salad, sliced cucumber, sliced ham, tuna salad, roast beef, and cheese with tomato sandwiches; all cut in petite shapes. Two pretty bowls, one filled with fruit salad and one with chips, caught our eyes. Chocolate covered berries, little individual pies, and slices of cake decorated pink plates. Small tulip shaped bowls held jams, and matching plates held breads cut in circles or squares. Some were spread with cream cheese or peanut butter. One corner of the table had long stem glasses, while the other end had tea cups. Tucked under a short stack of larger pink glass plates, flowered napkins

43

peeked out. Another table covered with a soft pink table cloth and flower-filled vases was surrounded by six chairs. It set mostly in the dining room and partly in the yellow kitchen.

Kate saw our excited faces and said, "The only rule here is that we eat anything we want!"

Art stood near their kitchen counter and announced, " We have cherry tea."

Lindsey said, "It's really cherry pop."

"We have orange tea."

"It's really orange pop."

"And we have coca cola tea."

Karen happily stated, "It's not tea!"

Lindsey nodded in agreement. We got our long stem glasses and chose our pops.

Art smiled and said, "Ok you three, we really do have tea. Let's see what the other young ladies would like."

Grand said she'd love a cup of tea, while my mom asked, "Would you be serving anything stronger?"

"How about a highball?"

"Perfect."

He made two highballs, one for my mom and one for Kate. Grand, holding her tea cup, looked longingly at their drinks. Art grinned and said, "Grand, yours is on the way." The ladies laughed and a budding friendship began blooming for Kate with Grand and my mom, who had been dear friends for many years.

Lindsey, Karen, and I filled our plates and sat together at the kitchen end of the table. Art gave us our pops in long stem glasses and smiled as he set them down, "Well, if you ladies will excuse me, I'll be outside planting a few plants in our yard. You're on your own."

Grand, Kate, and my mom talked nonstop. Kate listened while Grand told her how Brice and Karen came to live with her. My mom told Kate about my dad and his working for the FBI. Kate seemed surprised at my mom's rendering of his job. She quickly changed the subject, and told them that she and Art met in college, and that she was an elementary school teacher.

Lindsey, Karen, and I were a little slower getting conversation started. But once we did, we couldn't say enough. We told Lindsey all about Jimmy, Bobby, and Jeff

44

living down our street, and we told her things about them that made her laugh. We told her about our baseball games and that we heard she was a great player, too. We forgot about the arm.

Kate set up an ice cream station with all kinds of toppings on her raspberry formica kitchen counter. We made and devoured several concoctions.

Grand, my mom, and Kate moved into the living room. Grand and Kate were drinking hot tea while enjoying their desserts. My mom enjoyed her dessert with another highball. Their conversation continued with my mom's voice becoming louder.

Grand knew her so well. She knew my mom was on the verge of telling Kate about a bad episode between my dad and mom that happened early in their marriage. Karen, Grand, and I had heard it many times. Everything changed when she drank too much and repeated this story. Steering my mom from embarrassing herself was something Grand could do, and she effortlessly turned the conversation around.

Karen, Lindsey, and I escaped into Lindsey's bedroom. We'd filled ourselves with enough sugar to last a lifetime. I decided to tell Lindsey all about Sister Gladiola. I began with a re-enactment of my morning with Sister. In a rather loud screechy voice I mimicked her, "Where's Samantha Cole? Where are you? Raise your hand, Samantha." I hobbled all around Lindsey's room, screeching, "Where is she? Where's that Samantha? There you are. I found you." I hobble-charged toward one of Lindsey's stuffed animals and bopped it on the head. Lindsey and Karen were laughing so hard they had tears in their eyes. Even I thought it was funny, now.

It seemed Karen and I had figured out that not ever looking at the small arm was the way to handle this situation. We quieted down a bit. I remembered the bag my mom had with the gifts. "I'll be right back. I need to ask my mom something." They followed me out of Lindsey's bedroom.

Her voice got my attention when we walked into the living room. I looked at Grand for a second, and she moved her head a tad signaling that things were ok.

45

"Mommy, can I go to our house and get that bag?" She looked at me as though she'd never seen me before. I held still.

She swallowed some sips of tea Grand poured her. Grand repeated more slowly, "Joan, Sammy wants to go home to get a bag. Can she?"

Only a few seconds passed, but to me it seemed a long time. Finally my mom smiled and answered, "Sure."

I hurried across our street. My house was dark which meant my dad wasn't home from work. I opened the side door, hit the light switch, grabbed the bag, turned off the light, and ran back to Kate's. I looked at Grand first. She was smiling, and so was my mom.

"Well, that was fast." My mom held out her hand, as I handed her the bag. "Thanks, Sammy."

Smiling she said, "Lindsey, Grand and I want to give you a welcoming gift. We thought it might be fun for all three of you to have one." She handed Lindsey a small gift box and reached back into the bag for Karen's and mine.

As we were handed the small boxes, I had an Idea. I whispered into my mom's ear.

"That's a great idea, Sammy, but don't be too long. It's a school night."

"Kate and Grand, could we take Lindsey over to see our playhouse and open our gifts there," I asked. They answered we could. My mom held the bag open, and we dropped our gift boxes back in. She handed the bag to Lindsey.

Art was just heading toward his front door as we walked out. "Hey, where are you three chipmunks going?"

"To our playhouse," I answered.

The darkness and stillness at my house contrasted with Lindsey's. Once in my bedroom, I grabbed my lantern and playhouse key off of my desk. Karen flipped on the flood light switch lighting the back yard as we passed back through our kitchen and out the door.

We hurried to the playhouse and unlocked it. Walking inside with the lantern lighting it up, Lindsey said, "Gosh, this is so neat."

"Thanks," I answered as Karen and I looked at the bag of gifts Lindsey was holding with the small hand. We looked at her arm.

Long seconds later, I said, "I'm sorry your arm and hand are different."

"Me, too. Does it feel different? I mean, um," Karen asked and looked miserable that she'd asked.

Lindsey's blond curls surrounded her face as she looked down and softly said, "I know I look dumb."

"No, you don't." Karen and I answered together, not sounding convincing at all.

Then I very convincingly stated, "I'm the one who's dumb."

"Sammy, stop that! You aren't dumb. Remember what Grand told you," Karen questioned in a tone that stilled the sulkiness filling the small playhouse. "She said we're going to help you with schoolwork."

Listening to Karen and me, Lindsey said, "Sammy, this is the first time, ever, that anyone has told me something they think is wrong with them." She smiled, "My mom's a teacher. She'll help you, too." She set the bag down on a small table. "You know, I can do almost everything with this hand." She held out both of her hands and took turns squeezing ours with her small hand, then with her normal hand.

"They feel the same! One's just small, but they're both strong," I stated.

Karen was grinning ear to ear, "You can do everything with both hands, right?"

"Almost, my dad has taught me how to catch a ball with both hands. I have to do things differently with my small hand sometimes. I can do practically everything, I just look different. My mom says seeing someone different scares people sometimes. When people are scared, they can act mean."

"People are mean to us, Lindsey. They make fun of Karen, because her mom lives in New York City, and her family is different. They make fun of me because in school I'm always in trouble and there's other stuff, too."

We all were silent for a minute. Lindsey looked around our small playhouse. "This is neat."

47

"My dad built it for me. These windows open, and see the screens? This table folds down. Karen and I have sleepovers in here."

Karen said, "We sure do. The best part is, no boys allowed. It's just for Sam and me." She looked at me and I shook my head, yes. "Now, it's just for the three of us!"

Lindsey looked so happy. We opened our gift boxes and in each one found a dainty gold chain holding a gold heart. We happily locked the door to our playhouse, set the key and lantern down in my mom's quiet kitchen, and went back to Lindsey's.

Lindsey showed her mom the present and then hugged my mom and Grand. "Thank you for the beautiful necklace. I love it."

As Karen and I took our turns hugging them, I realized how very much I loved my mom. She and Grand told Kate how beautiful the tea party was and that we had a wonderful time. We all thanked Kate and Art and walked back to our houses.

That was the day my life lit up, and the loving friendship between our families and the three of us began. Karen with her peaches and cream complexion, dark brown eyes, and light brown hair cut in a pixie cut; Lindsey with her light complexion, huge blue/green eyes, and curly blond hair; and me with my rosy cheeks, blue eyes, and jet black ponytail; each of us ready and set to share our childhoods.

Nothing interfered with the love that grew between the three of us and our families during the fabulous 50's and the turbulent 60's. Nothing interfered; not Karen having a family consisting of a dad, a seventy year old grandma, and an uncle; not Lindsey having perfect parents and mismatched arms; and not me having an angry mom with alcoholic tendencies and a dad married to his job.

It's been two days, and she's still sleeping. Why?"
Jim asked.

"I didn't think it would take this long for her to wake.
She responds to stimuli, and her brain scan is clear. The
anorexia has taken a toll. Without her medical history it's
harder to figure out. She's getting nutrition. Apparently
she needs this rest. Talk to her. Reminisce with her." Dr.
Jameson paused and asked, "You've heard nothing from
her family? I would think they'd be worried."

"No one has called the Inn or returned our phone
calls," he sounded frustrated.

Jim heard Father Tom cheerfully saying hello to the
nurses telling them he liked the Thanksgiving decorations
and to have a wonderful Thanksgiving Day. He watched
him walk into Samantha's room carrying an armful of stuff
in a bag and heard, "Hello, everyone. 'It's raining cats and
mice' this morning. Might begin snowing later." Tom put
everything down and took off his wet raincoat.

Jim grumpily stated, "It's raining cats and dogs.' What
are you doing bringing all this stuff?"

"Close enough," Father Tom turned his head and
smiled. "I have an idea. I think she might enjoy some
music from the 50's and 60's. I stopped at Kate's to check
on things and borrowed a few items including her radio/
disc player and some compact discs."

"They're called CDs," Jim said not looking pleased.

"Come on Jim, you love this music." He set the CD
player on a counter along with several CDs. He unloaded
three afghans out of the bag setting one on Samantha's
bed and two on a chair. He pulled out a picture of
Samantha, Lindsey, and Karen taken on Christmas Day
1954 and set it on the night stand beside the bed. He also
took out two pillows, some napkins, more pictures, and a
few Christmas decorations.

"This is not necessary," Jim stated. "Why do this?
She should wake up any time, now."

"Look around this room. I wouldn't want to wake up in
here either. I brought it because I could, because
Thanksgiving's almost here with Christmas around the

corner, and because I wanted. I don't know why. It needs cheering up in here."

Dr. Jameson looked at both men, "It works for me. We'll begin physical therapy today. I'll check back later." He walked out.

It began raining as soon as the tea party ended. I spent the next hour sitting at our kitchen table doing my homework. My mom looked at me, "Samantha, it's getting very late. Go to bed and remember to say your prayers." She gave me a hug as I moved away from the table. "Hey, take your lantern and playhouse key to your room."

I flipped my bedroom light switch on and stood in the doorway searching every corner of my room before walking in alone. I wasn't sure what I might find, but I made sure it wasn't in my room! I set our key and lantern on my desk while checking out the stuffed animals on my bed. They looked undisturbed. Making sure my night light was on, I switched off the ceiling light and got into bed.

Arranging my stuffed animals around me, I knew my dad was home because I heard him shut and lock our kitchen door. Lindsey O'Malley filled my thoughts as I snuggled my head on my pillow. I pictured her small arm and wondered how it would feel to have different size arms. For sure, I was glad that my arms matched. I included her in my prayers. It was the one and only time I asked God to please fix Lindsey's arm.

Lightening lit my room in flashes as the rain poured down. I heard many of my mom's angry words coming from our kitchen. "I'm sick of this. Where have you been? Not safe. Kill you one day." Crashes of thunder exploded outside. My mom yelled, "You're never here. If there's someone else-" A door slammed shut.

I saw tree branches clawing at my bedroom window and pulled my covers over my head. I held so still. *Don't come in here.* Then I was dreaming that same awful dream where I heard a roaring sound, and then was alone in the woods. Ugly tree branches stretched close to me, trying to rip me apart. I wanted to run away, but I couldn't. No way to get out of the woods.

1954

Karen gently wrapped her arms around Grand's neck and kissed her cheek. Grand kissed her back on her forehead and tucked the soft homemade quilt around her granddaughter. Switching off Karen's bedroom light Grand said, "Sweet dreams precious one. I love you." Then she walked the few steps across the hallway to her own room.

Alone, Karen thought about Lindsey and pictured her small arm and hand. *I'm glad that didn't happen to me. I like Lindsey a lot and Kate. She's lucky to have a nice mom.* She pictured the beautiful tea party and closed her eyes. "Dear God," she whispered, "please help my mommy come back for me. I really need her. Please God."

Karen looked at the shadow of the tree swaying on her window blind and knew that the tree sheltered her house. She fell asleep, and although she didn't dream her familiar dream every night, tonight this dream lit up. She was walking down a sunny street with her mom. Her mom always wore the softest full length coat, and Karen loved snuggling close to her as they held hands and walked down the street. They never talked.

Lindsey loved her new pink bedroom. She looked at her bunk beds, decided on the top bunk, climbed up, and flopped down on her fluffy comforter.

Her mom walked in, "All set for sleep, beautiful girl?"

"All set! I loved our party. Sammy and Karen are really nice. They're fun. Sammy's playhouse is really neat." She touched the gold heart on her new necklace.

"I think Grand and Joan are wonderful, too," Kate said, smiling. "This is the place, Linds. We'll have a happy life here. The day after tomorrow you'll begin fourth grade. You know you'll be in Sammy's and Karen's classroom, right?"

"I know. Mommy, tonight when we were in Sammy's playhouse, Sammy said that she's dumb. I don't think she likes school very much."

"Yes, Grand told me Sammy has a difficult time at school."

"Do you think we could help her?"

"Sure."

"And Mom, did you know that Karen's mom isn't home very much? I guess she gets teased about that."

"Did she tell you that?"

"Sammy told me. I guess both of them hear mean things, too, from the kids at school." While she spoke, she looked at the strange shadows moving on her window blind along with the flashes of lightning streaking through.

"Everything's going to be fine, Lindsey." Kate said and closed the window curtains blocking the shadows and the lightning. "I think we'll all be dear friends. We'll help each other and take care of one another. I think we've found the right place." She stepped on the ladder and hugged her daughter. "I love you. Dad and I are always here for you. Tomorrow we'll talk more about going back to school. We've checked things out at St. Joseph's, and this time school will be a good experience. Now, say your prayers and go to sleep. Good night, honey, sleep tight."

"Good night, Mommy, I love you."

Lindsey lay awake thinking about going back to school in one day. She hadn't attended school since half way through second grade. School had been a nightmare for her. Some children constantly teased her and made fun of her. The rest ignored her. The teachers didn't help much regarding the teasing and taunting. Realizing she was very alone and unhappy at school, her parents withdrew her. Tonight Lindsey thought about all of this.

Luckily, her mom was an elementary school teacher. This last year and a half had been wonderful. She learned everything with ease and passed every test the state required. Her mom made learning fun. But the best part was, no one hurt her. She was happy and safe when she was home with her mom and dad. Lindsey knew they moved here so she could have a fresh start back in school. She thought about all of this while listening to the rain and thunder. She thought about Sammy and Karen and smiled. *This time I'll have two friends at school.*

Soon she was asleep dreaming her special dream: A distance away from where she stood there was a golden castle. More than anything she wanted to walk inside, but she couldn't get herself close enough. A beautiful person, a man, always stood between her and the castle. "Hello

53

honey," the man would say. "What are you looking for?
Tell me what you want." Although there was something
Lindsey wanted more than anything, looking into this
person's eyes always made her forget. Her dream would
end.

Father Tom sat holding Samantha's hand while sitting in a chair close to her bed. Lessening the sound of the monitors "Mr. Sandman" was playing on Kate's radio/disc player. Tom had made the decision to reminisce about Kate, Lindsey, Grand, Karen, and everything he could remember about Sammy's childhood. Hearing fifties and sixties music playing in the background fit his plan perfectly. He realized it would do his heart good as well. "I bet Kate's sending you a dream, Sammy," he said and patted her hand. "Your hand feels cold." Standing up, he adjusted the afghan he'd placed on her bed tucking her hand and arm under it. *That's better,* he thought.

Sitting back down he said, "Samantha, do you remember Father Aurther? You were very young when he was St. Joseph's Pastor. He died many years ago in Florida. He was a wonderful, old school priest. He met Art and Lindsey in the rectory on her first day of school. He had such a hard time understanding why any child should have to confront such difficulty. Concerning Lindsey, he asked me how he could explain to her classmates why any child should be born with deformity. You know, if he were alive today and could see her success and happiness, I think he would be celebrating God's answer to that question. But remember, everything was so different in the 1950's."

"Anyway Sammy, Father Aurther told me to keep a special eye on Lindsey. He told me he would not tolerate unkind behavior toward her. He, also, told me that her parents had requested that she be placed in Sister Gladiola's classroom. I even remember the year. It was the 1954-1955 school year when Lindsey arrived. Father thought, *A wonderful year for us and a heartbreaking year for another family in Bay Village.* He shook his head. He patted her hand, again. "Life has unbearable twists and turns; that's for sure."

1954

Sister Gladiola hobbled down the hallway, switched on the lights in her classroom, and hobbled to her desk. Sitting down she immediately thought about the new student they were adding to her classroom. *The new student with the deformed arm. I wonder what sins her parents committed to deserve that? Now, it's my problem, too. I suppose I deserve this considering everything I did all of those years ago. Everyone is talking about this murder in Bay Village. Well, I know about that. Pa never got the chance to hurt little MaryPat, did he?* She hid her face in her hands and cried.

Once she settled down, Sister looked at the paper on her desk and saw the name: Lindsey O'Malley. Her thoughts returned to the new student. *Lindsey with the small arm, I bet her mind is affected, too. Why me? I already have enough with that dimwit, Samantha Cole. At least I can scare the rest of the class into good behavior by making Samantha my bad example. The sins of the parents,* she thought. *God remembers and punishes sins.*

1954

Father Aurther walked slowly down the hallway to Sister Gladiola's classroom. The ringing of the tardy bell quieted the hallways except for the sound of classroom doors closing and someone running in the hallway. He turned around.

"Good morning, Father Aurther, I'm sorry for running in the hall." The young child apologized and looked down at the floor.

"You're a little late, young man."

"Yes, Father."

"Well, tell me your name."

"Thomas Miller."

"Thomas, let's walk together to your classroom. I think you just might have made it if we hadn't talked."

The boy's face lit up in a smile.

They walked down the hall just two doors from Sister Gladiola's room. Father knocked on the door. "Good morning, Sister, please don't mark Thomas down as tardy."

He walked back to Sister Gladiola's door smiling for a second remembering how difficult it had been for him to be on time for school when he was a child. He looked up and down the hall. *I'm going to miss all of this. I honestly can't believe how quickly the years have passed. How can I possibly be in my eighties?*

His thoughts turned to the beautiful child he met a day ago, Lindsey O'Malley. *How can I explain to a class of fourth graders why they are perfect, but this happened to her? How can I make them understand when I don't understand why this should happen to a child? How can I prevent many of them from teasing her?* He stood in the hall near Sister Gladiola's classroom contemplating God's plan and then knocked on her door.

SLEEPING MEMORIES 1954

Wednesday morning Karen and I rode our bikes to school, while Art drove Lindsey and walked with her into the rectory office as planned.

We finished saying our morning prayers and "The Pledge of Allegiance." Sister Gladiola stood by our classroom door as she told us, "In a minute Father Aurther is going to speak to you about a new student joining your class." As she spoke to us we heard knocking on the door.

Father Aurther walked in and quietly looked at us. Finally he said, "Good morning children."

"Good morning, Father Aurther."

"This morning a new girl is joining your class. Her name is Lindsey O'Malley, and she is nine years old like most of you. Lindsey is a wonderful child as all of you are; however, she was born with one of her arms being small. She is very kind, and very smart. She loves doing the things many of you like."

Standing behind Father, we saw Sister Gladiola roll her eyes.

"Lindsey O'Malley and all of you are God's children. Please make her welcome in your classroom. Remember that God is always watching you. Father Brown and I will be watching you, too." Leaving us with those thoughts, he walked back to his rectory where Lindsey and Art were waiting.

We'd just opened our social studies books when we heard another knock on Sister's classroom door. With her cane in hand, she teetered to the door. We heard her thank Father Aurther. She took hold of Lindsey's hand and walked, faster than we'd ever seen, to the desk right beside Karen, my old desk. Hobbling back to the front of the room she announced, "That is your new classmate, Lindsey O'Malley. Mary Elizabeth, you will be a friend to her today and the rest of the week. Help her with everything she needs."

Sister looked back at our new classmate, "Lindsey, you may come to me if you need help or if there are any problems. Do you have any questions?" She didn't.

"Put your social studies books back in your desks and get your crayons out. Mary Elizabeth, please pass these name tags out. Class, write your names and decorate them as you wish. You will wear them until Lindsey learns your names." Sister allowed us to talk quietly. Sitting next to her, I couldn't talk with anyone. I could see some of the kids standing up to get a better look at Lindsey, and I could hear some snickering. As we worked on our name tags, Sister Gladiola didn't stop any of it.

We finished and put on our name tags, then read out loud from our social studies books. Sister called on Lindsey, "Let's find out if you read at our level." Lindsey read with inflection and pronounced each word with ease. I realized I followed every word my new friend read. Looking amazed Sister said, "That will be enough. Tell me what you have just learned about Alaska."

I saw Lindsey smile ever so slightly, "In the spring of 1867, Secretary of State Seward told the United States to buy Alaska from Russia for seven million dollars. Not many thought it was a good idea because they thought it was a frozen wasteland. Seward told everyone that the fishing and mining industries in Alaska were rich." Linds added, "Of course, now we know he was right."

Sister Gladiola didn't look pleased. "Stop! That will do." She looked at me, "Samantha, tell me who our president was when we bought Alaska."

"Yes, Sister, Andrew Johnson was." I smiled at Lindsey and Karen.

"Samantha, you and Lindsey have surprised me. Please read next."

I looked down at the page and realized I'd lost the place where we'd stopped reading. "I've lost my place," I softly answered.

"What? Speak up. Don't use that whiny voice."

"I don't know where we stopped reading," I answered much louder.

"That's more like it. I actually thought you were paying attention for once. Head down on your desk. Tonight for homework you will write fifty times: Samantha Cole will speak up and pay attention in class."

59

1954

Whenever Father Tom had time, he enjoyed walking down St. Joseph School's hallways. It made sense to him that listening and getting an impression of how the Sisters and the children were interacting was valuable when discussing educational recommendations. He could hardly believe that he would be the new pastor after Father Aurther retired in December. He knew that many of the parishioners couldn't believe it, either! That being an issue, he wanted to do everything necessary to be knowledgeable about current church and school matters .

As he walked down the hall he appreciated the discipline the Sisters demanded, but he thought there should be more joy. He wanted to hear cheerful voices. Well, he thought, *This January I'll begin teaching eighth grade health and religion classes. I'm determined to make these classes great learning opportunities and great fun.*

His thoughts were interrupted when he neared Sister Gladiola's classroom. Father Aurther had asked him to pay particular attention to her classroom. This morning he heard her yelling at one girl, Samantha. *That poor child, I know Sammy Cole and her parents.*

We heard another knock on our classroom door and heard Sister say, "For Pete's Sake." She grabbed her cane, slowly stood up, and walked at her normal painful pace to the door.

A cheerful voice greeted her, "Good morning, Sister Gladiola. I have a little time on my hands this morning. May I join you for a while," Father Tom asked and looked around the room.

"Of course you may. We're reading about Alaska. Please sit down."

"Actually, I'd like to give you a chance to sit down. In fact, feel free to put your head down on your desk, if you'd like to rest."

While our class giggled, she glared at Father Tom. Young as we were, we could tell she really didn't like this priest. Somehow we also understood, once he entered our classroom, he was the boss, not she.

Father Tom tapped my shoulder and said, "Samantha, you may sit up. I want you to sit where you'd like while I'm here. Just take your chair and put it beside anyone you want to sit near. Go ahead. It's all right."

Sister Gladiola's face looked like a stoked furnace as I carried my chair and set it between Karen and Lindsey.

Father waited for me to settle in my seat, then began talking to us. "Close your books. I would like to have a discussion with you." He smiled at us. "You're fourth graders, now, and much grown up from first or second grades. I think you know the meaning of kindness. Tell me how to be kind. And, please stand up when you are called on."

Mary Elizabeth Lotis rose up, and said, "You can be kind by making a friend happy."

"Can we only be kind to our friends?"

"No, we can be kind to anyone," Jimmy answered and quickly sat down.

"What else is kindness?" Father called on everyone who wanted to answer. He kept us interested by adding comments and letting us do the same. Keeping this discussion going for a long time, Lindsey was one of the

61

last kids to speak. She raised her small hand. "Yes, Lindsey."

She stood up. "Kindness means understanding that what's inside a person's heart is more important than how a person looks."

Bobby looked at her.

Father shook his head, yes, and smiled at both of them. He looked at Sister, "I'm very proud of these children." Looking back at us he said, "I can tell you also know that kindness is a way to show you care about other people's feelings. Right?"

Everyone answered, "Yes."

He wrote on the blackboard: Kindness is caring about other people's feelings.

He asked Sister to leave that sentence on the board for the next few weeks. "Caring about other people's feelings is a great way to show kindness. We all should remember that, shouldn't we, Sister Gladiola?" He looked at her for a few seconds. "Well, you all have been very good. You're very dear children. Aren't they, Sister?"

She stared back at him and answered, "They're dear, all thirty-eight of them, Father Brown."

He looked back at her for what seemed a very long time. "Yes, every single one of them, including their teacher. Thank you for letting," Father didn't finish his sentence. He smiled at us and said, "Be very good children for Sister Gladiola. She is a very good teacher, and you are blessed to have her."

Our room remained silent for minutes after he left. I got up and carried my chair back to my desk next to Sister without being told. The next morning I found my desk in the first row.

Father Tom came to our room often after Lindsey's first day. He and Sister must have worked out a plan. He would teach us for two hours or so, and Sister would leave our room.

Lindsey's first day back in school turned out fine. Her second day wasn't as good.

1954

Father Tom left Sister Gladiola's room humbled. His mind was churning. *She has to be over seventy-five years old. I know she's the oldest teaching Sister at St. Joe's and in charge of thirty-eight kids, nine and ten years old. Dear God, what are we doing keeping these Sisters teaching forever? Sister Gladiola is worn out. I'm going to assist her as often as possible.*

His thoughts moved on. *I'm looking forward to becoming Pastor and implementing changes the parish school council has recommended for St Joseph School. I know many feel I'm too young for this responsibility. Earning the parishioners' trust, respect, and support is essential. I want and need to continue visiting the families. I'd like to meet Lindsey O'Malley's family. Tomorrow after school will work. I think they live near the Fry's and the Cole's.*

Jim was alone with Samantha. She remained sleeping in her hospital bed. "Sammy, I'm sorry," he whispered. "I didn't realize you were ill when I saw you at Kate's grave. I shouldn't have teased you." He rubbed her hand. He set her hand by her side and smoothed her hair back from her forehead.

"We've been looking for your cell phone hoping to find Rob's and your daughter's numbers in your contact list. We haven't found it, and Rob hasn't responded to the messages I've left on your home phone. Father Tom and I think I should book a flight to Portland. Hopefully one of your neighbors will know if he's out of town. Tom said that Rob's law practice keeps him away from home for extended periods. Maybe a neighbor will know how we can reach your daughter, too. We'll find them. In the mean time you have us, and we won't leave you alone." He looked at her sleeping face and smiled, "Once, you were the most important person in the world to me. I'm not sure when you captured my heart. Maybe it was when I found out you were great at baseball. I know you love Rob as I loved Liz very much. I'll find him and get him here for you."

He closed his eyes and leaned back in his chair.

About an hour later Tom made himself comfortable in the same chair Jim vacated. Excitedly he said, "Samantha, know what I found myself thinking about early this morning? That meeting Bette's mother, Wilma Lotis, had at her house after the boys got into that fight. Did you know about that meeting? Jim and I were talking yesterday about a lot of things that went on while all of you were growing up including Bobby getting into that fight with those boys who teased Lindsey. He remembered that Art and I played baseball in the street with all of you that afternoon. And yes, I handed him the perfect opportunity to point out our age difference."

"You know, now that I think about it, that was the day I met Kate and Art. Funny, I can still recall that Kate had her radio on in her kitchen, and Patti Page was singing 'How Much Is That Doggie In The Window.' Funny to remember that. It's been years since I've heard it."

64

"Anyway, Bette's mother set up a meeting at her house. That woman knew how to stir up trouble! The fight and the meeting happened during Lindsey's first week at St. Joe's. Did I ever tell you about my parents and the plan my dad and I devised to defuse Wilma Lotis and her meeting? My parents' business company was very successful and they became wealthy. Actually my brother, John, runs the company now. He's doing great, and he's extremely generous, too. My sister-in-law, Jen, is a gem, just a wonderful person. Back to the point, with my dad's generous help, he and I came up with a plan to stop Mrs. Lotis. Unfortunately our plan had consequences."

Lindsey's first day back in a classroom turned into a great day for all of us. Her second day was a different story.

Karen and I rode our bikes home from school and went over to Lindsey's house. She wanted us to help convince her mom that the three of us riding bikes to school the next day would be fine. She was so excited, "Mommy, please!"

Kate wasn't so sure it would be such a great idea even though Lindsey kept telling her that she would be careful. The three of us promised her we would stay together to and from school. After a lot of pleading, she finally gave in, "You girls have to understand you might be teased. There won't be any adults around to help you. You'll have to ignore any nasty remarks. Hopefully nothing like that will happen, but if it does, you'll have to get through it. Just keep pedaling your bikes. Don't stop, and don't tease back." Kate looked at each one of us, "Do you three understand?"

"Yes, Kate, thank you, thanks, Mom," we said at the same time.

The next morning Kate invited Grand and my mom over for coffee. The three of them stood on the O'Malley's front porch steps waving as we pedaled away. Kate called out, "Don't forget what we talked about, girls." We hollered back we wouldn't.

Sunshine peeked through the red, gold, and still green leaves as we rode our bikes down our street to school. My old bike made a rhythmic sound that usually made me think about how much I wanted a new bike. But this morning, it didn't bother me. We happily made it to school without incident.

The incident happened on our return trip. We pumped the pedals on our bikes toward home feeling the warmer afternoon air breeze passed our faces. Just reaching the turn to our street, several boys were waiting for us. They started yelling at Lindsey as soon as we made the turn. "Baby Arm. Here comes baby arm. We hate baby arm. We hate baby arm."

We pedaled faster passing some of them.

"Hey baby arm," Leland yelled, "why don't you feed your baby arm some spinach? Maybe it would grow like Popeye." Taunting laughter filled the air.

We kept riding those bikes as fast as we could. Some of the boys were ahead of us.

Wilfred yelled, "Does your baby arm work? Do you keep it in diapers? Diapers for baby arm. Stinky arm. Stinky arm. Stinky arm."

I'd heard enough, "Shut up, Wil."

"Sammy, don't. My mom said not to pay any attention to them."

"Stinky arm doesn't work. Stinky arm doesn't work," Wil kept yelling.

Karen rode her bike near Wil and yelled, "You better believe her arm works. She can hit a baseball farther than you can."

Lindsey pedaled her bike faster catching up to stop Karen from saying anything else, "Ignore them, Karen." Another boy, Mike, swiped his bike into Karen's bike causing her to crash into Lindsey. Karen and Lindsey fell to the street.

I yelled out, "I hate you, Mike. Look what you did!" I stopped, put my kickstand down, and ran to my friends.

Bobby and Jimmy sped up to us. Jimmy helped Karen and Lindsey pick up their bikes. Bobby tore down the street after Mike and shoved him causing Mike's bike to topple over. He got off his bike and ran over as Mike got up, "Why don't you leave her alone? Just leave her alone!"

Mike tried to punch Bobby, and they started fighting.

A few moms came outside to stop the fight and one hollered, "Boys, stop fighting this instant! Stop it. Stop fighting and get up." All of us could hear Bobby yelling at Mike. Two moms walked toward us. I recognized Mrs. Lotis as she asked, "Girls, are you all right?" Then she and her neighbor stared at Lindsey's arm.

In a quieter voice, Mrs. Lotis said, "Oh dear, that's the deformed girl in Mary Elizabeth's class I was telling you about. See the trouble a different child like this causes? And wouldn't you know she'd make friends with these two." Mrs Lotis pointed, "That one is Karen Fry. Her mother is off in New York City doing God knows what. The other one is Samantha Cole. Her mom's the drinker. Her father is FBI."

Having no idea that we heard every word she just uttered, she raised her voice, "Girls, go home now."

Karen immediately answered, "Mike made Lindsey and me crash into each other. Bobby is helping us, Mrs. Lotis."

She looked at Bobby and then us, "Girls, that will be enough. Get on your bikes and go home." Then she hollered, "Bobby Williams, stop fighting and come over here this minute."

Karen was in tears, "I'm sorry, Linsey, I made you fall. Are you ok? Our bikes are all dented and scratched."

As we got back on our bikes I thought about the things Mrs. Lotis said about us. I actually realized that she and the other ladies thought they were better than us, and I knew what she meant when she called my mom a drinker.

We rode our bikes up Lindsey's driveway and saw Kate sitting on her front stoop waiting for us. She stood up the second we got off our bikes and asked, "Lindsey, are you ok? Karen, your leg is bleeding. What happened?"

I blurted out, "I hate them for what they did and said. I just hate them all, Kate. I hate those boys and even those moms. Those moms aren't nice. Those moms are awful. My mom has told me never to tell them anything. They are so nosy. They're mean, dumb, and they aren't pretty!"

"Hey, hey, stop yourself right there, Samantha, that's not nice. What are you talking about? Where were the moms? What moms?"

"The dumb, stupid moms who stopped the fight."

"Sam, honey, stop talking like that. You three got into a fight on the way home?"

I snapped out, "No, no, we didn't fight. The stupid, dumb," Kate gave me a warning look, and I stopped talking.

She walked us inside, sat Karen down, and washed the blood off Karen's knee. "Lindsey, get the Bactine," she instructed.

"No, it'll hurt. I don't need anything on it, Kate."

Lindsey got it and came back saying, "It doesn't sting like that other stuff. It won't hurt at all."

Kate cupped Karen's face in her hands, "Karen, listen, I will never hurt you, not ever." She sprayed Bactine on Karen's knee and got out three more clean washcloths. She looked at Lindsey and me, "Are you two sure you're not hurt? Lindsey?"

We answered we didn't get hurt.

She looked at us with a not so happy look, "Ok you three, what happened?"

"On our way home; Wilfred, Mike, Leland, and some other boys said mean things to Lindsey about her, um, you know. They were saying mean things," Karen stammered.

She filled in the sentence, "You mean the boys were saying things to Lindsey about her arm? We talked about this yesterday. I told you to keep riding your bikes home, not to stop. So you stopped and got into a hitting fight with them? These boys actually hit you?"

I quickly answered, "No, Kate, this is what happened. We didn't get into a fight. Bobby, Jimmy, Jeff, and some of those guys were riding their bikes way behind us. Leland was yelling dumb stuff at Lindsey. When Mike rode his bike too close to Karen's bike, Karen crashed into Lindsey, and Lindsey's bike fell on top of Karen's on the street. Mike got really mad because Karen told Wil that Lindsey's arm was really good and that she could hit a ball farther than Wil could. So Mike got even by trying to crash Karen's bike. Then Bobby pushed Mike and yelled at him to leave Lindsey alone, and Mike tried to punch him. Then some moms came out, and they yelled at the boys to stop fighting. And, Kate, those moms were mean to us, too." I started to cry and Kate hugged me.

"Wonderful," she whispered, "whatever you just said, Sammy. You girls remembered part of what I told you. You stayed together." She wiped my face with one of the washcloths. She handed another cloth to Lindsey while looking out the window seeing Bobby, Jimmy, and Jeff standing with their bikes a little way down the street.

We looked out and saw them. "That's Bobby in the red shirt," I informed her, "and Jimmy and Jeff. They helped us."

"Sammy, go ask them to come here for a minute," Kate instructed. We walked outside, and I went immediately.

"Is she mad at us," Bobby asked.

"No, I don't think so. Lindsey's mom is really nice. Just come on." They followed me.

"Hi," Kate smiled and said, "I want to thank you for helping the girls. I don't want your moms to be worried about you. I'd like to treat you to some cookies and pop. You'll need to go home and ask if you can come back. Wait a minute." Kate hurried inside and wrote her and Art's names with their phone number on three note cards. Returning outside, she handed one to each boy. "Give these to your moms. I hope you can come back. Maybe all of you can play baseball in the street." The boys got on their bikes and left.

"Ok, Sammy and Karen, go home, change your clothes, and hurry back. We'll talk more about your bike ride home later. Bring your dolls and your baseball mitts. Hurry! Lindsey and I will need help with the cookies and pop. Just walk in when you come back. You'll find us in the kitchen."

1954

Lindsey sat on her front stoop with her head resting in her left hand, her elbow on her lap. Her fingers on her right hand were touching her lap. While she looked glum, the autumn sunshine kept the afternoon bright. Sunshine glittered her hair as she sat and contemplated her bike ride home from school. She kept spinning what happened through her mind. *I didn't do anything to make them be mean. Sammy and Karen didn't either. They just don't like me because of my arm.*

She noticed her friends walk up her driveway. She didn't look at them or say a thing as they dropped their baseball mitts on the stoop beside her. Kate waved them inside, and they went in carrying their dolls. *I wish I was either of them. I just want to look like them. I want to be the same as everyone else. That's what I want.*

She moved her left hand to her lap and sat straighter. A brand new thought circled in. *It was different today. I wasn't alone. Sammy and Karen were with me. They yelled at those boys and didn't leave me, and some other boys helped us. Bobby kept telling that kid to leave me alone. They were on our side.* Just like that, things seemed a lot better.

She heard some kids laughing and talking. Bobby, Jeff, and Jimmy were riding their bikes toward her house. She heard, "Hey Lindsey, do you want to play baseball with us?"

71

Karen and I changed into play clothes and hurried over to Lindsey's house. We dropped our mitts on the stoop where Lindsey was sitting and walked into Kate's kitchen. The wonderful scent of butter, chocolate, and sugary flour filled the air.

"Sammy, carry this plate of chocolate chip cookies outside please, and Karen, can you carry these three bottles of pop? I'll bring out a few more bottles just incase the boys can come back. Thanks," Kate said.

As we walked back outside we heard Bobby holler, "Hey Lindsey, do you want to play baseball with us?" Jimmy and Jeff were with him.

Lindsey stood up all smiles, "Sure. Do you want some cookies and pop first?" The next sounds we heard were kickstands going down. While we each drank a bottle of pop and ate several cookies, we talked about what happened on the way home. Lindsey actually ended up laughing when the boys mimicked the moms who stopped the fight. They made fun of Leland, too, telling her how he always causes trouble but never gets in trouble. We saw Kate laughing. She knew we saw, tried to stop, and ended up going inside.

"So, Lindsey, are you really great at baseball," Bobby asked.

"Well, I do a lot of things with my small hand like writing, school work, board games. With baseball, I catch with my left hand even though I'm right handed. I catch the ball, squeeze my mitt closed, and cover the ball with my small hand to keep the ball in my glove. It usually works."

"Linds, we all try to catch balls by squeezing our mitts and covering the ball with our other hand. You catch the same as us," Bobby shortened her name and informed her.

Her smile was huge. "My dad wants me to catch right handed and left handed. He had a mitt specially made for my small hand. He and I play catch, and I take turns with my mitts. I'm better catching left handed. My dad jokes, 'better reach!'"

"Can you bat," Jeff asked.

72

"Yep, I can. You'll see." Two more boys, friends of Bobby and Jimmy from public school, stopped by and wanted to play ball with us. We chose teams. Jeff, Karen, Jimmy, and I played against Lindsey, Bobby, and his friends.

Lindsey bunted the ball her first time up to bat and made it to first base. Karen and I were so glad. Jimmy told me to move in when Lindsey batted again. She smacked the pitch and made it to second. Bobby looked so happy. All of us were. The game was on!

We moved to the side of the street for a minute when Father Tom drove his red and white chevy down the street and onto the O'Malley's driveway.

1954

Father Tom waved to the kids as he walked toward the O'Malley's screened front door. Stepping up the three steps, he noticed the sweet aroma of homemade cookies and heard Patti Page singing "How Much Is That Doggie In The Window." He pressed the door bell.

Kate was about ready to watch the game outside when she heard the bell. "Hello Father." She was a little startled to see him. "I was just going outside to watch the kids play ball. Please come in." She smoothed the front of her slacks, slid her hands to her side, and thought, *Art said Father Tom is a young priest. He has the face of a teenager.* She finished her greeting, "It's so nice of you to stop by."

He smiled back, "I'd love to watch the children play. Let's sit on your front steps."

"Come in for a minute, please. I'll get us some ice tea or would you rather a coke? The kids just finished their snacks." *Oh Lord, stop thinking of him as a kid.*

"Coke would be great, right out of the bottle. Thanks." He followed her into her kitchen and looked around until he found the cookies.

She smiled as he eyed them. "Help yourself."

"Thank you. I could smell them the second I was at your front door. I loved the days my mom baked, especially chocolate chip cookies. Hands down, my favorite."

He looked all around Kate's kitchen and liked everything; the yellow walls, the raspberry and lemon print curtains, the raspberry formica counter tops with the chrome edge, and the cream colored floor tile. "You know, Mrs. O'Malley, it would be hard not to be happy in your kitchen." He remembered how safe and happy he always felt in his mom's kitchen. He took a bite of his cookie and added, "Great cookie."

She handed him his coke, "Thank you. Have more. Are you sure you don't want to sit in here?"

"No, it's a beautiful day. Let's watch the kids play." He selected another cookie.

Once they were sitting outside Father Tom said, "Mrs. O'Malley, I want to welcome you and your family to our

74

parish. I met your daughter yesterday and Mr. O'Malley, too. Father Aurther introduced us. I'm glad you moved here and are members of St. Joseph's."

"Thank you. We're already very happy here. I've met Father Aurther. I'm sorry he'll be leaving soon. He said he'll be retiring and moving to Florida."

"And that's the other reason I stopped by today. I'm trying to visit many parish families. You see, when Father retires at the end of the year, I will become the new pastor at St. Joseph's."

Huge surprise crossed Kate's face, "That's wonderful. But you seem so, um, oh, excuse me, never mind. That's wonderful news and congratulations!"

"I know I'm very fortunate to have this opportunity so soon. I'm hoping to meet most of our parish families by December. This change will be difficult for many parishioners. Sometimes new and unusual circumstances are hard to accept. Father Aurther is well loved."

"Well, it will be different and sometimes people struggle with things when they're different."

He noticed the quick sadness and then the returning kindness her eyes held. "You know, Mrs O'Malley, Lindsey's a beautiful child. These children she's making friends with are good kids."

"Yes, these are dear children, sweet and kind." Without hesitating she told him, "Lindsey wanted to ride her bike to school today, and I allowed it. I hoped it would be different, but on the way home there was trouble." She felt embarrassed that tears filled her eyes as she thought, *Why was my Lindsey born this way? Why?* She immediately banished that thought and cleared her throat continuing, "Father Tom, some kids just don't understand. Apparently some boys taunted Lindsey and called her names. Although she's heard these things most of her life, it still hurts her. These boys playing baseball helped her, and got into a fight with the other boys, and some mom's got involved."

He looked down and then back at her, "This world needs some changes. Your bright and beautiful daughter shouldn't have to hear anyone call her names or tease her. You're right that some people will behave stupidly when they have no understanding. Mrs O'Malley, yesterday I

75

had a talk with the children in Sister Gladiola's class. Please know that while Father Aurther is still at St. Joseph's, he and I will watch out for Lindsey. I'll continue to watch out for her as long as needed and so will all of the priests at St. Joe's. Karen, also, needs our help. Actually, Samantha does as well. I'm not going to explain why. I think your kind heart will understand in time."

"Thank you." She looked at him a second. "I hope this won't seem too unusual. Please call me by my first name. It's Kate. I'm certain my husband, Art, will want you to call him by his first name, too."

"Thanks, Kate. Tom works for me, too. That's hard for people to do. Even my mom calls me Father Tom."

"I can understand that."

"Getting back to the trouble Lindsey had today, I imagine Mrs. Lotis was one of the moms involved. She's friends with some of these boy's mothers. I wish I could tell you she'll dismiss what happened, but it's not likely."

"Father, believe me, I've dealt with many like Mrs. Lotis. One more won't be that tough. We'll get through whatever she does." They noticed Art's car turn into the driveway.

Art parked his station wagon behind Father's car and walked to the front steps. With a huge smile, he stuck his hand out to shake hands with Tom. "Hello, Father Tom, it's great to see you."

"Mr. O'Malley, It's good to see you, again."

"Father, please, it's Art."

He smiled at Kate and said, "Thanks, Art. I've been having a great afternoon chatting with Kate and watching the kids play ball."

"I bet you have. What do you say we join their game? I've got a couple of mitts in the back of the wagon. Whose team do you want to be on," Art asked as he handed Kate his suit coat, plus his tie, and rolled up the sleeves of his white shirt."

"I'll join Lindsey's. I've noticed she never strikes out."

"You're a smart man and a great priest. I've been watching Sammy and Karen play baseball, almost, everyday the last three weeks. I'll be on their team. We'll knock you guys out."

The dinner hour put an end to the game about forty-five minutes later. Art shook hands with Father Tom, "Thanks for stopping by today. I appreciate everything you're doing for us."

"Your family is wonderful, Art. I'm glad you're part of St. Joseph's Parish. This was fun." He waved to Kate, as he and Art backed their cars out of the driveway, and he drove back to St. Joe's.

1954

As soon as she ordered the children to go home, Wilma Lotis raced into her house straight to her phone book. Her mind was full as she looked at her daughter's, Mary Elizabeth's, class roster's phone numbers. *Honestly,* she thought, *letting plainly deformed children attend school with perfectly normal children. Who thought that one up? It isn't fair to anyone. Certainly our children shouldn't have to deal with such, such divine punishment. Even that poor girl shouldn't have to compare herself with the perfect children. This entire situation is plain stupid!*

First, she telephoned the two room mothers from the two other fourth grade classes and told them to get ten mothers from each room to attend a meeting at her house the next morning. Then, she made the phone calls for Sister Gladiola's room. Quickly getting nine mothers to attend, she called Bobby Williams' mom.

Knowing this was the person she needed on their side, Wilma knew how to get Ann Williams to her house the next morning. "Hello, Ann, this is Wilma Lotis. I'm fine, thank you. I want to tell you about the new girl in Mary Elizabeth's and Bobby's class. Have you heard about her? Oh, you heard she's a sweet girl? You say that Bobby and some other children are playing at her house right now. Well, I'll tell you how sweet she is. She's deformed! And of course, she's made friends with Samantha Cole and Karen Fry, two lost souls if I ever saw lost souls."

Ann rolled her eyes. Wilma was not her favorite person.

Wilma used her trump card. "Do you know there was a fight after school today because of these three girls? Your Bobby was in the thick of it."

"That's enough, Wilma. What do you need?"

"I'm having a meeting here, at my house, tomorrow morning at ten."

"I'll be at your house in the morning. Good bye, Wilma," Ann hung up.

We had so much fun playing baseball that day. When Art came home, he and Father Tom joined our game. Father Tom played on Lindsey's and Bobby's team, and Art played on Karen's and my team. My team lost by one run.

Just as we finished picking up the bases, Kate called all of us to her front steps. "This turned out to be a fun afternoon," she said. "I want to thank you boys for helping the girls today. However, I don't want you to fight with those other boys again. Fighting just doesn't solve anything. I understand it's hard to know what to do."

Bobby said, "Mrs O'Malley, Mike caused Karen and Lindsey to fall. The girls hadn't done a thing to bother him or Wilford and Leland. It just wasn't fair."

"Bobby, a lot of things that happen aren't fair. Just don't fight over the girls anymore," she sounded very tired. Trying to be more cheerful she said, "You're a great kid. All of you boys are. Anytime any of you need help, Lindsey's dad and I will help you. You better get home. It's getting near dinner time." The boys jumped on their bikes and rode to their houses where their moms were waiting for them.

"Girls, you're invited to dinner. This morning I asked Grand and Joan if you could have dinner with us, and they said you could."

After returning to the rectory and having dinner, Father Tom made two phone calls. Ann Williams was first. He learned that Wilma Lotis called her about Lindsey, the fight, and a meeting at Wilma's house the next morning at 10 a.m. Tom thanked her and made his next call.

The second phone call was to his dad. Tom explained about Lindsey, her bike ride home that afternoon, and about her kind parents, Kate and Art O'Malley. Then he told him about Wilma Lotis, "She has a way of stirring things up, Dad." They talked for about an hour, and his dad came up with an ingenious plan to defuse any actions Wilma might conjure to cause the O'Malley's trouble.

After giving Mass the next morning, Tom walked to the Lotis' house. Her meeting had been in progress about ten minutes. With a grin on his face, he rang the doorbell. She opened her door and looked at Father Tom with a 'deer in headlights' expression. It was all he could do not to laugh. "Good morning, Mrs. Lotis, I hope I'm not interrupting. It looks like you're having a ladies' meeting. This is perfect because I have exciting news that concerns you. It will be wonderful to share this announcement with others present as I bestow this honor to you."

She had no idea what Father Tom was talking about. The words: exciting news, announcement, and bestow honor; captured her attention. She ushered Father into her living room and needlessly clapped her hands to get everyone's attention. The complete silence that ensued had nothing to do with her clapping and everything to do with Father Tom's presence.

"Why Ladies," Father said, "please don't be startled and good morning to all. I promise this will only take a few minutes. Mrs. Lotis will continue with her important meeting." He glanced at Ann Williams with a smile.

He cleared his throat and looked at Wilma. "Now ladies, we all know what a fine wife, mother, and member of our church and school community Mrs. Wilma Lotis is." He clapped his hands and all of the ladies clapped theirs in agreement. "We all know how generous and kind hearted she has always been to those of you less fortunate than she, as she feels so many of you are." The ladies weren't quite sure what Father just said. Their faces formed puzzled looks as they glanced at one another. Wilma nodded her head in agreement, and Ann almost laughed.

He began speaking rapidly, "And of course there are those of you who look up to her because she is so well known for her appreciation of those who are mentally or physically handicapped." Everyone gasped, including Wilma. Very loudly he continued, "And so I'm very happy to tell you that Mrs. Wilma Lotis has been selected to be our parish representative to attend an important seminar on the handicapped. This meeting will be held in a beautiful location in Michigan next spring." Father thought of something and quickly added, "I believe there is Kennedy money involved." He saw a huge smile appear on Wilma's face and thought, *Dear Lord, forgive me. I'm not sure about that Kennedy money, but she loves Rose Kennedy.*

He continued, "Now, you'll have all expenses paid. I believe this seminar lasts four days and nights. You will travel by luxury bus. Of course you will give us a full written report on your thoughtful contributions as well as what you may learn from the honor of your attendance. We do have several months before you leave. During Mass near the date of your departure, Father Dennis or I will announce your name to everyone in church at every Mass explaining this honor you have been chosen to receive. You will come to the altar at the Mass you attend for all to see. Further, you will be given information, your reservations, and money allotted. So Mrs. Wilma Lotis, congratulations for receiving this high honor." He finished and smiled at Ann, again. He happily clapped his hands causing all of the ladies to join him. The ear to ear, toothy smile Wilma had on her face as Father Tom steered her toward her front door was perfect. He shook her hand, congratulated her, and walked out.

While he walked back to the rectory, he thanked God for his parents' generosity in donating the money for the seminar. His parents were extremely rich and very kind. Once his dad heard about the O'Malley's, he told his son he would do anything to help and called back with all of the arrangements made.

81

Tom laughed while he walked thinking, *Wilma Lotis will be traveling in the luxury bus for nine hours and spending four days and nights camping with many wonderful councilors, teachers, and parents who care for handicapped children. The seminar will include workshops, discussions, activities, and lessons on how to understand the needs and capabilities of these children. The campsite called, Million Star Hotel, is named for the beautiful night view of the stars. And in the dining cabin, there's a large portrait of Rose Kennedy!* As Tom turned the corner toward the rectory he looked back and noticed the ladies leaving. *Apparently the meeting has ended.*

~~~~~~~~~~~

Jim sat in the chair near Samantha's bed. "Hey you, you've got to wake up now. Christmas decorations are springing up everywhere even though we haven't had Thanksgiving, yet. Actually, Thanksgiving is this week. Rob should be returning home for Thanksgiving. I'll keep calling your home phone."

He noticed her legs moving and took hold of her hand. "Come on Sammy, open your eyes. You can do it. We'll help you, just open your eyes. She became still again. He rubbed her hand vigorously. "Come on Samantha." She kept sleeping. He patted her hand and watched her for a few minutes.

He said, "The other day I glanced at the Bay bike shop window and saw a bike decorated for Christmas. It made me think of the Christmas you, Lindsey, and Karen got bikes. I still remember seeing you guys riding your new bikes up and down our street. There were big bows tied on the handlebars."

SLEEPING MEMORIES 1954

Our three families had so much fun that first Christmas season we shared. A week before Christmas; Grand, Kate, and my mom took Karen, Lindsey, and me on a Greyhound Bus to downtown Cleveland. We arrived at Public Square just as it was getting dark seeing the square sparkling with Christmas decorations. Wide eyed, we jumped off the bus looking in Higbee Department Store's windows. Walking slowly as possible past each window, animated winter scenes of Christmas cheer filled our eyes.

We slipped into Higbee's revolving glass doors into the store. Our hands were held as we looked up at decorated evergreen roping swaged between and then wrapped around pillars in the aisles. We passed crowds of shoppers searching for gifts. Rows of glass showcase counters filled with jewelry, perfumes, scarfs, colognes, gloves, purses, wallets, speciality candies, all kinds of wonderful things; had sales men and women nearby helping customers.

We passed a crowd of people waiting for the elevator hearing excited chatter from every direction. Along with the line of people getting on the escalator, we got on and got off on the fourth floor finding the toy shoppe. Our ears filled with excited announcements from children seeing exactly what they wanted for Christmas. We looked around at shelves and floor displays seeing every toy we ever imagined. Grand, Kate, and my mom let us take our time while we looked at everything.

We got back on the escalator full of all kinds of requests to tell Santa Clause. After seeing Santa, we sat down for dinner at the Silver Grille which was on the tenth floor. The three of us excitedly waited for our dinners to appear in tin stoves that we got to keep and take home. All of us stepped back on the escalators and went all the way down to the basement store where the sale items were. The three of us were given the money we'd saved for Christmas shopping, and we searched until we found perfect gifts for our parents. Before we left to take the bus home, we met back at a crowded basement counter and ordered Frosted Malts, the best ice cream thing ever!

One week later we celebrated Christmas Day. "Sammy, wake up. It's Christmas! All of our presents are here at your house," Karen and Lindsey excitedly said as they jumped on my bed.

Just opening my eyes, I looked at them a second and asked the question that filled my mind most mornings, "Is everything all right?"

Karen answered, "Everything's fine. It's Christmas, and we're going to be together all day. Come on. Hurry and get up!" They ran out of my room.

I held my pillow for a moment as the lingering memory of angry words vanished. Sizzling bacon and percolating coffee aromas seeped into my bedroom. I got out of bed, and hurried into the kitchen seeing Karen and Lindsey holding mugs of hot chocolate topped with whipped cream. My mom was just setting a plate of sweet rolls down on the table and handing Grand a hot cup of coffee when she saw me. "Merry Christmas, Sammy," she said hugging me.

"Merry Christmas, Mommy."

Grand put her arms out, "Where's my hug?"

I hugged her, "Merry Christmas, Grand."

Then Kate gave me a hug and said, "We love you, Sammy. Isn't this the best surprise ever?"

Kate's words just filled my heart. I hugged her tight, "Yes, the best surprise ever."

My mom handed me my hot chocolate, and I carried it the few steps into our living room to find my dad. I saw him, Art, Brice, and Frank talking and laughing. My dad opened his arms, "Merry Christmas!"

"Merry Christmas, Daddy, I love you," I said and hugged him while looking at the bubbles in the lights shining through silver tinsel on our Christmas tree. My eyes discovered lots of presents underneath. I watched Brice put a log on top of the fire in the fireplace while Frank told my dad and Art something that made them laugh. Excited about the presents, for sure, I was even happier feeling the loving warmth and friendship that filled my house.

A few minutes later my mom, Grand, and Kate came into our dining room carrying dishes filled with scrambled eggs, bacon, sausage and potato casserole, fruit salad, and best of all, Karen and Lindsey came in carrying Grand's homemade doughnuts. Then we all were sitting around our dining room table eating, laughing, and just enjoying being together.

After breakfast everyone sat in our living room near our Christmas tree while the three of us opened our presents. We opened our gifts which included boardgames: Winner Spinner, Peter Pan, and Scrabble. Tiny Tear doll clothes and paint by number sets were in other wrapped boxes.

A little later, we all met at church to attend Pastor Reverend Aurther's final Christmas Mass at St. Joseph Church. We shook hands with him after Mass. He gave Lindsey a quick hug, and he blessed the three of us. We bowed our heads and stood very still. "May God fill your lives with many blessings."

We all met, again, at Lindsey's house in the early afternoon. Soon after arriving Art told Lindsey, Karen, and me to go to their garage to get some bottles of pop. When we lifted the garage door, we saw three, shiny, brand new, English Racer Bikes with one big bow and a name on each. We started jumping up and down. Our parents were right behind us. We were so excited. Art said, "How about trying them out?"

Uncle Frank began giving us instructions, "Girls, you don't use the pedals to stop. You stop by squeezing here on the handles. Always squeeze both. And you have three different peddling speeds. When you change speeds you must coast. Do not peddle your bikes when changing speeds."

"Yes, yes, we already know that, Uncle Frank," Karen told her uncle as she kicked up the kickstand on her new red bike. Lindsey did the same with her blue bike as I did with my purple bike. Soon we were riding up and down our street happy as could be.

1954

Brice smiled as he watched Karen on her new bike. He said, "I really think she's forgotten about her mother not being here for Christmas."

Frank snapped back, "Well, I certainly hope so. I still can't believe Sherry couldn't find a way to spend Christmas Day with her daughter. You have to face it, Brice. Your wife has no desire to be here with you two." He regretted his remarks as soon as he saw the hurt on Brice's face. "Look, I'm sorry. I was out of line. I'm sorry we mentioned Sherry. We're having a wonderful Christmas. The girls are happy. Let's go back inside. Mom will want us to head home soon to help her with Christmas dinner."

We had so much fun riding our new bikes and being at Lindsey's house. Kate made everything perfect. She had a buffet lunch serving chicken salad with cranberries and an assortment of breads. There was a large plate with sliced tomatoes, cucumbers, and lettuce. Another plate had sliced ham and cheeses. She had a plate of Christmas cookies and made sure we ate early in the afternoon. As soon as we finished lunch the three of us were back on our bikes.

This Christmas Day passed by so quickly. Before we knew it the sun was setting, and it was time to change clothes and walk to the Fry's house for Christmas dinner. Their house was amazing. It was small like ours and amazing because it was ever changing. Brice and Frank owned a furniture store. They were always placing different furniture in their house and painting their walls a cool color. Karen hated it, and I loved it because everything always looked new. Her house was especially exciting during the holidays. Every Christmas Eve they decorated a white Christmas tree with new decorations. I couldn't wait to see how they changed things and decorated their tree this year.

Lindsey couldn't believe it when we walked into the Fry's living room seeing a dark green sofa with several green and red pillows, two red print wingback chairs, and an over-stuffed chair; all new since we'd been here a few days before. This year their white Christmas tree sparkled with white lights reflecting on large shiny green balls hanging from the branches. Strings of red beads circled the branches, too. Presents under the tree were wrapped in red paper with white bows and green paper with red bows. The fireplace was lit giving welcoming warmth. Above it our eyes found the mantel covered with green branches all with red bows and hanging red stockings with our names.

Our parents relaxed on the new furniture while drinking their highballs. We sat near the tree on the soft dark green carpet drinking pops in fancy glasses containing stemmed cherries. Soon our parents watched us open our last presents, Diaries and Nancy Drew

Mystery Books. We found PJ's, socks, jacks, and candy in our stockings.

A little while after we finished opening our gifts, we heard the doorbell. We were so excited to see Father Tom. This Christmas dinner turned out to be the first of many meals we'd have with him.

Grand's dinner table was special, too, having white dinner plates on green place mats with crystal glasses, polished silverware, fluffed white napkins, and small gifts wrapped in shiny red paper with white bows placed at each setting. Lit candles and a low vase filled with red roses completed her pretty table. She sat at the head of the table while Brice and Frank served us beef tenderloin, whipped potatoes, crisp green beans bundled with thin strips of red pepper, her special Christmas salad, and warm homemade biscuits. Father Tom led us in saying grace. Soon conversation and laughter abound. We finished our dinner loving our bread pudding with caramel sauce and whipped cream.

Everyone played charades, and we had so much fun. Lindsey, Karen, and I fell asleep on the soft carpeting near the Christmas tree. We were covered with soft blankets and had pillows under our heads when we woke up in the morning. Although the three of us couldn't have known, only one other Christmas would be as precious.

Sometime during the week between Christmas and New Years our families went together to the White Oaks Restaurant for dinner. The three of us wore our Sunday church clothes and felt so grown up. It became a tradition for the next several years. Then our families spent New Year's Eve and New Year's Day together. Most years Father Tom was with us for these events. This first year it seemed all too soon that our Christmas vacation ended, and we found ourselves back with Sister Gladiola.

After the holidays our sad experiences returned. Nasty, hurtful things remained the same for my best friends. Most days Lindsey was teased about her small arm. Most days and nights Karen wondered about and missed her mom. In comparison, my problems weren't so terrible. I was ignored by Sister Gladiola during school days, and nights I lay in bed frightened by my mom's and dad's arguing.

We had a wonderful blessing, and it was Kate. She did everything possible to make our young lives joyful and safe.

Jeff, Bobby, and Jimmy liked hanging out with us, and we spent many days after school playing. We paired up without even thinking about it and ended up laughing about things that hurt us. Most weekend nights the three of us stayed overnight together at Lindsey's. Sometimes we slept in our playhouse. Kate and my mom would give us lots of blankets and my mom would make us hot chocolate.

The rest of our fourth grade school year wasn't terrible! Kate arranged for me to come over to her house every morning when my mom and dad left for work and every afternoon until my mom got home. I loved being with Lindsey and Kate. Lots of mornings Karen and Grand were with us. When we came home after school, Kate made us do and explain our homework before we played. She made sure we understood what we were being taught. While Karen always loved going to school, and Lindsey loved school at St Jospeh's, now I actually liked going to school, too. One spring morning I said to Lindsey, "Let's walk to school today."

"Walking's ok with me, I hope Karen doesn't want to ride bikes or want Uncle Frank to drive us." It was a glorious spring morning. Karen put her bike back in their garage. We talked while we looked at the houses we passed, and when we neared Mary Elizabeth's house, we looked to see if she was leaving for school. Through her dining room window we saw her still sitting at their table. We waved and then stopped walking and stared in the window.

Lindsey asked, "What's Mary Elizabeth doing?" She answered her own question. "She's feeding her mother. She's feeding her mother breakfast. Look! Mary Elizabeth just wiped her mother's chin." The blinds at the window snapped shut.

Lindsey kept looking at the window and the closed blinds hoping for another glimpse. "Jeez, that was weird," she stated. As soon as her words slipped out, she looked regretful. Still, she stood looking at the closed blinds. Karen and I knew she wanted to see inside again. All three of us did.

Very slowly we continued our walk to school. We heard the bell with it's usual sound and saw everyone in lines walking inside. It was unusual to see Father Tom near the arched wooden door we needed to walk through. Looking at him, we had the same thought, *Uh-oh.* We walked as slowly as we could while he watched us inch toward him. Once we were at the door he said, "Girls, I want you to go to the rectory. Mrs. Johnson is expecting you. Just sit quietly, and I'll be there shortly."

We hadn't waited very long when he arrived and sat down. He didn't seem very happy when he looked at us. I felt sick. He said, "I have some sad news to tell you. Mary Elizabeth's mother had an accident at a seminar she attended representing our Parish. She fell and broke both of her wrists and her ankle. For the next few months she'll be dependent on her family and friends for everything she does. As you three saw this morning, she needs help eating. Mary Elizabeth will be spending much time helping her mother."

Then he smiled a little, "I thought you might be wondering about what you saw Mary Elizabeth doing. Mr. Lotis phoned the rectory. He's worried she'll be teased about her mother needing to be fed like a baby. I assured him that you three would never hurt or tease Mary Elizabeth, right?"

I answered, "Father Tom, Mrs. Lotis has been mean to my mom and me. She calls my mom a drinker. My mom says, 'Never tell her anything. Just say, hello, and keep on going."

Karen added, "Oh, my mommy too. Mrs. Lotis says my mom is doing, 'God knows what in New York City."

Lindsey looked at us and then back at Father Tom. She made such an amazing decision for being just ten years old, a decision that would define her life. She said, "My mom says hurting other people back never makes anything better. People are nasty because they aren't smart enough to understand things." She told us, "I'm not going to hurt Mary Elizabeth. I'm going to help her. Maybe we all can help her."

Father Tom's face lit up in a huge smile. "Girls, the Lord our God works in wonderful ways. Maybe this happened to Mrs. Lotis because she needs some time to appreciate the wonderful things in her life. Hopefully she will remember that understanding and kindness make everyone feel worthy." He looked at each one of us and added, "Let the four of us be the first ones to tell Mary Elizabeth we're sorry her mom got hurt. What do you say?"

We shook our heads in agreement.

"Girls, let the four of us be the first ones to tell Mary Elizabeth we're sorry her mom got hurt. What do you say?" Tom looked at each face as they shook their heads in agreement. *I'm so fond of these children*, he thought. "All right, you go to Sister Gladiola now. She knows you've been delayed, and you will not be in any trouble."

After the girls left the rectory, with the slightest smile, he blessed himself. "Dear Lord, You are perfect in all things. You have given us a blessing. May we learn that even in tragedy, there is a gift. We will help Mrs. Lotis. I pray she'll receive some wisdom through her ordeal."

Apparently Father Tom called Kate after he was finished talking with us because she was waiting for us at the end of her driveway when we walked home for lunch. Bobby, Jimmy, and Jeff were standing with their bikes near her, too. When she got the six of us together she explained that Mrs. Lotis had an accident, "Mary Elizabeth will be helping her mother, and she will need you to be extra thoughtful toward her. You're great kids. Just be nice to Mary Elizabeth and no nasty remarks about her mother."

We looked at each other. Kate noticed and added, "I know she has been less than kind at times. However she is an adult, and the six of you will be respectful. Boys, no one told me that you make fun of her. I've heard you. To be honest, you've made me laugh, too." Smiles crossed all of our faces. "Don't do it anymore, understand?"

We understood. All of us were kind to Mary Elizabeth. Following Lindsey's lead, we took little gifts to her. Mr. Lotis and Mary Elizabeth were always happy to see us. We never once saw Mrs. Lotis. I said something about that, "Don't you guys wonder where she is? She never comes in the living room just to say hello to us."

Lindsey looked at me, "Sammy, she doesn't want us to see her. It's not her fault. She just doesn't want us to see that she can't do a lot of things and that she's different."

Karen and I didn't say a word back to Linds. We understood.

Even though we thought this fourth grade year would last forever, it slipped by. In the spring the three of us girls turned ten. Often we dreamed our recurring dreams. Karen dreamed she was walking and holding hands with her mom. Her mom always wore a snuggly coat. Lindsey dreamed about the castle and the man with the beautiful eyes who would ask her what she wanted. I dreamed about a horrible roaring sound and being in the terrible woods.

That spring and spending time with Mary Elizabeth sailed by as did the rest of our fourth grade year with Sister Gladiola. Soon it was glorious summer. Mrs. Lotis recovered, and after that we didn't see very much of Mary Elizabeth.

During this summer Karen's mom came home for a few days. Lindsey and I didn't get to play with her while Mrs. Fry was home. Kate told us, "Karen needs every minute her mother gives her. You two will be with her soon enough. Let her have this time with her mom."

She was right. Karen came over to my house as soon as her mom left to go back to New York. She came into my room, lay down on my bed, and buried her face in my pillow. Linds and I knew she was crying, but we didn't let on. We just sat with her and waited.

The three of us were together practically every day after that. Linds, Karen, and I had lots of sleepovers, sleeping in our playhouse several times. Kate and Art took us on vacation to a cottage they rented every summer. All of us went to the Sportsman Carnival in Westlake and loved the rides especially the scrambler and the Ferris wheel. Grand and my mom took us downtown on the bus to the Hippodrome Theatre to see *Lady and the Tramp.* Each family took turns having cookouts, several at the Huntington Beach pavilion. Jumping in the waves and playing tag in the water while hearing constant warnings about the undertow and not swallowing any water, was amazing fun. We hated getting out of Lake Erie and walking back up those thousands of steps to the outdoor shower and then to the pavilion, but seeing our picnic table set and our cookout ready made all of the steps and cold water worth it. That was the first summer the three of us went to an Indian's game. Art, Brice, Uncle Frank, Father Tom, and my dad took us to two games at Cleveland Municipal Stadium. Jimmy, Bobby, and Jeff came with us to one of them. They loved talking about pitchers. Uncle Frank and Father Tom thought left handed Herb Score would be the best pitcher in baseball. My dad thought right handed Bob Lemon and Early Wynn were great. They always kidded and argued about who was best.

One evening before our last week of summer vacation, Father Tom came to my house for dinner. He and my dad were sitting at our kitchen table having a beer and talking about the Indians. My mom was making dinner while having a highball. I came into the kitchen because my mom was talking more loudly. I didn't want her to get mad at my dad in front of Father.

Father Tom smiled, "There you are, Sammy. Things are fine." His voice was reassuring as I sat down at our table. "I was going to ask you at dinner, but now that you're here, could you help Sister Gladiola get her classroom ready next week?"

The happy look on my face soured.

My mom looked at me and yelled, "Samantha Cole, get that look off of your face right now!"

"Joan, it's all right," Father Tom calmly said. "Sammy, Sister needs help getting the desks and shelves in her classroom cleaned. Also she needs assistance getting books to her room and into the desks. It will take two mornings, Tuesday and Wednesday, to get these things done. On Monday morning we must sort text books for all classrooms. You'll still have the afternoons, plus two full days, and the weekend before the first day of school. I've already asked Lindsey and Karen. They've agreed to come. On Monday a lot of children are helping."

"Ok, I'll help, too."

"Thank you. Be in the gymnasium at nine o'clock. We'll have doughnuts and juice for everyone. Tuesday morning be in Sister's classroom at nine. I'll have a surprise, just for you three, for helping Sister."

These glorious summer days sailed by quickly, too. But before they did, the three of us gained more understanding and much wisdom.

96

Monday morning Sister sat alone at her desk thinking. She was dreading another long year teaching. *Most of them are spoiled brat children, who don't want to learn anything,* she thought. *They have no discipline. They have no brains. Today's parents expect me to do my work and their work in bringing up their children. They're all lazy. Pastor Reverend Thomas Brown thinks he's so wonderful giving me a few hours rest during the week. Why, he's the most spoiled of all from what I know.*

Her mind was racing. *There will be thirty-nine children in my room. And this year we have new books. I've had to read these damn books all summer and figure out the new way to teach these bloody, monster children. Let's have more Catholics. Who thought that having a baby every nine months was intelligent? Obviously male brains came up with that one! The husbands have to go to work and leave their wives all day to raise their babies. We must have more Catholics and then what, have less of everyone else? They expect me to handle thirty-nine children this year.*

She hobbled from her desk to the coat closet in the back of her classroom. Her mind registered the pain coming from both of her hips and legs. She grabbed a box of Kleenex from the shelf and hobbled back to her desk. Tears filled her eyes, and her expression grimaced. She opened the box of Kleenex, and got out a tissue. A prayer poured out, "Lord, help me, help me. Oh no, I forgot to bless myself. I'm sorry. I'm so sorry. In the name of the Father, the Son, and the Holy Ghost, Amen, Please let me forget. Oh, bless me Father for I have sinned. Help me, help me. I'm so sorry." She put her face in her hands and cried.

Finally she blew her nose, looked out the window, and saw her dead mother in one of the window panes. "Get out," she said with clinched teeth. "I'm telling you to leave me alone. You keep following me. Papa loved me, that's all. He loved me." She looked at the window at her mother. "Stop looking at me, Mama. You make me remember those things that happened decades and decades ago. You won't let me forget those horrible things he did to me. You knew, and you didn't stop him. Well, I did. I stopped him from hurting little Mary Pat. I saved her. Stop looking at me. Stop!" Sister Gladiola raised her cane, and the figure in the window vanished. Instead her father's dead, startled eyes filled the window pane. With amazing strength she threw the Kleenex box at the sight, then she hid her face in her hands.

A few minutes later, she heard laughing children carrying books into the classrooms. She recognized Karen Fry's, Lindsey O'Malley's, and Samantha Cole's voices. *Oh wonderful,* she thought, *Here come the three D's: the dumped, the deformed, and the dumb!*

We stayed overnight at Karen's the night before we went to help Sister. Grand woke us up Tuesday morning to scrambled eggs, toast, and juice. Then we were on our bikes heading for the second day of helping at our school. While we peddled our bikes, I realized the best thing. I wasn't afraid of Sister Gladiola anymore.

We walked into her classroom seeing we arrived ahead of her. We sat down and quietly waited. I looked at my friends and asserted, "Hey, we can talk if we want. School hasn't started. We're still on summer break."

"Maybe we should begin cleaning something," Lindsey said while looking around.

"We sure don't want to make her mad, summer vacation or not. She hates laziness," Karen stated. "There's no chores list on the blackboard. Maybe she left a list for us on her desk." She got up to look. "Good thing I checked." She held up a note.

Karen Fry, Samantha Cole, and Lindsey O'Malley,

Go to the door in our hallway that has 'Private' on it. Go inside to the janitors room   and get three buckets, a box of soap, a windex bottle, some rags, and towels.

The buckets can be filled in the sink in my room. You have permission to go into the janitors room and to be in the private hallway.

Thank you. You have been and are good children.

Margaret Elizabeth Burke   (Sr. Gladiola)

Karen looked at us, "That must be Sister's real name. I wonder why she can't keep it?" With Sister's note in hand, we went down the hallway. We stopped at the closed door with the word, PRIVATE, and enthusiastically opened it as it made a loud squeaking sound in the otherwise quite hall. "Wow," Karen said as we saw a pop machine, a hot chocolate and coffee machine, and a cigarette machine lined up against a wall. Across from them were two more doors. One door was open, and in this room we could see two sofa's, several comfortable looking chairs, side tables with lamps, one large table with chairs, and one window. The other door had Janitor's Room across it, and it was closed.

We opened the Janitor's Room door giving us a little more light in this dimly lit room. Our eyes slowly adjusted. We saw one bucket tipped over and a flashlight on the floor. The shadows were eery. "It's hard to see in here. Let's hurry up," I said. Standing very close together, we looked for more buckets and soap. Walking in further and turning a bit, we saw a standing ladder, a tipped over chair, a familiar cane, and something. A black, bulky thing pulled our eyes upward. I put my hand over my mouth and grabbed Karen's hand. We saw a big hanging sack, only it wasn't. It was Sister's clothes hanging! We kept staring and saw one shoe dangling. Sounds came from our throats as we realized Sister Gladiola was in that hanging heap.

Then we heard Father Tom, "Oh my God, No!" He pulled us all at the same time out into the hallway.

1955

Father Tom was having a hectic morning. He arrived late to Sister's classroom, and found it empty. *I hope the girls haven't forgotten about helping, again, today*, he wondered. *Maybe they're somewhere in the hallway or in the gym.*

He hurried down the hall and recognized the squeaking sound coming from the opposite direction. *Sister must be getting some coffee*, he thought. He kept walking, taking a few more quick steps, then stopped. He considered, *The girls know better than to open that door marked 'Private.' It's really quiet, no sounds from the gym.* He turned around and headed for the teacher's lounge.

Tom opened the private hallway door and kicked the stopper down. He noticed the opened janitor's room door and heard weak squeals getting louder as he walked in. The girls were right there. And then he saw, "Oh my God, no!" He grabbed Lindsey, Karen, and Sammy, and herded them out of the room into the school hallway. Then he hurried to close the janitor's room door, and kicked the stopper up closing the Private hallway door. "Let's get outside. Hold hands. I've got you. You're safe. Run. You need fresh air." He held Lindsey's and Karen's hands as Karen already had hold of Sammy's hand, and they ran down the hall.

They ran out into the sunshine. "Sit down. Are you ok? I've got you. You're ok. You're safe." He rubbed their backs and looked around. He saw the Chief of Police driving slowly in front of the school and waved him over.

Ken Heart, Chief of Bay Village Police, turned on his emergency lights and ran to them. "Everything all right here," he asked.

"No! We need help. Hurry into the janitor's room. Hurry."

Ken radioed for help then ran into the school.

Father Tom told the girls, "Stay right here. Don't move. I'll be right back. You're safe. Stay together right here." He ran back into the school.

Tom continued talking to Samantha while she remained sleeping. He was remembering Sister Gladiola's suicide. "Can you hear me, Sammy? I think all of this reminiscing is benefiting me the most. I'm hoping all of this talking will bring you back to us. Please wake up."

He held her hand. "I really haven't thought about these things much until now. I guess Kate's death and being with you has brought memories back. I do have regret, Sammy. The three of you were so young. I wish I could change how I handled Sister Gladiola's death. Of course things were so different then. She would not have been buried within the Church. Suicide was considered a sin back then. We were so stupid. Families, who already were devastated, were caused more pain."

"How Sister Gladiola managed to accomplish that I'll never figure out. I'll never forget cutting her down. Chief of Police, Ken Heart, was already on the ladder when I left the three of you and caught up with him. I held her as the rope gave way, and I fell to the ground with her. Ken jumped off the ladder and removed the rope from her neck. We made some fast decisions, Sammy."

Ken was on the ladder trying to cut Sister down when Father Tom caught up with him. Tom put his arms around the skirt of her habit and said, "I've got her, I think." The rope let lose. He fell to the ground along with her.

"I want to get this rope from around her neck," Ken stated. The police chief and the priest looked at each other for just a second. They could hear the approaching siren.

Father Tom shook his head, yes, and said, "Hide the rope. Let's move her into the private hallway." That easily they made the decision to hide the suicide. "Get her cane." He quickly gave Sister Last Rites.

Ken hurried back into the janitor's room to fix things. He put the bucket in the sink, placed the chair near a small desk, got the rope, and then folded the ladder leaning it against the wall. Quickly finding a bag, he stuffed the rope inside along with a flashlight. As he was leaving he picked up a piece of paper he found on the floor as well as her cane and shoe. The chief handed Father everything but the bag, then hurried outside. He saw one of his officers getting out of a police car.

Tom quickly put the cane near Sister, pushed her foot into her shoe, and returned to the girls seeing Ken talking with another policeman.

"We won't be needing help, Don," Ken stated. "It's an older nun, and she's gone. Dr. Pratt was in church, and he's pronounced her. He's contacted the funeral director, too. There's no need for an ambulance. The funeral car will take her to the funeral home. We're about done here." The parts about Dr. Pratt and the funeral director weren't true, yet. Ken knew they would be true within minutes. He turned his car's emergency lights off, grabbed a blanket, watched Don drive away, and hurried back into the school.

Kate just sat down on her front steps when she heard the siren and thought, *Gosh, it sounds near by.* The siren silenced. *Could something have happened at St Joe's?* She saw Frank next door in his yard and walked over. "Frank, did you just hear that siren? It sounded like it could have stopped at St. Joe's. The girls are there this morning."

"I know where the girls are." He looked peeved.

"Could we drive over to the school for a minute? I'm sure everything's fine. I'd just like to be certain."

The genuine concern on her face softened his mood. He put his hand on her back guiding her the few steps to his car. "Of course." He opened the passenger door for her. "I didn't mean to be grouchy. I'm sorry."

"You weren't grouchy. I worry too much. Probably the siren has nothing to do with St. Joe's."

They noticed a police car slowly pass them after they backed out of the driveway. "Checking things at school seems silly, now," Kate said. But less then a minute later, they saw another police car parked in front of the school and Father Tom with the girls sitting on the grass. They hurried out of the car and ran to them. "Are you all right? Lindsey, what's wrong?"

All three looked pale as Lindsey and Sammy put their arms around Kate, and Karen hugged Frank. He asked what happened. At the same moment, Sammy pulled away from Kate, looked at Father Tom and asked, "Was that the surprise you had for us? That was a terrible surprise!"

"Samantha, no, of course it wasn't. I never thought Sister would," he stopped a second, "I wouldn't ever do anything to frighten or hurt you."

He looked at Frank. "Take them to the rectory. I need to talk with Kate. We'll be there shortly. Keep them with you and don't talk with anyone else, not anyone." Realizing he'd been curt, he added, "Frank, Thank you."

Frank walked them into the rectory where the girls sat down on the sofa. All three were shivering. He asked the rectory secretary for a blanket. As he put the blanket around them he said, "Girls, whatever is wrong, you'll be fine. We love you. Can you tell me what happened?"

"No," Karen answered.

~~~~~~~~~~~

Tom got up from the chair and tried to settle Samantha down. Her eyes were closed, but suddenly she was very agitated. "Sammy, come on and open your eyes. What's going on?" She was kicking her legs and tossing back and forth. She let out a loud scream. He pressed the nurse call button.

Two nurses hurried in. "Father, go to the lounge."

Samantha yelled, "Why did she do it? Why? How could she go?" Then just as quickly she quieted down and became still again.

Father hadn't left. "She's settled down. I'd like to stay with her."

"I'm going to take her temperature and check a few things."

The other nurse walked toward the door. "I'll page Dr. Jameson."

Tom moved to the window and looked out at the falling snow. "Samantha, please wake up. We love you," he whispered. "I shouldn't have brought up Sister Gladiola."

Father Tom ushered Kate into St. Joseph School. "Sister Gladiola has died," he quickly said because the door marked private was wide open, and he knew Sister's body and Ken Heart would be in plain sight. Dr. Pratt was there, too.

"What happened?" She looked into the hallway and wasn't prepared to see what she gathered was Sister's covered body on the floor. "Oh, dear Lord, this just happened? The girls were the first to find her?" She stopped walking and leaned against the wall.

"I need to talk with you." He took hold of her hand. "Come with me to Sister's room. Sit at her desk a few minutes. I'm going to get you some water. I'll be right back."

As he hurried to the private hallway, Ken came toward him and said, "We've taken care of everything for Sister. Dr. Pratt told me she suffered a heart attack. He's close friends with Greg Spinner and has called him. She will be taken to the Spinner Funeral Home. Their car will be here in a few minutes. Father Dennis checked, and St. Joseph Church is to handle her funeral arrangements. She has no living relatives."

"Thank you, Ken, thank you. I will let you know if there are any problems." Tom shook his hand.

"There really can't be any problems. Doc Pratt will sign her death certificate. We're clear on this, right?"

He nodded and got a glass of water from the teacher's lounge, then walked back to Sister's classroom. Handing Kate the water he said, "I have something awful to tell you." She noticed his hand was shaking. "What is it?" "The girls found Sister this morning. They found her hanging in the janitor's room."

She set the water down and took some deep breaths. All of the color drained from her face, and she thought she might faint. She heard him add, "Kate, they thought that was my surprise for them." His voice gave way.

She was silent for a minute. She was thinking about the girls seeing Sister hanging and shut that thought off when she saw tears in his eyes. Touching his shoulder she said, "The girls know you and trust you. They don't know what they're thinking right now. We need to get back to them." Although she tried, she couldn't stop the word, *hanging,* from twirling through her mind. She looked around the room. "Why did the girls go to the janitor's room?"

Tom looked around and then remembered the paper Ken handed him. He got it out of his pocket and read it. "Oh my God, look at this! Sister told them to go there, and she knew they would do what she told them. That crazy old witch, let her go to Hell! I don't give a damn about her funeral Mass." He started out of the room.

His words startled her, and she yelled, "Thomas Brown, turn yourself around and get back in here." She closed the door after he walked back in. "Stop right now." Her voice was raised, "Just stop." She lowered her voice, "I can't even think."

He looked down, and quietly asked, "How could she be so cruel to these precious children? They are innocent, sweet, and kind. Why couldn't she realize that? How could I have missed all that was going on with her?" His wiped his tears.

"The girls need us. Let's go to the rectory and take them to my house." He shook his head agreeing, and they walked out of the classroom and the school.

Kate couldn't imagine the girls seeing Sister hanging. Her heart ached. *Dear God, help us,* she prayed.

Father Tom's mind was circling with thoughts realizing he still had more to tell. *How can I tell her about the lie I need all of us to keep?* He prayed, *Dear God, I'm sorry for all of this. I need help.*

They found the girls sitting together on the rectory sofa with their legs and laps covered with a blanket. Frank was saying something reassuring and looked genuinely relieved when they walked in. Father immediately said, "Let's go to Lindsey's house. Frank will drive you, and Kate and I will follow in my car."

While driving Tom asked, "Do you think Sister Gladiola should be given a Funeral Mass?"

"Absolutely."

He told her what he and Ken had done. Once Kate took the girls into her house, he told Frank what had happened.

Uncle Frank drove us to Kate's with her and Father Tom following. Lindsey, Karen, and I went with Kate into her kitchen. She dampened three washcloths with lukewarm water and patted our faces. Those warm wash cloths felt so good on our tear stained cheeks. When we went into the living room, Frank and Grand were just opening the front door. Frank said, "I've called Brice at the store. He'll be here right away." Grand hugged Karen first and then Lindsey and me.

"I'm going to fix us some lunch," Kate said, "soup and sandwiches. Girls, come help me."

After lunch, while still sitting at the table, Father Tom tried his best to talk to us. "Girls, I'm so sorry for what happened this morning. No one knew this was going to happen. Sister Gladiola was terribly wrong to hurt herself. What she's done isn't right. She shouldn't have hurt herself."

Kate said, "Excuse me, Father. Girls, when Sister wrote her list to you, I'm certain she didn't know she was going to hurt herself. Her mind was mixed up and broken, I think. It happened without her being able to think correctly. I want you to understand that she did not plan to frighten you or hurt you."

Father Tom added, "Remember what she wrote at the end of her list? She wrote that you were always good children. Remember that part. You are very good and dear children." He smiled at us, but his eyes and face looked so sad, "Would you like to play for a while? I must tell you not to talk with anyone about this morning, yet. We must make sure everyone close to Sister has been told what happened."

He looked at Kate, "I need to return to St Joseph's. Would you mind if I call Art and explain?"

She answered she would appreciate it and said, "Tell him the girls are playing here for the day, and we'll see him at dinner." Looking at us, "I want you to play inside. Sammy and Karen, go get your dolls. Lindsey, go with them. Hurry back, and I'll get out lots of blankets for you to make tents." Grand added that she'd go get Karen's doll and things.

Brice and Frank walked out with us and waited in Lindsey's front yard until we returned. They gave Karen a hug and left to go to their store.

We played all afternoon and really didn't say much about Sister. What we had seen was a hanging heap of clothes. I asked, "Did you guys see Sister's foot?"

"I saw a black shoe, I think," Karen answered. "I didn't see her face, did you?"

"No, but she was in those clothes," Lindsey said. "It's bad, what we saw." Then Linds asked, "She's dead, right?"

Karen and I looked at each other and shrugged our shoulders. Karen said, "They keep saying that she hurt herself, and I think we heard the siren coming. Maybe she's hurt."

"It was scary in there. That's what I remember," I stated. "It was cold, too. I'm glad Father Tom saved us."

It didn't seem as though we played very long. We were sitting at Kate's combined dining room and kitchen tables before we knew it. My dad and mom, Art, Kate, Grand, Brice, Frank, Father Tom, and the three of us awkwardly trying to act like everything was fine. Father said grace, a silent prayer, and we began eating the dinner Grand made us. Spatterings of conversation broke the silence while everyone avoided the reason we were all together. Finally my mom, Kate, and Grand cleared the table. Kate set down a plate of warm homemade peanut butter cookies. Lindsey, Karen, and I helped ourselves.

Looking a bit stern, Father Tom's eyes watched us. I looked at my friends thinking, *Uh oh, we should have waited to have a cookie.* In a tone unlike we'd ever heard Father Tom said, "Girls, earlier today I told you that it was wrong for Sister to hurt herself. Well, it was even worse than wrong. Sister Gladiola committed a sin against her Catholic Church when she hurt herself. Many religions don't teach this, but the Catholic Church does. She should not have hurt herself. Do you have any questions about this?"

"Yes, we do." Lindsey looked at us a second and asked Father Tom, "We want to know, is Sister Gladiola hurt or dead?"

109

"And I want to know why Sister Gladiola changed her name," I added.

All of the adults looked confused as they glanced at one another. They all quickly answered the first question at the same time, "She's at peace. She died. She's gone. She passed away. She's at rest. She's dead."

Lindsey's question sure was answered. Everyone forgot about mine. Father Tom reached for a cookie, and his hand was shaking.

Karen said, "God must be very angry with Sister."

I asked Father Tom something else, "God saw what she did. He knows we saw her.

Is God mad at us, too?"

Father Tom put his cookie down. He looked at the adults, and his face relaxed. He smiled when he looked back at us and answered, "No, God is not mad at you." He took a deep breath, "Girls, there are God rules and there are Church rules. Catholic and Protestant people believe in God, Jesus, the Holy Ghost, and the Ten Commandments. We all say the Lord's Prayer. But, each religion has their own rules."

He took another deep breath, "I'm sure when Sister Gladiola was young, she was happy. I bet she didn't limp, have any pain in her legs, or need a cane. When she was very young, she dedicated her life to serving God and teaching children." He looked at me, "She chose a new name when she became a nun and began teaching." He looked at all of us. "As she got older, we kept her teaching. Her legs got warn out and caused her pain all of the time. We continued to ask her to teach fourth grade, and we didn't pay any attention to her pain. She went on teaching as her Catholic Church still asked her to do. Everyone, including me, didn't think about her pain. She never complained to us. She did what we asked. I understand, now, that not only were her legs and hips old and hurting, her mind was too. Sister Gladiola had much pain and confusion in her mind. Everything got very mixed up in her mind."

For a second I remembered when I forgot my sweater and went back to her classroom and found it. She was looking at the window, talking to someone who wasn't there. I felt sad for her that day. I felt sad now. I never told anyone what I saw.

Father Tom continued explaining, "Yes, she did a very sad, bad thing. We believe that life is God's gift to us. We also know that sometimes people get sick and die. God blesses us and takes us with him when we get older or get sick and die. Sister Gladiola's mind was very sick. She died. I need to ask you if you can keep how we saw Sister this morning between us." Father Tom repeated, "I am asking the three of you not to tell anyone how you saw Sister in the janitor's room this morning. All of us can talk about it whenever you want or need. In order for Sister Gladiola to have a Funeral Mass in her Catholic Church, she loved and served her entire life, we must keep what we saw this morning between us."

I thought that Father Tom looked so kind.

He looked at each one of us, "Girls, this is a very important and giant decision. I want you to know that I will not be angry at what you decide. No one here will be angry. We all love you and that includes me. You think about what I've told you. Tomorrow morning we'll meet here for breakfast, and we'll decide about Sister's funeral." He looked at Kate, and she smiled and shook her head yes.

Karen and I stayed overnight at Lindsey's. We didn't have to think very long about our decision. Karen and Lindsey fell asleep quickly. For a while, I stayed awake remembering Sister in her classroom talking to someone who wasn't there.

The next morning Kate made bacon and pancakes with warm maple syrup for the three of us and Father Tom. We told him and Kate that we understood Sister Gladiola's sick mind made her die. We promised we'd never tell anyone what we saw. Father got up and gave each one of us a kiss on the top of our head.

Two mornings later St. Joseph Church was full of parishioners attending Sister Gladiola's Funeral Mass. I cried. Karen held my hand.

Jimmy, Bobby, and Jeff asked us if we saw Sister die. We told them the truth and said we didn't. Lindsey answered, "Her heart got so tired, it stopped beating."

111

And that was that. Our lives together moved on. The days passed by. The nights passed by. With eagerness to grow up, more years passed by.

Jim looked at the doctor, "Why isn't she waking up? I come in here thinking she'll open her eyes any second. She must hear us talking to her."

"Her body is recovering from years, most likely, of suffering anorexia. She is recovering and getting fluids and nourishment. Think of her as taking a break. We really don't know if she can hear us. Any news about her family?"

"No, not a thing! I'm getting on a flight to Portland late Friday night unless I talk with Rob today, Thanksgiving, or Friday. I've got her address and house keys. We still haven't found her cell phone or know for sure if she has one. I don't know what's going on with her family. Maybe a neighbor will know something. I've called her home phone daily and left messages at different times. Unless I hear from him or their daughter, going to Portland is the only thing to do."

"Hopefully someone will be home for Thanksgiving weekend." The doctor changed gears, "Her temperature is up this morning, ninety-nine point six. We'll watch that. We'll stay on course with physical therapy, talking, music, nourishment, and quiet time. Keep the faith." He started to leave and turned back, "When you find out anything about her family, call me anytime, day or night." He walked out into the hallway.

Father Tom and Jim looked at each other. Jim sarcastically said, "Well, that was informative. I'm glad I got here in time to hear that. I just can't believe this, and where in the hell are her husband and daughter?"

"It sounds like you're seeing the glass without any hope, Jim."

"What? What did you say, seeing the glass without hope? How about seeing the glass half empty or half full? Is that what you're getting at?"

"That's it," Tom turned away smiling and then looked back, "seeing the glass half empty. Actually, you're seeing the glass almost drained! Come on, Jim, maybe it's better that she's here with us. I'm glad you're going to Portland. Have you booked your flight? You could have trouble getting a seat with Thanksgiving weekend and all."

113

"My flights are confirmed, night owl flights both directions. I leave Friday night, and I'll be back Monday very early in the morning. The airline said I had perfect timing, the return flight just had a cancellation."

"Timing is everything."

"You actually got that right!"

"Yes, I did," Tom smiled. "Get to both airports in plenty of time. Flights are probably over booked because of the holiday. Another year almost gone, these days are flying by."

Without giving it consideration, the years flew by.
Each passing year, with each grade we passed, gave us
an exciting bit of independence. Our bike riding
perimeters grew and our curfews became later. We
gained independence from our parents to go bowling and
to the movies, and the first movie we saw without parents
was *King Kong*. We loved rock and roll music and listened
to "All Shook Up," "Party Doll," "Peggy Sue," "Jail House
Rock," "School Day," and many more. We went to Arthur
Murray Dance lessons and learned the box step, the cha-
cha-cha, and how to fast dance. Then twice a month on
Saturday nights during our eighth year at St. Joe's we
went to dances held in the gym. We wrapped our arms
around our dance partners and slowly moved our feet to
songs like "Love Me Tender," "It's All in the Game," "April
Love," "The Great Pretender," "Earth Angel," and "Chances
Are" until a parent chaperon, a Sister, or Father Tom
tapped our shoulders, and we resumed the box step. We
fast danced to "Purple People Eater," "Whole Lot of
Shaken Going On," "Hound Dog," "Rock In Robin,"
"Chantilly Lace," "At the Hop," and lined up for "The Stroll."
In eighth grade the boys were on football and basketball
teams. We were on the cheerleading squad, and no one
dared to make fun of Lindsey. The St. Joseph coaches
made sure of that. We moved on to Confirmation,
graduated, and excitedly looked forward to being freshman
in high school.

As these years passed Lindsey, Karen, and I became
sisters. We loved each other, and it seemed we'd been in
each other's lives forever. Our parents loved one another
as family, and they especially loved us. Kate was our glue.
She was the one always protecting us. Although she did
her very best, she couldn't save us forever. Time was
rolling along and the nineteen sixties were set to roll in.
Lindsey, Karen, and I couldn't wait!

At some point we told each other about our
reoccurring dreams. Mine started with a loud screeching
sound. It was always the very same terrible sound. I'd
feel very cold and realize I was alone in the woods. There

were clawing branches everywhere. I never knew how I got into the woods, and I never got out.

Karen dreamed about walking down a special street with her mom. Her mom always wore the same big, soft, furry coat, and Karen would snuggle beside it while they walked. They held hands and smiled at each other, but they never talked. When Karen woke up, she always wondered why they didn't talk. She mostly wondered why she didn't beg her mom to stay.

Lindsey dreamed about the golden castle and the man with the beautiful eyes. This man always said the same thing: "Hello, honey. What are you looking for? Tell me what you want." Lindsey could never get passed this man and get into the castle. Even though there was something she wanted so much, she could never remember what it was.

The six of us and a few others left the Catholic school system and joined students at the crowded Bay High School where we became the class of nineteen sixty-three. This first year in high school we had split sessions. Our baby boomer generation caused over crowding in thousands of schools across the country including ours. The seventh grade through Freshman school day began at 11:30 a.m. and ended at 4:00 p.m. Sophomores through seniors started their day at 6:50 a.m. and ended at 11:10 a.m.

We enthusiastically began our late morning classes maintaining good grades, but what really mattered the most to us was having fun. The friendships between Lindsey and Bobby, Karen and Jeff, and Jimmy and I evolved. We loved being together as a group and as couples we were beginning to love being alone! Like other classmates, we held hands in Bay High hallways between classes and passed each other lots of notes. On some weekends our parents drove us to the movies where our boyfriends put their arms around us. On other weekends we went to dances at the Bayway, and after the last dance we walked home together. We passionately kissed good night near our front doors until the flashing of porch lights got our attention.

These weekend nights sailed by along with our freshman year. The next year our class stayed at the uncrowded high school while the seventh, eighth, and ninth grades went to the newly built junior high school.

~~~~~~~~~~~~

Father Tom checked to make sure Samantha was warm enough. Her temperature was normal now. He felt her forehead and arms to make sure. She seemed a little cool, so he pulled the afghan up around her shoulders and sat back down.

He continued reminiscing, "Samantha, do you remember Henry Lowe, your principal at Bay High? He retired about twenty-five years ago and moved away. He used to come back to visit about twice a year, and he'd stay at the Holsten Inn. He really admired how Bette turned out. He couldn't stand her mother, however."

"Anyhow, about ten years ago he and his friend Jane had lunch with Kate and I. He and Kate laughed about that cheerleading meeting he and Lindsey had. You knew about that meeting, right? I'm sure Lindsey told you and Karen all about it."

During our sophomore year Bobby, Jeff, and Jimmy played football and basketball at Bay High without Lindsey, Karen, and me being on the cheerleading squad.

The summer football cheerleading tryouts didn't go well for Lindsey because some of the parents created a problem. The situation developed into a life altering experience for her. Our practices for tryouts were almost finished when Lindsey told Karen and me that she had to attend a meeting with Principal Lowe.

1960

Mrs. Wilma Lotis and a small brigade of cheerleader moms attended the Board of Education meeting. She stood up. "We can't have a deformed child cheerlead for our varsity teams," she whined. "The girls who are chosen to represent our high school are the best. They are the girls we want to show off. We've tolerated this, Lindsey O'Malley nonsense, in grade school through the freshman year. This is varsity level." She snapped out, "We cannot have deformed Lindsey O'Malley representing our varsity teams!" She sat down.

Henry Lowe, Bay High's principal, was told to attend this hastily arranged board meeting. He listened to Mrs. Lotis and thought how much he didn't like this particular parent. However, listening to her and the other parents caused him to consider how cruel certain teenagers might be to a cheerleader who didn't fit the norm. Henry knew about Lindsey because he and Father Tom were friends. Tom had made sure that he knew Bay High School's class of 1963 was enrolling some of St. Joseph's best former students including Lindsey O'Malley.

Finally Mrs. Lotis and the other parents quieted down. Henry had his moment to speak, "Please give me the opportunity to meet with Lindsey before you go any further with this. I'll do so immediately, and I'll inform the board when our meeting is concluded. This is a most simple request." He looked directly at Wilma Lotis, who he thought was just plain stupid, and said with space between each word, "Do you understand what I just said?"

Jane Smythe, the school board president, laughed out loud. She just loved Henry. She really did!

Wilma shook her head that she understood, and the meeting concluded.

Jane and Henry got into their cars and drove to Henry's house. They quietly sat in his kitchen, Jane drinking the perfect Manhattan he made and Henry drinking a beer. He finally let out the frustration she knew was coming, "I can't stand that woman. How can one person cause such a storm? Why does Mrs. Lotis have to be such a menace?"

120

Jane let him settle down for a few minutes then asked, "Can you stop her from going any further with this?"

His tone softened, "I sure am going to try. Let's go to bed."

"And sleep on it?"

"Not right away." Henry loved Jane, too. He really did!

Late Wednesday afternoon, Dr. Jameson walked into Samantha's room. He didn't find her alone very often. Music from the nineteen-sixties softly filled the room. He smiled and sang along to "Volare." I like this song, Samantha. Good old Bobby Rydell," He checked her monitors, looked at her chart, then washed his hands. He lifted her eyes lids and shined a small light in her eyes. "I wonder what's going on inside that mind. It's time to open your eyes. Father Tom and Jim Peterson are really worried about you. You just don't want to be in this old world for some reason, do you?"

He tried a new approach. "Now, listen here young lady. You have to make an effort to come back. This is going on too long. It's a tough battle, I get it. Well, choose to fight this battle and open those eyes of yours. I'm going to keep giving you these pep talks. Think of me as your cheerleader." He patted her arm and added, "Jim is traveling to your home in Portland on Friday. Hopefully he'll get some answers."

Looking toward the door to her room, he heard Father Tom and Jim entering. "I didn't realize you were here. Her vitals are good. She's coughed a few times. We'll keep an eye on that. Her color is better. Questions?"

Jim spoke right up, "How much longer can she stay like this?"

"As long as she wants. She's been mistreating her body for a long time, I'm sure. These things are hard to predict. I thought she'd be awake by now. I wish I could tell you how long." His smile was slight as he added, "I'm leaving here soon and won't be here tomorrow unless there's an emergency. My wife's family is here for Thanksgiving. I'm still invited over to see them when they visit. I'll be back in the hospital Friday."

After Dr. Jameson left the room Jim remarked, "Sounds like the doctor's separated or divorced." He changed subjects, "Do you have Thanksgiving dinner plans?"

"No, I have 9:00 a.m. Mass, and then in the early afternoon I'm helping serve Thanksgiving dinners near St.

Malachi Parish. I plan on stopping here for a while in late morning and returning here late afternoon."

"Bette and Ron want us to stop by the Inn sometime tomorrow for turkey dinner. She said to come whenever we want. Sound good?"

"Sounds great."

1960

The next morning Henry sat at his office desk in Bay High with a plan to halt Wilma Lotis. He made a phone call to Kate O'Malley and told her he wanted to meet with Lindsey that afternoon. He also said, "Mrs. O'Malley, of course you are welcome to attend this meeting. During these high school years we not only want to educate the children, we also want them to learn to make wise, independent choices. They must learn to make their own decisions." Henry got to the point, "Mrs. O'Malley, I have to inform you that there is a stupid, and I do mean stupid, leader of even less inspired parents who's trying to stop Lindsey from trying out for cheerleading."

"I thought most of that," her voice gave way a little, "was behind us. We,"

Henry felt awful about this situation, and with a booming voice he interrupted, "Please come with Lindsey to the meeting, but wait in my secretary's office. Let Lindsey and I discuss her options. I'm going to have my intercom turned on, and I'll make sure Miss Smith has her intercom on. There'll be no interruptions. Just the two of you will be in her office. You'll hear every word spoken between Lindsey and me. What do you say?"

In a very composed voice she answered, "Mr. Lowe, what time would you like us to be at your office?"

"Please be here at one o'clock. Thank you, Mrs. O'Malley."

They arrived on time for the meeting. Principal Lowe shook hands with Kate and Lindsey. "I'm happy to meet you both," he said. "Mrs. O'Malley, stay right here with Miss Smith while Lindsey and I talk a few minutes. Lindsey come in," he shut his office door as she sat down.

Lindsey looked around his office and liked it. She saw several pictures hanging on the walls of groups of students and noticed family pictures on his mahogany desk. She liked the school colors on the fabrics covering the chairs.

He smiled at her, "I'm very happy you're in the class of sixty-three."

"Thank you, Mr. Lowe."

124

"I have to tell you something. I hate what I have to say, and I don't agree with it." He swallowed and took a deep breath, "There's a group of parents who don't want you cheerleading at the varsity level."

She guessed this was the reason for the meeting. She'd noticed some of the girls at the practices staring at her small arm. She'd seen Mrs. Lotis talking to some moms who also stared. She'd seen it her whole life. At this very moment the anger, hurt, and embarrassment steeped inside her. Unlike her, she decided to make life difficult for her principal. "Why Mr. Lowe, why on earth don't some parents want me cheerleading for our wonderful varsity teams?"

He looked a bit surprised and replied, "It is because they don't know you or appreciate your abilities to be a great cheerleader. It is because they are narrow minded and stupid. It is because," he informed Lindsey, "you have one arm that is smaller than the other, and they don't have the brains to see that it doesn't matter."

"What are you telling me?" She stood up and held her arms straight out, looking back and forth at them. "Oh my God, look at my arms! I never noticed. They don't match!"

Kate was startled hearing Lindsey's remarks, but picturing that she must have held her arms out, she thought it was funny and actually began laughing.

At first Lindsey couldn't figure out how she could hear her mom laughing. Then she saw Mr. Lowe looking at the intercom on his desk. She got up, leaned toward the intercom and said, "Mom, why don't you just come in."

Henry's face turned red. Lindsey quickly considered her behavior, and she blushed. Kate slowly opened the office door, and her face was flushed. They all looked at each other. Then Henry, realizing they probably felt as foolish as he did, started to smile. In a few seconds they all were laughing.

"I'm sorry, Mr. Lowe. I really am sorry. It's just that when you said," Lindsey started laughing again, "when you said, I mean, it seemed like you were informing me, as though I hadn't ever once noticed my arm." Lindsey was laughing so hard she had tears running down her cheeks. Kate was laughing, too.

Still laughing himself, Henry said, "Lindsey, stop. I'm the one who needs to apologize. Every once in a while, as my dear wife used to say, I get a little full of myself. I'm sure I sounded quite stupid." With a kind expression and in a more serious tone, he continued, "Lindsey, I didn't want to hurt you. I disagree with anyone who thinks you shouldn't represent our school as a cheerleader. I want to add that there are many activities including: running for class offices, homeroom rep, joining the year book staff, the school paper staff, the choir, debate teams, competitive speech teams, and various clubs. Lindsey, there are so many worthwhile ways to spend your years in high school. Many activities could lead you toward a career. I'm not sure how little pleated skirts and yelling peppy cheers helps one." He looked down a second. "Let's pretend I didn't say that last part. Cheerleaders are bouncy, peppy, leaders of cheer, I guess. Ok?"

Lindsey and her mom glanced at each other.

Mr. Lowe looked a tad flustered, then smiled again and said, "Participating in the activities I mentioned are an asset when filling out college and employment applications. Lindsey, there are adults who may try to make things difficult for you because they are from a different generation. They are behind the time. You and your peers are beginning to see things as they should be, unlike earlier generations. Of course cheerleaders are a fun part of sports." He paused a second and said, "Things are beginning to change, and there are opportunities. You must choose your battles. If cheerleading is important to you, you have my support. Just know there are many opportunities at Bay High. You can accomplish so many things in high school with your friends who support you. Your classmates from St. Joe's know how intelligent and sharp you are. I'm sure classmates here already know. Lindsey, unfortunately you'll have more battles than most kids. 'Choose your battles wisely."

Kate stared at Henry Lowe. She was speechless. She felt really happy for her daughter, really happy. Earlier in the day she thought Lindsey would be told that she couldn't be a cheerleader for some dumb reason. Kate looked at her and saw a bright smile on her face.

His words kept running through Lindsey's mind, *Choose your battles. Choose your battles wisely.* Smiling she asked, "Can I think the cheerleading thing over, Mr. Lowe? I'd like to talk with my best friends, Karen Fry and Samantha Cole. We've been trying out together. Can I give you my answer tomorrow morning?"

"Tomorrow morning will be fine. Miss Smith will know I need to speak with you. And again, if cheerleading is your thing, I will support you. Mrs. O'Malley, you have a very beautiful, vibrant daughter. I have a feeling Bay High is in for a great three years. Thank you, both."

SLEEPING MEMORIES 1960

We were in Lindsey's bedroom as soon as she got home from her meeting with Mr. Lowe. We hated what she told us, "There are some parents who don't want me on the cheerleading squad." A new song on her radio "You Talk Too Much" also filled our hears.

I asked, "Who doesn't want you to be a cheerleader?" Without waiting for an answer I spat out, "I bet it was that witch Mrs. Lotis, and I bet Mary Elizabeth doesn't even know about it."

"You know what you guys? I don't care. Mr. Lowe told me about all of the activities high school offers. I hadn't given many of them any thought. He told me he'll support me if I want to continue with the cheerleading tryouts. He also told me to choose my battles wisely."

Karen said, "I'm sick of people hurting you." She looked at me and continued, "We both are. We don't want you going through any more of this shit."

"Wow, such a big word, shit!" Lindsey laughed. "Ok you guys, here's what I've decided. I'm not going to cheerleading tryouts any longer, the heck with it. I'm going to run for a class office. I'll get to know more kids in our class. Once they get over how I look, they may see that I'm not so bad. I'm going to do everything I can to help make the class of sixty-three a great class. I'm going to try to be a great student, and I'm going to have fun. I'm not going to let anyone hurt me. Those days are behind me. If running for a class office turns out to be a bomb, I'll do something else. I already have you guys, Bobby, Jimmy, and Jeff, and that's so cool."

"Well, if you're not trying out for cheerleading, we're not, either. Right, Karen?"

She looked at me, then she looked down for a second. "I wanted to make the cheering squad until hearing all of this." She looked up at us, "We've cheered together since St. Joe's. Linds, if you're done, we're done. You'll make a fab class officer. How about Sophomore class treasurer?" She smiled, "You stink at math, but Linds, you'll win!" We all laughed. Karen turned the volume up on the radio. Bobby Rydell was singing "We Got Love."

128

So, the three of us weren't cheerleaders any longer. Lindsey moved her life forward with new attitude filled with wonderful hope and love.

SLEEPING MEMORIES 1960

The meeting with Mr. Lowe shaped Lindsey's future, but everything changed for Karen that summer.

Every summer Art rented a cottage in Manistee, Michigan. The same place where he, his sister, and parents had vacationed. Every summer Karen and I went with Kate, Art, and Lindsey, and this summer we couldn't wait to be lying out in the sun while we listened to our transistor radios.

Linds and I talked on the phone the night before we left. "Lindsey, this will be so cool. We'll get the best suntans. What time should I be at your house in the morning? I think Kate said five." I turned the volume down on my clock radio. Connie Francis was singing "Lipstick On Your Collar."

I heard her answer, "Yep, five o'clock. I can't believe they want to leave that early. I hope Karen sets her alarm. Grand is already at her sister's house, and Grand is Karen's alarm clock. She's visiting her sister, niece, and grandniece, Jill. We've met Jill, right? This is the best. Yesterday, she dropped off her homemade doughnuts before she left."

"Grand's the best! We did meet Jill at a picnic. I think."

"Yes, we did. I liked her. My dad wants me to help him with something. See you in the morning."

Karen remembered to set her alarm, and the station wagon backed out of the O'Malley's driveway at ten minutes past five the next morning. There'd been lots of hugging and talking when Art told us to get in the station wagon. "Thank God we packed the suitcases in the carrier last night. We'd have never gotten out of here this morning," he said as we drove down our street passed Bobby's house.

We were a happy family driving to the cottage. Karen, Lindsey, and I fell back to sleep and slept for about six hours.

Lindsey woke up first. Karen and I heard her announce that she was hungry. I opened my eyes and added, "I'm hungry, too."

130

Art replied, "No need to say a word, Karen. I'll stop as soon as I find a shady spot."

It took him an hour to find the shady spot. He drove into a park complete with picnic tables, and restrooms. We helped Kate set Grand's doughnuts along with fruit, hardboiled eggs, crisp bacon, orange juice, plates, and glasses on the checkered tablecloth she'd spread out on the shady table.

I took a bite out of my doughnut and announced, "I'm on cloud nine!"

Art laughed, "Well, eat up because we're cutting out in twenty minutes." He sat with us a little longer, then got up and walked around by himself for several minutes. As we drove out of the park he said, "Kate, when we stop for gas, I need to call my sister." About thirty minutes later he found a gas station with an outdoor phone booth.

1960

While the girls took turns using the restroom, Art walked to the phone booth and dialed the operator. He gave the operator his sister's phone number telling her he would talk for five minutes. The operator told him the amount of money to put into the pay phone and said she would signal at close to five minutes.

He heard Cathy's, his sister's, phone ringing. She answered on the fourth ring. "Oh my God, Art, I can't believe you called. I tried calling you at home and remembered you were driving to the cottage today. I left a message at the rental office for you to call me. Art, mom died in her sleep last night. I found her this morning."

He didn't speak for a few seconds, then he asked, "Are you all right, honey?" His voice broke a little.

"Yes, I'm ok. I'm so sorry I have to tell you like this. I wish I could hug you. You're still my little brother, you know. Mom and I had a wonderful day yesterday. I will," she started to cry but still tried to talk, "I will tell you," her voice quivered, and she waited to speak for a few moments. In a stronger voice she said, "Mom's at Johnston's Funeral Home. I haven't made any decisions, yet. I was waiting to talk with you."

"It's so odd, Cathy. I just had this feeling that I needed to talk with you. We'll head back home. We have Sammy and Karen with us. We'll leave for your house in the morning. We'll do whatever you want, sweetheart. I love you. See you tomorrow."

Art hung up the phone and dialed the operator, again. He gave her Joan's phone number saying he only needed two minutes. When no one answered, he repeated this action giving the Fry's number with the same result. He put his coins in his pocket and told Kate about his mother. While hugging her, he looked at Lindsey. He thought, *I'll tell Linds just like I told her mom.*

He walked toward her and saw that she was walking to him. She asked, "Dad, is everything ok?"

"Honey, I have some sad news to tell you. Grandma died in her sleep last night. I just talked with Aunt Cathy." He hugged his daughter. He knew Kate was telling Sammy and Karen. Everyone got into the station wagon

132

and headed home. It was awkwardly quiet except for the radio.SLEEPING MEMORIES 1960

Kate told Karen and me about Lindsey's grandma. A few minutes later we were driving home, the three of us side by side in the back of the station wagon silently listening to records on the radio. With Lindsey in-between us we heard Dodie Stevens singing "Pink Shoe Laces," Paul Evans singing "Seven Little Girls Sitting in the Back Seat," The Crests singing "Sixteen Candles," Bobby Darin singing "Dream Lover," and Ed Byrnes and Connie Stevens singing "Kookie, Kookie, (Lend Me Your Comb). At first we knew Lindsey was crying, and Karen and I took turns gently rubbing her back or softly scratching her arms. After a while she smiled a bit.

Listening to a lot more records until about eight o'clock or so, we finally were back in Bay Village and turning into the O'Malley's driveway. We all hugged. Karen and I told them we were sorry about Lindsey's grandma. We really didn't know what to say.

"Tell your mom, Sam, and your dad, Karen, that I'll call them. If no one's home, come back here for the night. We'll be leaving early, but you can sleep in and lock up for us. I'll talk with one of them before we leave tomorrow."

"We'll tell them, Kate," I answered. Art gave us our suitcases. We dropped mine off at my house. No one was home.

We walked over to Karen's and found the side door closed and locked. We walked around to the front door and found it locked, too. "I guess my dad and Uncle Frank aren't home either. They're probably with your mom and dad." We walked back to the side door. Karen got the hidden key from under the flower pot. "They seldom lock both doors." She opened the door then put the key back. It was almost quiet as we walked up the three steps into the kitchen. We could hear music coming from somewhere.

I looked around and commented, "It's different when Grand isn't home, huh?"

"This is weird." We walked through the dining room into the living room. "We hardly ever close the dining room and living room curtains. Dad? Uncle Frank?" Karen set

133

her suitcase down. The music was louder, now, louder than it should be. Together we walked up the stairs leading to the second floor bedrooms. I had the strangest feeling that we should stop moving. I didn't say anything, and we kept walking. The music was very loud. We passed Karen's bedroom and Grand's and moved toward her dad's bedroom at the end of the hallway.

Karen's dad's bedroom door was almost closed. The music was too loud. We arrived at the door and Karen said, "Dad?" She pushed his door open.

That music was so loud. Brice and Uncle Frank didn't hear us. They were in bed. The music was too loud. They thought they were alone. It was private. Karen grabbed my hand. I pulled her back into the hallway. I turned us around, and I don't think she heard me say, "Come on, we shouldn't be here."

I kept hold of her hand as we ran down the steps through the living room, dining room, kitchen, and down the three steps back outside. We heard the phone ringing as we passed through the kitchen, but we didn't stop.

Karen's legs started to buckle once we were outside. Her hand felt cold as she pulled it away from mine. We sat down on the grass. She looked at me a few seconds then hid her face in her hands. She started breathing strangely and threw up. I tried to help her, then I got up and ran to get Kate.

1960

Kate called Joan to explain why we returned home. The phone rang ten times before she hung up and called Brice.

Frank answered their phone on the eighth ring, "Hello."

"Hello, Frank, it's Kate."

"Kate? Is everything all right?" He signaled Brice to turn the music down.

"No, Art's mother died sometime last night. We're back home. I think Karen and Sammy are heading to your house. I just called Joan, and no one's home."

"Oh God," Frank hung up the phone and got out of bed.

"What's wrong," Brice asked.

"The girls are home."

I ran into Kate's house to the kitchen and saw her hanging up her phone. "Kate, Kate, Karen needs you. She's throwing up. When we went to her house we heard music upstairs, and, and, Brice and Uncle Frank were in bed."

Art came into the kitchen. "What's going on?"

Kate looked at him and quietly answered, "Karen and Sammy saw Brice and Frank together."

"Oh for Christ sake!" He rarely swore.

Kate and I hurried to the front door.

"Stay here. I'll get her." In a more controlled voice he asked, "Sammy, where is she?"

"Sitting in their side yard. She's throwing up. Hurry." I was crying now, and I wasn't sure why.

He rushed out their front door while Kate sat me down in the living room. I looked at her, "I don't understand. What were they doing? The music was too loud." I stood up.

"It's ok," she answered and hugged me. "I'm going to try to explain."

Lindsey, dressed in pajamas, came into the living room. "What's the matter? Sammy, what's wrong?"

"Linds, just sit here with Sammy. Don't talk. Sit quietly, and I will explain when Karen gets here."

1960

Dear God, not today, Art thought as he quickly walked across his front yard. He immediately saw her sitting on the ground and jogged toward her. She'd stopped throwing up. "Karen? Karen, honey? Come back to our house." He squatted next to her.

She looked up at him, looked right into his eyes, and didn't answer him. He wasn't sure if she really saw him. Art put his hands on her arms. She was ice cold and shaking. "Honey, everything's going to be all right." He picked her up and carried her to Kate.

Lindsey sat down beside me on the sofa. She wrapped her warm hand around mine and said, "You're freezing." She got up, covered me with an afghan, and sat back down beside me. She started to say something just as Art opened the front screen door with Karen in his arms. We watched him carry her toward their bathroom. Kate followed him. We heard him close his bedroom door and very soon watched him walk back through the living room into the kitchen. He'd changed clothes, and now we heard the kitchen faucet. We also heard the shower being turned on. Lindsey looked at me, "What's going on?"

I simply shook my head and looked down.

We were silent until Kate, carrying a large quilt, walked with Karen into the living room. Karen was showered and wearing a pair of Lindsey's pajamas. We made room for her to sit between us, and she sat down without saying a word. I could feel her shaking, and certainly Linds could as well. Kate took the afghan off of me, then covered the three of us with the quilt. She patted my leg and said, "We'll figure this out togeth," she didn't finish. She turned her head as all of us looked at the front door opening. Brice and Uncle Frank were almost inside.

Karen whispered, "No, no, no," while shaking her head. She looked up still shaking her head and in a stronger voice said, "Go away." Then she screamed, "Get out" and covered her face with her hands. Art walked in from the kitchen.

The hope Brice and Frank had that she hadn't gone upstairs evaporated. "Karen, we need to talk with you. Honey, please," Brice pleaded.

"Go away. Just go away." And then louder than ever, "Get out!" Tears streamed down her cheeks.

Art immediately stood facing Brice and Frank, having his back to us and quietly said, "Go home. Trust us." He steered them back through the front door and went outside with them.

Lindsey whispered, "Has something happened to Grand, too?"

I didn't answer Lindsey. A list of words echoed through my mind, words that we'd heard tossed around our playground at St. Joe's and still heard when teenagers teased or kidded each other. Words that had sounded harmless until this minute. Words that took on hurtful meaning, now, as I watched Brice and Frank turn around and leave.

1960

Brice had huge tears in his eyes, "You're telling us, they saw us? This shouldn't have happened. We never imagined the girls would be home. We've been so careful. Never did we think anything like this could happen."

"I'm sorry, Brice. We'll figure this all out. I should've tried to call you, again. I called right away, but no one was home. I'm sorry. Kate and I know you would never hurt the girls." His thoughts circled. "It's just, God, I don't know. I'm thinking we should take them with us to my sister's. We're planning on spending a few extra days with her after my mother's funeral. I think the time away would be good for Karen. We're leaving early tomorrow morning. We never would leave you, right now, for any other reason."

Brice looked at Art and testily said, "You've got that right. Death is the only thing worse than what we've just done to Karen. Samantha, too, she was there, too." His tone changed, "I should have had the courage to tell Karen the truth about us. Just, how do you tell your child this? I can't undo what they saw. I'm sorry, Art. I can't undo it."

"I think it's a good idea getting Karen away for a while, Sammy and Lindsey, too," Frank calmly said. "It'll give us some time to think how we can explain to Karen and the girls." He paused a second. "Karen knows that Grand took care of me after my parents died. She knows we're not brothers. She also knows I was married for a short time, but doesn't know that my wife didn't die, we divorced. Look Art, it was difficult for me to admit who I am. I tried hiding from it." He wiped away tears and stayed silent a few seconds. "While this is who we are, it's not easy for others to understand. Anyway, I'm sure Lindsey and Sammy think Brice and I are brothers. We should have told Karen, then the girls, the truth along time ago. They were bound to find out soon. We felt so safe, though." He paused, again. "You obviously know we haven't discussed this with anyone. We've always wanted to keep our personal life private. In fact, we haven't even talked with Grand. She must know and just understands. When you get back home from your sisters, we'll try to explain to Karen first, then to the rest of our family."

140

"Kate and I figured things out. We've never discussed this with Jack and Joan. I think they know, too. I'm not sure why, but I think they know." He looked at his house and then back at them, "Would it be all right if Kate and I talk with the girls? We'll only talk with them if they're receptive. We don't really know if they have any understanding of homosexuality, what it is or what it means." Art felt awkward and looked away.

Frank answered, "We know you'll say the right things. Yes, please, absolutely, if Karen will listen. Brice, do you agree?"

He shook his head in agreement and asked, "Can they spend the night with you?"

"Of course they can. I don't think Joan and Jack know we're back home. Let me go with you to retrieve Karen's suitcase. At least she's all packed."

"We'll talk with Joan and Jack first thing tomorrow," Brice said as his eyes looked at Frank's. They both were devastated.

The three of them walked into the Fry's house. Art shook hands with them and picked up Karen's suitcase. "When we get passed all of this, we'll be better for it."

"There aren't many men with your insight. Frank and I are grateful for your friendship. Please call me immediately if Karen,"

Art interrupted, "Kate and I will wrap our arms around Karen. We'll do everything we can. The few days at my sisters will give you and her space."

Frank said, "We're very sorry your mother died. We couldn't have made a worse mess of everything."

"Please don't question yourselves. The mistake is not explaining to Karen. I sure don't know how or when you should have told her. We'll admit the mistake in not talking about this, and we'll fix it. We'll start by making sure she knows how very much you love her, Brice. We all love her very much." He looked at their sad eyes. "We'll get things figured out. I'll call you after my mother's funeral. We'll get through this. I need to call about the cottage, too. Maybe we'll still go for the second week. I'll call you." He patted Brice's shoulder and walked back to his house. He set Karen's suitcase down on his driveway, walked over to

141

the Cole's empty house, and got Sammy's suitcase. He put both back into the carrier on top of his station wagon.

We were quietly sitting on the sofa when Art walked back into his house alone. Each of us was holding a warm cup of tea. He stopped in front of Karen and me, "I'd like you to come with us to attend Lindsey's Grandma's funeral. We need to be together. We need to talk."

"No talking!" Karen stated. "We will not talk about it ever." She gave him an angry look. He escaped into the kitchen.

Instantly Kate was standing in front of us, "Yes, we will talk. There are things that will never change. One of those things is how much all of us parents love you girls. No matter what we do or who we are, we love you. We'll give you an explanation. We'll get started talking about this now, and we'll continue talking about it over the next few days, weeks, months, how ever long we need."

She looked at Karen, "Honey, you should have been told. All of you should have been made aware. All of us adults haven't ever discussed this. We should have trusted our friendship and love for one and other."

Lindsey looked at all of us and asked, "Will someone please tell me what's happened?"

"Kate, Shut up!" Karen yelled.

In stunned silence, Lindsey stared at her.

Art came back into the living room. He looked right at her and said, "Karen, we know you're shocked, angry, confused, and I'm sure a lot of other feelings because of what you saw. You can yell at us, if yelling will make you feel better."

She glared at Art. Then giant tears fell from her eyes. She got up, ran to him, and cried in his arms.

"It's all right," he said with tears in his eyes, too. "We all love you, honey. That's what matters the most." He looked so sad.

"Mom? What's happened? Has something happened to Grand?"

"No, honey, Grand is fine. She's still with her sister, niece, and grandniece. We just have to tell you something that we should have explained sooner. Everyone is fine. We need to calm down and just talk about this."

Kate asked me, "Sweetheart, are you all right?" She covered us when Karen sat back down.

"I'm not sure what we saw. I'm just positive we shouldn't have been there."

Karen put her hands over her ears and shook her head, no.

"Honey, stop. We need to talk about this," Kate said and held her hands out for Karen to hold. "Please let us talk about it." She gently patted Karen's hands. "Love has many faces. You already know this. Usually a family has a mom, dad, and children. Grandparents, aunts, uncles, and cousins visit, but most families have moms, dads, and children living together. Most families have dads who go to work and moms who stay home during the day to take care of their families and homes. Most families have children who are the same as most children. However, sometimes things are different. As long as love, respect, and kindness fill a home, different can be a blessing. Being different can lead the way toward understanding and compassion for others. Girls, our three families are different. You must realize that." A small smile appeared on her face.

I looked out the living room window at my house. Her words, *love, respect, and kindness,* scratched my heart. Those things were missing at my house. I felt sad about everything, and I think Art noticed.

His eyes returned to Karen. "We're happy together. Our families love one and other and think of each other as part of one large family. We share understanding and kindness. We give each other support concerning our differences, our problems, and our blessings. We've made this mistake, and for sure it's been most unfair to you, Karen. Your dad, Uncle Frank, Grand, and the rest of us have never mentioned this between us. Maybe we should have, but we haven't." He took a deep breath and said, "As Kate," he looked at Lindsey a second, "as mom said a minute ago, love has many faces. There's the love between friends and the love between families. Kate and I feel that all of us are family. We all do."

Then Kate softly spoke, "There's the love between husbands and wives. This is the usual way romantic love works. Sometimes love is different. Sometimes honest,

144

sincere, romantic love happens between two women or two men. And even though our religion begs to differ, love is sometimes different from what people expect."

Lindsey quietly asked, "Kind of like me, mom?"

Kate looked at her daughter and smiled, "Honey, like you in this way: beautiful, wonderful, smart, a million other fantastic things and, also, different from the usual."

Karen's tears streamed down her cheeks. Lindsey and I held her hands tight.

As I reasoned things through my mind, I asked, "So, Brice and Uncle Frank love each other the same way you and Art love each other?"

Lindsey, squinting her eyes, looked from me to her mom. She seemed to be trying hard to put my sentence into some kind of order.

Karen shook her head and straightened her back. "I can't hear this. They're supposed to be my dad and my uncle. Does Grand know?" More tears filled her eyes, and she sank back down on the couch. "Of course, she must know."

Art said, "Grand hasn't ever spoken about your dad and Frank to us. I imagine she understands. Just as Kate and I keep our personal life between the two of us, your dad and Frank want to do the same. Grand respects their privacy. Honey, Grand's at your great aunt's house for three weeks. Your dad and Frank knew you were with us at the cottage for two weeks. They thought they had some private time for themselves. They had no idea you'd be home."

Karen wiped her tears and started to say something. She stopped and seemed to consider what she just heard.

I asked, "So, Brice and Uncle Frank aren't really brothers?"

"They are not brothers."

We silently sat for a minute or two contemplating this new development in our lives when Kate said, "Girls, you know, it could have been, I mean, you could have gone away with Jack and Joan or Brice and Frank for two weeks and come back home unannounced to our house. You could have walked in on Art and," Art looked stunned, but she didn't hesitate, "You could have walked in on Art and me while we were being intimate."

145

With a horrified look on her face, Lindsey put her hands over her ears and loudly said, "Ewww, Mom, that's awful. Stop. Ewww!" She shook her head and shut her eyes.

Equally shocked at Kate, I ordered, "Kate, stop, enough!"

And Karen was startled, too. She looked from Kate, to Lindsey, to me. It was quiet.

Then Art, who was staring down at the carpet, broke the silence by making the strangest, silliest sound. It sounded like a snort, a belch, and a toot all mixed together. We all looked at him. He tried to look innocent by still staring at the floor. He looked so funny when he looked back up and saw all of us with our eyes on him. Karen actually began laughing, then Lindsey was laughing, then Kate and Art. And as outrageous as laughing at this situation seemed to me, I began laughing with them.

Within seconds Kate was hugging Karen. "All of us love you very much and care your thoughts and feelings, honey. Nothing in this world is more important."

Art touched her shoulder and asked, "Would you like to stop talking for now?"

"Yes."

"We want you and Sammy to come with us to my sisters. We can talk more at her house. Please remember that your dad and Frank love you very much. The last thing they would ever do is hurt you. Keep in your heart that there is no one in this world your dad loves more than you. Don't ever doubt that."

Karen hugged him and didn't say a word for a minute, then said, "I'd like to stay with you and Kate for a while."

"Ok. Just remember we all love you very much, especially, your dad loves you." Then he smiled and said, "I have a crazy idea. I know we've spent a ton of time in the station wagon today, but let's get out of here and go to the drive-in movie. Sammy, go get into pajamas. I'll buy snacks, whatever you want. You already have pillows and blankets in the car. I'll get the paper and see what's showing. Kate, I've talked with Cathy again. She doesn't want us to leave here before noon tomorrow. She found a letter mom wrote stating her funeral wishes. The funeral director has the letter. We can sleep in tomorrow morning."

We were relieved with his idea. The three of us disappeared into Lindsey's bedroom to find some pajamas for me.

Friday morning Jim came into Samantha's hospital room. "Any changes?"

Father Tom got up, stretched, and said, "Well, no, except that her temperature is up a little. The nurse notified Dr. Jameson. He's coming in today, and he's on his way. Are you packed for Portland?"

Jim felt Sam's forehead. "She does feel warm. Where's the doctor?"

"I said he's not in the hospital. He's on his way. He'll be here any minute. She's comfortable. Her breathing is steady. So, are you ready for your flight to Portland?"

"Yes, I have what I need packed and in my car. I've got some things at St Joe's I need done by Monday morning. Just wanted to stop here first. I'll be back later. Maybe we can get some dinner. I'll go to the airport from here. Let me know what the doctor says, ok?"

"Will do. I'll be leaving after the doctor checks Sam out. I'll stop by the school office."

"Ok, sounds good."

Tom watched him walk down the hallway. He walked back to Samantha. "Where are you child?" He took hold of her hand. "You do feel warm. Dr. Jameson will be here any minute to see what's going on." He wrung out a wash cloth with cool water and patted her forehead and cheeks with it. He placed it on the inside of her wrist and gently held it there. Then he said, "What are your thoughts while you're sleeping? I hope you can hear me reminiscing. You three were just starting high school when you learned about Brice and Frank. I've always felt that their situation was a big reason why Karen became passionately involved with civil rights. We just got back to feeling comfortable with each other and then such sadness filled out hearts. You, Karen, and Lindsey were so young to have so much happen. You three had Kate, though. She was our blessing."

Art found the drive-in movie listing in the paper. He tried to talk us into *North by Northwest,* but the three of us insisted on *Pillow Talk.* Kate helped our cause by suggesting that a lighthearted movie would be just right. Funny, I left that movie thinking any girl who won Rock Hudson's heart would be so lucky.

As weeks passed Karen talked with Lindsey and me about her dad and Frank. The three of us really didn't understand homosexuality. Eventually we figured out it wasn't a choice, and we understood it was something we needed to keep private. Many people simply hated the thought of it.

Although it took the rest of the summer and most of autumn, before the first heavy snowfall, our family got back to feeling safe and comfortable with each other.

We began our sophomore year in our uncrowded high school with everyone excited about the first ever live televised presidential debate between Richard M. Nixon and John F. Kennedy. Kate invited our family and our boyfriends to her living room to watch. Karen was still staying at the O'Malley's and Brice and Uncle Frank didn't join us. Grand was at Kate's almost everyday and was there for the debate. The six of us teenagers felt like adults as we ate pizza and discussed how nervous Mr. Nixon and Mr. Kennedy looked at the beginning of the questioning. As the questions continued, we thought that John Kennedy gained confidence, and Richard Nixon continued to look uncomfortable.

Huge harsh realities faced John Kennedy after he won the election in November and became president in January. We three sisters faced some harsh realities in our own lives. Mine was not so bad compared with Karen's and Lindsey's. Simply, when my mom drank, she drank too much, and her behavior became unbearable. We knew that my dad was angry and preoccupied with something that took up most of his time. Precious Karen's relationship with her dad and Uncle Frank hadn't healed yet. At this point, she knew her mom wasn't ever going to come home and stay with her. All of us knew she wouldn't ever be cared for by the one person she needed so much. Although most of our classmates no longer taunted and teased Lindsey, no matter what she accomplished, many adults could not get her small arm out of their thoughts. She was different, and that caused them to keep her at a distance.

Just before Thanksgiving 1960, Karen told Kate she was thinking about returning home. Two days later she did just that. It was the Fry's turn to host turkey dinner and the busy activity gave them opportunity to begin feeling comfortable with one and other. Christmas passed by and finally the new year came.

One winter afternoon, while her dad sat near the warm fireplace reading his newspaper, Karen asked him if they could talk for a few minutes.

"Sure, honey," Brice folded his paper and set it on the end table.

"Dad, my mom isn't here because you are homosexual, right? I mean, did she know? Did she always know?"

He took a deep breath. He'd wanted to talk with his daughter about this without forcing the conversation. With no warning his opportunity was here. He looked at his daughter, who was becoming a beautiful young lady, and began explaining, "Your mom is an amazing person. She's a million things all in one package. We became friends, honey. She knew about my homosexuality and remained my friend. I loved her so much for that. I still do."

He looked away for a second. "We lived in the same apartment building in the lower east side in New York City. We were very young, very poor, and very lonely. We became friends. We enjoyed talking with each other. We shared our hopes and dreams with one and other. We trusted each other with secrets. We told each other the great things happening in our lives, and we were happy for each other. We shared the bad and sad things that happened, too. Sometimes we cried with each other. We became very close friends."

"One night we were both so lonely. Honey, you just happened. I was very excited about you and so was your mom. We got married right away. At about the same time, I became a buyer for a furniture store and got a big raise in salary. Your mom and I were happy planning and getting everything ready for you. We were intimate just that one time." His face flushed, and he looked down and then back up. In a determined voice he looked at Karen, "Nothing happened between us again, but we were so happy about you. We remained dear friends. For the first several months after you were born, we were fine."

"Well," he paused a second, "things got difficult for both of us as time went on. Your mom just loved singing in night clubs and acting in plays. Her dream was that someone would discover her talent, take her to Hollywood, get her movie scripts, and make her a movie star. That was and I imagine will always be her dream. I realized New York City wasn't where I wanted to raise you. When Grand came to see you shortly after you were born, she just loved you. I mentioned I wanted to move out of the city, and she wanted to know if I'd consider moving to Bay Village."

"Your mom liked it here. She'd travel back to New York City to try out for parts in plays. If she got a part, she'd go back and stay for rehearsals through the run of the play and then come back here. But as time passed, your mom wilted here. We watched her spirit change. It wasn't right for her here. Karen, your mom loves you, but acting and singing are her passion. She loves the attention and the applause. She didn't choose that life and not you. It's who she is, if that makes sense. She saw how much Grand loves you and loves taking care of you. She saw how much Frank loves you. Your mom knows we do everything possible to make you happy and take care of you. She loves you very much, Karen. It's hard to understand, I know."

"Honey, your mom always knew about me. She never questioned or judged me. She gave me all of her loving friendship. I will always love and care about her. I help support her financially, and I always will." Tears filled Brice's eyes as he said, "Our marriage never stood a chance, but everyday I thank God for the gift of you."

Karen looked into her dad's kind, sad eyes. "Thank you for telling me this." She hugged him. "Thanks, dad. I love you."

He hugged her close, "I love you."

In the space of about ten weeks, during the spring of 1961, we turned sixteen. On that coolest of birthdays we took our temporary driver's test and got our temporary license. We practiced driving and parallel parking while our parents gave us instructions. Less then a week after our birthdays, we passed our driving tests and hit the streets being inexperienced, licensed drivers. For a while our parents limited our driving to Bay Village. Weeks later, our boundaries expanded to the surrounding communities. We drove to Beatty's Big Steer Inn, Bearden's Drive-In, and Manners Big Boy restaurants hearing the revving cars circle passed the parked cars. Our teenage concentration was devoted to who was inside the parked cars much more than not bumping into them!

Our bodies made some spectacular changes by the time our sixteenth year arrived. Jeff, Bobby, and Jimmy were as tough as they could be. Like many guys in the class of '63, they had crew cuts. They also needed to shave stinging themselves after with cologne. The fragrances of English Leather, Brute, and Canoe Colognes waffled through Bay High's hallways causing curious excitement. Karen, Lindsey, and I looked like young women, sometimes, just like most of the girls in our class. We ratted and backcombed our hair into beehive flips, put on make-up, and wore nylons with our white sneakers. Our sixteenth year amazingly improved our brains, too. All of us were much wiser than our parents and our teachers.

With all of the growing up, some things didn't change. The three of us still dreamed our reoccurring dreams. I still dreamed about the screeching sound and being in a cold woods. Karen still dreamed she was walking down a street holding hands with her mom, and Lindsey still dreamed about the man with the beautiful eyes, who asked what she wanted as he stood near a castle. Our problems didn't change either. My mom still drank too much, and my dad still was in too deep at the FBI. Karen still had Brice's and Frank's secret to keep and no mom. Lindsey still had mismatched arms, and for many people that's all that mattered.

153

During this time in our lives we had wonderful things, too. Kate was a strong influence in our lives. She loved her Lindsey, Art, and every one of us in her family. She always watched out for us. Art fixed up the basement in their house at her request. Actually Brice, Frank, and my dad helped Art, and they fixed up the basement recreation room complete with a television set, pool table, and Hi Fi record player. Kate always welcomed us making sure there was plenty of pop, chips, and snacks. She wanted to keep us happy and safe. Our families, Father Tom, and our boyfriends spent most Friday nights in the O'Malley's recreation room. Kate would get Rosie's Pizzas, my mom was in charge of making salad, and Grand took care of dessert. We ate after Jimmy's, Bobby's, and Jeff's football or basketball games. I loved those nights.

Jim returned to the hospital early Friday evening and met Father Tom. Tom told him Samantha's temperature was still elevated. The medication to reduce her fever helped, but it wasn't back to normal.

Dr. Jameson stopped in her room before leaving the hospital and reassured them that she was being closely monitored. Then he said, "Mr. Peterson, when you speak to Mr. Green in Portland, have him call me immediately. I hope he'll return with you. That would be the best solution." The doctor left. They decided to get a quick dinner at the hospital cafeteria, then went back to her room.

Now Jim walked through the jetway into the plane and settled in his seat. He smiled slightly thinking about the questions he'd been seriously asked and the obvious, yet truthful, answers he'd given when he checked in. *Did I pack my own carry on? "Yes." Had I left it unattended? "No." The twenty-first century is rapidly approaching and this is still our best strategy?* He fell asleep trying to think of better strategies and woke up hearing an announcement that trash items were being collected in preparation for landing.

His flight landed safely at 6:30 a.m. Cleveland time, which was 3:30 a.m. in Portland. No one tried to steal the jet. He smiled and thought, *Thank God for those great questions!* Two hours later he was in Samantha's home town in his motel room showering and contemplating his day.

Jimmy and I were the first ones to go steady. He gave me his ID bracelet on a Sunday afternoon in January of our junior year. We were so happy. We loved each other and everything else. When he told me that Jeff and Bobby were planning on giving Karen and Lindsey their ID bracelets, I was beyond excited. He swore me to secrecy. In the space of five days all of us were going steady.

The following weekend Bay's basketball game was on Saturday afternoon giving our boyfriends a free Friday night. Like most Friday nights, everyone was going over to Lindsey's. We told our parents we'd be there by 10:00. Jeff, Karen, Jimmy and I told our parents we were going bowling, first. Lindsey and Bobby told Kate, Art, and Bobby's parents they were going to the Beach Cliff Theatre to see a movie with some other kids. No-one was telling the whole truth.

1962

Lindsey and Bobby hopped into their friend's car waving to Kate and Art. They drove around in Bay Village driving down Wolf Rd. for a few minutes, then down a side street turning on Lake Rd. Basically they drove a huge rectangle as they passed the Holsten Inn heading back toward Bobby's passing the parallel to his house. They turned on the next side street then crossed Wolf Rd. and turned on their own street stopping in Bobby's driveway. His mom and dad were in Columbus, Ohio visiting their daughter, son-in-law, and new grandson. They wouldn't be home until the next day.

"Thanks, Tim. You guys have fun at the movies," Bobby said as he got out of the back seat. He held the door for Lindsey. She happily got out quickly walking with him to the Williams' front door. He got the key from under the welcome mat. There was just one light on in the living room. His house was quiet and empty.

"Bobby, this is so cool. We haven't ever been alone before without the chance someone could show up."

He took hold of her hand, "I love you so much. Will you go steady with me?" He took his bracelet out of his coat pocket and put it on her wrist.

She had a huge smile, "I love you." She hugged him.

"Linds, this means more to me than just going steady. It's like a first step. I want you to marry me after we graduate from college. This is the first step."

Tears filled her eyes. "I love you so much. I've been so happy since the day I met you. You've made my life so much fun, and you've made me feel so safe. But marrying me comes with-"

"I don't care. You're beautiful, sweet, intelligent," he loved her smile as he said, "and I'll never be in love with anyone but you. All I care about is our life together someday." His hand was shaking as he held hers, and they walked into his bedroom.

SLEEPING MEMORIES 1962

Friday night Lindsey and Bobby drove off with friends to a movie they weren't really going to see. Jeff, Karen, Jimmy, and I drove to Bay Lanes where we weren't going to stay. After bowling one game I announced, "Let's walk over to Cahoon Park."

We watched Karen and Jeff walking around the iceskating ponds. The ice had melted and in the moonlight we could see ripples in the water. Soon Jimmy and I were sitting on a bench making out with our winter coats on. The wind was blowing off the lake, and we were freezing. We were kissing, and laughing, and trying to watch Jeff and Karen.

"Has he given her his ID bracelet? Can you see them," I asked Jimmy.

"I can't tell. I think they're talking. Let's find out."

He hollered, "Hey Jeff, did you ask her, yet?"

"Ask me what?" Karen answered.

"Nice going, Ace," Jeff yelled back.

I laughed and yelled, "Karen, Jeff wants to go steady with you."

"Way to go, Sammy. What if I've changed my mind."

"Tell Jeff I'd love to go steady with him. No chance he'll change his mind."

Jimmy yelled, "It's yes, Jeff."

"Thanks, I got that part."

A few minutes later, the four of us happily walked back to Jeff's car and drove to Kate's. When we arrived in the rec room, we saw Lindsey and Bobby sitting on the couch. Lindsey was wearing his letter sweater and looked so pretty and happy. As soon as she saw us she held up her arm to show off his ID bracelet. Karen quickly showed her Jeff's. The three of us were a little too excited and loud.

Grand hollered down the steps, "What's all the excitement?"

"Look," Karen walked to the steps to show her Jeff's bracelet.

Seconds later all of the adults were downstairs. It got quieter. Karen and Lindsey showed everyone their bracelets. I noticed the only smiling adult was Grand.

Art finally spoke, "Wow, this is great, going steady, all of you. I just can't believe you'll be seniors in high school this fall."

Hearing those words, Kate turned around and ran up the steps with my mom and Grand right behind. Minutes later she leaned into the stairwell and said, "Just warming the pizzas in the oven. We'll be right back down."

We heard Father Tom's voice after hearing the side door close. A couple of minutes later Brice and Frank arrived. Father came downstairs saying, "Well, I hear congratulations are in order." He checked out our bracelets. Then he goaded Jimmy into a game of pool.

Art got out cards and poker chips. My dad arrived, and the guys sat down at the card table.

Kate, my mom, and Grand carried plates, napkins, pizza, and salad downstairs. Kate said, "Help yourselves everyone." Then immediately, "Hey Linds, how was the movie?"

She and Bobby answered in unison that the movie was great.

I realized discussing a movie they hadn't seen wouldn't be easy, so I asked Kate, Grand, and my mom, "What were your favorite date night movies?" I noticed Father Tom looking at me.

Grand answered, "When I first had dates to the movies, they were silent movies. A person working in the theatre played a piano or organ to the action happening on the movie screen. Sometimes intertitles, large cards with short written descriptions, were carried across the stage. Movies got much more exciting when these title cards were included in the movie, but they were still silent. The piano or organ player still had a job!"

While Grand was talking, I saw Father Tom looking directly at Lindsey and Bobby as he ate a bite of pizza.

This Friday night was unusual, but it did get back to normal. The guys played cards and pool, and all of us girls sat together and talked. Everyone helped clean up at the end of the night. One last thing was not normal, though. Father Tom reminded the six of us not to miss Saturday Confession. He hadn't ever done that.

Then, Linds, Karen, and I stayed overnight at my house for the very last time.

1962

After everyone but the girls went home, Kate finally looked at their bracelets. She smiled and said, "I'm happy for the three of you, for the six of you." She gave each one a hug and told them not to stay awake all night. They left, and her smile lessened as she watched them cross the street and walk into Sammy's house.

Kate's mind was full as she settled in bed. "Art, are you still awake?"

"Yes."

"Can't you just feel the energy between the kids?"

"If *energy* means they can't be together as couples often enough, yes, I feel it."

"We've always been so happy with the friendships the girls have with the boys. They've always paired up, and that seemed fine until recently. I'm worried about them. They haven't even considered going out with any other boys. What are we going to do?"

"Well, you're going to keep talking with them about respect and waiting to be married. I'm going to tell the boys how much I care about them and that I'll kill them if they ever hurt our girls. How about that?"

"That won't work. I'm so worried about Lindsey. We haven't ever talked with her about the possibility of her someday having a baby born as she was."

"With what these kids have been taught in health and biology classes, she knows. We'll talk about that when she wants. We have lots of time."

"Yes, well, maybe we don't." She thought about Brice and Frank for a second. "It's just that all of a sudden everything's happening so fast. In a year and a half the girls will be in college. I feel as though time is running out. We're almost obsolete. And this thing in Vietnam, some reporters say we really aren't getting involved in the conflict. Others suggest the United States is getting hugely involved. Boys almost the same age as Jimmy, Jeff, and Bobby are signing up for the armed forces thinking they'll be stationed in Europe. Some of them could end up in Vietnam. The whole thing could turn into another Korea. My God, kids in their class could be just like you were in Germany. They're just approaching seventeen, and all of this is so close."

"Now, Kate, settle down. You've always been the strong one. We are not in a war in Vietnam. It's a military police action in Asia. The United States is acting as military advisors for the region. President Kennedy does not want a war in Asia. Why, remember those people in Washington who wanted the president to confront the Soviets in Germany when Berlin was divided last summer? Remember President Kennedy thought a wall was better than a war? I think Germany is more important to us than some remote place in Asia. Our boys, acting as military advisors, will be home before our kids graduate from high school. Honey, this is a wonderful time in their lives. Our kids will make it through. I know they will. We just have to keep them talking, busy, and close to us. They need to know what we expect from them and that we love them all very much. Now, let's go to sleep."

"Ok, you're right. I love you, honey."

Art didn't sleep very well. For the first night in years, he dreamed about the war in Germany. He could hear the gunfire, the roar of the fighter planes, the screaming and yelling, and the sound of the bullets being fired from all directions. He could feel, smell, and see the mud, and feel the dead cold, and see the mangled bodies, and the arms, the small arms covered in blood. He was consumed with the feeling he had to stay awake, had to keep his eyes open, had to make sure no enemies were out there in the cold, dark, night sneaking and creeping toward them. He felt so tired, but he had to stay awake, and watch, and listen. He couldn't close his eyes for one sweet second. "Can't sleep. Can't sleep," he spoke from his nightmare.

Kate heard his words and knew what he was dreaming. *Why did I upset him before he fell asleep,* she thought. She carefully woke him up. She hugged him and held him close until he fell back to sleep, then she got up to take an aspirin.

161

I loved the nights we stayed overnight together. We usually spent one of the weekend nights talking, listening to music, giving each other wise advice, even doing homework until the wee hours of the night. We were just a few months from our seventeenth birthdays, and we positively knew everything there was to know! We were so happy to be going steady. We took turns telling each other how the guys asked us. "Tossin and Turnin" and other songs filled my room as we drank cokes and ate chips, pretzels, dip, and chocolate chip cookies.

"Gosh, it was so cool being alone with Bobby and not having any parents to worry about." Lindsey told us how Bobby asked her to go steady. Then she told us they went into Bobby's bedroom.

"Linds, are you being careful?" Karen interrupted sounding very adult.

She looked at Karen. "I need to know the name of that doctor who gives out the pill. I just don't know how much longer we can wait."

I couldn't comprehend Lindsey and Bobby even thinking about taking this chance on getting pregnant. "Lindsey, don't you want to wait? Everyone has always said to wait until we're married. My mom and Grand have told us, your mom has sat us down and talked with us about this a bunch of times, and let's not forget the Church! You guys need to think about everything that could happen. We're still in high school. Lindsey, think!" I was pleading with her.

I looked at my bedroom door a second. "Do you guys hear anything?" We didn't turn the radio down, but we stopped talking and listened. "Never mind. It must have been on the radio."

Lindsey looked at me, "I've thought about this a lot. Have you ever just known that something is absolutely the right thing? I just know that for Bobby and me this is right. I trust him, and he trusts me. We know we'll always be together." She looked at Karen, "Tell me about this doctor."

Karen looked so superior. For just a split second, I wanted to dump my coke on her. She had the information.

I turned my radio up louder thinking my parents wouldn't hear what we were talking about. We leaned in as she began, "The doctor doesn't want to know your real name. If everything's all right, he'll give you a six month supply of birth control pills. It costs about eighty dollars. That includes the exam and the pills."

"Eighty dollars!" I was appalled and couldn't believe he'd give a test, "And, what's he giving you an exam for? Does he ask questions to know if you're really in love?"

They burst out laughing. With space between each word Karen said, "Sammy, he gives you a m e d l c a l examination." She quickly added, "It's a physical exam to make sure everything's ok down there."

I hadn't a clue what she was talking about. My mom hadn't ever given me this information. I said, "My mom told me about needing to have blood tests before getting a marriage license, but that was all. What are you talking about, medical exam down there? I honestly don't know anything about this. And stop laughing!"

Now Karen really looked superior as she said, "Well, brace yourself, Sammy. This is a little gross, but I'll tell you."

I interrupted her, "How do you know all of this?"

"Do you remember last November when I went to visit my cousin, Jill, at Ohio State? We spent a night talking with each other. She told me something. I know you guys remember when we found out about my dad and Uncle Frank," she looked at Lindsey, "and your gramma died, Linds. Remember that Grand was visiting her sister, her niece, and her grandniece? Her grandniece is my cousin, Jill. You've met her. Actually, she isn't a first cousin. She's my cousin once or twice removed."

"What! What's that?" I was angry. "What are you talking about removed cousins? What in the hell is that?"

Annoyed, Karen answered, "Sam, forget it. I'll explain later. It doesn't matter. Just listen."

Lindsey spoke up, "Actually, I don't get that part about your cousin being removed either."

"Will you guys shut-up and listen! The summer before Jill's senior year in high school she had a baby girl. That was the reason Grand had gone to stay with them. Jill told me giving birth was very painful. Nothing had ever hurt so

163

much. But very soon after giving birth, the most heartbreaking pain she'd ever experienced was when the Sister took Jill's new born baby from her arms and carried her away."

"A few days before her baby was born, Jill's grandmother, Jill's mom, and Grand had a long talk with her. Jill's grandmother is Grand's sister. Anyway, they convinced her that giving her baby to a married couple, who wanted a family but couldn't have children, would be the most loving thing she could do for her baby. They told her that they would help her as much as they could if she wanted to keep her baby. They also said giving the baby to a married couple, who had their own home and desperately wanted a child to love, would be the sweetest gift she could ever give her baby."

"Only a few hours after giving birth to her daughter, Jill had to say good-bye forever. Her face was covered with tears when she told me this part. She said she'll always remember those moments holding her baby and looking at her precious face for the very first and last time. She'll remember that precious face and awful moment when her baby was forever taken from her arms. She said her heart will never mend. She'll always remember the sound of her own mom's quiet sobs as her mom's granddaughter was taken from her reach, too."

"For the next month her mom, her grandmother, and Grand helped her as best they could. They kept telling her that the baby is with a wonderful couple who loves and is giving their new baby everything she will ever need and want. Jill knows this is true because she has read the documents from the adoption agency stating the couple's qualifications. She knows they are and will continue to be great providers and loving parents."

"We talked for a long time. She told me she didn't finish high school with her class. She went to night school to get her high school diploma. She's been taking classes year round at Ohio State. She'll graduate in just over a year, I think. She's happy and has met a guy she really likes. He knows about everything that happened. Jill says he's kind, smart, caring, fun, and handsome. They go to bars and love dancing, and they enjoy going to museums, lectures, plays, and just love being together."

164

The three of us smiled. "Let There Be Drums" vibrated from my radio. "So, Grand wanted me to visit Jill last November because she wanted her to talk with me about being responsible for my actions. Jill promised me that what I told her would stay between us. After we talked, she gave me the name of a doctor and told me about the exam."

She looked my way, "This is how I know, Sammy."

We all were quiet for a minute. "Ok Karen, tell us about this doctor's appointment," Lindsey said.

"Here we go. It's a little gross." She told us about the exam. When she finished, Linds asked for the doctor's name and phone number.

I couldn't imagine what she was thinking, "Again, I ask Lindsey, don't you think you should wait? I mean after hearing all of,"

BANG! An enormous loud noise silenced me. Wide eyed I turned my radio off. We grabbed for one and other while hearing a terrible screeching noise and the huge sound of a roaring engine shrieking down our street. My mom screamed, and we ran out of my room.

The front door in our living room was wide open. As we ran outside we saw my parents, and we saw Kate running down her driveway into the street toward us. She hollered, "I saw a huge truck leave your yard and speed down the street." She ran to Lindsey, Karen, and me asking if we were all right. Seconds later Art ran across the street and stood with my parents. All of us stared at my dad's car.

"Oh my God, Jack," my mom looked then yelled, "What's this? What's this all about?" She hit him in the chest with closed fists. "We aren't safe in our own house?" My dad seemed oblivious to her punches as he stared at his car.

Art got hold of my mom. "Joan, stop, the girls are here." He put his arms around her. "Look around. Neighbors are out." There were several neighbors on their front porches looking in our direction.

All of us gravitated toward the car. The trunk and most of the back seat were smashed because of the weight of a large boulder. As we walked around to the front of the car we read words painted with white paint across the hood,

YOU'RE NEXT. "Everyone stop moving," my dad ordered. "Back away from the car. Don't touch it. There could be shoe prints and fingerprints. Art, take everyone to your house and lock the doors. I'll call the bureau."

Kate held my mom's hand and Lindsey walked beside my mom, too, putting her arm around her. Art walked with his arms around Karen and me. I broke away from Art and ran back to my dad. "Dad, I want to stay with you." This was the only time I ever saw my dad working as an FBI agent.

I thought he didn't realize it was me with him as he said, "This is my family, my home. I'm going to kill this bastard myself." He grabbed my hand as he hurried us into our house.

Once inside my dad called his partner, "John, get agents to my house, now! His threat from this afternoon wasn't enough. That bastard has actually sent his thugs to my home frightening my family. Code of ethics, bullshit," he yelled into the phone. He listened a few seconds. "Yes, I still have it." He took a crumpled paper out of his pocket and slammed it on the counter. "Threatening me with a message on my windshield in the bureau parking lot is one thing. Smashing my car in my driveway to frighten my family; son of a bitch, I'm going to get him!" My dad's voice softened, "They're ok, very shaken up. Just get over here."

I smoothed the crumpled paper as my dad turned away and talked. I read, DON'T SHOW UP MONDAY. I watched him hang up the phone and look at me, "I'm sorry, Sammy." He hugged me and rubbed my back. "Everything will be fine. Don't be afraid. We're safe, honey." He put the paper back in his pocket, then he kept his arms around me.

We heard a car. John Simon, not only his partner but his closest friend at the FBI, arrived. He lived in Bay Village, too. He walked inside, looked at us, and asked, "You guys all right?" While he and my dad talked, more agents arrived. They were sent to Karen's and Lindsey's yards. Mr. Simon hugged me and told me not to worry. My dad and I walked over to Kate's.

Karen and Lindsey came into the living room as soon as they heard my dad and me. Still crying my mom glared

166

at my dad, "I can't stand any more of this. It's always been frightening, but this is the worst case ever. It's been on going for years. If you aren't frightened for yourself, aren't you worried about Samantha? What if they come after her, or Karen, or Lindsey?"

"Good God Jack, what have they gotten you into," Art asked.

Matter of factly my dad answered, "You know I've been working undercover. I told you about the bastard we arrested several years ago. I told you about him when his release was reported in the papers. Remember we had to let him go because no one would testify in court? Since then I've gotten a lot more evidence against him. We've got an airtight case. We've arrested him again. Obviously he's learned my identity. His day in court has arrived, and he doesn't want me testifying."

My mom was furious with him. She yelled, "How can you be so calm? This has gone on long enough. You're never home. Sometimes you're unreachable for days. I worry that you're hurt or dead someplace. I wonder what else might be going on. It's gotten to be too much. We can't go on pretending we're these normal married people, Jack. I don't know from one day to the next if they're going to hurt you or kill you." Her face looked so angry, but her voice quieted a little, "One thing's for sure, I've never been afraid for Samantha, the girls, or me before. All of these years wondering if this is the day they win and you lose. I drink to numb myself from worrying. I'm so angry inside, I could scream myself silly!"

All of us stood quietly still for many seconds.

In a controlled voice she said, "I'm done with this. You do what you must. Tomorrow you're taking Samantha and me to my aunt's house. When this is finished, you retire or I'm divorcing you." My mom turned toward the front door and walked back to our house.

It was silent for a few minutes. We didn't move. Kate hugged me, and a second later Art asked my dad, "Are we safe, Jack?"

"Yes. There are agents in the Fry's yard, in yours, and ours as well. Some are in cars parked in all of our driveways. I'm testifying this Tuesday. By Tuesday night he'll be in prison for the rest of his life. His people won't be loyal or fear him any longer once he's in prison. The agents will remain here until he's locked up for good." He asked Kate, "Can the girls stay here the rest of the night?"

"Absolutely," she answered.

"I'm sorry about all of this. I never thought this, son of a," he looked at Karen, Lindsey, and me, "I never thought he'd do this, never! You're safe, don't worry. I better get back to Joan. Girls, you're ok, right?"

We shook our heads and answered, "Yes."

"Sammy, I love you, honey." He turned and walked out.

I didn't want him to leave. I needed him. I wanted to stay with my dad, and I ran out after him. "Dad, Dad, wait," I hugged him, "I love you, too. I didn't understand. I didn't know any of this. You haven't ever said anything, and mom hasn't ever told me. I don't want anyone to hurt you."

"Sam, I'm fine. We don't need to be afraid of this guy. He's nothing. In a few days he'll be in a prison far away from here. I need to talk with your mom now."

"All of the fights, were they mostly about work?"

"I know we've had awful arguments. I'm sorry, Sammy. We'll figure everything out. I think mom is right. It's time I retire from this crazy job. I need to talk with her, honey. Go back with Karen and Lindsey. You're safe. We all are. I'll see you in the morning." He hugged me and watched me go back inside Kate's house.

Kate woke us up early Saturday morning. My mom wanted everyone to come over for breakfast. I couldn't believe my mom thought this was a good idea. She was so angry just hours ago. I felt sick thinking what it would be like at my house.

We walked into my mom's kitchen surprised at seeing Father Tom. He was holding a corning ware dish full of scrambled eggs and cheerfully said, "Good morning," as he set them on our kitchen table near platters filled with bacon, sausage, fried potatoes, toast and jelly. I looked at my dad and mom, and they seemed surprisingly good. Karen shrugged her shoulders as she glanced from them to me, and I knew she was assessing what was going on, too. We sat down at the card table extension to our kitchen table, and my mom smiled handing us mugs of hot chocolate. The adults sat down and Father Tom said grace. As I watched my parents I thought, *My mom and dad seem somewhat happy.*

Disjointed conversation filled the room. Finally Grand said, "We saw that boulder on your front yard, and Kate told us what happened very late last night." She looked at my mom and dad, "What's going on here?" I was so grateful she spoke up.

My dad said, "Ok Grand, let me try,"

My mom interrupted, "I'd like to go first." She looked down a second and smoothed the napkin on her lap. "Last night, well actually early this morning, Jack called Father Tom. I got very angry again." She made eye contact with each one of us. "I won't go into all of it, but I do understand that my drinking is a problem. I have to admit, for a long time I've been aware that I drink to ease my worry and anger. I've tried to overlook the fact that when I drink, I drink way too much." Sounding more hopeful she continued, "I do think I'm different from an alcoholic because I can go days without drinking."

I watched my dad, Kate, and Father Tom glance at one and other.

My mom noticed, too. "Nevertheless, I understand it's a problem for me. I know that my behavior changes. I say and do things I don't want to say or do. I can't seem to control myself. I think I'm having a drink to relax, and I get wound up instead. Anyway, I'm going to face this problem, and if I must quit drinking alcohol, I will. I can't just apologize and make the past nasty things I've said disappear. I want you to know that I didn't ever mean to hurt any of you." My mom looked at me now, and she looked so beautiful yet so sad. "This has been most unfair to you, Samantha. I'm so sorry."

I loved my mom more than ever that moment. "Mom, I can't even remember the things you've said. I knew you didn't mean any of it. I just brushed it off."

She smiled and said, "Do you mean brushed me off? Well, good because my behavior has been inexcusable."

I sat back and absorbed the huge truth in her last sentence.

"Well," my dad looked at Father Tom, and then he looked at my mom and me for a few seconds as he said, "we talked about a lot of things with Tom. Together with God's help, we'll get everything figured out. We're on the right path. In a while I'm driving Joan and Sammy to stay a few days at Joan's Aunt Julie's house." He smiled at me, "Good with you, Sammy?" He didn't expect an answer as he kept talking. "I want all of you to know how sorry I am about last night. I never thought this guy would try to intimidate me at my home near all of you." My dad's expression hardened, "This guy is scum. Even his own people hate him. He's done despicable things to friends and foe. Once in prison, he'll be dead within a week."

Father Tom looked startled, and so did the rest of us. My mom took hold of my dad's hand.

"I'm sorry. My dad looked down and took a deep breath. "I am sorry." He smiled at my mom. She let go of his hand. "Please know that all of you are not in any danger. Our agents will stay here until he's transferred to prison. The judge already has read my signed written testimony. It was delivered to his home early this morning. He called me less then an hour ago, and he changed my court appearance from Tuesday to Monday. With my written testimony, with all of the evidence that has been presented so far, with what happened last night, and with my testimony on Monday; this guy will be in prison by Monday night. Do not repeat any of this." He looked at Karen, Lindsey, and me. "Girls, I know it will be hard not talking with your boyfriends about all of this, but you must not. You cannot tell them a word about this. Understand?"

We shook our heads and answered, "We won't."

Karen smiled at him and said, "Wow, Jack, this really is exciting jazz. I guess work never gets boring."

Brice admonished her, "Karen, this is serious."

"It's all right, Brice. Girls, I seldom discuss my work with anyone. I wouldn't be discussing it now if last night hadn't happened. Get some more hot chocolate and go to Sam's room. Just remember our agreement. And Sammy, you need to pack a few things. We'll be leaving soon for Aunt Julie's."

"Gosh Sammy, I haven't ever seen your dad so serious before," Lindsey commented once my bedroom door was closed. Karen turned on my clock radio. We heard Roy Orbison singing "Crying."

"Now I know the main reason for their arguments. Actually my mom cleared up a lot of things in the time between last night and this morning. I understand her anger and even her drinking. I'm amazed she talked about her drinking. That's something she hasn't ever done. I'll be right back."

Walking out of my room, I heard my dad talking, and I stopped short of our kitchen. "This guy is finished. He has no friends. No one he's done business with wants him talking. He's just hours from becoming powerless and meaningless. It was stupid that he made his attorney request a bench trial. He thought his attorney could get a judge they could bribe."

I heard my mom say, "That's more information than Grand, Kate, and I need. Let's stop talking about this."

"I'm sorry, ladies. You're right." He patted my mom's shoulder and looked out the kitchen window. "Looks like rain. As soon as the car gets here we should leave. Joan, agents will follow us for a while. You won't notice them. And agents will remain on our street until this guy's in prison."

I stood near the kitchen watching and listening. My parents looked so happy. Grand was drying the last dish. "We'll see you back on Wednesday," she asked.

"Yes, maybe even Tuesday night," my dad answered.

"Well, I'd like to stay until Wednesday morning," my mom stated while smiling, "Sammy loves my Aunt Julie, we haven't seen her in almost two years, and Julie loves doting on you."

"Wednesday it is. I would rather stay over Tuesday night, too. And I love Aunt Julie, too, not to mention her damn, lumpy, sleep sofa," my dad added with a grin.

I just stood there watching. My mom and dad were joking and smiling. I forgot my question. I went back into my room and put some clothes in my suitcase.

My dad called us into the kitchen. Kate hugged my mom and said, "Things are going to be great now, Joan. You and Sammy relax for a few days."

Father Tom winked at me and whispered to Karen and Linds, "Confession's in a few hours."

171

Kate gave me the biggest hug. "Love you," she whispered.

Everyone left.1962

Grand took out the chocolate chip cookies she baked yesterday and wrapped a dozen in wax paper. Quickly, she made some baked ham and tomato sandwiches spreading on her special mustard and mayonnaise combo. Then she got a large bag of chips and put everything into a basket. She put her coat on, hurried back over to the Cole's house.

Seeing Joan in the kitchen, Grand opened the side door. "Joan, I thought you might like a lunch for your drive."

"Thank you. We'll love that." Joan gave her a hug.

"You have a good rest these next few days. You and Sammy mean the world to me. I love you as my own. You know my Karen loves you and Sammy, too." Grand hugged Joan, again, and hurried out the door feeling silly that tears were filling her eyes.

I went over to Lindsey's before we left to go to my Aunt's because Jimmy wanted to see me. He and Bobby only had a few minutes to stay before leaving for their basketball game, and both had a ton of questions about my front yard. I told them my mom and I were going to my aunts for a few days and tried to explain without saying anything I couldn't tell them. Looking really worried Jimmy said, "Sammy, we saw your front yard and those agents sitting in their cars." He kept asking me more questions, and I'm sure Art and Kate could hear. Calling all of us into the kitchen, Art explained to the guys that everything was settled, and there was nothing more to say.

The car from the agency arrived in our driveway around three in the afternoon. A momentary scurry of activity occurred as my dad put two suitcases in the trunk and sat down in the driver's seat, my mom put Grand's lunch and six cokes in the car and sat down in the front passenger seat, and I threw my pillow and blanket on the back seat and got in. A few minutes later we were happily moving along and talking as though we'd been planning this trip forever. The serious matter of the night before didn't come up, and as we talked and laughed I realized the three of us hadn't had fun together in a long, long time. I thought about spending time with my aunt and mentioned that I was excited to see her. Both my mom and dad reminded me of long past visits and fun things Aunt Julie and I had done together. Then I asked the eternal question all kids ask, "Dad, about how long until we're there?"

"It's about six hours from our house to Julie's. These roads are clear and dry so far. There's not much traffic today. It looks like rain though. In about two or three hours we'll be driving through the hills where there's a lot of curves and hills, and I'll have to slow down. With rain the driving time will be longer."

"Your father has always loved challenging the speed limit, Sammy."

"Hey, this job needs some perks. You know Sammy, I can't get your, Lindsey's, or Karen's tickets fixed. I don't want you kids speeding and getting into any accidents."

173

"Dad, please don't worry about that. We don't either. Just put that out of your mind. Let's have the lunch Grand made us. I'd like a coke, too.

"Good idea! Grand is wonderful," my dad remarked.

We talked more while we ate our sandwiches. About an hour later, after the three of us finished eating some cookies and drinking our cokes, my dad found a gas station that had restrooms. Very soon we were back in the car, and I snuggled down on the roomy back seat. With my head on my pillow and my blanket around me, I felt happy and safe as I listened to my parents laughing and talking. I loved how they sounded, and I fell into a peaceful sleep.

I woke up because I heard a familiar noise. I looked out the window, seeing it was dark outside. I listened and realized I heard a noise like the roaring sound in my dream. It was getting louder. "Dad, what's that noise?"

"What, Sam?"

"That noise. What is it?" I looked out the rear window and saw headlights.

"Sounds like a truck. Oh, shit!" He stepped on the gas pedal, speeding up. The truck's lights were streaming through our rear window, now, lighting the inside of our car. My dad maneuvered a curve going very fast, and my mom and I slid into our passenger doors. Driving on the straight way, the light in our car dimmed as we gained distance from the truck.

"Jack, what's happening?" My mom turned looking through the rear window.

As soon as the truck got to the straightened road it gained speed. It's headlights filled our car and my mom shielded her eyes. Within seconds it slammed into our bumper causing our car to swerve. My dad got control and sped through the next curve.

"What's he doing? He's bumping our car. Oh God, Jack, they found us."

Mom and I started crying. My dad yelled, "Stop it! Listen to me, both of you. I'll go as fast as I can on the next two turns. He'll have to slow way down on the turns."

It worked and our car gained some distance from the truck. "Ok," my dad said, "after the next curves, I'll slow down near the curb. You both open your doors, jump out, and roll down the hill. I'll gain distance again and jump out, too. I'll find you. He'll think we're in the car when it crashes."

"Dad, no."

My mom took hold of his arm and resolutely said, "I'm staying with you."

His next dreadful words still echo in my brain. "Climb over the seat and get Samantha out of the car. I'll tell you when to get her out."

My mom climbed over the seat and opened the curbside door. My dad was driving so fast. We could hear the truck's engine roaring closer. My mom sternly said, "Samantha, you must do this. Dad and I will jump together after the next curve. You have to be first. You must do this. We'll find you."

I couldn't do it. "No, Mom, I want to stay together."

My mom didn't hesitate for a second. She gathered my pillow and blanket and pushed them into my chest and wrapped my arms around them. "You must do this, now, Samantha. We love you. We'll always love you."

My dad sped into the next curve and then everything seemed to happen in slow motion. He yelled, "Ready?"

My mom pushed me to the curbside door. "Sam, we love you." She was crying.

"Mom, stop!" I couldn't make her stop pushing me because I didn't let go of my pillow and blanket.

Why didn't I? Why didn't I grab hold of the front seat?

My dad slowed down on the straight road and yelled, "Now!" I remember being pushed hard against the door, and the door giving way, and then an explosion of pain, then rolling and spinning. I remember hearing an enormous thundering, roaring, screeching sound. And at some point, I felt and heard nothing. Everything was gone.

175

Father Tom returned to the hospital and stepped near Samantha's bed. He spent most of the previous night talking to her then sleeping in the chair by her bed. At about six in the morning he went home to the rectory and showered. He said eight o'clock Mass and heard Saturday morning confessions. Now he felt her forehead and said, "I think your temperature is up a bit, again. They'll be checking on you soon. Dr. Jameson won't be here today. It's Saturday." He felt her forehead, again. "I'm not sure, Sammy, maybe your temperature is normal." He changed the subject. "Jim should be in Portland. He's going to your house. Hopefully he'll find Rob at home." He kissed her forehead, said a short prayer, and sat down.

"I've been meaning to tell you that several months ago Jim and I were at a principal's conference, and we actually saw Doug Nolan's name on the principal's roster list. Jim found him. Doug's a principal at a public school in Akron. He's still a great guy. He asked about you. I've never stopped thanking God for him and his friends calling the police when you needed help. Doug talked about that night in detail. He said he hadn't thought about it for decades until recently. He smiled when he remembered the police officers, Lyle and Otis."

1962

Four teenage boys were already late driving home from one of the boy's grandparent's cabin. They hadn't encountered many cars on this dark, windy road. They were talking when bright headlights from the opposite direction caught their attention. The headlights quickly disappeared in a curve then reappeared in the straight way. Tim, the driver, watched the car slow down and head to the side of the road. "Is that guy having car trouble? What's that noise," he asked. Another set of headlights momentarily filled the windshield and disappeared in a curve.

Doug, sitting in the backseat behind Tim, looked as they neared the car. He watched. "Bummer! Did you guys see that? That car door opened, and they threw something out and split. It looked like, I think a body was shoved out!"

Tim yelled, "Hold on!" He swerved out of the way as a semi truck cab nearly hit them and roared past. He stopped his car on the side of the road.

Doug said, "We gotta do something. I'm sure it was a body." They all heard a thundering screeching noise. "God, I think that truck cab wiped out."

One of the boys said, "Stay cool. I don't think we should get out of the car. There's a road sign ahead. Maybe there's a town where we can get some help."

Tim answered, "Ok, but remember this spot. It's near the sign, and it's less than a quarter mile back where Doug saw something thrown out."

"It was a body thrown out a quarter mile or less behind us," Doug stated.

Tim drove to the sign and stopped a second, "Hopkinville is two miles ahead. We'll find a pay phone and call the police."

About fifteen minutes later the Hopkinville Police weren't buying the tale a male teenage driver, Tim Marshal, called in about a body being thrown from a car. It was a slow night in this town like most of the nights. Checking the situation out would be a diversion from the normal routine. Two policemen drove to the gas station

177

and were surprised to see the kids waiting and waving their arms.

SLEEPING MEMORIES 1962

Near the bottom of a very steep hill, I opened my eyes. *What happened? Where's this? That roaring and awful screeching noise. Where am I? I'm so cold, shivering, so cold. Too many trees, too many branches scratching.*

1962

Otis Greer, one of the policemen, looked at the teenagers. *This is some hooey these boys are cookin up,* he thought. *They did drive ahead and lead us right to the Hopkinville sign, though.* Otis drawled out, "Now, who thinks he saw a body thrown from a car?"

Doug answered, "I did. I was looking out the window, and this car slowed way down, and the backseat curb door opened, and the interior lights went on, and I saw, I think I saw someone push someone out. Then the car sped away."

Lyle looked down and let out a short laugh, "So, now, you aren't so sure? You just t h i n k you saw something. Might you been haven yourself a little nap?"

"No, No, I'm sure. It looked like a person. I positively saw something thrown out. And then this semi truck cab came speeding right at us."

Otis put his hand up to stop Lyle, looked at the teenager and said, "What's your name son?"

"I'm Doug, Doug Nolan."

"All right Doug. Is this the place where you think you saw someone throw out a body?"

"Yes, sir, well, just a little further ahead."

"Yes, sir? You know what Doug? I like you. You're one polite teenager." Otis smiled, "You haven't been havin yourself a couple of brewski's, have you?"

"No, sir." Doug spoke quickly, "I'm telling you, this car came bookin toward us. Then it slowed down. The back door opened and, and I saw something. I saw a body pushed out. Then a truck came out of nowhere going about eighty miles an hour. Tim swerved out of the way, and we heard a loud screeching noise. We stopped a few minutes. Then we drove to find a phone, and we saw the Texaco Station and called you from the phone booth."

"Ok, Doug, you weren't driving?"

Tim answered, "I was driving, sir. Doug was in the backseat, street side. I called you."

Otis said, "You're Tim Marshal?"

"Yes."

180

He looked at the four boys, "All of you get in your car and drive near the spot you're talking about. We'll follow you."

Officer Otis Greer walked back to his partner. "I can't tell. They seem like good kids. Let's check this out." He was aware of a fuel smell which often hung in the night air in these hills especially on damp nights. With the police following, the boys drove away from the Hopkinville sign and stopped less than a mile away. Both police officers and all of the boys got out of their cars. "Wow, that fuel smell is strong now," Otis said, then asked, "Are the flashlights in the trunk, Lyle?"

"Yep," Lyle answered and stood still.

"Do you think you could get them, Lyle?" He asked and thought, *It bugs me when Lyle forgets who's in charge.*

Lyle got the flashlights and handed him one. "Thanks. First let's look near that curve ahead for some fresh swerve marks." With flashlights on they saw the tire marks on the road. "These were caused by a truck all right," Otis said.

"Wow. Was going darn fast, skid marks all over. Looks like smaller tire skids over here," Lyle stated.

The teenagers were about ready to jump out of their skin. One of them yelled, "Hey, what about the body?"

"Now, mind yourselves. We're gettin there," Lyle yelled back. He smelled the fuel and agreed it was unusually strong. He quietly said, "Otis, if I'm not mistaken, there's a curve about two turns or so no truck could make goin as fast as these kids claim it was goin."

"Now that's why I keep you around, buddy. You're right. Let me get these kids off to the station, then we'll drive farther and check it out."

Otis asked Tim and Doug for their Drivers' Licenses, then copied down their information. He copied down their license plate number and got their phone numbers. "I need you kids to drive to the Police Station. It's just down the road from the Texaco station, same side. I'm going to radio Officer Jenkins and tell him you're on the way. He'll need all of you to give him written statements about what you saw. He'll call your parents from the station. Hopefully, you'll be on your way home soon."

181

SLEEPING MEMORIES 1962

My eyes opened. *Where? Where is this? I'm dreaming. I'm so cold. These branches. I'm freezing, so cold. Ugly trees. I've got to get up. Just dreaming.*

The two policemen drove slowly around the first curve. There hadn't been another car passing by since they arrived. Not many drivers use this unlighted, hilly, winding route after dark. They saw it as they neared the third curve. "Look at that. Boy, we have ourselves something here."

"Why yes, Lyle, we sure do." Several yards ahead, they saw the cab of a semi truck sprawled on it's side with debris everywhere. They got out of their car and ran toward the truck stepping in spilled fuel, glass, and around a mangled cab door.

Lyle climbed up to the opening where the driver's door used to be. "No-one inside here," he hollered.

Otis was shining his flash light all over the street and edges of the road looking for anyone injured. Lyle jumped down and did the same. Otis walked toward the hillside edge of the curve and shined his flashlight on the low guard railing. Lyle pointed his flashlight and looked on the opposite side and then joined Otis. They hoped the poor truck driver hadn't gone over the railing. As they neared the edge, they saw that it was more like a cliff, than a steep hill. The two of them began walking along the roadside shining their flashlights along the railing and saw part of the guard railing ahead ripped apart. They ran toward the opening. Way down the hill they saw a fire. Otis ran, while pointing his flashlight on the road, toward the truck and saw skid marks everywhere. Running with him, Lyle said, "These are from a car."

"Lyle, get the flares and set 'em up away from the fuel, beyond the ripped railing. Grab the rope, too. I'll radio the fire department and get them here. Then I'll radio Billy and tell him to call Gallipolis for help. They'll have floodlights to light the hill. Meet you back here." Otis thought, *I need to tell Billy he's got to have those kids stay put, and make sure their parents have been called, too. I'll tell him to get Clare to muster up some food for them.*

They met back by the ripped railing. "We gotta get down there, Otis. Just ahead it's not so steep. I've got the rope tied there."

"Good." They ran ahead. "We'll hang on as far as it goes and slide the rest of the way." It didn't take long for them to reach the fire. They got as close as they could. "That looks like someone in the front seat, beyond help," Otis said.

Lyle looked away, "Poor soul."

"Someone could be lying near here or on the hill. Come on. Let's look the best we can with the flashlights."

Lyle hollered, "Hello, anyone hear us?"

~~~~~~~~~~~~

Father Tom patted Samantha's face with a cool cloth. "Samantha, I want you to talk with me. I wish I knew what was going on inside your mind. Can you hear me, honey? Squeeze my hand if you can hear me." After he felt nothing, he gently squeezed her hand. "Oh well, I still think you must be hearing me." He smoothed her hair back and relaxed back in his chair.

He continued reminiscing, "So while Doug and the other boys waited at the police station, it was your Aunt Julie who called Art. She'd fallen asleep while waiting for you. It was late when she woke up and realized you should have arrived. In no time Art was outside telling the agents about your aunt's call."

Shivering, I was so cold as my eyes focused on my mom. She wrapped my blanket around me and had my shoulders and head resting on her lap. "Mom, I was dreaming I was in those woods." I looked at her and she looked radiant, "Mom, you look so beautiful."

She smoothed my hair and gently moved her fingers across my forehead. "Honey, you'll be all right."

I looked around as much as I could. "Mom, I don't like these woods. It's so cold. I feel sick. I want to go home. Where's Dad?"

"Sweet girl, he's coming."

"Here I am, Sammy," my dad said and smiled at me.

"Daddy, I hate it here. Let's leave. Get us out of here, Dad."

"Sammy, you have to be brave, now." He knelt in front of me and gently felt my arms, sides, and legs. "I have to lift you a little." He moved stuff and gently lifted my leg onto a soft pile. He smiled so magnificently and said, "Sammy, remember the time, you were very little, when mom and I went away for a few days, and Aunt Julie stayed with you? You missed us and told her that you were all alone because we weren't with you. Do you remember what she told you? She said that you could never be without us. She told you that the second you are born, mom and dad love is always with you. Even when they have to go away, their love is always with you and surrounding you forever. You're never without them. You're never alone. Honey, do you remember Julie telling you?"

"I remember. It was a long time ago."

"Never forget. We love you forever. You're never without our love."

"I'll remember, Dad."

"I love you so much," my mom gently said and kissed my cheek. "We, both, love you so much. You've become a beautiful young lady. Soon you'll be out in the world, meeting new people, starting a life of your own. Go places, Samantha. Make new friends. See everything you can. Make your life special, honey. Be sure and go places before you settle in. There's so much to see." She gently cradled me in her arms. "You sleep, now, our precious girl. We'll stay with you. Dad and I won't leave you. We'll stay until help comes. Your dad took care of everything a long time ago. You'll have everything you need. Remember, there's such a lot in this world to see. Just close your eyes for now. We love you, sweet Sammy."

1962

Julie was angry with herself for falling asleep. She looked at her watch. It was after ten o'clock. *Joan and Jack should be here by now,* she thought. She walked into her kitchen to her phone and dialed her niece's phone number thinking it was a dumb thing to do. *Of course no-one answered,* she thought. She went to her front window and looked out. *I know, I'll call the O'Malley's and find out if they know what time Joan and Jack left.*

She dialed information to get the number. Art answered on the fourth ring. "Mr. O'Malley, Art, this is Julie Lynn, Joan's aunt. I'm sorry to call so late. Joan, Jack, and Sammy haven't arrived yet. Do you know what time they left?"

The next minute Art was in his yard telling the agent about Julie's call. Jack's FBI office contacted every agency and police department along the route Jack had mapped out. About two hours later the boys were showing agents the place where Doug Nolan saw a body thrown from a car.

"Sammy, you must wake up now," I heard my dad say. I was trying to wake up, but I didn't want to.

"Sammy, we have to leave," my mom told me as I opened my eyes to the most brilliant light. "Bye sweet girl," my mom said and kissed my cheek.

"Everything is taken care of, Sammy. You don't have to worry. Our love is with you forever." My dad said and smoothed my hair from my forehead, kissing it.

He took my mom's hand, and they began walking away.

I looked around. The light was magnificently bright. "Mom, Dad, where are you going? Don't leave me. Don't walk away. I need you with me. Don't go."

They kept stepping away while I watched. I wanted them to turn around. I heard my mom say, "Way ahead, can you see her, Jack?"

"Yes, Yes, I see, so beautiful. She'll be safe and sound," My dad answered. He turned back and winked.

Such magnificent light safely, gently surrounding my mom and dad. I watched the distance between us grow. I couldn't make them stay.

1962

The boys stood near the FBI agents and near Lyle and Otis showing them where they had seen the car near the side of the road. Doug still insisted that he'd seen a body thrown out of the car.

Flood lights lit the way down this steep hill the same way the hill was lighted a few turns further where the car was still smoldering below. Agents pointing flashlights spread out and began their way down both hills. They yelled Jack's, Joan's, and Samantha's names. An agent hollered, "I found a shoe over here." Several agents came together and gained momentum slipping and sliding down the steep hill shouting the names.

"We found one," an agent yelled. He and another agent knelt down checking for a pulse. "She's alive. I think it's the daughter, Samantha." Four agents stayed with them and called out for medical help. Other agents spread out still looking. The two agents beside Samantha didn't move her. One said, "She's trying to say something."

"Don't walk away. Don't leave me," Samantha softly whispered.

"Honey, we won't leave you. You're safe. You did a great job covering yourself with your blanket. We're getting help. We're staying right here with you." The agents near her took off their jackets and gently put them on her blanket.

A while later a doctor was kneeling beside Samantha. "Samantha, we're going to get you to the hospital. I just need to check you over a minute." He gently removed the jackets and untucked the blanket seeing her leg was resting on a mound of sticks and leaves. He could feel at least two bones pushing through her skin. He saw that her right arm was broken and that she was bruised everywhere. "Okay," the doctor told the agents, "we've got to slide the med cot under her very carefully."

She moaned as they gently moved her. "It's going to be tough getting her up that hill. Two of you walk ahead of us to make sure of our footing. Five of us will carry her up, two to a side, one at her feet. Two walk behind. Try to keep the cot level. We've got to get her to a hospital now.

I don't know how she covered herself with that blanket, let alone how this mound of leaves got under her leg."

Father Tom noticed that Samantha was getting restless. He stood up from his chair. He watched her legs moving. She began moving her head from side to side. He leaned over her and said, "Samantha, I'm right here with you. You've been sleeping. Open your eyes."

With her eyes still closed she whispered, "Why did she leave me? Why did she go?"

"Why did your mom leave you? Honey, she didn't want to leave you." He picked up her hand. "Samantha, you just squeezed my hand. Open your eyes. You can do it. Open your eyes."

"No, no, no. Why didn't I stop her? I let her go. I let her leave me. Don't leave me. Please stay." Her voice was just a whisper.

"Samantha, I will not leave you. Open your eyes. You'll see me. I'm right here." Tom pressed the nurse call button as he spoke.

She let his hand go and turned her head away from him.

"Wake up, honey. The nurse is coming. Stay with me. Come on. Open your eyes." He vigorously rubbed her hand. Her hand was limp in his. Her eyes remained closed. A nurse rushed in as his cell phone buzzed.

Another nurse came in, "Father Tom, go to the lobby and answer your call. You need to leave while we check Mrs. Green."

"Ok, I'll be in the lobby on this floor. I'll be right back."

"We'll find you. Answer your phone."

The first nurse said, "Her temperature is up, 103.5."

He held his phone. "I can't believe I didn't notice her temperature."

"These things can happen quickly. Dr. Jameson is in the hospital this morning after all. We'll notify him right away."

Tom left for the lobby while flipping open his phone, "Hello, Jim, I'm glad you called. You arrived in Portland all right?"

"Yes, I'm actually in front of Samantha's and Rob's house. It looks nice. No lights on inside, though."

"I hope he's home. Glad you took her keys with you." Tom took a deep breath and exhaled.

"Are you ok? You sound out of breath."

"I'm fine. I just hurried to the lobby when you called. Nurses are in Samantha's room. You called at a good time, they wanted me to leave." He decided not to mention Samantha's high temperature and changed the subject back to Portland. "So, for sure you'll go into their house even if no-one answers the door, right?"

"You know, I've been thinking about Rob. I must say, I never liked the guy. Not because of what happened between Samantha and me. She left me before she met him. The few times I was around him, I just didn't like the man. I think that's why I called you instead of knocking on their door. I want him to answer the door, but I don't want to spend time with him." He thought, *Way to act.* "Hey, I'm sorry I said all of that. For God sake, Samantha needs him and so does Dr. Jameson. You know, Tom, I am sorry, but I feel better admitting this."

"Well, I'm glad you got that off your chest. It'll be good if he answers the door, better than you busting and entering."

Jim smiled, "You mean breaking and entering."

Father smiled, too, "Yes, exactly. Don't get yourself thrown in the slammer. Seriously, stay safe and call when you can."

"Will do, thanks, Tom." Jim flipped his phone shut and put it in his jacket pocket.

193

Kate stayed with me day after day and many nights for the first weeks I was in the hospital. She only left when she was sure I wouldn't be alone. My Aunt Julie stayed with me for the first two weeks, too. She and Kate took turns staying over night. After two weeks, Aunt Julie traveled back and forth between her house and the hospital, staying for a few nights, and then returning home. Father Tom was with me for the first several days. Of course, Grand was always near. Art was with me every night after work. He came on the weekends, too.

I was utterly heartbroken. I tried to convince the adults that my mom and dad couldn't be dead. I tried explaining that they stayed with me in the woods, that they helped me and kept me safe. I kept saying that I saw and talked with them. How could they be in St. Joseph's Cemetery? But then I somewhat remembered the spectacular light, and at times as I remembered being with my mom and dad, I remembered that light seemed to be coming toward me, too. I wasn't sure, but it seemed I was encouraged *away* from it. I didn't tell anyone about the amazing light. But for a while I did talk about being with my mom and dad. Only Father Tom seemed to believe me. He told me he believed that my mom's and dad's love kept me safe. "Above all, Samantha, God's love is full of wondrous gifts. I believe you, honey. I believe you." He would bless me.

Karen, Lindsey, and Jimmy came to the hospital everyday and stayed as long as they were permitted. Eventually, Kate and Jimmy's parents persuaded my doctor to allow Jimmy spend as much time with me as he could. On Sunday afternoons Bobby and Jeff came, too, with Lindsey and Karen.

I was completely dependent on everyone for everything. My leg and arm were in traction, my other arm had a cast, and I was covered with bruises. When Jimmy saw me for the first time, he cried. He told me that he would never leave me, that he loved me and would stay with me and love me forever. I was so afraid of being all alone. I held on to his words. I did feel a little guilty that he was stuck with me. Without hesitation, he took over feeding me and made the situation seem perfectly normal.

194

He actually got me laughing about it. "One day, seventy or so years from now, I'm going to sit back, watch T.V., and let you feed me."

"Jimmy, just don't drool."

"Ok, that did it. See all of these vegetables? Down the hatch."

I loved that he could make me laugh. So could Linds. She kidded with me when she fed me, "Having one small arm doesn't seem so awful, now!"

"Smart ass!"

Those moments made my sadness bearable.

After weeks, my leg and arm didn't have to be in traction any longer. My leg and both arms were wrapped in new plaster casts. I couldn't put any weight on my leg. Of course, I couldn't use crutches. I was finally able to leave my room, if Jimmy or someone pushed me down the hall in a wheel chair.

With each passing day, I missed my mom and dad more. With each passing day, I wondered where I would live once I got out of the hospital. Would Aunt Julie want me? Would I move in with her and have to leave everyone else I loved?

Late one Friday afternoon Art, Kate, Lindsey, and Father Tom came into my room. Jimmy had only arrived about an hour earlier. He smiled, gave me a kiss on my cheek, and left.

Art was the first to speak, "Sammy, soon you'll be leaving the hospital. It would mean the world to us if you would come live with us. We love you so much. We want you with us more than anything. You don't have to give us your answer now."

Lindsey took hold of my hand and rubbed my fingers below my cast. "It would be a dream come true for me, Sammy. I couldn't love you more than I do. Do you know that you were the first person to tell me that I was beautiful? Well, the first one except for these two." She smiled at her mom and dad. "You changed my life that day at our tea party, Sammy, when we met. You were the first person who saw me and not my small arm. You made my life light up. I love you. You've been a sister to me since that moment."

Kate gently said, "Never would we try to take the place of your mom and dad. No one can ever do that. We love your mom and dad and miss them." Her voice gave way and tears filled her eyes."

Art finished her thought, "We miss them with all of our hearts. When we're with you, though, we have them near. We want you with us because we love you, and we need you, too."

Father Tom took a hanky out of his pocket and wiped his eyes.

"I love each one of you more than I can ever tell you. Living with you will save me. I was so afraid. What will happen to my mom's and dad's house? Can I still go in it?"

Lindsey got a Kleenex and wiped my eyes and cheeks. I smiled at her and said, "You, Karen, and I are sisters. Always have been, always will be."

Art answered my question, "A long time ago your dad made me the executor of your mom's and dad's estate. I told him at that time if anything ever happened, we'd want you to be with us. We can keep your house just the way it is for as long as you want. Forever, if you want. Everything your parents had is yours. When you're ready, your lawyer and I will explain everything to you. Yes, honey, you can go into your house whenever you want."

"Thank you," I whispered. I felt so relieved and happy that they wanted me. Yet right then, for the first time since my parents' deaths, I wanted some time alone.

Kate hugged me and said, "We'll leave you for just a little while and get ourselves a coke. We love you, Sammy."

She always knew what to do for me. "Thank you. I love you very much. See you in a few minutes."

I had three other visitors before I left the hospital: Doug Nolan, John Simon, and the agent who found me. John introduced me to Doug Nolan. He explained that Doug saw my parents getting me out of the car and called the police.

Hearing those words, two shots of pain surged through me; one jolting my bones and one breaking my heart. Tears filled my eyes without me being able to control them.

196

I whispered, "Thank you." Looking at Doug, I saw he had tears in his eyes. He smiled and shook his head.

John introduced me to the agent who found me in the woods. This agent said, "You did an amazing job securing your leg and wrapping yourself in that blanket."

I'd given up trying to convince anyone that my mom and dad did those things. I just said, "Thank you."

Then John took hold of my fingers, gently rubbed them, and said, "Your dad was greatly respected at the bureau. All of us will always remember his great dedication. We were proud to work with him. He was my closest friend at the agency." He smiled and added, "He was my great friend. I miss him. He was proud of you, Samantha. He talked with me about you all of the time. Your dad loved you so much."

He looked at the other agent, "We want you to know that you are safe. We've found everyone involved in hurting you and your parents. It's all over. You and your friends are safe." He awkwardly tried to hug me. Then he put his agency card on my nightstand. "If you ever need anything, you call us. This agency will help you anytime, anyplace." He smiled at me and added, "I miss your dad's friendship. I loved the guy, too." With tears falling down his face he turned and left. The others followed him out.

I still have that FBI card.

The day finally came when I, wheel chair and all, went home with Lindsey, Kate, and Art. Brice came out of the O'Malley's house as soon as we drove into the driveway. He leaned in the car, hugged me, and said, "Welcome home. This is a good day, honey." He and Art carried me into the living room. I didn't look toward my house. Karen and Grand had big smiles when I got inside, and I could smell Grand's dinner in Kate's kitchen. I smiled knowing how lucky I was to have them, knowing they were trying so hard to make me happy. But inside my broken heart, my feelings were tangled.

This day ended, with more weeks and months following. Karen stayed close to me. It seemed as though she was living with us, too. The adults understood that the three of us were sisters and that was that. I didn't return to school the rest of my junior year. Kate taught me at home with guidance from Bay High teachers. Brice or Frank took me to physical therapy appointments. I completed months of physical therapy until the injuries I'd suffered were no longer evident.

The first place I drove alone one evening was Huntington Beach. I stood near the dozens of steps leading to the beach and looked down. I walked closer to the pavilion while watching the waves roll onto the beach and then seep back into Lake Erie. They moved in perfect rhythm without hesitation, rolling in and out, in and back out. I heard the three life guards blow whistles and then climb down from their chairs encouraging the last swimmers to move toward the steps for the journey up to Lake Road. One blond life guard climbed back up his chair's ladder and slowly searched the water finally sitting down and looking only west. The life guard, just a few people who'd finished walking up the many steps, and I watched the pink sun nearing the waves and a minute later disappearing partly behind the cliff and seemingly into the lake. The life guard and a few others watched the sunset awhile before leaving. And in perfect rhythm, the waves continued to roll in and out, in and out. The sky and the water displayed beautiful shades of pink, lavender, and blue. And the waves rolled in and out, in perfect pace, in and out as daylight faded away. These things had not changed.

By September no one could tell I'd been severely injured the previous winter. Although my emotional well being took much longer, I was back in school the first day of our senior year. Sometimes on windy fall evenings I would walk alone to my backyard, lay down on the grass, and close my eyes. I'd take a deep breath and listen. Smoky scented air and soft noises from children playing would fill my senses. I'd picture my dad raking his leaves while Karen, Lindsey, and I played. My heart would fill as the memory seemed so real, and I wished I could have those moments again.

The weeks passed by as did Bay High football games. Jeff, Jimmy, Bobby, and the rest of the Bay High Rockets and the Westlake Demons rivaled to win the Brown Jug Trophy. Homecoming with Karen, Jeff, and Bobby on the Homecoming Court slipped past. Bay Varsity Basketball games and the dances following in the gym, winter formal

198

dances, movies at the BeachCliff Theatre; cokes, milkshakes, burgers, and fries on the car window trays at Beatty's and Bearden's, bowling at Bay Lanes, iceskating on the ponds, and fun nights all together in the recreation room at our house with Grand, Brice, Frank, Father Tom, Kate, and Art; all of these things we excitedly let pass as we eagerly looked forward, not realizing our childhood was vanishing.

Thanksgiving and Christmas without my parents and the first anniversary of my parents' deaths passed by. On that anniversary Father Tom said Mass in the chapel with just our family, Aunt Julie, Bobby and his parents, Jimmy and his parents, and John Simon attending. That night Lindsey, Karen, and I finally talked in depth about my mom and dad. I cried, and they cried with me. We got through it. I didn't tell them about the woods and my mom and dad helping me.

When spring set the trees, shrubs, and flowers to bloom, I began feeling like my old self. Laughing and really enjoying life happened without me anticipating it. As our senior year rapidly moved toward conclusion, Grand and Kate took us downtown to shop for our prom dresses. We went to all of the stores: Higbee's, Taylor's, Lerner's, Bailey's, May Company's, Halle Brother's, and Bonwit Teller's. We bought and wore long empire waist dresses and new shoes that were dyed to match our dresses.

Jeff, Bobby, and Jimmy, each wearing a rented tux, picked us up in sparkling clean cars and gave us pretty corsages. Our classmates, including us, met groups of friends and ordered dinners at fancy restaurants. The six of us met friends at a restaurant called The Blue Fox. Teacher chaperones greeted us when we arrived in our high school gym that we'd decorated. Then we danced to music we loved. "Shout Shout," "The Twist," "Surfn' U.S.A.," "Shout," "It's Mashed Potato Time," "The Loco Motion," "Peppermint Twist," "Let's Dance," "Go Away Little Girl," "Town without Pity," "I Can't Stop Loving You," "Wonderful Wonderful," "Only You," "Georgia," "Moon River," "You Belong to Me," "Theme from the Apartment," and more.

Before we knew it, we were standing in graduation gowns. My Aunt Julie and Karen's mom came to graduation. Just like that high school became a memory, and we were in college: Jimmy at the University of Tampa, Jeff at Wisconsin, and staying in Ohio; Karen and Bobby at OSU, and Lindsey and I at BGSU.

As all of this passed, Karen still dreamed about walking down the street holding hands with her mom. Lindsey still dreamed about the castle and the man with the beautiful eyes who asked her what she wanted. My dream never returned.

~~~~~~~~~~~~

Jim finished his phone call with Tom, "Will do, thanks Tom," closed his phone, and put it in his pocket. He got out of the car, locked it, and walked up Samantha's and Rob's driveway. Noticing the curtain move in the neighbor's window, he backtracked to the neighbor's front steps and rang the door bell. No one answered. *Friendly people,* he thought as he walked to Rob's and Sam's back deck.

He looked around seeing outdoor furniture and mums that were still colorful. *This looks nice.* He knocked on the sliding glass door. No one answered. With Sam's keys in his hands, he walked to the front door and rang the bell. After ringing the bell three more times, he tried two keys before sliding the correct key in the lock. He called out, "Hello, Rob. Hello, anyone home," as he opened the door.

He stood still inside the foyer for a minute. He called Rob's name, again, got no reply, and walked from the marble tile foyer into the living room seeing a fireplace. He looked all around. *Yes, this is very nice. I can picture Samantha here,* he thought. He heard the furnace click on. It was quiet, just the soft sound of warm air through the vents. He called out again, "Rob, anyone home?" Walking into the dining room, he saw the stilled pendulum on the circle wall clock. His eyes surveyed everything while walking through the kitchen. His mind was taking in every detail. *Oh this is great. There's a family room with another fireplace and a sunroom. Lots of windows everywhere, I like this.*

Jim walked back through the living room into a hallway and saw a bedroom at the end. Walking just inside the doorway he thought, *Rob's and Sam's bedroom.* Feeling weirdly uncomfortable as he saw their large bed, he moved his eyes around the room. *The decorating in here and everywhere is great.* He saw paintings on the walls and stepped further inside to find some family pictures. There weren't any. He quickly walked back through the other rooms, again, and didn't see any family pictures anywhere. He stepped through another hallway off the kitchen and found two more bedrooms. One was set up as a library. He noticed family pictures on one of the shelves.

Suddenly Jim had a feeling. *Maybe they're separated.* He quickly walked back into Sam's bedroom and opened the closet door not seeing men's clothing. He walked to the other bedroom, opened this closet door noticing it was not as large as the other but still a good size. He saw more women's clothes. He spoke, "Huh, these could be Sam's daughter's things." He decided to check the library for a closet. He looked in the smaller closet, "Rob, apparently Sammy doesn't share closets." He saw men's clothing. He closed the door, went to the bookshelf with the pictures, and picked three up.

As he walked to the kitchen he said, "Where in the hell are you, Rob?" His mood softened as he gazed at the pictures. In one he saw a little girl in a soccer uniform. In another he saw Rob with a young girl wearing a graduation gown. He thought, *You haven't aged much, Rob.* Then he looked at the last one and saw a very thin Samantha standing with her arm around a beautiful young version of herself. *Sam's daughter all grown up. This must be from her college graduation. I just can't for the life of me remember her name. It's an easy name. What the heck is it? Sam must have her daughter's phone number in a phone book or written down somewhere. I'll know the name when I see it.* He put the pictures back in the den.

He returned into the kitchen and opened the refrigerator. *Wow, hardly anything in here; just bottles of water, one carton of orange juice, one quart of skim milk.* He opened the milk, and it smelled awful. He poured it down the sink. Without tasting the orange juice, he did the same with it. He saw ketchup, mustard, pickles, jelly and a few other things and shut the door. He looked in the freezer. It was practically empty just frozen vegetables, orange juice, and packaged meals. He opened her cupboards. Most were empty, but a few had dishes, glasses, and bowls. He said, "Samantha, what in the heck are you doing?"

He walked back to the master bedroom. He opened the night stand drawer and found a TV remote. He looked in a couple of drawers and found women's clothes folded. He walked through the living room and went outside. He

202

went back to the same neighbor and rang the doorbell, and still no-one answered. He walked across the street and rang two more doorbells having no one answer. He tried the house on the other side of Samantha's with the same result. *It is Thanksgiving weekend, guess everyone's gone.*

Something occurred to him. Quickly, Jim made his way into Sam's house back into the Library. He opened the closet door and didn't find any men's shoes. He realized he didn't see that many clothes either. He went back into the master bedroom and looked in every drawer and found no men's anything anywhere. He found himself smiling. *Maybe they're separated or divorced. Still, she must have his phone number someplace in here and her daughter's.*

Jim searched for phone books in all of the drawers in the house and didn't find any. He walked into the family room and sat down. *Comfortable. Samantha, what in the hell's going on around here? He's a jerk and not worth what you're doing to yourself.*

Then he stood up and said out loud, "I forgot about the garage. Stupid ass!" He went to the kitchen and opened the only door he'd missed thinking he'd see the garage. Instead, he saw the laundry room. Once he opened the door next to the dryer, he stared at one very sharp sports car parked in the middle of the garage. He said, "That's a girl. Go for the bucks!" He walked around the car thinking, *This beauty must have cost over sixty grand.* He opened the driver's door and tried to get in. The seat was moved up for Sammy to drive. He couldn't fit in, and he realized neither could Rob. He shut the door.

He returned to the laundry room and looked in the cabinets. He smiled while thinking, *Here they are, phone books.* He picked up a small local Oswego Lake and a large greater Portland, Oregon phone book. One more was on the shelf, and he took it out. It was a city phone book for Santa Barbara, California, where Samantha used to live. He looked in the Portland books first. He thought, *These are fairly new, published eight months ago.* He looked for Green listings in the local phonebook. There were only two with R. initials and nothing with Robert. He found Samantha's listing seeing just her name. *They must be separated.* He smiled. He looked in the larger phone book and circled the two matching R. Green listings from the local Oswego Lake book and found Samantha's name and number, again. He took out his cell phone to see if he had this number for her, and he didn't. He pressed the numbers and a recording said this number was not a working number. *That's right, Bette gave me a new private number for Sam.* He pressed her name with that number and heard the phone ringing in her kitchen. He closed his phone and put the local book back in the cabinet. He looked for a personal address/phone book and noticed two empty Nokia phone boxes. *One for Sam and one for her daughter, I bet. That answers that question, too. I'm assuming Rob also has a mobile phone.* He grabbed the city of Portland and city of Santa Barbara books, walked into the kitchen, and checked every drawer looking for a personal phone book not finding one. Walking through the house, again, he looked for a desk thinking she'd have it there. He opened cabinets and drawers in the library without any luck. He picked up both phone books, locked the front door, unlocked the car, and got in.

He sat in Samantha's driveway looking in the Portland phone book. He decided to call the two Green listings from the local book he'd circled. Neither person was Samantha's former Rob.

I'm going to get something to eat and get to work on more of these Green phone numbers. Then I'll return to Samantha's and try to talk with her neighbors, again.

He drove around Oswego Lake and found a seafood restaurant. After eating he got a black coffee to go. He drove for a few minutes finding a spot to park the car and called every Robert Green listing in the Portland book. He was lucky that every call was answered. His bad luck was that none had a connection to Samantha. He called a few R. Greens with the same bad luck. He checked his cell phone battery and saw that it was very low. *Ok, enough of this for now. I'll head back to Samantha's and knock on her neighbors' doors, again.*

Only one neighbor, who lived across the street, answered her door. Jim explained who he was and showed her his driver's license. He briefly explained

204

Samantha's situation. "I'm trying to locate her family," he told her.

The lady told him she'd only spoken with Samantha a few times. "I really don't know anything about her family. A man stops by her house kind of often." She told Jim she thought they could be friends. "He waters her plants when she goes out of town, too,"

"Do you know if this man is her former husband?"

"She never told me that she was married. We really aren't friends. We're just acquaintances. He waters another neighbor's flowers, too. I doubt he's her former husband."

"I doubt it, too. Do you know this man's name?"

"No."

"Could you show me which other neighbor has him take care of their plants?"

"Sure, the people right next door. They really stay to themselves. They moved in early this year around the same time as Samantha." She pointed to the same house where he'd noticed the curtain move.

"Yes, you're right about that. I think someone was watching me from a window. They didn't answer their door when I went over. Have you met Samantha's daughter?"

"No, I've seen a younger women at the house, although I haven't seen her for a long time."

"Can I give you my phone number? If you happen to talk with anyone who might know Samantha's husband or daughter, could you ask them to call me? I'll give you the hospital phone number, too. Thank you for talking with me. Merry Christmas. I like your wreath."

She smiled, took the phone numbers, said she was sorry she couldn't be more help, and wished him a Merry Christmas.

Jim walked to his car thinking. *It hasn't felt like the holidays are near one bit.*

He decided to return to his hotel to call the rest of the Green phone book listings. He thought, *Tomorrow, I'll return the phone books. I'll leave a note on her kitchen counter with my name and phone numbers. I'll ask whoever reads my note to please call me immediately. Hopefully other neighbors will answer their doors tomorrow. Maybe some of them went out of town for*

Thanksgiving weekend and will have returned. Anyway, after that I'll go to the airport and try for an earlier flight.

After showering and getting into sweatpants and a long sleeve t-shirt, Jim finished calling the last R. Green listings in the Portland phone book. Each call was answered with no one knowing a Samantha Green from Ohio.

He began calling the Robert Green listings in the Santa Barbara book. The first number had a recording stating the number was no longer in service. The second number was answered by a much older lady. "Hello," she said.

"Hello, I'm trying to locate a Robert Green, who has a wife who grew up in Ohio. My name is Jim Peterson."

"My Robert died a long time ago," the old voice answered, "and I grew up in Seattle. I'm sorry. I wish I could help you. You sound very nice."

"You sound very nice, too. I'm sorry your Robert died."

"Oh, young man, he's been gone over twenty-five years, now, but thank you. I still use his name in phone books. It's been a long time since anyone said they're sorry he died."

"Well, no one has called me a young man in a long time, so thank you, too."

"Now, my dear," Jim heard the old voice about to give him a lecture and sarcastically thought, *Great.* "You sound to me to be in your fifties or maybe even in your sixties. Why that's young! You should be having the time of your life and enjoying all of your gifts. You've got another thirty, forty years to party. Don't get rusty. Keep your mind and everything moving, and I mean everything!"

Dear Lord, I think this might be turning into an obscene phone call! He stayed silent too long.

"Oh, now, please don't be embarrassed. Hello, are you still there?"

"Yes, I'm still here."

"Well, I just know because some of my friends haven't taken this advice. They've wasted so many years thinking they were too old or too sad to do so many wonderful things. Every year of life is a gift. So live smiling, stay or fall in love, and think young. Life gets more precious and beautiful with age. I'm telling you to use it or lose it. I'm a

206

retired history teacher, and I'm 91 years old. Just live all of your life fully no matter what happens. Don't let the turkeys get you down. You're as young as you behave."

He laughed, "You know, that's the best advice I've heard in a long time. Thank you, and you're right."

They both said good bye and hung up.

High school, graduation day, summer vacation, fall college semester, President Kennedy and Camelot, Christmas vacation, and all of 1963 disappeared into thin air. 1964 came upon us with cold days, freezing nights, lonely hearts, and a sad country. After we returned to college, Jeff broke up with Karen which didn't surprise us one bit. Just like Jimmy and me, they were attending universities in different states. But not like Jimmy and me, they didn't miss each other. Jeff spent Christmas vacation skiing with friends from college. Plus, Karen had changed a lot. Brice seemed ready to explode at her several times during our Christmas break.

I was sitting on my dorm room bed watching a few snow flakes falling amid unusual bright sunshine when Lindsey walked back into our room. She'd been on our dorm floor's phone at the end of our corridor. "Sammy, I just talked with Bobby. He's really worried about Karen. He thinks we should come visit tomorrow and spend the weekend with her. Apparently she's cutting a lot of her classes. He thinks we need to make sure she's ok."

The next afternoon we signed out of our dorm and drove to Columbus. Bobby was waiting in Karen's dorm lobby when we arrived. As usual kids stared at Lindsey's small arm. Some began smiling watching Bobby and Lindsey hug as though they hadn't seen each other forever. "I've missed you so much, Linds," several of us heard Bobby say as he let go of her.

We signed into the dorm. Bobby told us he'd be back in an hour, and we'd walk to the bar. Linds and I took the elevator to Karen's floor. Her roommate greeted us with a big smile and said, "I haven't seen much of Karen this week. You guys can hang out with my friends and me." We explained that she promised to meet us later at a bar on High Street.

We waited in line for over an hour before our drivers licenses were checked and our wrists were stamped for low beer. Like many college bars, we walked in finding the space unnoticeably smoke filled, crowded, dimly lit, loud with music, and streaked with strobe lights. We made our way to the bar and got 3.2 beers. Bobby saw some friends, and we joined them. The band began playing "You Can't Sit Down" and heeding the lyrics, we got up and danced.

While dancing, I turned and saw a somewhat familiar face, and couldn't believe how she looked. Grabbing Lindsey's arm, I pointed at Karen. She was smiling at us. The look of disbelief on Lindsey's face was undeniable, too. The three of us danced our way to the bar. Everyone was singing with the band and yelled out, "High Street" as Linds and I stared at Karen's new look. She was wearing a terrible outfit, had on small wire rimmed glasses, no make up, and her hair was stringy and straight. She looked like she'd given up eating. We couldn't take our eyes off of her. Lindsey blurted out, "You've changed a lot. Are you ok?"

"Well, nice to see you, too." She gave her a hug, then me.

I just couldn't believe how much she'd changed since Christmas break. "Karen, what's going on? Something's happened to you," I said as loudly as I dared.

We'd made her mad. She looked us up and down. Mockingly she said as loudly as she could over the band, "There isn't anything wrong with me. You two are the ones with something wrong. You don't know anything about what's happening! You both still look like high school, all dressed up for the guys. God, you are stupid!" She started yelling at us and every other girl who made eye contact, "Why do you do it? Who do you get all cutesy for? You don't need to get all pretty for them anymore." She spread her arms toward a group of guys standing at the bar. "Why do you think you have to please them? Please yourselves, that's what I'm doing. You can do and be anything you want!"

Lindsey and I just stood there.

Suddenly, her eyes filled with tears. She yelled, "There's so much hatred in this world, so much nasty discrimination." She pointed at the dance floor. "Do you see colored faces? Imagine what it's like not being welcomed or permitted into a restaurant, a bar, or to use a bathroom or drinking fountain. Think about it!"

Lindsey loudly answered, "You're right, Karen." She patted Karen's arm.

209

Karen glared at her, "People mock you all of the time, Lindsey. The three of us were ridiculed in Bay Village. Didn't you hate that? We weren't ever invited to anyone's house. Think about it. My dad and Uncle Frank are lucky they haven't been killed like your parents, Sammy. They get hate mail all of the time." She looked all around, "I mean look around, everyone's staring at us. And our boys are dying in a war." She looked around at everyone and shouted, "We are in a war, you know."

"Ok Karen, you're right," both of us said, again. We'd taken Psychology 101.

Lindsey looked at me and said as quietly as possible, "Go get Bobby. We need to get her back to the dorm." The band was playing a Beatles' song, "I Saw Her Standing There," a record we heard all of the time on the radio.

I found Bobby and yelled in his ear, "We need help getting Karen out of here." I grabbed his hand and pulled him toward the bar.

When Bobby saw Karen, he smiled at her and hollered, "Hey, lets get out of here. Come on." He took her hand. *He must have taken a psychology course, too,* I thought and smiled with him.

She pulled her hand away. "Bobby, you know Lindsey will never get a job with that small arm. No one will ever hire her."

Both of us stopped smiling. Bobby put his arm around her and pushed and moved her toward the door. Linds and I followed. I was furious with Karen.

Karen yelled, "You boys are all gonna die on a rice paddy field in Asia."

Bobby got her outside. Karen, while crying yelled, "It's so sad about Lindsey. She'll never get a teaching job with that arm."

Everyone outside heard her and looked at us, especially at Linds. Bobby had heard enough. His face was so red. He looked at Karen with his teeth clinched and quietly said, "Stop it. You don't know what you're saying or doing. What are you on? You're going to get kicked out of school."

Lindsey told him, "Bobby, it's ok. Let's just get her to her dorm."

210

"She won't get a teaching job, Bobby," Karen clinched her teeth, too.

Bobby slapped her and Karen crumbled to the ground crying. He put his arms around Lindsey, "I'm sorry, Linds. Don't listen to her."

"Bobby, I know she's out of it. I'm fine. We need to help her."

"He helped Karen stand up, "I'm sorry about what I just did. I've never done anything like that before." He looked around at everyone staring and repeated much louder, "I'm sorry." With Karen in between Bobby and me, we started walking toward her dorm.

Off and on Karen kept yelling about the war, boys dying, colored people, and Lindsey. Finally, she passed out. Bobby carried her the rest of the way. He said, "We can't take her into the dorm. She's done more tonight than just drinking too much. I think she's on something. She'll get kicked out of school if she's caught like this. I think you should take her home for the rest of the weekend. Let's put her in the back seat of your car."

Lindsey answered, "That's what we need to do."

"Sammy, will you stay in the car with her while I go with Linds into the dorm? We'll get your bags, and a pillow and blanket for Karen." He looked at her sleeping in the back seat. He said, "I'm sorry I slapped her. I can't believe I did that."

"If you wouldn't have slapped her, I would have," I said.

"She didn't mean what she said," Lindsey hugged him. "Come on. We need to get our stuff before curfew when the doors get locked. We've got to sign all of us out, too. I hope we can." She told the student dorm resident assistant that Karen was sick, and we were taking her home for the weekend. The RA helped her carry our things down to the lobby where Bobby was waiting.

After putting everything in the trunk, Bobby leaned in the back seat and said, "Tell her I'm sorry. I'll tell her myself next time I see her." He pushed the pillow under her head and covered her. She was snoring. He gave me a hug and hugged and kissed Lindsey. "Call me as soon as you can in the morning. Drive safely."

We began backing out and Bobby ran back to our car, "Hey, what about gas? Do you guys have enough gas to drive home?"

Lindsey got out of the car as I stopped, hugged and kissed him, and answered, "Yes, we got gas when we arrived. I love you, Bobby." She got back in.

Hours passed midnight, I'm sure Kate and Art couldn't imagine who was ringing their doorbell. They opened the door and saw the three of us standing on their front steps. Lindsey and I were on each side of Karen holding her up. She really looked terrible and said, "Oh God, I'm going to be sick." Art grabbed hold of her, got her down the steps, and held on to her as she threw up.

At the same time Kate told us to get in the house. "What on earth is going on? Are you all right? Did Karen come to visit you at BG," she asked.

We explained everything we knew. About ten minutes later Art carried her into the house toward the bathroom. With a less than happy look on his face, much less, he said, "Kate, turn the shower on. She's a mess. Girls, she's all yours." He walked into his and Kate's bedroom. Once we finished in the bathroom and took her into my bedroom, we heard Art turn the shower on again.

Kate got her into a nightgown. She brushed Karen's washed hair back and loosely gathered it with a circle clip, while I got the bucket and some towels, just incase. Lindsey pulled the covers down on the extra twin bed, and we got Karen in it. She mumbled how sorry she was. Kate pulled the covers up, kissed her on the cheek, and smoothed a few strands of hair from her forehead. Lindsey gave her a kiss on the cheek. I passed on that. I was so angry about the things she'd said. The light was turned off, and we went back into the living room. A few minutes later Art came in.

He didn't look pleased with us. "Girls, I'm not a happy man right now. What's going on?" I was startled how disappointed and angry his voice sounded.

Lindsey spoke up, "Dad, Bobby called to tell us he was worried about her. We went to stay with her for the weekend. When we saw her, we didn't recognize her. She's a mess. Mom, we're sorry. We don't know what's

212

going on." Linds looked at me for a second. "We think she could be in trouble with drugs. We don't know."

Art looked at us. "Are you two all right?"

I finally spoke up, "Yes, we're fine." I wanted him to know we hadn't let them down, too. "Art, we didn't even finish one 3.2 beer. We hoped we'd be able to talk with Karen over the weekend. She's into so many new things. When she met us tonight, she looked awful. She started talking about the colored people's injustices, and boys dying in rice paddies in Asia, and more about discrimination." I glanced at Lindsey and knew she didn't want me to tell the rest. "She just fell apart in front of us. We brought her home."

"All right girls, that's enough for tonight. Don't you think so, Art? Let me make all of us some tea and toast, and then we'll get some sleep."

Art answered, "As long as you two are fine. I'm proud of you, both. You did the right thing bringing her home. We'll have to tell Brice what's happened tomorrow morning, which is about three hours from now. I don't want any toast. I'm going to bed." He rubbed his arm while heading to his bedroom.

Kate smiled a little. "I have some pie, if you'd like that."

We both were starving and answered we'd love some pie. Soon we were sleeping in Lindsey's room.

Brice was sitting on the side of Sammy's extra twin bed when his daughter opened her eyes. "What's going on," he asked in a determined tone.

Her dad came into focus as her eyes opened. "Nothing is going on." She sounded very irritated as she looked around, recognized Sam's room, and tried to figure out how she got here.

"Karen, this is serious. You need to tell me how much you had to drink last night and what else you're doing to yourself." He raised his voice, "Tell me, now. You've lost weight, you're pale, and there's obviously a lot more going on with you."

"Leave me alone," she answered and turned her head toward the wall.

"I will not leave you alone. Get up, now. We're going home." He was close to completely losing his temper with her.

"Ok, ok, I need to use the bathroom."

He waited until she stood up. As he walked into the kitchen he thought, *I can't let her life turn into a mess like her mother's. I don't know what to do. She's changing before my eyes.* He sat down in the kitchen. He was glad to see Samantha and Lindsey sitting at the table. He wanted to have a few minutes to talk with them without Karen. He wanted to hear what they thought.

Brice was listening to the girls when he realized Karen was taking a long time in the bathroom. "Lindsey, would you please see what's taking her so long?"

The next morning Lindsey and I sat in Kate's kitchen with Brice, Art, and Kate. Brice asked us a million questions. We told him everything we knew. I was getting very angry that we were explaining her behavior while she was hiding out in the bathroom. Just as I was thinking it might be a smart move for Karen to get herself in the kitchen, Brice noticed she'd been in the bathroom a long time. "Lindsey, would you please see what's taking her so long," he asked.

Not wanting to be questioned without back up, I followed her to the bathroom door. Linds knocked. "Karen," she called and tried the door. It was locked. "Karen, we're in the kitchen, come on."

I had it with her, banged on the door, and loudly called, "Karen, get out here." Apparently Art was on edge, too. He came to the hallway, backed us away, and called her name while loudly pounding his fist on the door. Brice and Kate came as Art broke the door down. We found her on the floor.

Karen's hospital stay lasted over two weeks. She admitted to her doctor and dad that she'd been taking some kind of pills a friend kept giving her. She, also, admitted to smoking pot and drinking too much. Brice withdrew her from her classes at OSU for the semester. Although her mom didn't come to see her, Grand visited her every day. Kate sent things from us: cookies, paperback mysteries, and new pajamas with slippers.

The Thursday Karen left the hospital for home, Linds and I came home for the weekend. We studied, and she read more mysteries. We didn't talk very much, but we were with each other for three days and nights. Karen began counseling sessions on the first Monday she was home. Her dad or Frank took her to counseling three or four times a week. By the time June arrived she looked healthy and actually appeared happy.

During the first half of summer break, she still went to counseling twice a week. While she didn't tell us what was said, she confided with Lindsey and me that during these sessions she talked about her mom and dad. She finally had the opportunity to let lose the sadness she felt concerning her mother. It seemed to us that opening her broken heart to doctors by discussing the pain she'd held inside forever, gave her wonderful relief. Her doctors listened, guided her, and let her speak everything her mind and heart were hiding. She talked about everything including her dad and Frank. By the middle of summer the transformation in Karen was amazing. She seemed joyful.

She was allowed to return to OSU for the second summer session. The stipulation was that she had to come home every weekend after her Saturday morning class. She didn't mind that one bit. She'd been worried her dad and uncle would keep her home forever.

This summer turned out to be a great summer for all of us because we were busy and back together. Father Tom asked Bette Lotis, who we previously called Mary Elizabeth; Jimmy, Bobby, Lindsey, and me to volunteer at the children's summer program being held at St. Joseph School. All of us already had summer jobs at the Holsten Inn. When we weren't working, we helped out at St. Joe's. Being with the kids that summer, pointed Jimmy and Lindsey toward careers in education. Linds noticed how quickly the children forgot about her arm once she joined in their activities, read to them, and played games with them. And because Karen was back at OSU, on some Friday nights, we went to bars in Lakewood. We drank 3.2 beer and danced to records or bands.

The summer of 1964 really belonged to Karen. After everything that happened early in our second college semester, by the middle of summer she'd never been happier. She gained needed weight, was drug and alcohol free, and looked beautiful. She loved her summer classes at OSU. Her one problem: she was having difficulty getting all of her classwork completed. She solved that problem!

And that summer, everyone heard The Beatles. "I Want to Hold Your Hand," "Please, Please Me," "Love Me Do," "Can't Buy Me Love," "She Loves You," and "I Saw Her Standing There" filled the airwaves.

Dr. Jameson walked down the hospital corridor to the lobby and found Father Tom. "Hello Father, I've checked Samantha and given her medication for her temperature. She-"

Tom interrupted, "She spoke and squeezed my hand. I was talking to her about the car accident she and her parents were in years ago. Her mother and father died at the accident scene. She spoke, squeezed my hand, and said, 'Why did she leave me. Why did she go?' I'm sure she's hearing me reminisce with her. She was referring to her mother's death, I think." He looked at Dr. Jameson for reassurance.

"I honestly don't know if she's hearing you, but keep talking to her. It can't hurt. Squeezing your hand is a good sign. Her fever should come down in a while. You can put cool compresses on her forehead. I'd like your temperature checked. The nurse is waiting for you. I'll be leaving soon. I'll see her, again, before I leave. By the way, I enjoyed listening to the Beatles while in her room. The music is a good idea."

"I think so, too." They left the lobby walking in opposite directions.

Tom arrived at the nurses' station on Samantha's floor. Her nurse said, "I'll walk back with you to Mrs. Green's room and take your temp."

His temperature was normal. He got himself comfortable in his chair and reached to hold Samantha's hand. "Well, honey, your hand and arm don't feel too warm. Hopefully, the medication is already working." He set her hand on top of her covers. "Reminiscing with you has reminded me that we sure had our heartaches. Now that I'm talking to you and remembering with you, well, you kids had enough heartbreak, that's for sure. When Kate and I reminisced, we talked about all of the good times. Remember meeting Phillip?"

She moved a little and turned her head, just a bit, toward Father.

He sat up straighter and moved to the edge of his chair. "Samantha, Sammy, can you hear me?" He vigorously rubbed her arm. "I think you hear me. You

217

jump into this conversation anytime. Now, honey, we really did have so many blessings, too. All of us had so much fun together. We were like one large, be it a little unusual, family. Jim and I have stayed very close friends all of these years. We stayed close to Kate. She always took care of us, and we took care of her, especially these last years. She was so proud of you, Karen, and Lindsey."

He stood up and felt her forehead. She didn't move her head away. "Ok Sammy, let me sit back down. I've been thinking about Karen and Phillip. Kate loved remembering the day we met him. It was just a perfect evening in her and Art's backyard. Karen was healthy, beautiful, and so happy. I can remember how excited she and Phillip were to be with all of us. We sat all night by that bonfire. Sammy, do you remember? Can you see their faces?"

SLEEPING MEMORIES 1964

Karen was so happy with Phillip. She didn't tell us about him right away. Her history professor introduced them. Linds and I knew that someone special had stepped into her life. We all met him in Kate's backyard. It was a wonderful day helping Kate and Grand get everything ready. The party that night was perfect.

We all were so happy, Lindsey and Bobby, Karen and Phillip, and Jimmy and me.

1964

After her second class Monday, Karen stopped in the student union to get some coffee. She was on her way to meet with her history professor. Just inside the door, on the huge bulletin board, she read a large printed message stating several classes were canceled for the day including her sociology and English literature classes. All were cancelled due to a maintenance issue in the building. *My lucky day,* she thought as she walked to the coffee machine. She pressed the right buttons, watched the coffee cup drop down and fill with coffee and then cream, tasted it, and snapped the lid on. She picked up her folder holding her history lecture outlines and her books.

Back outside, she walked across the oval to her professor's office. After she attended his lecture last Friday, she confided to him that she was getting behind and needed help knowing what to prioritize. He told her, "Come to my office on Monday at one o'clock."

Professor George, energetic as always and sincere with concern that his students get help when they need it, bounced up from his chair to greet her as she walked in. He looked down where he'd written her name. "Hi, Karen, glad you came this afternoon. It's better to get help sooner than later. Easy to fall behind in these summer session classes. There's so much information crammed in." Her eyes were locked on the other person standing in the office. Professor George looked at both of them a second. "Karen, meet Phillip Avenston, my assistant."

"Phillip, this is the student I was telling you about, Karen Fry. Karen's falling behind in history and some other classes as well. She missed much of spring semester due to illness. She's trying to regain, in this summer session, the credits she lost. She wants to graduate on schedule."

He looked back at her. "Right?" Karen shook her head while smiling at Mr. Avenston. "She needs help organizing her time and highlighting the important information. You know, the usual stuff."

Phillip smiled at her. *My God, she's beautiful,* he thought. He replied, "I think I understand. I have time later this afternoon. Would you like to get started today?"

She didn't answer. She kept looking at him with her big, puppy-brown eyes. "Could you meet me in the student union at four?" He waited for an answer. "Karen?" "Yes, I'd love you." *Oh, God, I can't believe I said that.* Her face flushed. She laughed and said, "I meant to say, I'd love to. I'd appreciate getting started right away. I can meet at four." She tried to regroup still gazing into his perfect blue eyes.

"I'll find you in the student union. See you soon."

She finally looked back at her professor, "Thank you, Professor George." She picked up her folder, books, and left.

After she left the professor asked, "Have I made your day, Phillip?"

"I think you have." He thought to himself, *She's amazing, really amazing.* Then he considered, *She's a freshman, and I'm twenty-five. I'm acting ridiculous.* He shook his head.

Karen decided to go back to her dorm and change clothes. She took a quick shower. After wrapping herself in the large beach towel she loved using and returning to her room, she rolled her hair onto large rollers and sat under her portable dryer. Holding a hand held mirror, she applied some make-up: a little soft pink lipstick, blush, a touch of eye shadow, and a tad of powder on her nose. Her sandy blond, shoulder length hair dried, and she took the rollers out. Quickly she put on culottes, a short sleeve madras blouse, and flats and then brushed her hair. She sprayed a bit of perfume on her neck. As she walked through the lobby of her dorm, she stopped at the desk and signed out for a one hour late return.

Karen heard a lot of activity and chatter as she opened the student union door. She was about twenty minutes early. To her delight, Phillip was already there. He stood up as soon as his blue eyes spotted her. She smiled at him looking at his curly blond hair and beautiful eyes while thinking, *He's the most handsome man I've ever met. I feel so happy!* She couldn't stop smiling, realizing he'd been watching for her.

"Hi, Karen, by the way, please call me, Phillip."

"Hi, Phillip," she answered giving him a most enchanting smile.

221

He cleared his throat, "We can study here, or I know of another place that's much quieter." *What am I doing?*

"Let's go there." She tilted her head upward to look into his eyes.

As they walked outside, they looked as though they'd known one and other forever. Phillip held her hand as they hurried down the steps to the sidewalk. *Her hand feels so soft and warm, and she's the most beautiful girl. I can't believe how she makes me feel.* His mind was racing. *This is crazy,* he thought to himself. He looked down at the top of her head just in time to see her look back up at him as she smiled. *Control yourself. You're not thinking clearly.* He opened the passenger door to his two seated sports car and let her in. When he got in he asked, "Want the top up?"

"No."

They sped away listening to the radio with Steve Lawrence singing "Go Away Little Girl," and the thought, *exactly,* sailing through his mind. She closed her eyes and leaned her head back. He saw her hand resting on her lap and couldn't stop himself from wrapping his hand around hers. The warm wind swept around them as they sped to his apartment. His car didn't seem to slow down much. It just sailed into his parking spot and stopped. He got out and opened her door noticing she left her books. Grabbing them, he held her hand as he led her to the lobby of his apartment building. All the while he kept smiling, and she kept smiling, too.

He unlocked his apartment door, and they walked into his living room. He turned on some soft lights and went into his kitchen which was open to his living room. Karen looked around. *His apartment looks sharp,* she thought. She saw it was mostly beige with some different shades of gray and blue. She took her flats off, and her feet sank into the thick, dark gray, shag carpeting. Looking at dark blue pillows on his light gray sofa and cream pillows on his dark blue overstuffed chairs, she also saw lots of beige framed pictures on end tables and blue framed pictures on his light beige walls. She walked toward the wall pictures and saw groups of colored and white people standing together. Some people were smiling, and some were looking determined. A picture on an end table stole her attention. Phillip was standing near Martin Luther King. Karen turned toward the kitchen and gazed at Phillip. *He's amazing!*

"Hey, would you like a coke or something?" He called from his kitchen.

"A coke would be great, thanks." She walked into his kitchen and saw more light beige walls and a perfect shade of blue on his formica counter tops. *Gosh, my dad and Uncle Frank would love this apartment.*

"How about a sandwich or something?"

"Maybe later, a coke is just right."

He handed her the coke in a glass filled with ice and picked up her books. They walked into his living room.

"Your apartment, I think it's great." Karen looked up at him. He set her books down on an end table next to his large, comfortable looking couch. As she looked up, he looked into her big, brown eyes and saw a trace of tears. "Phillip," he heard her say, "you touch my soul when you look at me."

"I don't know what's happening. No one, ever, in my life has made me feel like this. I haven't ever, not once, brought a student here. I want to hold you, just hold you." He turned his stereo on. Johnny Mathis began singing "Chances Are." He held his arms out, "Dance with me." She slipped her arms up around his neck as they held each other close and danced to the music.

The mention of meeting lips encouraged him. He gently kissed her. He thought, C*hances are very good that someone special is in my arms.* Phillip wanted to hold her forever. He wanted her so much. He kept dancing with her as the next song "All the Time," began. They danced and his heart beat faster as he thought, *I could be with you all the time. I think.* He looked at her and said, "Karen, I never want you to be hurt by anyone." He looked down into her eyes, "You're killing me here. As much as I want to-" He stopped dancing, took hold of her hand, and walked her to his kitchen bar counter. He pulled out two bar stools. In a different tone of voice he said, "Let's sit and talk awhile."

"Phillip, I love you. This is so amazing. I just know that I love you. You love me, too, I know it. I just know you do."

223

He looked up at his ceiling. *God, is this some kind of test?* He smiled, "Ok little one, we've got to slow down. I'm twenty-five and you're, what, maybe eighteen or nineteen? My feelings are real. I think. Listen here, you've got me way off balance. Ok, the first thing we need to do," he walked to his stereo, "is get Johnny, here, turned off and get more lights turned on. Then we'll look at your history notes."

She watched him and smiled a huge smile. *Oh my gosh, I love him. I love him so much.* She glanced below his waist and said, "Looks like Johnny has a mind of his own."

He saw where she glanced, "Oh great, I've fallen for a little devil. Wait, I haven't fallen. Let's just talk."

"Phillip, maybe you could help me with English Lit? Maybe we can go over Romeo and Juliet? Juliet was very young when she fell in love."

"Indeed she was," he tried sounding very knowledgable. "Many think that Romeo was considerably older, and the whole thing didn't end well."

"Maybe we should move on to philosophy. Let's think. Love, is love ageless, Phillip? Are there age boundaries when two people want to be together more than anything else in this world," she asked and winked at him.

My God, she winked at me. It's as though she's older. He felt flustered. "Listen, young lady, just listen to me. We'll talk for a while. We don't need to rush anything. In fact, we're done talking about this. I'm taking you back to your dorm. What time are your classes tomorrow, Tuesday?"

She was surprised by his sudden decision, "Um," she thought for a second, "I'm done by two."

"Perfect. Can I pick you up at your dorm about three tomorrow?"

"Sure." She slid off the stool.

He picked up her books, and they left for his car. Before he turned on the ignition, he turned to her and pulled her into his arms. He kissed her so tenderly, he took her breath away. While hugging her he said, "You're amazing, little one. You've changed everything. We don't have to rush anything."

224

She settled back into her seat. He drove out of his parking lot and sped down the street.

1964

Phillip returned to his apartment, and that night he didn't fall asleep easily. He couldn't stop thinking about the young girl he'd met just hours before. *Somehow everything feels different now.* He tried to convince himself that he couldn't be in love with her. *We just met. She's too young. And yet, when I'm with her, she doesn't seem so young. She seems to control me. I think I would do anything to make her happy. Her smile, her beautiful, enchanting smile fills my heart.* He finally fell asleep with a smile on his face.

At three o'clock the next afternoon, he walked into Karen's dorm lobby. She was ready and waiting for him. His face looked so happy as she handed him her books.

"Where's your history folder with the lecture notes," he asked.

"Let me think. Where did I leave that folder," she asked with an impish grin.

"You're kidding. I didn't notice your folder at the apartment. All right, let's go get it. Then we'll come back to the campus library and begin figuring out your history lecture outlines. When we're done, let's have dinner together. It's a good, safe plan."

When they got into his car, she kissed him on his cheek. "Hello sunshine," she said as though she'd known him forever, and then showed him that grin.

His heart melted. "It's a little chilly. Do you want the top up?"

"No, I've got my sweater."

"I like that sweater. It's as long as your skirt. Looks sharp."

"Thanks." Karen turned his radio up and buttoned a few buttons on her sweater. The Tymes were singing "So Much In Love."

He turned the heater up and happily thought, *I can picture walking down the aisle with her,* then he considered that getting married wasn't possible. He took hold of her hand and watched her lean her head back against her seat and close her eyes. *She's so beautiful. I'll never do anything to hurt her.* He thought about Michael spending the month with his parents and shut

226

those thoughts down. It made him realize: *No walking down the aisle.* He put both hands on his steering wheel.

He parked his car in his parking space and said, "Wait here, and I'll get your history notes."

"I need to use your bathroom," she answered.

They walked to the elevator hand in hand and then into his apartment. "Don't even take your sweater off. We need to get out of here, get to the library, and get started organizing your notes. I want to take you to a great restaurant tonight. Your dorm curfew is eleven on week nights, right?"

"Yes, eleven, I'll hurry." He saw that impish smile.

He decided to unload his dishwasher. A few minutes later, he turned toward a slight sound he heard. At first he was startled by what he saw, but very quickly his face formed a smile. Karen stood there wearing only her sweater. "You know, little one, I only have so much strength to fight this. Thank God I didn't tell you to keep it buttoned! Are you sure this isn't happening too soon?"

"I'm so sure." She stepped into his arms. He picked her up, carried her into his bedroom, and closed the door.

Hours later she opened her eyes. She was beyond happy and turned toward Phillip. He wasn't there. She sat up and looked at the bathroom door in his bedroom seeing it was open, and so was his bedroom door. It was very quiet. She still had a smile, but a slight unease edged her. She put her hand down feeling a piece of paper on the sheet. The next second, everything she felt in her heart and knew in her mind filled her eyes. She read, *I love you, now, and always. I'll be back in a few minutes. Our dinner plans have changed. Hope you like pizza. I put a sweatshirt on the chair. Look in the drawers if you want a different one. I love you. Phillip*

She slipped his sweatshirt on. It hung a few inches above her knees. She saw her clothes on the arm of the same chair and put on her underwear. Then she found her purse and walked into the bathroom near the living room.

He was in the kitchen when she walked out of the bathroom. He hugged her as soon as he saw her. "I have something for you." He handed her a small box wrapped in gold paper with a fancy gold bow.

Karen started to say something, and he stopped her. With the happiest expression, she opened the box and saw a gold bracelet with four gold charms: two small gold letters, U R, and then two letters attached together MY, and then a solid gold heart. "Phillip, it's beautiful. You are my heart. I love it." She put it on. "I'll wear it always. Thank you." She hugged him and kissed him. "Where did you get this?"

"The jewelry store my parents have always used is just around the corner. The owners are very good friends of theirs. Both owners were there. I told them how much you mean to me, and they helped me put this together. I have to take it back tomorrow. The soldering needs to be permanent. They said it will be ready for you on Friday afternoon."

"Ok, Friday afternoon." She took the bracelet off and set it in the box.

"I've got a little bad news. There's no pizza!"

"You're joking. That would have been the best part of the day!" Karen showed him that devilish smile.

"Oh, really? The best part?" He picked her up and carried her back into his bedroom.

"Well, maybe not the very best part." She wrapped her arms around his neck.

When they left his apartment they had time to get some pizza. While they waited for it, Phillip asked Karen for her class schedule. "I promise we'll start getting your classes figured out tomorrow. Don't worry. Everything will be great. What time can we actually go to the library tomorrow?"

"My classes start at eight in the morning, and I'm not done until six."

"I'll meet you in the library at six thirty."

They talked, laughed, ate their pizza, and got Karen back to her dorm at three minutes to eleven.

During the next weeks Phillip helped Karen with all of her classes. He helped her organize her time and gave her ideas on how to know what to prioritize in each class. "The important thing," he said, "is to read your notes often and try to apply what you read to conversation. Don't just get through your classes, apply what you're learning. Bring it to life. Just try it. You'll see."

Also during these weeks, they learned everything about each other. Karen told Phillip about her Dad and Uncle Frank. She told him about her mom living in New York City explaining that she really hadn't ever spent much time with her. "The last time my mom and I were together was at my high school graduation. I could never let my children grow up without me, let alone love and be with anyone who could. I couldn't be with anyone who could let a situation develop where they missed precious time raising their child."

Phillip looked away. He felt a jolt in his heart. "He started to say, "But Karen, sometimes things,"

"It's ok, Phillip." She didn't want him to make excuses for her mom. "When I was younger, I used to pray that she'd come and stay with me forever. I grew to understand things. I love her. I dream about her. It's ok. My grandmother, Grand, has been my mom. Kate O'Malley has been a mom to me, and Joan was, too. One thing for sure, I will never do that to my children."

He looked away for a few seconds.

"My dad and I are very close. He's the best. And really, I have three dad's. I used to have Jack, too. My Uncle Frank and Art O'Malley, Art is Lindsey's dad, have always behaved like fathers toward me. And speaking about fathers, Father Tom, our parish priest, is part of our family." She continued talking telling him about Samantha and Lindsey. "Sammy and I met Lindsey at a tea party her mom, Kate, gave us. We've been sisters since that day. I couldn't love them more." She told him everything that happened when Sammy's parents died.

He told her about his childhood and all of the traveling and different countries he'd seen with his mom and dad. He said, "My parents worked hard, and the company they started is successful in many countries. They sold it several years ago. My dad's still involved in it. They're very kind and generous. You'll love them. They're living in their home in Italy right now and have a house here in Columbus. They travel back and forth."

The two of them were never at a loss for words. Both of them loved that they shared concern for all who faced discrimination and oppression. They talked endlessly about ways to bring people together with understanding and compassion.

They told one other almost everything. They each kept one secret. The only thing Phillip didn't tell her was about Michael. He just couldn't figure out how to tell her all of that, especially after hearing about her mother. The thing Karen needed to tell Phillip was the trouble she'd gotten into during early spring quarter. She needed to tell him the real reason she left school spring quarter and why she didn't drink alcohol.

One afternoon as he was driving to his apartment she turned her big, brown eyes on him and said, "Let's drive to the park for a while. We need to talk about something."

He let go of her hand. To him the words, we need to talk about something, had the hidden meaning: I need a little space, which led to breaking up. He'd given the "we need to talk" speech to a few girls himself, and he knew what was coming. Suddenly he felt angry. He stepped on the gas peddle until they were going way over sixty.

"Hey, slow down. You're driving too fast. What's the matter?"

He slowed down as they entered the park. He parked, got out of the car, slammed the door closed, and walked away with his hands in his pockets. Karen sat still for a moment, then got out of the car, ran after him, and got in front of him. "I just want to talk with you about something."

"Oh, I bet you do!" He glared at her.

She'd never seen him look angry, let alone how angry he looked right then. She thought he looked kind of funny, and she smiled a tad.

"What are you doing? Just get to it. And this isn't funny, young lady. I'm as in love with you as possible. You mean everything to me. I know you're younger and this relationship my not mean so much to you." He yelled louder, "I love you." He looked around and less loudly said, "Do you get that? I've never loved anyone as much as I love you, and here you are playing games with me. I should take you back to your Bay Village so you could finish growing up."

She had to turn her back to him, because he looked so damn funny. She knew she was going to laugh.

"Hey, hey, don't you turn your back to me!"
She turned around, laughing as tears filled her eyes.
Phillip looked at her, "What in the hell is wrong with you? Just say it and get it over with."
Her smile vanished. *Well, fine. Let's get it done.* Now, she was angry, too. Her voice raised, "I was smoking pot and taking pills last winter, and I almost killed myself on them. And, oh yes, I forgot, I was drinking a lot, too! My dad, Art, and family found me near death on Kate's bathroom floor. And I had to stay in the hospital clinic for days to free my system. I had to go to weeks of counseling. When I came home, my dad and uncle took me to counseling three times a week for most of last spring. That's why I'm behind in my hours."

She was so wound up and angry hearing herself say everything out loud, she took a deep breath. In a controlled voice she finished, "I don't have to go home each Saturday to work as I told you. My dad makes me come home each weekend because he doesn't trust me, yet." She swallowed, "So-" Her voice gave way and tears spilled down her cheeks. She whispered, "How do you love me, now?" She turned to walk back to the car.

Phillip's face lit up in a smile, and he got in front of her. "I love you even more. That's how I love you, now." Lifting her off the ground, he held her tight. "I love you more than ever. I'm sorry." He set her down and held her hands. "I thought you were going to tell me that you wanted time apart. I'm sorry I acted like a jerk. I won't do it again. If your feelings for me change, you'll need to tell me, and I'll listen."

"Phillip, I will never, ever, want time apart from you. My feelings for you will never change. The second I saw you I knew I could never love anyone else."

They drove back to his apartment. She filled his arms as soon as his apartment door closed. "I could never leave you. I can't breath without you. Don't ever leave me," she whispered.

"You're my life. You're everything to me. I'd do anything for you. I'll never hurt you." They walked into his bedroom.

Later they made pizza and salad and talked about their future and the things they wanted to accomplish

231

together. Karen told him more about growing up with Sammy and Lindsey. Phillip asked, "What if I drive you home this Saturday?"

The next day, Karen waited until her classes were over to call home. It was early in the evening when she called hoping either Lindsey or Sammy would answer the phone. Linds answered on the third ring. "Hi, I want to tell you something. I met someone wonderful several weeks ago. I love him so much. He'd like to drive me home this Saturday, so he can meet all of you. What do you think?"

"Sammy and I knew it. We knew it! You've been so happy these past weekends, and you sure couldn't wait to get back to school. No one likes their classes that much!"

"You guys will love him, too. He's fun, smart, kind, caring, great looking, and we share the same interests. He is a little older than we are. He just finished grad school."

"How old is he?"

She swallowed, "He's twenty-five. You just have to meet him. Don't tell Kate or Grand how old he is. Please, give him a chance."

"Come on. If you love him, and he's making you this happy, we'll love him."

"Thanks, Linds. After you get to know him, you two tell me if you think the age difference matters." She got back on subject, "So do you think it could work this weekend? I need to call my dad, still. Is Sammy there? I want to tell her."

"Absolutely this Saturday will work. Let mom have everyone over Saturday night. You know she'll love doing it. Grand and mom will make everything perfect. Let me ask her, and I'll call you right back. Sammy should be home any minute."

"Ok. I'll call my dad right now, and let me call you back in a half hour. Oh, one more thing, do you think Phillip could stay at your house? You and Sammy could crash with me."

"Sure. Let me talk to mom about everything."

"Thanks. Love you."

Karen called her dad. She had a strategy she was sure would work. They talked for a minute and then she said, "Dad, I met a guy, several weeks ago, who I'm beginning to like very much. I want you to meet him. I think he's great, and what you think matters to me."

"Honey, you're supposed to be at school to catch up."

"I met him when I went to my history professor's office for help. Professor George asked him to help me. My grades are excellent, now. Phillip has helped me so much."

"His name is Phillip? Is he in class with you?"

"Yes, that's his name, Phillip Avenston. No, he's not in any of my classes," she paused and breathed in. "Could he bring me home this Saturday? I really want you to tell me what you think about him. You, Uncle Frank, and Grand look him over. If you guys have reservations about him, tell me. Would this Saturday work? Sammy, Lindsey, and I will stay at our house, and Phillip will stay at Kate's. Could you check with Kate tomorrow about everything?"

They finished talking, "Dad, I love you, and I'll call you back tomorrow night."

Karen called Sammy and Lindsey about fifteen minutes later. She heard Kate's voice. "Kate, hi."

"I was hoping it was you calling. Sammy's right here. I just want to tell you not to worry about a thing. Phillip can stay here Saturday night."

"Thank you. He's really wonderful. I can't wait for him to meet you. He feels like he already knows you. My dad's ok with this weekend. I talked with him.'

"Good! Honey, the weather forecast is perfect for this weekend, according to weatherman, Dick Goddard. How about if we have an outdoor picnic?"

"That would be wonderful."

"Grand and I'll have fun getting things ready. Love you, Karen, here's Sammy."

"Linds and I knew it. We could tell. Can't wait for Saturday."

"You'll love him, Sam. He's so fab. Did Lindsey tell you that he's twenty-five?"

"That's so cool!"

"He has a graduate degree and is an instructor at Ohio State. He's helped me this quarter. That's how I met him. He goes to Italy once a month and works at his parent's new company as well. Guess what? He's an active supporter of the equal rights movement. He's wonderful, Sam."

"We're so happy for you. We can't wait to meet him."

"Make sure Jimmy and Bobby are there."

"Absolutely, and Father Tom has already been invited, too."

1964

Conversation came in spurts on the drive to Bay Village. Finally Phillip said, "Hey what's going in? Don't you think they'll like me? I'll turn on the charm. Who could resist!"

"No, they'll like you. I just hope you like all of them. My family is a little different."

They arrived finding Art's backyard beautifully set up for a picnic. They heard lots of chatter as they stepped on the patio. Brice saw them and immediately greeted them, hugging and kissing his daughter and shaking Phillip's hand. He steered them to Frank and Grand, and then Phillip met Kate, Art, and everyone else. Father Tom arrived a few minutes later and introduced himself. In no time, he took Phillip over to the bocci ball set and challenged Jimmy and Bobby to a match. Soon Phillip was kidding with Jimmy and Bobby, who he called Jim and Bob.

Karen smiled as she watched how easily everyone welcomed him. The laughing and happy kidding filled her heart. *I'm so lucky to have this family.* She turned and walked inside to help Kate and Grand carry food to the back yard.

"Grand made everything here," Kate stated. "She absolutely insisted."

"Not everything, you made a bunch of things, and Art has the yard looking perfect and the barbecue ready. We're having a beautiful day." Grand gave Kate a pat on her arm.

"I love you, both, thank you. Phillip is having a great time."

Kate gave Karen a hug and said, "Let's get these snacks outside. We'll eat dinner after six, right Grand?"

She shook her head, yes, as she looked at her granddaughter's bracelet. "What a pretty bracelet, honey, is it new?"

Sammy and Linds walked in as Karen was showing Grand and Kate. "Isn't it perfect?"

Sam and Linds looked at it, and Lindsey softly said, "You are my heart. Phillip gave you this?"

"Yes."

"It's beautiful. We've known him for over an hour. And so far, he passes in my book. Jimmy and Bobby, Jim and Bob," Linds smiled more, "sure seem to like him."

"Sometimes Phillip calls me Kar! He shortens names. However, he hates to be called Phil."

"See, even perfect people have quirks," Sammy laughed and added, "Most everyone at school call them Jim and Bob, now. We should tell them Phillip likes to be called Phillip."

"He's having such a great time. I bet he hasn't even thought about it." They all carried snacks to the backyard.

Everyone had a wonderful time. The couples played bocci ball, horse shoes, and yard jarts the rest of the afternoon, and the guys enjoyed needling each other. Later Art grilled chicken, and once Grand's and Kate's side dishes were carried outside, everyone enjoyed a delicious picnic. With the sun setting, Art asked for help to build a bonfire. After a lot of laughing at not being able to keep it lit, they finally got a great fire going, and everyone remained around it until past midnight.

About an hour before Phillip and Karen left Sunday afternoon, Phillip asked Brice if he could talk with him for a few minutes. They walked outside and sat in chairs in the Fry's side yard.

Brice broke the few seconds of awkwardness, "I'm glad you brought Karen home yesterday. It's been good meeting you and spending time with both of you. I can see my daughter's very happy."

"Meeting all of you has been wonderful. Yesterday was great, thank you. Mr Fry, I want you to know that I love Karen, absolutely. I will never hurt her, not ever. I understand that she is younger than I am."

"How old are you, Phillip?"

"I'm twenty-five. Everything changed for me the moment I saw her. Nothing like this has ever happened to me. I love her. I would ask your permission to marry her right now, but I know she's young, and the time isn't right for her or for me, now." He looked away for a second, "A lot of times, she seems wiser than I." He looked directly at Brice. "I'm certain that Karen loves me as much as I love her. I don't want you to worry that I'll hurt her. If the time ever comes that she needs space, I won't hold her back.

I'll step aside. I'm certain her feelings for me are genuine, but if they change, I will be a gentleman. Also, I want you to know that I will always support her sobriety. I'll watch over her and protect her, always. I've told her I'd stop drinking if that would help support her. She's told me that she does not need or want me to do that. If she ever wants me to quit drinking, I will." He finished speaking and just looked at Karen's dad for a few seconds.

"Thank you, Phillip." They stood up. "I appreciate you telling me these things. I trust you. My daughter means the world to me. I've never seen her so happy and confident. I absolutely want her to complete her bachelor degree before getting married. If she wants to be in school year round to graduate sooner, I'll support that." Brice shook Phillip's hand and patted his arm. They talked a few minutes about the picnic and Buckeye football before walking back inside.

Grand thought she'd walk over to Kate's for a few minutes. The girls were there, and she wanted to spend some time with Karen. She walked out the side door and took a step toward the side yard, hearing Brice talking. She stopped.

Immediately she knew she should turn around or just say hello and keep walking, but she took one step back near the shrub and stood still. She heard, "Mr. Fry, I want you to know," *This is wrong of me. I shouldn't do this.* She remained very still. "that I love Karen, absolutely. I will never hurt her, not ever. I understand that she is younger than I am." Not making a sound, Grand heard every word. "I'll watch over her and protect her, always."

Standing very still until she heard, "Thank you, Phillip, I appreciate you telling me," she turned, quietly opened her side door, and stepped up the three steps into her kitchen. She quickly wiped tears dropping from her eyes as she looked out the window above her kitchen sink. *I know, dear Lord, what I just did was wrong. I'm so grateful I heard every one of those words. Thank you, Thank you! I'm so happy for my precious, Karen.* She smiled. *Well, my Saturday confession with Father Tom will have a little more pizzazz. Although, is it a sin to confess something that you're thankful happened?* She stood looking out for a few seconds longer.

Ok, now, in a minute, I will go to Kate's. She went upstairs to her dressing table to put some powder on her nose.

Everything went perfectly for Karen and Phillip during the next days, months, and few years. They spent their time together pursuing their hopes and dreams. They attended equal rights rallies in support of opportunity and rights for all. They set up informal discussion groups giving groups of people the opportunity to hear from those who had experienced segregation. Karen became a business major. Phillip excelled in making his parent's new company in Italy very successful. And of course, during this time Karen neared the completion of her bachelor's degree.

They loved being together. They loved being Buckeye fans. They loved each other's families. When Karen met Hubert and Roslyn Avenston, she liked them instantly. The four of them had dinner together often when Hubert and Roslyn were in Columbus. Karen and Phillip went home to Bay Village for dinners and overnights. The two of them and Bobby went to visit Sammy and Lindsey at Bowling Green and the girls visited them at Ohio State. Phillip became part of their family, and he loved it.

There was only one problem lurking. Even with his parents' urging, he still hadn't mentioned Michael to Karen. He spent one week a month in Italy with Michael when his parents had Michael with them. In Columbus, whenever Michael's mother permitted, Phillip played games with him outside in her yard. He knew he should have the two people he loved so much, Karen and Michael, meet one another. He knew his mom and dad were right telling him that he needed to tell her everything. And yet, he didn't. Karen's words, *'I could never let my children grow up without me, or be with anyone who could,'* had placed the fear of losing her in his mind and heart.

239

1966

The door to Bobby's room was open. He liked when his friends stopped in. Mid afternoon he was at his desk reading for his evening class when John walked in. John had transferred to OSU this quarter. He grew up in a suburb of Columbus and was glad to be finishing his degree near home at the university he always loved. "Hi, Bob, what's happening?" He sat down on the bed and looked at the new picture of Sammy, Jimmy, Lindsey, Bobby, Karen, and Phillip on the desk shelf. He got up and looked closely at the picture. "What are you guys doing in a picture with that guy? That's Mr. Avenston, and he isn't cool."

Bobby looked at him, "What are you talking about? Phillip's a great guy. We've known him for a long time. He and Karen have been dating for years. How do you know him?"

"Mr. Avenston is married. He has a couple of kids. His wife lives next door to my parents. He's separated from her, but sometimes I see him in the yard playing with his older son. I've said, hi, to him a few times. He's waved, but that's all. I think his wife's name is Maureen. Apparently she's Catholic and won't divorce him. My mom thinks being Catholic has nothing to do with staying married, but the Avenston's money sure does. The Avenstons are loaded. Anyway, she and her young son moved into the house next door to my parents. Soon after she moved in, she had another baby. My mom took dinner over. Your Phillip, our Mr. Avenston, hasn't lived in the house, I don't think. Maureen has a terrible reputation in our neighborhood. She has different boyfriends over all of the time. Phillip could be there, sometimes. Here's the thing, she's pregnant. She told my mom, just the other day, that Mr. Averston is very excited that they're having another baby. She said he wants to end their separation and make their marriage work."

Bobby put his head in his hands a second and then he stood up. "God, this is terrible. I've got to call Lindsey. I can't believe this. He seems to love Karen so much. You're sure about this?"

"I'm really sorry, but all of this is true. I've seen his wife, and she's definitely expecting. Good luck." John patted Bobby's shoulder and left.

Bobby walked to the end of the hall, picked up the receiver on the phone, and waited a few seconds for the operator to answer.

In their dorm room, Sammy and Lindsey heard a voice on their room intercom saying Lindsey had a phone call on their floor phone. She walked down the hall to the phone and answered, "Hello."

"Lindsey, I have something I need to tell you. It's bad."

"What's wrong? Are you ok?"

"A friend of mine, John, you met him, he transferred here this quarter. He just told me that Phillip is married and has a couple of kids."

"What? That's crazy!"

"Just listen. He saw that picture you just sent me. He recognized Phillip and said that Phillip is separated from his wife. His wife and two children live next door to John's parents. He's seen him playing in the yard with his oldest son."

"No way, John's got to be mistaken."

"Please just listen. His wife won't divorce him because she's Catholic, but everyone thinks it's because the Avenston's are wealthy. From what John told me, Phillip's wife is a terrible person. Here's the worst part. His wife is expecting another baby, and she told John's mom that Phillip is very happy about their baby and that he wants to get back together."

"It can't be the same Phillip. He loves Karen so much. They've been going together almost three years. No way, I can't believe this!"

"We have to tell her."

"This just can't be true."

"There isn't any reason John would make this up."

"Let me tell Sammy right now. We can't tell Karen this over the phone. Both of us have a class in an hour. I'll need to get permission for us to leave for the night because it's a week night. Unless I call you right back, we'll meet you in Karen's dorm around seven-thirty, eight o'clock.

"I can't miss my evening class that starts at seven and ends at nine. I'll get to her dorm as soon as I can. See you tonight. I'm sorry I had to tell you about this. I love you."

"I love you, too."

Lindsey was in the adult resident's dorm apartment asking for permission to leave campus for the night. Sammy was in their dorm room with everything she'd just been told about Phillip circling her mind. The intercom startled her. "Phone call for Samantha or Lindsey." She hurried down the hallway to answer the phone.

"Sammy, I'm pregnant, and Phillip has a wife and family." Karen began crying.

"Karen, Linds and I..."

Karen interrupted, "I was, huh, huh," she cried, "at our apartment, and this lady knocked on the, huh, door. Oh Sammy, she knew my name! She said she was a friend of Phillips, and I let her in. She had a picture," she cried more, "a family portrait of her, Phillip, and two little boys. She told me Phillip is her husband. She showed me her driver's license." More crying. "How could he? She's pregnant, too. Her baby's due in a few weeks," Karen cried and cried.

Sammy began crying. "Karen, Linds and I want to be with you."

"Phillip loves me. He's told me he loves me a million times. I love him so much. She's having his baby, too. How could he?"

Lindsey was standing next to Sammy, now. Sammy was crying, and she took hold of the phone. She heard, "Oh God, I still love him. He never told me. He never said a word. I'm pregnant, too."

Lindsey lost her breath for a second. *Oh, God.* "Karen, it's Lindsey. We're leaving to be with you right now. We'll be there soon. Try to rest. We'll figure this out. We love you. We'll be with you soon. Just rest. Love you."

She hung up the phone, picked up the receiver, again, and collect called her mom. "Mom, Karen's in trouble. She needs us. Our adult resident, Mrs. Link, was going to call you to get your permission for us to leave. We were

242

going to leave after our next classes. It's a week night, and we need permission. We're going to skip our next classes and leave right away. You call Mrs. Link. I'll tell her that you'll be calling her immediately."

"What's going on?"

"Mom, Karen's pregnant, and we need to be with her. There's lots more going on."

Our Karen, one wrong decision in the wrong moment can undo one's life and set everything on an unintended path.

Mrs. Link was so kind. She came to our room to tell us that Kate called and gave permission for us to leave right away. "If you need to be home longer than one night, call me." She handed me a paper with her name and number. She helped us carry our things to our car. "I hope everything works out for Karen. I've met her, and she's sweet. Mrs. Link gave us a hug, "Drive safely."

Then we were on our way.

1966

Smiling, Phillip turned the key in the lock to his apartment door knowing his Karen was waiting for him. His smile disintegrated the second he saw Maureen sitting on his couch.

"Hello, Darlin," she grinned at him.

"What are you doing here, and how did you get in?" He hated her.

"Now Phillip, is that any way to speak to the mother of your children, one of whom is about to bust out of me any day now?"

He glared at her middle, "That certainly isn't my baby. We know Jeff isn't, and you lied about Michael, too, you witch." He despised Maureen. Their history together was brief. He met her eight years ago, when he was almost twenty. During the short time he was attracted to her, she told him she was pregnant with his child. In one month, Maureen's mom planned a small wedding in a Catholic Chapel. About five months later he was married, holding a new born baby they named Michael.

Phillip's parents rented a nice apartment for him and his new family near their home in Columbus. His mom, Roslyn, took care of Michael during the week when Phillip had classes. Roslyn and her husband, Hubert, loved being with their new grandson. Phillip adored his son and took care of him. Unless he was on campus in class, Phillip was with his baby son. Maureen had little interest in her baby or her marriage. She spent her time shopping, partying, and sleeping. She just couldn't get her hands on enough Avenston money.

Phillip and his parents absolutely loved Michael. However as the months passed, Hubert began having doubts that his son had fathered this baby. He spoke to his wife and son about his doubts. Phillip, although devastated, and Roslyn admitted they had their doubts, too. "Dad, I love Michael. I can't bear the thought of him being with Maureen and without us. I consider him mine."

"We love him as well and feel the same way. He's our grandson," Hubert smiled at his son.

One night after Maureen came home intoxicated, Phillip lost his temper with her. She screamed back that

245

she was going to take Michael away from him and that he couldn't stop her because Michael wasn't his. As soon as those words slid out, she tried to take them back. Phillip, controlling his rage at her, told her he and his parents had figured that out. Late the next morning she told Phillip that his parents were not to get near Michael.

Their marriage lasted less than a year. Maureen was pregnant. This time Phillip knew he wasn't the father, and she knew he knew. They hadn't been together since way before Michael was born, not once. They separated, but she wouldn't divorce him. She used her first born son as leverage to keep her grip on Phillip's money. In vengeful greed Maureen kept her son away from the grandparents the child loved and, as often as possible, from the father who adored him. Because her mother hadn't ever been interested in her grandson, everyday and many nights a babysitter cared for Michael. Shopping and partying were her priorities.

Hubert and Roslyn hated how Michael was being raised. They knew Phillip was trying to be with him and was heartbroken at missing precious time with him. Their son told them that Michael was no longer the happy baby he'd once been. Hubert set up a meeting with Maureen, her attorneys, and his attorneys. He offered her a substantial check each month in return for equal time with Michael. It took her two-seconds to agree.

Now, Phillip looked at Maureen sitting on his couch with her huge belly, her puffy made-up face; and couldn't stand the sight of her.

She amusingly looked back at him and said, "I suppose having two pregnant women in your life is a little overwhelming."

"What in the hell are you talking about?"

"Now, don't tell me she hasn't told you." She saw the surprised look on his face and began laughing. "Oh my, you don't know. Little Karen happens to be going to the same OB/GYN as I, stupid! My, my, that was two days ago, and she still hasn't told you her wonderful news? Little Karen and the teeny bopper receptionist at the doctor's office are friends. I heard the receptionist say how nice it was meeting you and your parents the other night. Oh, I can see by that silly look on your face that you

246

remember meeting her. The day before yesterday, I was sitting near the reception desk, listening. Imagine the chance of that! Just as Karen's name was called to see the doctor, her receptionist friend congratulated her and said that you must be thrilled. You are thrilled, right?"

Phillip yelled, "Where's Karen? What did you say to her?"

"She left rather abruptly after I showed her our recent family photo."

"What family photo? There's no family photo with me in it."

"Oh sweetie pie, yes there is. It's the recent one of you, me and the kids." She showed him the photo. "I don't think she noticed your hair cut was a tad different. Why, she just came undone, picked up her purse, and ran out of here. That must have been way over two hours ago."

"Oh God, if anything happens to her, I'll-"

"You'll what?" A smile slithered on Maureen's face.

He picked up his keys and ran out to the waiting elevator. Once outside, he got in his car and sped out of the parking lot. *I've got to find Karen. I've got to tell her everything. She'll understand.*

He was speeding between seventy and eighty mph. There wasn't much traffic. *God, I've hurt Karen. I promised I wouldn't. I can't imagine what she's thinking. That damn photo. That bitch took an old picture of me and added it in that photo. How did she do that? Why didn't I listen to my parents and tell Karen about Michael?* Tears filled his eyes. *Karen's pregnant. She'll be the sweetest mom. We'll love this baby so much. I can't lose her.* Tears flooded his eyes. *God, she is my heart. Please, help her forgive me.*

Phillip slammed on his breaks seeing the stopped truck. His car rapidly spun around several times, missed the truck, and crashed into a brick wall.

247

Lindsey and I arrived in Karen's dorm about four hours after we talked with her on the phone. Knocking then opening Karen's dorm room door, we saw her sleeping on her bed. She didn't stir as we announced that we were there. We looked down at her and Lindsey said, "She must be exhausted."

I patted her arm. "Karen, we're here." She didn't move. I stood looking at her sweet face streaked with dried tears. I tugged on her quilt, and her arm slipped down beside her mattress. Fear shot through me, "Karen!" She remained still. I called her name, again, louder and covered my mouth with my hand.

Lindsey grabbed hold of Karen's shoulders and shook her a little. She reached for her hand as I ran into the hallway yelling for help. I banged my fist against closed doors yelling, "We need help. Call for an ambulance." I ran back into her room with the Resident Assistant hurrying in with me. Several girls followed us but stayed outside the door opening. We heard Lindsey calling Karen's name while holding her wrist trying to find a pulse.

The RA pushed Linds away and pulled the covers off the bed. I saw a small bottle roll on the floor. She pressed her head on Karen's chest listening for a heart beat. "One of you go to the phone by the stairs and dial the posted emergency number for an ambulance, then dial the adult resident's number." She threw the pillow under Karen's head on the floor and started artificial resuscitation.

"Judy's calling right now," one of the girls who'd gathered at Karen's door hollered.

The adult resident was with us a minute later. She told the other girls to go back into their rooms and walked Lindsey and me into the hallway. "I'm Mrs. Shore. Tell me what happened."

We explained how we found her while watching the campus police running toward us into her room. They took over resuscitating her. In minutes the ambulance attendants were in her room doing the resuscitation. We watched them lift her onto the gurney. Her eyes were still closed while they continued to help her and quickly rolled her passed us out into the waiting ambulance.

Tears filled our eyes as we watched Mrs. Shore talking with the campus police then locking the dorm room door with a master key. She wrote DO NOT ENTER and a message to Karen's roommate on note cards pinning both to the small message board on their door. Linds and I felt helpless hearing the noise of the siren lessen with the growing distance of the ambulance.

Mrs. Shore walked us to the lobby. "The campus police are waiting outside and will take you to the hospital right now. Please answer their questions. I have Karen's home phone number. Do you know it or should I go copy it down for the campus police?"

"We know it," Lindsey answered.

"Ok, her parents will be notified once she arrives." She walked us to the door while saying, "I recognize you girls from other visits. I know the three of you are very close. You have my prayers."

Lindsey reached in her coat pocket for her keys. "Bobby Williams is meeting us here after his last class. He should be here soon. Could you give him my car keys?"

She got another note card from her sweater pocket and wrote down his name. "I'll be at the lobby desk waiting for him. Don't worry. I'll make sure he gets to the hospital."

The police sped us to the emergency entrance with their siren blasting. We listened as one policeman said, "Once you find out how your friend is doing, we'll need to get a statement from you. Do you know your friend's home phone number? I'll give it to the emergency room nurses to notify her mother and father."

I don't know why Kate's number sailed out of my mouth. Linds didn't correct me.

We walked with the policemen through the ambulance entrance into the hospital seeing a nurse walk toward us. One of the policemen simply said, "Karen Fry."

"Girls, come with me." We followed her into a small room. "Please sit down. Are you relatives of Karen?"

Lindsey answered, "We're sisters. We grew up together. We're family." Then in an unfamiliar voice she sternly demanded, "Please tell us how she's doing."

Very softly and distinctly the nurse replied, "Karen's heart isn't beating on it's own. The doctors are doing everything they can. She remains unconscious. We need to notify your family."

Lindsey and I sat very still for a second. I remembered the small bottle I picked up and got it out of my pocket. "This rolled off her dorm bed." I handed the nurse the bottle and felt like I'd betrayed Karen.

Lindsey stood up, held my hand, and said, "They told us her heart was beating. Her hand felt warm. Let us see her. Please, take us to her."

"I can't right now, but I will keep you informed. I need to speak with her parents. Please sit back down and stay right here. Can I get you some water?"

"No," we answered and remained standing. The nurse left. We saw the campus police standing near the door.

"Lindsey, should I have given her that bottle? I don't want to talk with the police."

"Yes." She hugged me and started crying and trembling all over. I held her and realized the sobbing sounds I heard were mine.

1966

Bobby got to the hospital, ran through the emergency entrance, and almost knocked an ambulance attendant off his feet. "Hey, watch it."

"Sorry, I'm sorry," Bobby said running passed them through the emergency room to the first nurse he saw. "I'm here for Karen Fry. Do you know where Lindsey O'Malley and Samantha Cole are waiting? I was told to find them here."

The nurse was just going to call Karen's home residence. She looked at Bobby and asked who he was.

He explained and the next minute he was holding Lindsey and Sammy in his arms while they cried and tried to tell him what happened. "Linds, I'll be right back. Both of you sit down a minute."

Quickly Bobby found the nurse he'd spoken to before, "Could you please call a priest for Karen and for us?"

"Yes, I'll do that after I speak with her family." She looked down at the small paper she was given with what she thought was the home phone number. She looked back at him, "Please remind the girls that the policemen need to speak with them. I'll make sure the priest finds you."

"Thank you."

Kate and Art were sitting at their kitchen table drinking a cup of tea. "Art, the girls are at OSU visiting Karen. They may come home in the morning. Apparently Karen has a problem." Kate was interrupted with the phone ringing.

Art got up and answered it, "Hello."

"Hello, this is Mercy Hospital calling. My name is Cathy Evans. Are you the father of," Art rubbed his chest. "Karen Marie Fry?"

He cleared his throat, "No, Karen is our dear friend's daughter. They live next door to us. She's very much like a daughter to me." He didn't know why he was saying all of this. "Is Karen all right?"

Kate heard Art and watched him rub his chest. She knew something had happened.

The nurse continued, "I really need to speak with her father or mother. We were given this phone number. Could you give me Mr. Fry's phone number, please?"

Art told her the number and asked, "We're family. Should we be with them?"

"Yes."

"Can you tell me, was there an accident? Is anyone else hurt?"

"There are two girls and one boy here at the hospital. Could you tell me your name please?"

"Art O'Malley."

"Mr. O'Malley, the girls' names are Lindsey O'Malley and Samantha Cole. The boy is Bob Williams. The girls arrived with the police, and the boy just arrived. They are fine and were not in any kind of accident. I will call Mr. Fry right now."

Art hung up the phone and sat very still. He looked at Kate but couldn't speak, yet. Long seconds later the phone rang again. "Dad," crying into the phone Lindsey said, "Karen's in the hospital, Daddy."

He cleared his throat, "I know, honey." She was crying so hard he couldn't understand what she was saying. "Is Bobby with you? Let me talk with him a minute."

Kate looked at him. He held her hand and said, "Go to Brice. I'll be there in a minute. Linds and Sam are not hurt. They're at Mercy Hospital, Bobby's there, too. Something awful has happened to Karen."

She let go of his hand and turned toward their back door. Art continued on the phone, "What's happened?" Bobby told him how the girls found her.

1966

"Oh no, God no," Kate whispered as she hurried to Brice. She thought, *I was waiting to hear from the girls. I just didn't want to worry Art before going to sleep tonight.*

As she closed the Fry's side door and walked up the three steps into their kitchen, she saw Brice handing Frank the phone. Grand was tying her bathrobe just walking into her kitchen. Kate heard her asking, "What's the matter in here?" She followed Grand's eyes and saw a broken glass on the floor.

"Mom," Brice looked as though he was going to crumble to the ground. "Mom, something happened to Karen. She's in the hospital on a ventilator. She isn't breathing on her own." He wrapped his arms around his mother as quiet sobs poured out of him.

"Sweetheart no, that can't be true. Who told you that?"

Kate quietly swept up the glass and put the broom back into the broom closet. In the background she heard Frank on the phone asking, "Please can you tell us what happened? Is anyone else hurt? Yes, Mercy Hospital. We'll leave right away."

Brice put his hand out toward Kate and walked with Grand and her into the living room. He sat in a chair and stared at Karen's picture which was on the end table. Grand and Kate sat on the sofa. A few minutes later Father Tom and Art were with them.

Gentle tears began falling from Grand's eyes when she saw Father Tom. *It must be true. My sweet, precious Karen, how can this be?"* She cried much harder, now, and Kate's arms held her.

It was decided Art would drive Brice and Father Tom to the hospital in Columbus. Frank would stay in Bay with Grand and Kate and wait to hear from Brice.

The kindest, older priest, Father Martine, sat with us until Brice, Art, and Father Tom arrived. When they did, Nurse Evans immediately escorted Brice to Karen. Then she brought Father Tom and Art to us. Father Martine blessed us and left, while Father Tom and Art held us tight. Nurse Evans waited and told Father Tom that Karen was given Last Rites. "She is breathing with the help of a ventilator, and she's in intensive care."

"I think I spoke with you on the phone," Art said.

"Yes, Mr. O'Malley, you did. I'm Nurse Evans."

"Is there anything else you can tell us?"

"She needs the ventilator to breath right now, Mr. O'Malley." She looked directly at Father Tom, "Prayers are so amazing. I've seen miraculous things happen." She squeezed Art's hand and left.

Father straightened his back and said, "I'm going to find Brice and Karen." He smiled and said, "This collar gets me in everywhere. She needs all of us near her. I'll be back to,"

Suddenly we were staring at Phillip, who looked like he'd been in a fight. His face was all bruised and his arm was in a sling. "No-one will tell me where Karen is," he said. "I've been here for hours, and no-one will tell me."

I looked at him, and I wanted to hit him myself. I yelled, "Get away from us. How could you lie to all of us? How could you hurt her this way? I hate you. Get out!"

Father Tom put his arm around me. "Samantha, sit down. This isn't his fault. What are you doing?"

Lindsey glared at him, "You are the most despicable,"

Art took hold of Lindsey. "What are you doing? For God sake, Karen needs us, and this is no time to argue about anything."

Bobby interrupted, "Phil, just get out. We know you're married, and have children, and your wife's expecting, and you've been lying to Karen all of these years. We don't want you near us. Your next door neighbor, John Woodward, had a lot to say.

Phillip answered, "John Woodward?" *Oh God, the Woodward's next door to Maureen.* "Please, give me a minute. If you don't want to hear me out, I'll leave."

"Just get away from us," I yelled again.

"Let him talk to you," Father Tom said in a raised voice.

Art looked stunned absorbing everything Bobby had said and began rubbing his arm.

Phillip thanked Father and said, "Sammy, you're right. I didn't tell Karen something I should have told her from the start. Please listen," Phillip pleaded. "I was in undergraduate school when I met Maureen. I thought I loved her. After we'd been dating a couple of months, she told me she was pregnant, and her mom arranged a wedding in a Catholic Chapel. We got married, and a few months later she had a baby boy. We named him Michael. I loved Michael from the first second I saw and held him. I thought he was my son. And my parents felt the same way, and we still do."

I glared at him and stated, "I've heard enough. Get out!"

"Samantha!" Father Tom pointed at me shaking his finger.

Phillip continued, "I love Michael," his voice broke as tears filled his eyes. "After he was born, a few months later, my parents suspected Michael wasn't my son and told me. I told them I thought the same, but I loved him very much. My parents said they loved him, too. We kept quiet. Maureen and I didn't have a marriage. After Michael was born, she never cared for him. She hardly ever held him, and she went out most every day and night shopping and partying. All she did was spend money. I never even slept in the same bedroom with her again after she was expecting Michael," he looked at Lindsey and me, "not ever." I thought I was in love with her in the beginning but not for very long. One night she came home very drunk, and I lost my temper with her. She yelled back that she was leaving with Michael, and I couldn't stop her because Michael wasn't mine. She tried to take those words back. She pleaded with me. I told her that my parents and I had figured that out months ago. The next morning she announced that my parents were not to see Michael ever again. I knew she could also do that to me. My dad offered her an allowance, and they got Michael back in their lives."

Father Tom asked, "What happened to you, your arm and everything?"

"When I returned to the apartment to find Karen, I guess it was late afternoon yesterday, Maureen was there instead. I think Karen must have let her in. Maureen showed me a photograph with herself, her younger son, Michael, and me. She told me she showed it to Karen. I don't know how she had a photograph like that. I was never in such a picture. I hurried to find Karen and got in a car accident. Just my car was involved."

Phillip looked back at Lindsey and me, "Karen told me about her mom. She told me how much she missed having her mother with her. She'd never understand how any parent could be away from their child. She told me she couldn't ever be separated from her children while they grew up and couldn't be with anyone who did that. Michael isn't mine, and Maureen could take him completely away from me. If she were to meet another stupid, rich man; she'd take Michael away from me in a second. Because my dad pays her, she lets him live with my parents several months a year. She limits my time with him. Here, in Columbus, I get to see him at the house next door to the Woodward's. She has a younger son living with her and him in that house. When I've gone to Italy without Karen, I've been with Michael at my parents' house. But the truth is, I'm apart from him more than I'm with him. My mom and dad love Karen very much. They've argued with me that I should tell her. They don't understand I'd lose her if she knew. I was afraid I'd lose her."

Father Tom touched Phillip's arm. "God bless you." He looked at Lindsey, Bobby and me and rather sternly said, "Sit down and stay put. Art, make sure they understand that Phillip is a good man." Then he looked at Phillip, "Come with me."

257

1966

Karen couldn't comprehend what was happening. *Where am I,* she wondered as she looked around. *I don't recognize this place. My dad's crying.* She looked at the doorway. *"Mom, is that you?"*

Sherry's eyes captured her daughter's eyes as she moved near Karen's hospital bed. Her smile was radiant when she took hold of her daughter's hand and steered her toward the doorway.

Why is Dad crying? She held her mom's hand and walked with her outside to the same street she had dreamed about forever. *I never realized that this street seems to continue forever.* She snuggled into the side of her mom's soft coat. She'd never felt so peaceful and safe.

They stayed together walking for a very long time until the street split into two paths, and her mom stopped. For the first time her mom spoke to her, "Honey, do you know what this is?"

Karen looked at her mom, "What did you say?"

"Do you understand what this moment, the division in our path, means? Honey, you must make a choice. Karen, I love you. I've always loved you. You are my beautiful daughter, and you're amazing. You are loved so much. One path will take you directly to God's perfect Heaven, right now. The other path leads you back to the rest."

"The rest of what, Mom?"

"The rest of everything: happy/sad, beautiful/ugly, wonderful/terrible, peaceful/hectic, amazing/horrible, lovable/unbearable; you know, honey, the rest of life on earth. Nothing is perfect. Well, Heaven is, and that's the choice you have."

"Mom, the paths look exactly the same. How do I know which path leads where?"

"You'll see," her mom kissed her and hugged her. Sherry walked away and looked back, "Nothing is perfect, Karen, only Heaven."

Father Tom and Phillip walked into Karen's room in intensive care. Brice, with tears running down his face was sitting beside his daughter's bed. They could hear him telling her how much he loves her. Staying still for several seconds, Tom then put his hand on Brice's shoulder and gently asked him if Phillip could be with her for a few minutes.

Father looked at the machine keeping her alive. Brice backed up, and Father Tom leaned over her while taking hold of both of her hands. "Karen, stay with us. We need you and love you. Your time here on earth cannot be over. Stay with Phillip. He has had evil in his life. He needs you and loves you so much. Stay with him. His love for you is honest. Hear him, honey." And then he prayed, "God in Heaven, lead Karen on the path back to us. In your gracious wisdom, grant this prayer. In the name of the Father, and of the Son, and of the Holy Ghost, Amen."

He reached for Phillip's hand, placed it in hers and said, "Tell her." He left Karen's room and walked with Brice back to Lindsey, Bobby, Sammy, and Art.

1966

Phillip held Karen's hand, and he didn't feel her hand respond. Tears fell from his eyes onto the sheets. "Karen, I've been so stupid. I should've told you about Michael. He's my son. I love him so much. His mother, Maureen, isn't a good mother. She isn't a loving mother to him. She means nothing to me. I'm so sorry she hurt you. And I'm a million times more sorry that I've hurt you. I haven't been with her for years, long before I even knew you. I have never been unfaithful to you. My mom and dad begged me to tell you about Michael. I thought I would lose you if I told you about him. He's so amazing. You would love him. He spends several months a year with my mom and dad in Italy. I go to Italy to be with him. I thought I would lose you if you knew I wasn't always with him. Karen, I love you. Please listen to me. I need you. I love you. I have never been unfaithful to you. Please come back to me."

Softly, in measured rhythm, the finger tips of his other hand moved from her elbow to her wrist back and forth, back and forth. "I love you with all of my heart. We have something so special. Please stay with all of us, with me. I will always love you. I'm so sorry I didn't tell you about Micheal. I want to be with him all of the time. You must meet him. You two will love each other. Please don't leave us. I love you, Karen, forever." He gently lay his head beside her and cried.

Father Tom returned to intensive care and waited a few minutes near Karen's room. He walked in and patted Phillip's shoulder, "Come with me. You can come back in a while." He walked him to a private waiting room and said, "File for divorce, Phillip. I will help you get the annulment."

"This all seems so easy. Why have I let Maureen get away with this all of these years? She's caused this to happen to Karen."

"And to you. Come with me one more place." He took him to the elevator and went to the first floor. They walked to the hospital's chapel. Opening the door Father said, "I'm sure many prayers have been heard here. Trust God and pray for Karen."

Karen was standing alone on the street where it divided into two separate paths. Her mom was no longer there. She looked down one path, then the other unable to make a decision. Both were filled with sunshine. Trees with gentle swaying branches grew on the sides of the paths and flowers in every color graced the landscapes. The paths looked identical. She couldn't move and kept looking down one path and then the other. For a long time she was stuck in place.

She put her hand above her eyes to get a better look down one of the paths and saw her mom walking alone. Karen smiled as her choice seemed clear. Finally she and her mom would be together. She began to take a step as she glanced down the other path. Her eyes captured a young boy, about eight years old, motioning for her to follow him. His smile was huge as he kept waving for her to follow. And then she heard the little boy holler, "Come on. I need you."

1966

Art really didn't know what happened earlier. Kate told him that Karen had a problem and that the girls were probably coming home in the morning. Then the hospital nurse called. Now, hearing that Phillip was married and had a son was shocking to say the least. But, the pain on Phillip's face resonated with Art. He felt no-one could look like that if his heart wasn't broken.

He looked at his daughters and Bobby, "I do not understand much of what has happened in these last hours. Right now our Karen needs all of our prayers, and love, and understanding. None of you have ever encountered a situation like the one Phillip is in. I haven't either. I'm a pretty good judge of character. For certain Father Tom is. I think Phillip was wrong not to tell Karen the circumstances in his life, very wrong. But he most certainly loves her, and I believe that he has not cheated on Karen. He is a good man who has made a terrible mistake. His heart is breaking, too."

Brice and Father Tom walked in. "Karen is in the intensive care wing," Tom told them.

Brice looked at everyone and said, "The doctor told me that Karen was in the early stages of pregnancy. She's had a miscarriage. She took too many sleeping pills." He looked at Sammy and Lindsey, "If you two wouldn't have been there, she, she wouldn't have had a chance."

Everyone was silent for a few minutes. "Girls, do you want to see Karen? And you, too, Bobby," Father Tom asked. "She needs to know you're here, I'll take you."

"I need to call Frank and mom," Brice said and left to find a pay phone.

Sammy held Karen's hand. "Karen, we all love you so much. Please come back to us. Phillip loves you, too. You must be so hurt finding out about everything the way you did, but you can get past it. He loves you so much. You know what your heart can forgive. Please open your eyes and come back to us. Lindsey, Bobby, and I will help you. Jimmy is coming home. He'll be here today. Come back to us. Karen, I can't lose you, too. If you're at a crossroad, think about all of the living you have left to do. Think of all of the people you want to help. We all want you with us.

Lindsey patted Karen's leg. I'm here, too. So is Bobby. We're sisters, you, Sammy, and me. Stay with us, Karen. We're at a wonderful time in our lives. You have such a caring heart. Don't leave us. We need you."

The doctor walked into the room. "Well, Father, I see you've brought more visitors."

"Yes, all family, doctor. I remember you instructed only family can be in here."

When the opportunity came, Phillip talked with Brice and told him about Michael. He apologized profusely and as much as he tried to control his emotions, he cried when he told him about Maureen and everything she'd done to Karen. "It's my fault, Brice. If I just had listened to my parents and told Karen everything, none of this would have happened to her. I thought she'd leave me. She told me about her mother. I thought I'd lose her. I'm so sorry. My mom and dad told me to tell her. I love her so much. I was afraid."

Brice had no doubt about Phillip's sincere love for his daughter. He sadly said, "You're forgiven."

Frank drove Grand and Kate to Columbus the next day arriving in the hospital before noon. About the same time, Jimmy arrived at Port Columbus Airport where Art picked him up.

Later that day Linds, Bobby, Jimmy, and I walked with Grand, Kate, Art, Frank, Brice, and Father Tom into Karen's room. Within seconds her attending doctor opened her door and seeing all of us said, "I know. You're all family."

Grand looked at him with tears in her eyes, and for the first and only time, ever, I heard her swear, "Your damn right we're family," she answered and began crying.

"You're Miss Fry's grandmother. I remember, we met earlier today. I think every one of you being here, telling her to come back, telling her you love her, is most helpful." He gently touched Grand's arm, "I sound sarcastic at times. I apologize. I wish all of my patients had a family like yours. I need to check Miss Fry. Go to the waiting area just through the doors near the nurses' station. I'll find you. I need to speak with Miss Fry's father."

"I'm Karen's, Dad," Brice answered.

"Yes," he looked at Brice. "Sorry, again, I remember we spoke yesterday. I'll find you when I finish."

We left, and I realized I forgot my purse. Just before I knocked on Karen's door I heard the doctor say, "Young lady, hear me. Listen to the plea from your family. Have confidence. They need you, and I want to get you off this ventilator."

I quietly pushed the door open, got my purse off the nearby chair, and walked down the hallway.

That evening when Jimmy and I were alone and he hugged me, everything inside of me broke. I cried in his arms. He held me and never said a word. He just held me tight.

We spent four nights in Columbus. Phillip made reservations for all of us at a hotel near the hospital. His parents made arrangements to return to their home in Columbus.

Each day we visited Karen, in smaller groups, and repeated how much we loved her and needed her. Mid morning, on the fourth day, she opened her eyes.

Brice, Phillip, and I were in Karen's room. Phillip was holding her hand telling her over and over and over how sorry he was and how much he loves her. He was crying, again. I was just moving near her bed to say something else, anything else, when I watched her move her other hand on top of Phillip's. Brice and I heard some new enthusiastic sentences pour out of him, "Karen, honey, you're hearing me? Open your eyes. Can you hear me? Everyone's here. Open your eyes."

Brice leaped off his chair, went to her, and Phillip stepped aside. He patted her hand and said, "Come on, Karen. Open your eyes."

I went to the other side of her bed, and loudly demanded, "Karen, do it now! Open your eyes!" Very slowly her eyes flickered open, and then she opened them wider.

She stared at her dad for what seemed several minutes as he spoke to her, "That's right. Keep them open. Grand is here, too. Everyone is here. I'll go get them."

Her head turned toward me, and she stayed still several seconds, then she looked back at her dad. With tears and a big smile, Brice patted her hand and stepped back to let Phillip move closer. Her eyes stayed on Phillip. He took hold of her hand, and she moved her other hand back on top of his. She tried closing her eyes and Phillip said, "I love looking into your beautiful eyes, honey." They opened wide.

Brice hurried to the nurses station, and I went back to the waiting room to tell everyone Karen's eyes were open. Grand and Frank hurried to her room while the rest of us stayed put.

By that night we all visited with her. She was breathing on her own. We were told that her throat would be very sore from the tube. She barely talked, but she smiled quite a bit considering everything. Phillip brought her a cooler full of several flavors of sherbet and soft ice cream from a speciality ice cream shoppe. When we returned to the hotel, he had dinners delivered to our rooms. He stayed all night with Karen.

Lindsey and I spent the next morning with her, just the three of us. We told her we were sorry about the miscarriage. Karen softly said, "Phillip told me a while ago. He cried when he told me, and I didn't. I just found out for sure a few days ago. I think it was a few days ago. Time is kind of blurry. I hadn't really comprehended the realization of a baby, yet. I'm sorry you guys. I would have loved it, but,"

Lindsey held her hand, "It's ok. Too much has happened in a short time. We all love you, and it's ok."

Karen shook her head as tears formed in her eyes. It was quiet for a few minutes. "Phillip told me that you two were unmerciful when he found you in the hospital. Sammy, you told him you hated him. And Linds, you told him he was despicable, and Bobby told him to get out and called him Phil. The Phil part made me laugh." She grinned, "Thanks."

Again, no one said anything for a while. She put her hand on her throat. "The doctor said my throat should be somewhat better later today. Thanks, you guys. He deserved it. Phillip says you saved me and Father Tom saved him." She reached for our hands, "You saved me. I love you." Now huge tears fell from her eyes. "I'm sorry for all of it."

We hugged her and Lindsey said, "We love you, too. All will be fine. We all still love Phillip, too. Maureen is sick and awful and," she looked at me, "and that's the last time she's ever going to take a second of our thoughts."

Karen touched her throat, again, then motioned for us to wait a second. A minute later she smiled, "I like that plan. Phillip's dad told him, he thinks with all that happened to both of us after she lied to me, there might be a way to get full custody of Michael. He also thinks she'll agree to divorce Phillip, now, and Father Tom will help him get the annulment. Michael and I are going to meet each other at his parents' house soon, and I'm excited about that." She seemed lost in a thought or memory for a second as she stared out the window at the sky, smiled, and added, "I'm very excited about that. My dad is taking me home when I leave here. He and Phillip have talked and hopefully I won't be home long. Also, Phillip is going to help me catch up in my classes."

"Outta sight," I said.

Father Tom patted Samantha's hand. "It was magical that you and Lindsey arrived in Karen's dorm room at the exact moment you did." A slight smile crossed his face. "God's magic, do you remember that, Samantha?" He watched her move just a little. "Even in the worst of times, God's magic."

Tom looked closely at Samantha's face. He noticed inside her closed eyelids her eyes were moving. "Samantha? Honey come on, open your eyes. I think you're hearing me reminisce with you." He rubbed her hand and patted it. "Come on, come back to us."

She turned her head away just a bit. Her eyes stilled.

Father Tom continued rubbing her hand a minute and then stopped. "I really think you'll wake soon." He got up and stretched.

Phillip couldn't believe how nervous he felt. It was just a phone call. He dialed the Fry's phone number. "Hello, Mr. Fry, it's Phillip. Yes, I mean, Brice. Could we meet for lunch tomorrow? I could be in Bay Village by early afternoon." He listened. "You could meet me in Mansfield? That would be great. Ok, one o'clock at the Sohio gas station, and we'll decide where to eat. Thanks, see you tomorrow."

The next day shortly after one, they sat in a bar that advertised great burgers. They were having a beer and just ordering lunch. After the waitress walked away Brice looked at Phillip, "Everything good with Karen? Is she feeling ok and getting caught up in her classes? I know she's excited about graduating in December." He thought Phillip looked worried.

"Karen's doing great. Her grades are excellent, and she's very excited about graduating." He changed subjects. "I know I let everyone down, especially Karen. She knows I will never keep anything from her again."

"Stop. That part of your life is behind you. It's way passed. I really do understand, really. Let's not discuss it anymore. It was a horrible time for you, those years with Maureen. She's out of your life, now. Michael is with you and your parents. He's a great child. I know Karen loves him."

"Michael is crazy about her. She has his heart. Brice, she has my heart, too. I would like to ask Karen to marry me. As you wanted for her, she'll have her classes completed for graduation in December. I'd like to ask her this Thanksgiving. Would that be ok with you? I've loved her from the first second I saw her, and I'm certain it was the same for her. This is the other part. Do you think we could have a small wedding just before Christmas, this Christmas?"

Brice just stared at him.

"Getting married this Christmas is my idea. Karen doesn't know. I mean, she's told me she'd love to be a December bride and have a family wedding. I'm just preparing you incase it all works out. I mean, I know it will work out. I mean, I know she'll say yes." He looked down, "I'm messing this up."

"Phillip," Brice stood up, walked toward him, and said, "yes, ask her, and I think she'll love getting married this Christmas." Both were standing as he continued, "We'll have a wonderful Christmas, and her grandmother will be so happy planning her wedding." Brice hugged him and then just looked at his face while having hold of his shoulders.

With a huge smile Phillip answered, "Thank you. We'll call you the minute she says yes!"

Brice let go of Phillip's shoulders and looked around the bar. "Uh-oh." The noise level had stilled as everyone was staring at them. He whispered, "Oh Lord, this isn't good. This isn't good at all." Phillip looked around, then started laughing. In a few seconds they both were laughing while Brice's hand squeezed Phillip's arm.

One giant man walked toward them, and Phillip quickly held up his beer, "My future father-in-law," nodding at Brice, "gave his permission for me to marry his daughter!" Everyone clapped and cheered. The huge man stared at both of them. Finally he grinned and shook Phillip's hand and Brice's. He bought them a round of beer.

Brice said, "Let's not tell Karen this part."

"She'll love this part!"

1966

Bobby walked up Lindsey's driveway to the back door knowing Lindsey was Christmas shopping with Sammy, Kate and Grand. He opened the side door and called, "Art, are you home?" He felt anxious as he tried to put the scramble of words circling his mind back into the sentences he'd been repeating over and over. He realized his hands were clammy.

"Bobby, hi!" Come on in. All of the ladies have gone shopping." Art looked at him a second and thought, *He doesn't look so good.* "Everything ok?"

Bobby looked directly at him and said, "I need, I mean, I'd like to talk with you."

"Sure. Sit down. Would you like a coke or something?"

"No thanks, not right now." He took a deep breath. "I love Lindsey with all of my heart. I think, without understanding it at the time, I've loved her since grade school. I'll always take care of her, protect her, keep her safe, and love her. I'm asking for your permission to ask Lindsey to marry me."

Art just sat and looked at him for long seconds. He was remembering the young kid he played baseball with so many times, the young boy who'd been a part of Lindsey's life for what seemed forever. He smiled as he realized Bobby looked like he was about to pass out. He answered, "You have my blessing and my permission. You're a wonderful young man. I've thought of you as a son for years. Kate and I love you as family. You know that. Kate will be so excited. Does Lindsey know about this?"

"You and Kate have been a second mom and dad to me. You've been wonderful to me and to Jimmy. To answer your question, I don't think she knows. We've talked about it many times. She may be thinking we'll become engaged when we graduate this spring. She's so excited about Karen and Phillip's wedding." Bobby took a small box out of his pocket. "Here Art, this is the ring I want to give Linds." He opened the box.

"It's perfect."

"We've looked at rings in jewelry store windows lots of times. My dad sent me to the jewelry store he goes to. I think she'll like it. My parents are very excited."

"So I can tell Kate," Art asked. "I'll swear her to secrecy. I'm very happy for our Lindsey, very happy for you both." He put his arms around Bobby and gave him a hug. Bobby hugged him back and thanked him.

1966

Jimmy knew this was his chance. He knew Sammy was with Grand baking Christmas cookies and finishing favors for Karen's and Phillip's wedding reception. He dialed the O'Malley's phone number and Art answered.

"Hi, Jimmy. Of course you can come over. Yes, Kate's here. Ok, see you in a few minutes." He hung up and had a wonderful feeling about this visit.

He walked back into the living room where Kate was watching Art Fleming and Jeopardy on TV. "Jimmy's stopping over in a few minutes. He wants to talk with us."

Kate got up and turned the TV set off. "Does he know Sammy's over at Grand's?"

"I think he's aware of that."

A few minutes later the front doorbell rang, and Art opened the door. "Hi Jim, wow, it's cold out there. Come on in."

Jimmy unzipped his coat and sat down on a chair across from the sofa where Kate was sitting. "Would you like a coke or anything, Jimmy," she asked.

"No thanks. I just want to talk, ask-" Jimmy hesitated.

Kate looked at him. "Jimmy, is everything all right? You know,"

The words poured out as he interrupted Kate. "I would like to ask Sammy to marry me this New Year's Eve. I mean, I want to ask her on New Year's Eve. I love her. I love her so much. I'll do everything to keep her happy, and I'll take care of her always."

Art smiled and looked down a few seconds. Kate had a huge smile and quickly wiped away tears.

Jimmy stood up and got a small box out of his jacket pocket. "Here, look. I'm giving Sammy my grandmother's ring. It's just that I want her to have a ring that's a story of life and love, a ring that has a strong and loving history. Kate and Art, I'm asking for your permission to ask Sammy to marry me."

This ring's perfect and beautiful. I'm so happy for you and Sammy," Kate said as she hugged him.

"Kate's right, it's perfect. We've loved our Sammy from the first moment we met her. We know you'll always do what's best for her." He looked at Kate a second.

273

"We've loved you kids forever. We couldn't be happier. I know Jack and Joan are looking down and celebrating, too. You have our blessings." Art shook Jimmy's hand and then hugged him. "You're the one for Samantha."

They heard the back door opening. Kate hurried into the kitchen giving Jimmy the chance to put his ring back into his pocket. "Sammy, is that you?" She blocked her path. "Jimmy just got here. Good timing!"

Karen's wedding weekend was crisp, bright, happy, intimate, joyful, and just a little unconventional. The night before her wedding, Karen, Grand, Roslyn, Lindsey, Kate and I stayed overnight at the Holsten Inn. We had a blast spending that night together watching Roslyn fuss over Karen and Grand. She made no attempt to hide how happy she was to be getting a daughter, "Not an in-law," she said. And she hugged Grand and added, "I finally have a sister, too, Grand. I've wanted a sister my entire life, and I'm so lucky it's you." Then she looked at Kate, Lindsey and I, "Didn't Phillip mention this package deal?"

Karen hugged her and told her that the package deal must include all of us, or the deal was off. Roslyn looked at all of us, and with a smirk answered, "Well, nothing is perfect, only Heaven!" And we all laughed as Karen stared at her for a minute. Roslyn quickly added, "I'm blessed to be getting every one of you for family. I love each of you." She raised her wine glass, and we followed with our drinks as she said, "To our blessings!"

Then Karen took hold of Lindsey's and my hands looking a tad thoughtful and quietly repeated the words, "Nothing is perfect, only Heaven." She smiled telling us that sentence sounded so familiar to her, like she'd been right here before, like she was reliving this moment."

"Deja Vu!" Lindsey said.

Late the next afternoon at exactly five minutes to five Lindsey and I, dressed in floor length violet-blue dresses, stepped through the front side door of St. Joseph's Chapel. With huge smiles we walked to our places on the altar steps and watched Bobby, Jimmy, and Micheal, who were Phillip's best men, escorting the last guests to almost full pews. The wedding invitation list had grown a bit. Three violinists softly played music while we watched the last guests seated and saw Bobby escorting his parents near the front of the chapel. Seconds later we watched him escort Kate, who held one light blue rose, and Art to the front pew three seats from where Frank, Grand, and Brice would be. Soon Roslyn came to the arched doorway. She looked beautiful, holding her single blue rose, dressed in a long blue skirt with a silver sequin jacket. Little Micheal took hold of her hand, and she happily and proudly walked with her grandson. He looked so cute in his tux as he escorted her with Hubert following to their front aisle seat. We saw Grand at the archway, and she was beaming. She looked so pretty wearing a full length, long sleeved, deep violet dress. It had silver sequined buttons, and she was holding a blue rose. Jimmy and Bobby escorted her to her seat directly across the aisle from Phillip's parents and next to Kate.

Everyone turned and stood up seeing Karen centered in the archway. Looking so beautiful, her dress elegantly fit around her shoulders and almost touched the floor. We saw the string of pearls around her neck that Phillip had given her one morning ago knowing they matched the pearls buttoning the back of her gown. She held a white bouquet containing three blue roses. Smiling, she stood still as the best men, Phillip, Pastor Martin, who was the Avenston's minister, and Father Tom stepped through the side door and found their places on the altar step. Brice joined Karen on one side and Frank stood on her other side. The violins paused and trumpets began playing "Trumpet Tune" as our sister and her dad and uncle walked down the Chapel aisle. The long train attached to her dress moved in perfect timing with each of their steps. She looked so happy. Near the front pew where Grand was seated, she hugged her dad and uncle. She hugged and kissed her grandmother and then Brice walked her to Phillip. Father Tom wiped tears from his eyes as he and Pastor Martin began this Wedding.

We had so much fun at Karen's and Phillip's wedding reception at the Holsten Inn. The band played everything from nineteen twenties music through our favorite songs. Grand danced the Charleston with Hubert and everyone loved it. Bette Lotis, who was a guest but also an employee at the Holsten, kept her eyes on every important segment of the reception. Lindsey and I remarked that she did this without notice. Much later that night she told Lindsey and me, "One day I'm going to own this place."

Karen, Michael, and Phillip went back to Columbus following Hubert and Roslyn the next day. We were all together again, a few days later Christmas Day, in Bay

Village. They stayed over night, and Christmas afternoon, we celebrated Lindsey's and Bobby's engagement. Karen and Phillip left for their honeymoon in Italy two days later. The rest of us drove to Hubert and Roselyn's house on New Year's Eve. We had a blast in their beautiful home. Just before midnight, Jimmy asked me to marry him. We were so happy. Roselyn gave me a card and gift from Karen. Jimmy said, "I had to tell Karen." I cried happy tears as I read her sweet hand written card.

It was this new year that defined our lives. Linds and I, wearing engagement rings, went back to BG to finish our senior year and graduate. Bobby returned to OSU, and Jimmy went back to the University of Tampa in Tampa, Florida. And on Kate's radio several times each day, The Mama's and the Papa's could be heard singing "Monday, Monday."

SLEEPING MEMORIES 1967

There was another reason for excitement when we returned to college that January. The guys, especially, were eagerly anticipating the first ever AFL/NFL World Championship Game. At first Lindsey and I didn't understand what the big deal was. Art changed our attitude. On that Sunday, he got us excited by giving his permission for us to leave campus for the afternoon and night. He made it known we had to be back at B.G. in time for our first Monday morning class. We eagerly drove to Roslyn's and Hubert's house in Columbus and met up with almost our entire family to watch the first ever Super Bowl! Karen and Phillip were back from Italy, but Jimmy was in Tampa. Roslyn, Grand, and Kate made so much food. Phillip and Bobby called him before the game and kidded him about all of the home cooking he was missing. The things I still remember most about the first Super Bowl Game: great food and missing Jimmy.

We enjoyed this last winter in college, well three of us did. Jimmy enjoyed summer weather in Tampa. The two of us wrote long letters to one and other and talked on the phone at least twice a week. All aspects of our lives were happy as we anticipated everything ahead. The cold months, three of us experienced, passed by getting us to the last weeks of spring and warm weather. The four of us enjoyed warm days at our college graduations. I went with Jimmy's parents to Tampa to see him graduate. His mom was so nice.

I had one little problem. I just couldn't decide on a wedding date. Jimmy wanted to be married this December. I didn't know what time of year I wanted to be married. When my mind wondered off, thoughts about traveling and seeing new places filled it. Maybe I had two little problems. Also, a pang in my heart quietly rumbled that Jimmy's fate had been decided when my parents died. After they died, he told me he'd love and stay with me forever, and his sweet words formed a promise he seemed stuck in keeping.

The night Lindsey and I finished studying for our last exams at BG, we celebrated by getting pizza at the cozy Italian restaurant we loved. Lindsey's mind was full of the

278

plans she and Bobby had made concerning their future. "Sam, do you ever think that we owe something back," she asked as we sat down at our table. In the background we heard the jukebox with Frank Sinatra singing "Strangers in the Night."

Our waitress appeared immediately lighting the candle at the center of our table. The candle was in an empty chianti bottle. She took our pizza and beer order as the candle began adding a new color of drips down the sides of the bottle. "What do you mean, Linds, 'owe back?" I didn't have a clue what she meant. I listened to her answer while I watched our waitress pin our pizza order to a cord above the counter in front of the opening to the kitchen.

"Bobby and I have been talking about our future. We think with everything that's happening in our country and in the world right now, we should do something about it. We've been given so much. We feel we should volunteer some time back. We should do something to help others."

I looked right at Linds and said, "Well, the way the war in Vietnam is going, Bobby and Jimmy just might find themselves doing plenty. It really scares me." Our waitress set two beers down on our table.

We talked about Vietnam for a while. Our pizza arrived, and we each took a slice. "Sammy, Bobby has already enlisted in the army. He'll be leaving for basic training before summer."

I put my pizza down on my plate. "What? Why did he,"

"Just listen for a minute. He wants to have a career in politics. President Kennedy said in his inauguration speech, 'Ask not what your country can do for you. Ask what you can do for your country.' Bobby hasn't forgotten that. He wants to do something for his country. His mind is filled with so many ideas. He believes the changes Martin Luther King and so many colored people desire are very important and necessary. He's concerned about the spread of communism. You know that he, Jimmy, and I have talked about the problems that exist within our public school systems. Bobby wants to be involved. He's so excited about the future. He's serious about a political career. Serving his country in the army is the first step.

279

Sammy, I'm going to tell you the rest. I've signed up with Care Core. I'll be leaving this summer, too. We want to get married right after graduation. We want a small wedding."

I set my glass down and just looked at her. I thought, *How could they have done all of this without me knowing?* I felt a bit hurt and blurted out, "Are you, both, crazy? What will mom and dad say when they find out? Kate's so excited about our graduations and you teaching soon, not to mention planning our weddings. Linds, how could you guys?"

"Sammy, stop." She said with her voice raised. We were quiet for a few seconds. We heard the jukebox with Aretha Franklin just beginning her song, "Respect." In a calmer voice she said, "Karen was right. I'll never get a teaching position because of my arm."

I interrupted, "She was on drugs when she said that! She didn't know what she was saying that night. You'll be a wonderful teacher."

"I hope to be a wonderful teacher. Care Core will be the perfect place to begin my teaching career and gain experience. I'll be busy while Bobby's gone, and both of us should be back home about two years from this fall." Smiling, she looked at me and waved her finger, "No telling mom or dad about any of this, and you'll have to help me figure out how and when to tell them. For now, mum's the word, ok?"

I grinned back. *She was still including me in her secrets after all.* "Mum's the word!"

"One more thing, you and Karen are our maids of honor and Jimmy and Phillip are our best men. Father Tom, you, Jimmy, Karen, Phillip, Bobby, and me in the Chapel at St. Joe's. And our immediate families, of course. That's what we want."

I looked shocked and then smiled, "Of course we're your maids of honor, ditzy. Actually, Karen will be your matron of honor! We'll be there. I love you, and I'm excited for you guys."

Things came to a halt in Portland. Jim's plan to get on an earlier flight home didn't happen. Now his Sunday flight was delayed. While he was frustrated being stuck in the Portland airport, he wasn't as annoyed as he would be normally. He spent the previous night at the hotel calling the rest of the Robert or R. Green phone book listings in the Santa Barbara book. Only five times, he didn't reach anyone. Each of those times he was able to leave a message giving his phone number. He wrote these five numbers down. He spent the rest of his night considering the likely prospect that Samantha was no longer married to Rob. That thought put him in a mood he hadn't experienced for a long, long time.

He got his phone out of his pocket and called Father Tom. "Hi, my flight is delayed. How's Sammy doing?"

Tom was asleep when his phone buzzed and he heard Jim's voice. He answered, "She's doing fine. Can you hear me? I'm in her room. She's good. I think she'll wake soon, Jim, I really do. I honestly think she's hearing some of the things I'm reminiscing with her. She's coughed a few times. I'll tell Dr. Jameson about the cough when he gets here. Did you have any luck calling the Green listings?"

"Yes, I had luck, none of them were Rob."

"What?"

"None of them were Rob. We'll talk about it when I see you tomorrow, or I guess today. Were you sleeping? I'm sorry, forgot about the time difference. I won't get to the hospital until after school."

"Maybe I'll see you at St. Joe's. I have morning Mass, Monday, seven a.m. I want to be back at the hospital before noon. I'll stop by your office. Get some sleep on your flight."

Jim looked out through the large window. "There's a plane at our gate. Thank God."

"Always a winner, thanking God! See you tomorrow."

Father Tom set his phone on the table next to his chair. He walked out of the room, down the hall, and back. He looked at the few pictures he'd placed around Sam's hospital room. He smiled at the one of Sammy and

281

Lindsey wearing college graduation caps and gowns. He moved to Samantha and covered her arm with the sheet and light blanket.

Sitting down, wide awake now he said, "I'm not sure whether Lindsey got my letter telling her that her mom died. We sent a telegram, too. Linds told Kate and I that she'd be in very remote places in Africa this next year. It's the main reason she came home for three weeks a while back. Anyway, she said her mail would be held for her at the hotel address we've been using."

"Lindsey, Kate, and Karen had a great time when she came home. Karen came home, too, and stayed the entire time Lindsey was here. I know they tried calling you to see if you could come home. The phone number they had for you was disconnected. The operator said she didn't have a new listing with your name. They actually tried finding your number using Cole instead of Green. Who would have imagined that Bette Lotis, I mean Stein, would have your new phone number and not us? Oh well, glad Bette had it to call you about Kate."

"Samantha, no one is mad at you. Kate never once was upset about the life choices you and Lindsey made. Life gets away from us sometimes. We all understand that your life has been with your daughter and husband these years."

Tom saw that the covers had slipped down and covered her arm again. "Tell me about your daughter. I imagine she's beautiful just like you. Samantha, is she in college or has she graduated already? It doesn't seem possible that she could be graduated from college. Is she?"

He looked back at the graduation picture of Lindsey and Samantha. "I remember you, Lindsey, Bobby and Jimmy graduating from college, all about the same time. Karen graduated earlier. Well, I remember the graduation party at Kate's, that's for sure. Gosh, that was way over thirty years ago. Wow. Such memories we have. Memories are our mind's gifts, don't you think so, Sammy? And they're strange, sometimes, the way memories from long ago can be so clearly reminisced."

"Sammy, remember your graduation party? It was the same night that Lindsey and Bobby told Kate and Art that they wanted to get married in two weeks. Of course they had a good reason."

He watched Samantha move her arm back on top of the covers. "Well, I guess you're not chilly." He patted her arm. "I think I'll head back to the rectory soon. I'm really wide awake, now. I'll be back later this morning."

Grand came with Kate and Art to Lindsey's and my graduation ceremony. Bobby came, too. Jimmy still had finals at the University of Tampa. Grand and I held hands as we walked to our college's reception. "I love you, Grand. I'm so lucky to have you in my life. I can't wait to see Karen."

"You two were my dear little girls. Then Lindsey came along, and I loved the three of you. I'm very proud of you always. You, especially, have overcome such sad things." She looked at me and smiled, "Today, I can feel your mom and dad here with us cheering you two on. You know she loved you in a most precious way, Sammy. Your mom was a daughter to me. They'll be dancing in Heaven celebrating your and Lindsey's success. I love you, too, honey, since forever."

"Sometimes I can just feel their presence. You do understand, don't you, Grand."

A few weeks later, near the end of May, Kate had a huge graduation party for Lindsey, Bobby, Jimmy, Karen, and me. Everyone was invited including Hubert, Roslyn, Michael, Jimmy's and Bobby's families, Lindsey's aunts, uncles, and cousins, my Aunt Julie, Grand's sister, Karen's cousin Jill, her husband and their little girl. We all had so much fun together.

Our party began in the afternoon and lasted until almost dark. Kate and Art held the party inside their house and out in the back yard. Our families made and brought food. Bobby's and Jimmy's moms, Kate, Grand, and Roslyn made lots of snacks, salads, and desserts. Art set up games and chairs in the back yard. He grilled ribs, chicken, and hot dogs. Everyone had a blast.

After our party ended, Lindsey and Bobby told Kate and Art that they wanted to get married right away. Two weeks later we all gathered in St. Joseph's Chapel to celebrate their wedding mass.

1967

After cleaning up from the graduation party, family members went to different places for the night. Hubert, Michael, and Roslyn walked across the street to Sammy's house. The renters had moved out. Her house was comfortable having freshly painted walls and new furniture. Roslyn loved the cozy home. Karen and Phillip went to Grand's house for the night. Jimmy and Sammy drove Aunt Julie back to the Holsten Inn. They circled three rocking chairs on the veranda and sat down realizing this was the only time just the three of them would have together. Plus, Sammy knew Bobby and Lindsey wanted to talk with Art and Kate about their immediate wedding plans. It was a perfect time to be with Aunt Julie. They talked while hearing the waves gently rolling onto the beach.

Bobby and Lindsey were just walking into the living room after checking the back yard for anything else that needed to be put away. Kate and Art were sitting down on the sofa when they walked in. "Mom and Dad, the party was perfect. Everyone had a blast. Thank you," Lindsey said, then looked at Bobby.

Kate answered, "It was fun. Enjoyed seeing your sister, Bobby."

"Dad, Mom, we need to tell you something, I mean ask you something. We want to get married right away."

Art and Kate looked startled. Kate answered, "Why? I mean, that's wonderful! We can put a wedding together this summer. How about late August or September?"

Bobby spoke up, "Kate, we want to be married in two weeks. I've,"

"Two weeks," Kate interrupted while straightening in her seat looking at Lindsey, "honey, what's going on?"

"Mom, please, just let Bobby finish."

He tried to conceal a slight smile as he thought, *Oops, they think Lindsey's pregnant.* "I've enlisted in the army. I'm leaving the second week in June for basic training. With your permission, we would like to get married before I leave. We want a small wedding with immediate family attending. Lindsey knew I enlisted. We talked about this before I asked her to marry me. We have a plan. I hope

285

to have a career in politics. I want to run for political office within the state. If we succeed winning state elections, I would like to run for congress someday. My serving our country in the military is a first step." He looked at Lindsey. "Linds has decided what she wants to do while I'm away."

"Dad, Mom, think about what the two of us will accomplish. I'm so excited about all of our plans. I definitely want to take advantage of my degree in education, but I'm going to have a difficult time getting hired." She looked at her Dad. "Dad, I've joined Care Core. In my correspondence with them, they've written they have many opportunities for teachers. I wrote them about my arm. Their answer was that they were impressed with my collage degree and that they have many teaching positions available. Bobby will be away for two years, and I will be helping people during that time, too. We'll be working toward our goal. And, having teaching experience will benefit me when we're both back. Wouldn't it be amazing if Bobby becomes a United States congressman someday?"

Art smiled while rubbing his right arm. Kate stood up and held her arms out. "Lindsey, come here." Smiling as tears filled her eyes, she hugged her daughter. "Seems we'll be shopping for your wedding dress tomorrow. Hey, do Sammy and Karen know about all of this?"

Not giving Lindsey a chance to answer, she asked Bobby, "Have you talked with your parents, yet?"

"Tomorrow, we're talking with them tomorrow. My mom and dad know I've enlisted and when I have to leave. We wanted to ask you, first, concerning our getting married."

"Ann and John didn't say one word to me about you enlisting." She looked at Art.

"Me either," he answered the question before she inquired.

"I asked my mom and dad not to say anything. They know I wanted to tell you about enlisting, and they know about Care Core. We haven't told them; asked them about getting married, yet."

"Bobby, we love you. Thank you. You could have eloped." Kate thought about that a second, "I'm so glad you didn't. We're going to have a great wedding! Let me know when I can call your mom. Now, tell me some things you want. Do you plan on wearing a tux or a suit? Are you having any friends in the wedding?"

They talked for a while.

Art got up and walked into the kitchen. He hollered, "Hey Bob, come here for a second." Walking into the kitchen, Bobby was handed an armful of food. Art put his index finger to his lips, "Shhh." They heard chatting in the other room. Art moved to the edge of the kitchen and called out to Kate that he and Bobby were going out, and they'd be back later. Then they carried food and left over beer to the station wagon.

They saw Jimmy's car coming down the street as they were driving out of the driveway. Art stopped and said, "Great, I won't have to come back for him. Bob, get him in the wagon."

Jimmy and I had said good night to my Aunt Julie and were on our street stopping in front of the house when we saw Bobby get out of Art's car. He hollered, "Jimmy, drive your car home, and Art and I will pick you up."

I got out of the car and hugged Bobby. Then I went to Art's car window and asked, "What's new?"

"I'll give you 'what's new!' You better hurry into the house. I'm sure they're waiting for you. Look, who's already been called!" We watched Grand and Karen hurry across the front yard and open the side door.

When I went inside I saw Kate filling the tea kettle, then turning on her stove. There was a pad of paper and a pen on her new, swirled yellow and cream, formica counter. I heard, "I was feeling a little tired but not anymore. We need to make a list. We've got a lot to do in fourteen, yikes, thirteen days."

Lindsey laughed, "Yes, we have lots to do, and Mom, do Sammy and Karen know about our plans? Is the Pope Catholic?"

Karen had a huge grin and hugged Linds. Then Grand's blue bathrobe sleeves were surrounding Lindsey as she enclosed her in a sweet hug. When I hugged her I said, "I love you, Linds." Kate wiped happy tears from her eyes, then went to her stove and poured steaming hot water over tea bags in the teapot. I set plates, forks, spoons, and napkins on our table as Grand did the same with the sugar bowl, a pitcher of milk, and some lemon. Karen found an untouched cherry pie, and Lindsey set some left over cookies and brownies down. All of us sat and got comfortable as love, laughter, and wedding plans filled Kate's kitchen.

It was close to noon when Tom walked back into Samantha's hospital room. "Samantha," he vigorously rubbed her arm, "Jim's back from Portland. He'll be here later this afternoon."

He sat down and said, "While driving back here, I was remembering when Art, Bobby, and Jimmy woke me up at the rectory to tell me that Bobby and Lindsey wanted to get married. As I recalled everything, I laughed myself silly. It's still my all time favorite night. I could never get away with a night like that again in the rectory or anywhere, not in this day and age."

Tom heard Samantha cough and thought she sounded a little congested. He felt her forehead and adjusted her covers knowing Dr. Jameson would be there soon. He continued, "Bobby was so happy he and Lindsey were getting married. You know Sammy, that night is the closest thing to a bachelor party I've ever attended. Well, the closest thing to a bachelor party I was ever equally involved in. There was my brother's bachelor party, but that was years earlier, and it wasn't in Bay Village."

1967

Tom had just finished his prayers and turning down the covers on his bed when he heard someone banging on his rectory door. He had a hunch who was making that racket. He pulled his sweat shirt over his head and walked down the steps to his front door. "All right. All right!" He opened the rectory door seeing three grinning faces. Looking at Art he said, "Apparently it was a mistake telling you that Father Doug and Father Tony are visiting their families until later morning Masses tomorrow."

Carrying lots of food and some beer, they pushed past Father into the rectory kitchen and set everything down on the table. Following behind Jimmy, Father Tom waved a finger, "You know Jim, this isn't the best way to impress the guy who just hired you for a teaching position at St. Joseph's, not to mention recommending you for a graduate school scholarship."

Art heard him, "Oh, now, Tom, we came here to continue partying because we have something new to celebrate."

"Dear Lord," he replied while smiling.

Art opened a bag of chips, pretzels, a carton of dip, and a bottle of whiskey. "Good thing we had a lot of non drinkers at the graduation party."

Jimmy took four beers out of the case. Father Tom handed him the bottle opener. Then everyone was handed a beer and Jimmy raised his bottle, "Congratulations Bob. We wish you and Lindsey the coolest life ever."

Art needed to clue Tom in on the recent events. As he filled two shot glasses with whiskey he said, "Jim, Bob, go to the car and get the rest of the food we grabbed from Kate's fridge."

As soon as they walked out, he handed Tom a shot. "Bobby and Lindsey want to be married in the Chapel one week from this Friday evening, and Bobby has enlisted in the army. He leaves the week after that for basic training, with Lindsey leaving soon after to work for Care Core. So what have you been doing in the hour since you left our house?"

"Dear Lord, bless them." Father closed his eyes for a few seconds and prayed that everyone in the parish stay happy and alive for the next hours. He raised his glass and said, "To Lindsey and Bobby," then he and Art drank their first shot.

Art gazed at Tom a few seconds and commented, "Sometimes I forget just how young you are. You have a wise heart, and it makes you seem much older. Realistically, it looks like I'm the only one who'll be able to handle his booze."

"Is that a challenge, my friend?"

"Is what a challenge," Jimmy asked as they set leftover appetizers on the table.

"Oh, you'll find out, precious children," Art answered as he swallowed some beer. Seconds later they all sat around the kitchen table listening to Father Tom tell his priest jokes. "Have you heard the one about the rabbi, the priest, and the bartender?" The celebration began.

Soon everyone was laughing so hard they had tears streaming down their faces. "Oh God, Art, I wish you could have been there." Jimmy was telling Art about a prank they'd pulled on Father Tom when they were in eighth grade. "Our Father Tom had made all of us boys remain in Sister Veronica's room during afternoon break. We'd done some dumb thing to annoy Sister. He told us to sit quietly until he returned to teach our eighth grade boy's health class held in her classroom the next period." Jimmy drank some of his beer and laughed at the memory. "Think about it Art. He left about forty, eighth grade boys with nothing to do, alone, in a classroom for fifteen minutes."

Art interrupted and looked at Father Tom, "He has a wise heart; not so sure about his brain." They all laughed.

"Plus, our punctual Priest here," Jimmy said smiling at Father Tom, who was trying hard not to smile, "was about ten minutes late for our health class. So, we had lots of time with nothing to do. One of the kids, and I swear it wasn't either of us, noticed a bottle of instant adhesive glue on the window sill. Well, one thing led to another. By the time Father returned, we all were quietly sitting like perfect angels. Father Tom walked in looking very stern.

He unrolled a health chart that was clipped to the top of the blackboard, sat down, and began teaching."

Bobby started laughing and said, "Jimmy, I remember. This was the year health class included learning about sex. Father Tom called it, 'our young enthusiasm,' remember?"

Art laughed out loud. Tom couldn't hold back a smile, and they all laughed while drinking more beer.

Jimmy continued, "So, Father bumbled on and on trying to keep a positive, informative lecture with forty, thirteen and fourteen year old boys eagerly wanting to hear every word about their 'young enthusiasm.' And then the moment we'd really been waiting for came. Father Tom looked over at that chart covering the blackboard that had the word: sperm. He tried to stand up. Very quickly he realized he was very literally glued to his seat. And you know what, Art? He shifted in his seat and didn't even react. He kept right on sitting and talking while we watched him try to pick up the ruler we'd glued to a pile of papers on Sister's desk. Then he casually tried to lift a book. He tried doing these things all while talking about the sperm, sketched to resemble tiny fish, indicating swimming movement to somewhere on the chart that was clipped to the blackboard about four feet from his reach."

Art was really laughing now, and so was Bobby.

"We could just see Father's mind figuring out that we'd glued down everything we could get away with. He tried Sister's ink well. It didn't budge. A bowl with rubber bands and paper clips was stuck down. While trying to lift things, he kept right on teaching. We saw him looking at the Bible. He hesitated speaking for a few seconds and looked at us as we sat trying to look innocent of any wrong doing. Then he went for it and lifted the Bible with no problem."

"Ya, you didn't want to burn in Hell," Art injected. Father Tom was laughing.

"Meantime, the final bell rings," Jimmy went on, "and Sister walks the girls back into her classroom. Father Tom smiles and tells her to let the girls get their things because the boys would be staying for a while. Sister asks if everything's ok. Father assures her that all is well."

Jimmy swallowed a big gulp of beer then continued, "So the entire school empties out. Silently we sit, and sit, and sit. Father Tom keeps watching us with a big grin on his face. He opens the Bible and begins silently reading. He knows he's gotten even with us because we're missing football practice. I'm sure he was picturing us, because of our tardiness for practice, running endless laps, and doing push ups, and sit ups for our overly zealous eighth grade coach."

"After an hour, Father Tom finally says, 'So you idiots, just how long is this glue guaranteed to hold?' And we all burst out laughing. Then he adds, 'I hope you geniuses have saved your allowances. Seems you'll be purchasing some new items for Sister's classroom.' He finally stands up, and we all hear cloth ripping. Our entire class laughs even more, and so does our great Priest." Jimmy slaps Father on the back and ends his story saying, "Father stands a second, then tells us, 'Don't move for three more minutes,' as he backs out of the room."

Father Tom opened more beers. They sat talking, laughing, and drinking. Father asked, "All right, while we're at it, which one of you asses altered and switched the remembrance letter your class wrote me? You know, the one you begged me to read at the end of your Eighth Grade Graduation Mass? Remember the Monsignor was there because he had a niece in your class, and he and I celebrated your Mass? The Bishop confirmed you. Monsignor had to get up and hand me his copy of your original letter. I know it was you, two. Fess up. You and four other kids were the altar boys for your Mass."

Bobby slapped the table, "Oh, that was great." He gulped more beer. He was beginning to have trouble forming his words as he remembered, "The Mass is just about done. Father juss needs to read his b e a u t ee ful letter from our class." He looked at Father Tom a second, "Didn't sha? Anyway, we see him looking a little skept, uhm, spek, a little worried because the letter we put on the po dee um, is written on blue paper and not white paper like the orginal, you know, the first one."

Bobby shakes his head and laughs as though he can see the whole thing again, and says, "St. Joe's is juss packed with parents and famlies, and its hotter than heck.

Our Bishop is wiping persration, you know, sweat off his forehead. All of our parents and everyone is squirming thinking, read the darn letter and end this two hour Mass. Father Tom looks at us altar boys, and we're trying our dammist. damdest not to even crack a smile. And of course we told our class about the swish, swittsh cause what fun would it be without them knowing? We're all smiling at him looking insol, inn-o-cent, like angels. So now, he's silently reading his new letter on blue paper to himself, stuff like: 'Hi. We love you, Father Tom. Gotcha last! Don't sit on any more glue. No more spitting contests during lunch break. No more bragging that you can stuff more Bubble Double, Double Double gum in your mouth than anyone else on earth.' Finally Father smiles at all of us, and at the packed full fews, I mean packed pews, and says somethin like,"

"I remember exactly what I said," Father Tom interrupted. "I said, 'Before I share their kind message, let us all bow our heads and pray that our graduates, here, receive much intelligence and wisdom as it seems they're going to need all of our prayers!' With that, all of you graduates burst out laughing and then everyone else began laughing. And Monsignor Schaunacy handed me his copy of your letter, that I made sure he had. Bet you never knew I'd done that."

Now Jimmy looked at Father, then at Bobby and said, "Nooo. We didn't know, did we, Bobby? Always wondered how come he had a copy. Thought maybe his Katherine Mary, you know, his niece, gave him a copy. I'll be dammd."

"It's a possibility." Father Tom said.

"Father Tommy," Jimmy slapped the table and asked, "Rememer when you got us out of our lass senior high esxams?"

Bobby slapped Jimmy on the back and said, "Oh God, that wasss so great!"

Art was laughing, looking at the two boys he loved as sons. "Tommy, I give them about ten more minutes before they go nite-nite."

"I'd say that's about right." Tom got up and got two glasses of water. "Drink some water and eat some salty chips."

"Ok,"Jimmy said. He began his 'final exams' story, "We got through the firss three days of exams and decided to cebrellate, cel e brate that we only had one day of hise skool left. Sooo, we got some low beer and the girls."

"Ok, you two, remember that I am their dad and this," he pointed at Tom, "is their priest."

Jimmy tried to look very serious, "We've never hurt our Lindsey or our Sammy, never!"

"Anyhew," Jimmy smiled and got back to his story, "We were soo escited about hise skool gradjuassion that we all got a lille smashed. Huh, Bobby? Right here behind the rectory."

"Oh yes, I remember," Tom said. "We heard this laughing out back as Father Doug, Father Tony, and I sat down for dinner. Mrs. Flannagan, bless her heart, wanted to call the police. I told her not to, that I'd go check it out. Well, I found these two," he smiled at Jimmy and Bobby, "drunker than skunks along with Lindsey, Samantha, Jeff, and Karen. All of them just having a great old time. So, I asked them, 'All done with our exams, are we?'"

"Oh, Lemme tell it!" Bobby jumped into the story. "Well, after Father asxs that quession, all a sudden Lindsss starts to cry and then Samss starts crying. Jimmy, here," he slaps Jimmy's back, "Jeff, Karen, and I juss can't stop laughing. Then Jimmy answers Father's quession, 'Nope, we have more xamna...tessts in the morning.' Sooo, our favorite Priess," he slaps Father Tom's back, "sits down with us and opens one of our lass beers, drinks it, and doesn't say one word. Then Father opens our very lash beer, never speeching, saying one word to us. All the while, Linnss and Samss are sobbing and the ress of us can't stop laughing."

"Lemme tell Artie this part, Jimmy interrupted. "So then Father says, 'So lemme make sure I understand your sishuation. You genussess are plastered, and you have more fian, testss in the morning?' And Bobby, who happens to be the bess friend a guy could ever have, answers, 'Father, you have asssesshed our sishuation."

"So Artie," Father Tom stops Jimmy, "I'll finish this story. I tell the little shits to get into my car because I'm taking them home. The girls are still crying and Karen's crying along with them, now. The boys are trying hard to stop laughing, but they just can't make themselves stop. And you know, Art, I could hardly stop myself from laughing. They all looked so hopeless. I get in my car with them and yell at them. I tell them to set their clock radio's for the morning, to say they're prayers, to go to bed for the night, and to get themselves to school the next morning. I tell them I'll have their hides if they miss their exams."

Bobby finishes the story, "So the nexx morning, eash of our teashers tells us to go to the office immeat, really quick. And there's Father Tom in the office. He's told our Pris, our Princbul Lowe that he needs us for the day. And jus like that we're saved. Howdge you do it, Father?"

"Well, first of all, I didn't do it for you two asses. I did it for the girls. At least they had the good sense to be remorseful. Principal Lowe and I are great friends. I told him the truth, that you all had gotten plastered drinking, not very many, three-two beers. He actually thought it was funny. He knew you all were eighteen. Plus, he knew you all had excellent grades. Henry Lowe said he owed Lindsey a favor. Art, I took them all out for breakfast and then fishing on Lake Erie, off Vermillion."

Bobby smiled at the memory and laid his head down on the table and said, "You're the bess, Father." About four seconds later, Jimmy joined him.

Art and Tom looked and saw them face down, snoring.

"Well, that didn't take long," Father Tom said. He looked at Art, "Tell me what Lindsey and Bobby need me to do."

"They want to be married in the chapel one week from Friday."

"Done."

"Thank you, Tom. I'm sure you'll be hearing form Kate and Lindsey tomorrow."

"Well, yes, I'm planning on that. So tell me," Tom looked down at Bobby, "What has this young fool gone and done?"

"God, Tom, he's enlisted in the army, and he leaves in three weeks for basic training."

The two close friends sat in silence for a few minutes. Then Father Tom poured two more shots, and they talked until the wee hours of the morning.

It was early afternoon. Father Tom was talking about Lindsey's and Bobby's wedding when Samantha began moving her legs and then her arms. He stood up and took hold of her hand. "Samantha, I'm right here. Can you hear me? I think you just squeezed my hand." He squeezed hers. "Come on, hold my hand and open your eyes. Jim's back, and he'll be here later this afternoon. I know he'd be so glad to see you awake."

He felt her forehead. *Her temperature is up,* he thought. He got a wash cloth and dampened it with cool water. Pressing it on her forehead, he said, "Please open your eyes. Dr. Jameson will be in here soon. It's time you open your eyes, Samantha."

She was very still, again. Father took the cloth off Sam's forehead. He rinsed it with more cool water and held it on one of her wrists. The he rinsed it again and placed it on her other wrist. He walked to the hallway and saw the doctor at the nurses' station. *Good, he'll be in here soon.*

He sat back down and turned the cloth over on her wrist. "Well, we were remembering Lindsey's wedding. Do you remember that I said, 'Lindsey and Bobby, may God in heaven protect your loving hearts, hear your precious prayers, and make your time together full, blessed, and happy.' Remember that? I've never forgotten."

SLEEPING MEMORIES 1967

We saw Father Tom standing at the front of the full
chapel looking at the candles outlining the center aisle.
Shining through stain glass windows, the late afternoon
sun beautifully reflected colors of light throughout.
Flowers in soft shades of violet with a touch of white and
pink graced the altar and matched Ann William's and
Kate's corsages and Karen's and my bouquets.

The guests were seated. All of us except Bobby were
together in the front vestibule. Father gave him the signal
to join him. After Bobby walked through the side entrance
and up the front altar steps, the organ music concluded
and two violinists began playing. Father Tom and Bobby
had huge smiles as Phillip offered his arm to Grand. Brice
and Frank followed behind as Phillip walked Grand to the
front pew, sat all three two seats from the aisle seat, and
returned down the side aisle. Jimmy escorted Bobby's
mom, Ann, with Bobby's dad, John, following to their front
pew seats across the aisle from Grand. Jimmy gave Ann
a kiss on her cheek and shook John's hand.

In the vestibule, Kate looked back at Lindsey and Art
and whispered, "Love you" as Jimmy walked back down
the side aisle to escort her. We watched him give Kate a
kiss on her cheek and help her sit down next to Grand.
Then he returned to escort me to our places on the altar
steps. Phillip and Karen happily followed us. We all
smiled as we walked down the aisle and found our spots
near the altar. The violinists hesitated some seconds, then
began playing the song Kate had requested, "Love Never
Fails." Everyone in the Chapel stood up to watch Art walk
Lindsey down the aisle.

Bobby stepped down two steps to meet them. I hadn't
ever seen Art look more proud and happy as he and
Lindsey slowly made their way to Bobby. Lindsey's white
silk dress swept around her body perfectly, and her white
bouquet beautifully complimented her elegant dress. As
they arrived in front of Bobby, Art shook his hand and
hugged him. Then he took his daughter's hand and
placed it in Bobby's, and the bride and groom turned and
walked up the two steps into their future.

Father Tom lovingly said Lindsey's and Bobby's wedding Mass. He ended by blessing them, "May God in Heaven protect your loving hearts, hear your precious prayers, and make your time together full, blessed, and happy. In the name of the Father, and of the Son, and of the Holy Ghost, Amen."

Those words sent Lindsey and Bobby Williams into the waiting world.

1967

After enjoying their dinner reception at the Holsten Inn, the newly weds were finally alone in their suite on the third floor. Their friends and family still danced and celebrated downstairs.

Lindsey and Bobby hugged one another. Looking out at the gentle ripples on Lake Erie, they saw fading shimmering pink and purple light blending the sky with Erie's easy movement. Lindsey kissed Bobby's cheek. "I'm so happy. This day, I've been waiting for this day and these next hours with you forever," she whispered in his ear, then went into the large bathroom to change out of her wedding dress.

When she walked back toward Bobby he had a huge smile, "You're so beautiful. I love you so much, Linds."

"Do you like my negligee?"

"I'm the luckiest guy in the world. In church you looked amazing. But now, never have you looked more beautiful." Bobby looked at her and admired his bride's perfect curves.

"So you've seen me in my negligee, and you like it?"

"I love it! Are you going to wear these things every night?"

"Bobby," she was grinning, "If you don't get this thing off of me this second, I'm going to attack you."

"Gosh Linds, that's so old, you attacking me," he kidded and then looked very serious. "We've waited for so long. I love you so much." One slender blue strap slipped down her shoulder and arm, then the other one. They both felt the short silk gown slide down Lindsey's body onto the thick carpet. He looked at her and gently said, "Lindsey, you're so beautiful." He picked her up and carried her to the large antique bed where they both sank way down into the feather mattress. The room filled with laughter as they realized they were sinking and were almost stuck in the thick feather thing.

Later, she was gently rubbing his chest. Her head was on his shoulder as she said, "You make me so happy."

"Isn't it amazing? We don't have to worry anymore, you know?"

300

"I know. All of a sudden we have everyone's blessing. Silly, isn't it. Our mom's gave me all kinds of skimpy, stringy things to wear."

"Linds, I almost forgot." He got up and walked across the large, beautiful, slightly out dated room toward his suitcase in the closet. He came back carrying a small box.

She looked at him standing beside her and smiled. "This is amazing." Then her attention returned to the gift he handed her. She unwrapped it and opened the box finding a round gold pendent hanging on a shimmering gold chain. She held it up. "Bobby, this is beautiful. I love it. Thank you." She turned it over and noticed two dates engraved on back. One date was their wedding day. She looked at the first date for a second. "Bobby, this must be the date I started fourth grade."

"It is," he answered. "It's the very first time I ever saw you. Somehow I think I knew, that first day, that I'd be with you forever." He took the necklace from her small hand and set it on the night stand. Bobby held Lindsey close and began kissing her slowly, gently, long passionate kisses. A while later they were in the place only they shared.

Much later, Lindsey woke up and walked over to the dressing table. She looked into the mirror and thought, *I look really great. Must be the 'guilt free' sex.* She smiled at the thought while combing her hair and putting on some lipstick. She picked up the room service menu, then the room phone, and ordered a boatload of food.

Bobby woke up hearing her on the phone, "Out of energy, tiger?"

She smiled, yet felt a slight bit embarrassed. She picked up a pillow off the couch and threw it at him. It landed on his face.

"Hey, you," Bobby laughed and threw it back with more force than he'd intended. It knocked Lindsey right off her feet and onto the carpet.

Bobby leaped from the bed. "Linds, are you ok? I'm so sorry." He picked her up and saw that she was laughing so hard, she had tears streaming down her face.

"Bobby, I love you so much." Her embarrassment disappeared, and she laughed even more.

"You never finished looking at your necklace."

"I'm sorry." She walked to the night stand and picked it up. "It's a locket." She opened it and saw one picture in each side, a snapshot taken when they were about ten years old and a recent picture from their graduation party. "I love this, Bobby. I'll always wear it." She smiled and put it on.

"When we get our wedding pictures, could you put one of them in where our graduation picture is? I'd like you to do that."

"Then that's what I'll do." She put her arms around her husband. "Thank you."

Lindsey and Bobby had their three night honeymoon leaving only a few days before he had to leave for basic training. Karen and I knew Lindsey was dreading staying with either of their parents for their first nights of marriage. We told Art and Kate and came up with a great plan. Before Karen and Phillip returned to Columbus, all of us made everything at my parents' house just right. We placed pictures of Bobby and Lindsey around, placed their unopened wedding gifts on the dining room table, cut the grass, and trimmed the shrubs outside. After Phillip and Karen left, the rest of us stocked the refrigerator and cupboards, and placed some fresh flowers around. Brice and Frank did a little decorating making my house just right for Linds and Bobby. When the newlyweds returned to Kate's, I got to walk them over to my house and hand them the keys. They were so excited.

Bobby and Lindsey were thrilled having their own house for the few days they still had. Staying in Sammy's house was the best gift ever, but the days passed so quickly. Bobby kept telling Linds, "Honey, we'll get through this. I'll be back home in eight weeks. You'll be leaving for Bolivia a few days after I leave for Vietnam. We'll put our experiences to good use toward our future, just the way we planned. Two years will pass by in no time, and we'll have the rest of our lives together."

"I know. These days have been so perfect, and we've had the best beginning. I love you so much. I wish these two years were already over."

Bobby's mom, Ann, had everyone, including Bobby's sister and family, over for dinner the night before her son left for basic training. The next day just his parents took Lindsey and Bobby to Cleveland Hopkin's Airport, and then he was gone.

Lindsey brought her things back to her parents' house. She stayed in Sammy's bedroom sleeping in the other twin bed instead of returning to her own room. She didn't want to be alone. "Sammy, this is the first time since I met Bobby that I can't see him or talk with him when I want. I've never felt so lonely."

"Get ready for Bolivia. Keep busy. I love being with you. We'll go to the movies. Let's do some things we haven't done for a long time. Let's go to Huntington Beach, the art museum, a play, the zoo. Jimmy wants you to hang out with us. Please let us help you through this. I love you, Linds. Keep busy these next weeks. We'll help you."

She heeded the advice and mainly concentrated on getting ready for her two years in Bolivia. She already had several hours of Care Core orientation and training meetings on her calendar. Actually, she hadn't really considered how much she had to do before she left. There were several vaccinations she needed to have, so she made appointments with her doctor. Limitations on how much she could take with her combined with the things she needed to take, prompted her to make thoughtful lists and go on several shopping excursions to stores she hadn't frequented before. She noticed that she needed to purchase several different size, see through plastic, zipper garment bags.

The first time she walked into the building and entered the room where her meetings were held, Linds was greeted with quick hello's and the same avoidance she'd always experienced. This orientation staff was very friendly, however, and welcomed her with helpful information. The meeting began and her next hour was spent listening to a speaker while looking at projector slides. They had a ten minute break and were promised this meeting would end soon after that. Standing up, Lindsey noticed a girl looking at pamphlets and thought, *I'll give her a try.* "Hello, I'm Lindsey O'Malley, I mean Lindsey Williams. I just got married and keep forgetting I have a new last name."

"You did," she smiled. "Well, congratulations. I'm Pam Grady. Are you and your new husband volunteering together?"

Lindsey saw that Pam had the most beautiful smile while explaining that she and Bobby weren't volunteering together. "So, I'll be off to Bolivia while he's in Vietnam."

"Bolivia? That's where I'm headed. Now, I'm really glad to meet you," Pam laughed. "Would you like to get a coke or cup of coffee when we're done here? How about we get a beer at the bar down the street. It's a great place. Nice, kind people own it."

"Let's go to the bar. I need a packet like the one you have. They said they'd get me one during the break. They ran out of them," Lindsey answered. I'll meet you by the door when we're done here."

Twenty minutes later, Lindsey and Pam sat down in the bar, ordered their beers, and began non-stop conversation. Lindsey watched Pam's animated way of expressing herself and loved it. *She's so pretty,* Linds thought as she listened. *She has the biggest dimples and the greenest eyes that look gorgeous with her flawless complexion.*

"So," Pam said, "the way I look at it is, you take what the good Lord gives you, and you run with it." She continued, "Do your best. Look your best. Work your hardest. Learn everything possible using that brain God passed out. By all means make life fun, and things will usually turn out just fine."

"That's the best advice ever!"

After that first orientation meeting, they always sat together at their meetings. They talked about a lot of things during breaks. Pam loved hearing about Bobby. "Gosh, I hope I meet someone who makes me as happy as you are. I'm looking forward to meeting him." Although there were over twenty volunteers heading to South America, they were the only two being sent to Bolivia and that suited them. Finally having everything ready for their two year commitment, they made certain they were on the same flights.

Knowing that Sammy would love Pam, Lindsey invited her to dinner one Sunday. Kate had the entire family come to dinner, including Bobby's parents, Ann and John, and everyone thoroughly enjoyed Pam. What made Lindsey the happiest was her new friend really liked her family, too.

An invitation was returned for Lindsey and Sammy to come to Pam's house the following Saturday. They never had more fun! Pam's family was loving, funny, kind, generous, and numerous.

Having so much going on, the eight weeks without Bobby passed by much quicker than Lindsey ever imagined. Her orientation and his basic training were history. She was so excited that it was time for him to return home.

1967

Lindsey had Bobby home with her for ten days before he'd be leaving for Vietnam. She stocked the refrigerator at Sammy's house full of his favorite food. She cleaned everything and had their bedroom looking perfect, placing a few candles and wedding pictures in just the right spots. She realized she didn't care what anyone thought. If they wanted to stay in that bedroom for ten days, they would!

Bobby's mom, Ann, wanted to go to Hopkin's Airport to pick him up, too. His dad asked Linds if they could drive her. When the three of them watched Bobby walk down the steps from the plane into the bright sunshine, Lindsey thought he was the most handsome man she'd ever seen. He was in his uniform, and he looked lean, tan, and strong. Bobby's smile was huge. She couldn't take her eyes off him as she stepped back to let his mom hug him first, then his dad. In seconds she felt herself being lifted off her feet as his arms surrounded her, and she buried her face in his chest crying happy tears. She heard, "I've missed you so much, honey. I love you." Her hair filled his hands as he looked at her smiling, tear streaked face. "Don't cry. We have all of these days together."

"Just now, when I first saw you," her voice quivered," you look so handsome I'm so happy you're home. I love you." She held him tight. John drove them to Lindsey's parent's house where everyone waited. Ann, Kate, and Grand had made a wonderful welcome home dinner for Bobby. After lots of hand shaking and hugging, everyone settled down with their drinks and enjoyed this night together.

Around ten o'clock, Bobby and Lindsey, sat beside each other watching and listening to everyone laughing and talking. "Lindsey, are we staying here tonight," he whispered.

"No," she quietly answered. "We're staying across the street, alone, by ourselves, with no one else there, just you and me." She smiled at him.

"Get us the hell out of here before I attack you in front of our parents and our priest," he whispered while grinning at her.

Lindsey stood up and called out, "Good night everyone. We're a little tired. Thank you for everything." She grabbed Bobby's hand and pulled him toward the front door. She tried to pick up his duffle bag, which he picked up, as they exited together. They hurried across the street, unlocked Sammy's front door, and walked inside. She grabbed the duffle bag from Bobby, dropped it, and began unbuttoning his shirt.

"That's a girl," he joked. He worked on his belt buckle and zipper. Linds pulled her shirt off over her head and unbuttoned her skirt letting it fall to their feet. She stood in front of him wearing her new baby blue lace panties and bra. His eyes welled up in tears as he looked at his wife. "God, Linds, I've missed you so much."

She hugged him and began kissing him. They laid down on the living room carpet and soon found themselves in the best place. "Bobby, I'm going to make you so happy." She stayed with him on the floor for a while and then went into their bedroom.

A few minutes later, she came back into the living room and softly said, "Come with me." She took hold of his hand helping him up and led him into their bedroom. He saw flickering light from candles dancing around the walls as he sat on the edge of the bed. Lindsey smoothed lightly scented oil on her legs and arms. When she finished, she set her arms on his shoulders and looked at him so tenderly telling him that he was going to love their nights and days together. He kissed her slowly, leisurely as she molded her body against his.

This first night passed. They spent much time inside Sammy's house, just the two of them, laughing, reading, spending rainy days and nights inside, hearing the rain in the background when they made love.

Three nights before he left for Vietnam, Bobby and Lindsey sat at their candle lit table in the White Oaks Restaurant. She looked through the window at the swift moving water rushing down the Cahoon Creek thinking how quickly their days together were passing. Smiling at him, she tried concealing how frightened she felt. She'd missed him so much during the eight weeks he was in basic training. She couldn't comprehend missing him for two years. Reaching across the table for his hand, she couldn't hide her feelings. "I don't want you to leave! When we decided all of this, I didn't realize how much being apart would hurt, how much I'd miss you. In college we could visit each other when the time apart was getting too long. I didn't think all of this through."

He felt her hand trembling and saw tears forming in her eyes. "Linds, even when we're apart our memories, our hopes, and plans keep us together. When I leave this time, you'll be leaving for Bolivia. You won't be here waiting; you'll be on your way, too. We'll both be in different parts of this world doing things to help others. We'll experience and learn so much. Remember all of our plans." He grinned at her, "I love you." Wanting to get her thoughts on something else he said, "Tomorrow night will be a blast. Our moms invited everybody we know to the party. I'm really looking forward to meeting Pam. How many things are we celebrating tomorrow?"

She knew he was trying to cheer her up. She quickly wiped away the tear that escaped and smiled, "Well, they want to celebrate the five of us turning twenty-two late last winter and this spring, our graduations, especially Karen's. Last December Karen finished her exams and had her diploma mailed home."

"Well, she was getting married about then, too," Bobby reminded her.

Linds laughed, "True enough!" She continued, "We're celebrating Jimmy's being hired to teach at St. Joseph's and getting into graduate school, our recent marriage; remember that! Phillip's new successful company, and it's a going away party for those of us leaving town, whoever they are!"

"Might be easier to tell me what we're not celebrating. I'm glad they planned it so we'll have the next nights just for us. You know, Linds, after this time apart, we'll have the rest of our lives together. Someday when we look back, we'll realize this time away was a small part." He felt so lucky she was his as he gazed into her blue green eyes. "You make me so proud. Nothing ever stops you. You've heard unkind words and left them in the air. You've changed people's attitudes by showing them you can do everything. You've given me so much happiness. I can't

309

imagine anyone being happier than I am. The way I feel about you is timeless. You and I will go on forever, always and forever. Nothing will ever change us.

The rest of that night and the next three nights were memories so quickly it seemed impossible. They were back at the Airport. Lindsey stood watching Bobby walk away from their parents, family, and her. *I need to hold him one more time.* She ran after him, he turned, and they held each other close. "I love you," she said smiling even though her face was covered with tears.

I'll hold this moment forever. He held her so tight and said something in her ear. Then they let go of one and other, and he quickly turned away. Lindsey stood still and watched him walk up the steps and disappear inside the plane's cabin.

Everyone understood she needed to be alone. They watched as she hurried past them and ran up the stairs to Hopkin Airport's outside observation deck. Ann and John were already up there waving to their son. Lindsey didn't see them. Tears deluged her face as she watched the DC8 taxi toward the runway. She waved with both hands hoping Bobby could see her. Then she stood still and watched the DC8 speed up as it lifted toward the sky and disappeared into the bright sunlight.

He'd looked so handsome a few minutes earlier when he'd said to her, "I love you always and forever. Those people in Bolivia are so lucky to be getting you. We'll do what we need to do, now, and we'll be holding each other again before we know it. Linds, remember, 'always and forever, before we know it.'"

"Always and forever, before we know it," she softly repeated out loud as the plane that held him faded from sight. She ran down the deck's steps into her dad's arms.

Bobby's homecoming from basic training passed by so quickly. Jimmy and I went out with them just one night. We all were together three times, once at Bobby's parent's house, once at our house, and at the party. All of us knew that they just wanted time alone. Kate, Ann, and Grand threw a huge party for everyone a few nights before Bobby left. It seemed we were back at the airport sending Bobby off to Vietnam before we could comprehend it.

After we watched Bobby's plane depart and watched Lindsey run into Art's arms, Karen and I stood still as Bobby's dad hugged Linds next. His sister hugged her and told her to write letters. Ann and Lindsey held each other and cried. Then we all quietly left the airport. Bobby's parents followed his sister's family to her house in Columbus. Ann told all of us that their hearts would brighten spending time with their grandchildren.

Art drove the rest of us back home where Grand, Brice, Frank, and Phillip were waiting. In Kate's kitchen we found fried chicken, corn on the cob, fluffy mashed potatoes, golden gravy, and mandarin orange marshmallow salad; all Lindsey's favorites. "We made you dinner and thought maybe we'd go to a movie after," Grand told Lindsey as she hugged her.

"That sounds like a great idea." Art tried to be cheerful. "Thank you, Grand. Dinner looks delicious." We sat down looking at all of the food when he spoke up again. "You know what? Let's put this away in the fridge and have it for dinner tomorrow. Let's go to the early movie. I hear *Barefoot in the Park* is funny. Art slid his chair away from the table.

None of us had seen that movie, yet. We all agreed going to the movies was a good idea.

Three days later all of us except Karen and Phillip were back at Cleveland Hopkin's Airport sending Lindsey and Pam off. Our families met for the first time at the boarding gate. Names were exchanged, warm greetings were exchanged, and then boarding was announced. Suddenly Pam's family was hugging her, and we were hugging Lindsey. Smiles and tears appeared on many faces as the reality of saying goodbye for at least one year sank in.

As Brice watched Frank hugging Lindsey, he put his arm around me and said, "I really can't believe that you three girls are off on your own."

Lindsey came beside me and held my hand a second. Grand wrapped her arms around her and said, "We all love you, precious one."

"I love you, too, Grand. You and," she smiled at me as tears trickled down her cheeks, and she quickly wiped them away, "Sammy take care of each other. I'll be back in one year for a visit. Karen told me to let her know exactly when I'll be home so she can be home, too. We talked on the phone almost an hour last night."

"I'm proud of you, sweetheart." Art hugged her.

"Thank you, Daddy." I hadn't heard her call him that in years. "I'll call you as soon as I find a phone. For sure there are phones at the airport, and I'll write you, mom," she looked at me, "and Sammy everyday. I love you, Dad."

Kate opened her arms, "They're lucky to be getting you and Pam, two wonderful angels. I'm happy for you, Linds. Enjoy this experience. You have all of our love."

Then it was my turn. Since the day we met, we'd never been apart. I hugged her and didn't want to let her go. "I'm going to miss you so much. Stay safe, and I'll write you about everything that's happening here. I love you." Tears poured down my cheeks, and we felt Kate and Art hugging us both at the same time.

And then everyone was hugging everyone. Dark skin, light skin, medium skin, both Pam's and our family entwined as though we'd known each other forever. Linds and I watched everyone for several seconds, and she said, "This is so easy, all of us being together. Just people bonding friendships, desiring similar things. Karen and Phillip would love this."

"They sure would." Then with a smirk on my face I said, "You know, I'll be mom and dad's favorite child now."

"They've always loved you best! I'm the one who gave them fits. Take care of them, and I love you back." She hugged me and added, "And remember, I'm always your sister." Then she said the silliest thing, "If you ever need me, come find me in the jungle. You'll always have me, Sammy."

Kate and Art were back with us. "Dad, remember when I was little, and I used to tell you that I was going to marry you someday? Remember that I loved you first." Lindsey hugged him tight, then wiped the tear rolling down his face.

He kissed his daughter's cheek and let her go. Kate put her arm around him and smiled a huge smile. I leaned against his other side with my arm around him, too. We stayed like that watching Lindsey and Pam board the plane.

~~~~~~~~~~~~

Dr. Jameson entered Samantha's room, washed his hands, and picked up her chart. "Good morning or I guess it's afternoon. I've gotten a little behind today. Have you noticed any changes, Father? I see the wash cloth." He took hold of her hand.

"I think her temperature is up. She seemed warmer to me just a while ago. I saw you at the nurses station and knew you'd be in here soon. She's been moving her legs and arms more. I think I felt her put a little pressure on my hand, too.

He put his hand on her forehead and then on her cheeks. Dr. Jameson pushed the nurse call button. "I want to do a thorough exam on her," he said as he wrote on her chart. "Take a little break. Go to the cafeteria for lunch. The sandwich special sounds good. Read about it on the board when I got some coffee this morning. I'll find you there or in the waiting room. Let me see what's going on here."

Tom looked very concerned and the doctor added, "It's not uncommon for coma patients to run temperatures. Her moving more and possibly trying to hold your hand are positive signs. I'll find you when I'm finished."

Father Tom left the room as two nurses came in. He walked down the corridor and pushed the elevator button for the cafeteria.

Dr. Jameson saw Samantha's temperature had reached 104.1. He decided to move her back into intensive care. She was shivering as she was lifted from her hospital bed onto the gurney. They covered her and rushed her upstairs. Once back in a hospital bed, they took her temperature, again. It was 104.3. One nurse took blood samples and left, another nurse began fluids, then gently wrapped her arms and legs in cool terrycloth towels. After ten minutes, she removed the towels and replaced them with fresh damp towels and pulled her covers back up.

Samantha continued to shiver. *Jungle, find me. It's so hot. Get these damn covers off. I can't get them off. I'm freezing. Father Tom, I can't hear you. Where are you? Are you with me? I'm dizzy. I feel sick.*

314

Twenty minutes later her temperature was down to 103.9. "That's a little better. I'm going to remain in the hospital the rest of the day and tonight. I'll check back after I finish with my patients. Notify me immediately if anything changes," Dr. Jameson said and left to find Father Tom. The nurse replaced the towels, again.

1967

"How are you doing," Pam asked Lindsey after they'd walked through the first and standard class sections of the plane. They were buckled in their seats in coach class. "We haven't talked in a few days. Have you heard from Bobby?"

"Yes, he called me when he landed in San Francisco. He sounded really happy. He said that he sat next to an army general during his flight. The stewardess saw his uniform, and because first class had open seats, she moved him up front. After Bobby sat down, this general changed seats to sit next to him."

"I don't think anyone's going to move us up to first class. We need uniforms," Pam joked.

"Let's move to the lounge table when the seat belt sign turns off." Lindsey remembered that someone at their party told her that the lounge table seats were for everyone's use.

"That's a good idea! What happened on Bobby's flight?"

"Lindsey continued, "Apparently, Bobby and the general talked during the entire flight. He told him that he and I graduated from college in May and just got married. He talked with this general about our future plans and told him his plan to run for political office. He explained that we're taking these two years to volunteer. When they landed in San Francisco, the general asked him to join him for dinner. That's when he told Bobby he would like to get Bobby's orders changed. That's all I know. His mom and dad don't know anything more, either. He called them, too. His mom thought he sounded really excited."

They sat quietly for a minute, then Lindsey asked, "How about you, Pam, are you doing all right?"

"I'm doing fine. Glad to be with you, and glad we're on our way. Have you heard for sure that you'll be teaching?"

"I haven't been told the age group of the kids, but I've been told I'll be teaching. It's one of the reasons we thought Care Core would be a good place for me. With my unique hand and arm situation, I would've had a hard time getting hired for a teaching position."

316

"Unique,' I like that. There weren't any hospitals employing 'unique' doctors either."

"Doctor? You're a doctor? I didn't know that!" Lindsey looked surprised, "I thought you,"

Looking upset, Pam joined her saying, "were a nurse." Then she snapped out, "And you were damned surprised to meet a colored nurse, too, I bet."

"Pam, no, I didn't mean it like that." Her face turned bright red.

"It's all right. That's the way it is. I'm used to it."

"No, really I'm sorry. I can't believe I said that. All of the doctors I've gone to have been older, and they've been men. You're right about the female part. Women are nurses, not doctors. That's what people expect. It's what they're used to. I'm so sorry."

"Lindsey stop, I'm being difficult. I shouldn't have said anything about being a colored nurse. You've never questioned my capability."

"No, of course not, but I never considered that you could be a doctor. I assumed because you're female, you'd be a nurse. Just like men aren't nurses. You told me you'd be working in the medical field. Remember? I immediately thought nurse." Lindsey thought about Pam's parents calling her Dr. Pam and wisely decided against saying she thought they were kidding around. Then she thought, *How could I be so stupid.* "Pam, I am sorry."

"I suppose being female is giving me as much trouble as being colored. Getting into medical school was hard, but not as hard as trying to find a hospital to begin my internship, residency. I just couldn't get in anywhere. And my grades are outstanding, if I do say so myself!" She smiled and looked at Lindsey, "So, here we are."

"Karen and Phillip, would be very unhappy with me right now. Given my status," she held up her small arm, "I ought to know better than to judge people on sight."

Pam changed the subject, "I'm so happy I met them and Bobby at your party. Bobby is one of the coolest guys ever. You two are perfect together. Karen and Phillip certainly are happy, and Phillip's son is a neat kid. Where did they meet?"

"She fell in love with Phillip while attending Ohio State. They got married last December. They should have arrived in Italy yesterday; otherwise they would have been at the airport with us. Phillip's parents live in Italy and in Columbus. Pam, I'm sorry I hurt you. I didn't mean to."

"Me, too, I didn't mean to be nasty."

Both sat quietly until the seat belt sign turned off, and they moved to the lounge table. An older couple, sat down seconds later, looked them over, shook their heads, and went back to their cabin seats.

"I wonder what it was, color or deformity?" Pam asked as they began laughing. A young couple sat down with them, smiled, and said hello.

Pam and Lindsey ordered two beers from the peppy stewardess, and each one paid a dollar in exact change. "So, what do you think it'll be like in Bolivia," Pam asked. We watched the stewardess carrying small bottles of alcohol on serving trays to waiting passengers. We heard another announcement for the economy class passengers to please pay the one dollar for alcohol in exact change. We noticed the glow of recently lit cigarettes along with cigarette smoke filling the cabin and some passengers turning their over head air vents on higher.

"I think it'll be hot. I don't know, run down I guess."

After they finished their beers, they moved back to their cabin seats, still talking about Bolivia. "Pam, do you speak fluent Spanish?"

"I think I do. The problem is not speaking it often."

"I'm a little worried about it. I've taken several Spanish courses, but I never speak the language. I didn't lie, I aced all of those classes. But,"

"You'll be fine. The four volunteers we're joining are from Indiana, Pennsylvania, and Atlanta. I'm pretty sure it's their second language, too. You and I will practice speaking Spanish. In a few days, we'll be cool. Besides, they told us many of the people we'll be helping will be speaking different dialects."

"Yes, I've been wondering about that, too."

Later their plane landed for 30 minutes and several passengers departed for good. Their flight made one more stop and finally landed a third and final time at their destination in Bolivia.

Two Care Core volunteers were certain they saw their new recruits walking from the jet into the open air airport. "You two must be Pam and Lindsey. We're glad you're here. I'm Stan and this is Jackie."

"Hi, it's good meeting you. I'm Pam, this is Lindsey."

"You've got to be tired." Stan said as they walked and saw an airport employee already stacking luggage on the open-air luggage stand. The girls saw their suitcases. "I'll grab the heavy ones," Stan told them. "You ladies carry what you can, and let's get this done in one trip to our luxury mode of transportation." Pam and Linds were led to what they hoped was not the car. It looked like an old jeep, a really old jeep, that probably never had any windows except for the windshield. They watched Stan put two suitcases on the back seat. "All right ladies, you two sit on top of these." Jackie put one bag on the floor in front and got in while Stan fit the rest where he found space.

Once they drove away from the airport, Lindsey couldn't believe how dark it was. It seemed a very long time that they held on for dear life as they rapidly traveled on bumpy roads in the old luxury mode of transportation. They hadn't gone far, though, when Pam grabbed Lindsey's small hand and pointed to the sky. The magnificence of so many stars sparkling everywhere their eyes could see, seemed like a beautiful welcome. Jackie turned to tell them that they were more than half way home and saw them looking up. "It's amazing, isn't it?"

Not too much longer, the jeep suddenly turned beside a building and came to a stop. "We're home," Stan announced. "I'll get your bags to your room."

Jackie told them to follow her and unlocked a door leading to a bathroom. She got nightshirts, and wash cloths out of a plastic bag. "Use these tonight. They're clean. There's hooks for your clothes right here," she pointed. "Get washed, and I'll show you where you'll be sleeping. I'm going to get you a hot cup of tea and some cookies. You had dinner, right?" They answered that they had. "I'll be back in a few minutes. We'll help you unpack tomorrow morning. Then we'll drive and show you around this place."

"Truthfully, Father, I'm not sure what's going on with Samantha. Of course, we're working on getting her temperature down, It shot up to 104.3. We've got it down to 103.9 now, and it should continue to drop. She did cough a few times. Her lungs sound clear. We'll know more tomorrow. We moved her to the intensive care floor for tonight." Dr. Jameson continued, "I'm going to finish my rounds, and then I'll check back on her. Are you ready to leave the cafeteria? I'll walk with you to the elevator."

"I need a lid for my coffee. She seems so close to waking sometimes. Maybe it's just wishful thinking on my part," Tom said as he got the lid, and they left.

"No, I agree with you. I think she seems close. Coma patients do run fevers. In Samantha's case we don't have a history. That makes everything more difficult. She's being closely watched. I'll check back."

Tom walked into her room and washed his hands. *I wonder if I've forgotten to wash my hands sometimes. Oh, Lord, I hope I haven't given her a cold or something,* he thought.

She seemed to be resting comfortably. "Samantha, I'm here." He looked in a tall cabinet and saw her things. Then he noticed two bags on the floor that held the blankets, radio, pictures, and other things he'd brought to her former room. "Ok Samantha, everything has been moved to this room. All is good." He picked up the graduation picture, looked at it, and set it back in the bag.

He sat down, "Jim should be here soon. Oh my, I need to call him about your floor change. This room isn't very comfortable, only one chair. Sammy, we were talking about Lindsey's wedding, and the going away party, and meeting Pam. Remember how much we missed Bobby and Lindsey when they left for Vietnam and Bolivia? Everything changed for all of us."

Tom sat quietly for a few minutes remembering. He stood up and said, "I really think you're hearing me reminisce." He patted her hand, "I'll be right back. I need to call Jim. Continue without me if you wish."

All of us missed Lindsey and Bobby so much. It took us awhile to get used to life with them far away.

Also, that was the summer things changed between Brice, Frank and us . They seemed different. They were quieter and didn't always come to dinners or hang out with us. Maybe they felt bad that Karen, Phillip, and Michael were spending so much time in Italy with Hubert and Roslyn. Things just changed. They seemed preoccupied with something that they didn't share with us. Along with missing Lindsey and Bobby, I missed them.

We hadn't had a family dinner with everyone in several weeks. Kate came into her kitchen one morning and said, "Sammy, we're acting crazy. We need to get our family together. Are you and Jimmy free for dinner tonight?"

"We sure are."

"Great, I'll call Grand and Father Tom. Do you think Jimmy's parents would join us?"

"I'm not sure. It would be wonderful if you asked them."

"All right, I will. I'll call Ann and John, too."

Everyone was able to come. Conversation came easily, and we had a great time. After Art went to bed, when Kate, Grand, and I were doing the dishes, Kate remarked, "This was a fun night. Brice and Frank seem good, don't you think?"

"Yes, much more like their old selves," I answered. "Frank has lost a little weight, but he seems fine."

"Yes, I've noticed that, too." Grand chimed in, "He's just fine. I'm sure."

"I'm so sorry I haven't invited Jimmy's parents to dinner before. They've always been invited to our parties, but never dinner. That was really stupid of me. They're wonderful. I wish they weren't thinking about moving to Florida."

"They've always been wonderful. Now they're fun because Jimmy's dad no longer drinks alcohol."

"Oh, I never knew that was a problem. I'm happy for them, Sammy. We'll get together more often."

"I'm happy for them, too. I really love them, especially Jimmy's mom. I'm glad his dad figured things out. Jimmy and his mom are really happy he quit drinking. I think he used to embarrass them. They're really serious about moving to Florida. His dad is older, I think he's sixty-six. He doesn't look it. His mom is almost ten years younger. Anyway, I think they plan on moving next spring."

While Kate and I dried the last of the pots and large bowls, Grand put tea cups, small plates, the sugar bowl, and a pitcher of milk on the kitchen table. The left over dessert was already on it. She poured hot tea into the cups, and we sat around Kate's table talking, reminiscing, and laughing. We had a wonderful time that night. It was the night we got to our new normal, and it included Jimmy's parents.

I forgot about Jimmy's parents. How can I just forget about people? I know they moved away. Father Tom, I can't hear you. Are you here? Where are you? God, I'm freezing. No, this isn't right. I'm with Kate and Grand. Stay with me. There you are. I see you, now.

"I love you guys, good night." I hugged Grand, then Kate and went into my room to write Lindsey about our night.

Lindsey and Pam were sleeping early the next morning when Paulette stood in the back doorway banging two pots together. "Hey, you two, wake up! I know your names, just don't know which name goes to who. I'm Paulette. We've got a lot to do today including shoveling cow manure out of an old structure. So get a move on it. We'll show you where to put your clothes and things as soon as you get done in the bathroom. The shovels are await-in."

"Shit, and I'm Pam," she quietly answered.

"Shit's it, you've got it! Glad to meet you, Pam," Paulette grinned as Jackie arrived standing next to her. "We'll see you back here in five minutes. We've got Old Nellie, our luxury mode of transportation, waiting for us outside of the bathroom. Get moving!"

"Double Shit," Lindsey echoed. "Not back in that truck, again. My butt still hurts and I'm not even sitting on it. I'm twenty-two, and my bones feel like one hundred and ten."

"Hi, Lindsey. Don't tell us you don't like Old Nellie. Jackie and I think she's the best. Now, rise and shine. You're down to four minutes."

"God Lindsey, what have we done and gotten ourselves into?" Pam whispered as they got out of their beds. "I sure didn't think it would be like this." They both looked around their room.

A few minutes later they heard a knock and then a door opened. Paulette smiled and said, "Follow me. The bathroom is just outside your door." They only needed to walk a few steps to the bathroom. Lindsey and Pam glanced at the old jeep as Paulette unlocked the bathroom door. The inside looked familiar. "All of the facilities here look alike. We lock this bathroom door at night and when we're all away."

Pam and Lindsey looked at each other thinking the same thing, *What if we need to use the bathroom at night.* They didn't ask.

When they returned to their room, Paulette and Jackie were sitting on the ends of their beds. Jackie told them they'd help them put their things into the cabinets that lined up along the bedroom wall. "Keep everything you have in the plastic bags with the zippers zipped," Jackie instructed. "You did put things in separate bags? Your underwear in one, P.J.'s in one, shirts and shorts in one, jeans and long sleeve shirts, you know, the way it was written in the brochure?"

"We did," Lindsey answered as they began getting the different size zipped bags out of their luggage.

"Good." They put most of their things away in about ten minutes. "Ok you guys, you can finish this later. Get changed into jeans, long-sleeved shirts, and put on your mud boots. You brought rubber mud boots, right?"

"We brought them," Lindsey answered.

"Good, we really need to get moving. We'll give you a tour of this little place later. Hurry and get changed. We'll be waiting in Old Nellie outside your back door. You'll get to see the landscape this morning."

A few minutes later Paulette locked their bedroom door, got back onto the front passenger seat, Jackie stepped on the gas pedal, and the four girls were rapidly traveling down a dirt road. Lindsey and Pam, sitting in the back seat, were holding on to the backs of the front seats. Riding in the back seat of Old Nellie was equal to being shaken like a rug. The jeep only had the front windshield window.

They tried to take in the scenery as they sped down the road seeing mountains in the distance and crops planted in rows filling parts of the landscape. Then there were structures on both sides of the road making it clear that this street was very narrow. They slowed down passing people and buildings. Moving rapidly again they noticed more farm land, adults and children in the distance, then more old buildings on one side of the road with fields on the other side.

Without warning, the jeep slid to a stop. "We're here," Jackie announced. "Let me give you some things to carry to that," she pointed, "table over there near the grill." She handed Lindsey a basket with napkins, paper cups, stir sticks, powdered creamer and sugar packets, four oranges, and two boxes of Pop Tarts. She gave Pam a plastic table cloth. "I'll be over in a minute," she said as Paulette carried two large thermoses of coffee.

Lindsey commented to Pam as they walked to the table, "Right here, it's beautiful. Look at the spectacular color in those flowers near the table."

"And the leaves on everything, the shrubs, plants, trees, are so many shades of green. It looks like a painting with this perfect blue sky," Pam remarked.

"That's right," Paulette said. "Bolivia is beautiful and messed up. It's especially messed up in some of the favelas. There's always turmoil. No-one knows who's really in control; the military, mafia, communists, or some other self-serving bastards. Things are always changing here. Two things are constant, however: turmoil and poverty. People trying to live their lives and feed their families need help, and that's what we're here to do."

Jackie was there now, and she added, "Most of the people near here are very poor and uneducated. I'm sure you were told this at orientation, and I'm sure you noticed the poor villages we drove passed a while ago. Three things I'll tell you right now. Don't go anywhere alone. It's a rule that if at least two of us find it necessary to go someplace, we must tell the others where. Don't trust anyone outside of our little compound. We need to be friends and need to trust one and other, but do not trust anyone outside of us. And, don't eat any of the food they, absolutely, will give you." Jackie smiled, "The food rule is a little flexible. Most of the people are very kind, but we need to be aware of the sanitary conditions."

"Jackie knows what she's telling you. We must be able to trust one and other completely, but no-one else. It really isn't safe to trust anyone else. It's impossible to tell who might know someone who could cause trouble. Our job is to help educate and give aid to the poor children and their families. And, what ever you do, don't express any political opinions. You never know who's listening. It would be wonderful for these people to embrace democracy, but we can't advocate it for fear of causing them and us trouble," Paulette stated. She laughed and added, "I guess that makes more than three things."

"We heard and learned about this at orientation, but being here really wakes one up," Lindsey said and then swallowed more of her coffee. "Well, one thing's great, the coffee."

325

"This coffee is amazing," Pam agreed. "And I just found out, I love Pop Tarts."

"Well, bon appetit!" Paulette laughed, "and hurry up. We need to get going on our little project. The place we want to clean out is over there. See it?"

"That thing just down the road with the side boarded up a little," Lindsey asked.

"Yep, that's it. Some cows had been inhabiting it. The animals are gone, and the guys boarded up the opening to keep all animals out. We thought if we could clean it up and if the guys could fix it up, it would be a great building for the children. It has a wood floor, the roof is sturdy, and the other walls are intact. We checked it out and think we could do something cool with it."

Jackie said, "You haven't met Ken, yet. He and Stan left early this morning to pick up supplies. They should be back soon. They'll help us when they get back. Including you two, there's six volunteering here, now."

Jackie climbed back into Old Nellie and drove close to the shack while the three others walked the short distance. Getting the shovels and buckets out of the jeep, they walked toward the mostly boarded up opening and then to the door. There were dozens of flies. "Opps, forgot the bug spray and some things in Nellie. I'll be right back," Jackie said.

"You get that stuff, and we'll start digging some holes in the field. That's where we'll bury the mud and manure," Paulette said.

Lindsey and Pam started digging holes with Paulette as though they'd been doing this sort of thing all of their lives. "You guys look like you've done this before. Hey Jackie, these two are pro's."

Finished spraying the flies, she took off her mask and gloves and hollered back, "So, they're not pansies?"

"So far so good!"

"Lindsey, I think they just referred to us as pansies."

"If we can stop digging, they can call us anything they want."

"I like these two," Jackie smiled as she picked up a shovel. "Let's keep digging a few more minutes, then we can get in there and get this over with." A bit later she announced, "Ok, that's enough. I think we've got plenty of holes dug. We need to get masks and gloves on before going inside. Change your masks if they get damp or uncomfortable. You can see we've got lots of them here on the front seat, gloves, too. Just remember to take your gloves off after your mask is off and get new ones on before you put on a clean mask. Ok, we look like surgeons! Let's start doctoring this place up!"

They picked up the buckets and shovels and walked inside the shack. "Oh, the smell in here is terrible. This stinks to hell," Lindsey coughed and gagged, "It's awful."

"I see you're not a farm girl," Jackie tried to kid. "It stinks for sure, but look around at the great space in here. If we can get it cleaned out today, and if we can get these floors and walls disinfected and scrubbed this week, and in the next weeks we repair it and do some painting; don't you think it will be a great place to teach the kids? The guys have already picked up donated windows and doors. Churches from the states are donating and sending all kinds of supplies."

"For the first time ever, we have three teachers and three doctors here," Paulette carried on the plea. "This place will make a great school for the children."

Lindsey apologized, "Ok, I'm sorry. I'll knock off the complaining. Bobby wouldn't be happy with me right now." She looked away at something.

"Ditto for me, even the part about Bobby," Pam said.

"Bobby," Paulette repeated his name. "I hope we get to meet him someday. We'll have some beers later and hear all about your man, Lindsey. He must be the guy attached to that locket around your neck and ring on your finger. By the way, tuck your locket under your shirt."

"He sure is," Pam answered for Lindsey.

She tucked her locket while looking at two, huge, brown eyes on the thinnest little boy, who was peaking in on them. He was hiding near the boarded opening. As she walked closer to it, he ran away through the field.

Jackie patted Lindsey's arm, "Luckily he's avoiding the holes! Don't worry, he'll be back. And, he'll bring lots of children."

"Really?"

"Yes, really, so let's get this poop out of here. And you know what? Let's take this boarding down. It'll give us some fresh air. The guys will put it back up later. It'll be quicker getting to the field using that opening, too." They got tools out of the jeep and got the boarded wall opened up. Taking turns shoveling and carrying the full buckets to the field, they finished shoveling all of the manure and mud out of the building much sooner than they'd anticipated. With the open door and the wall open, the floor started drying out.

They scraped the mud and dirt off the floor with spade shovels and were finally able to use brooms. "Hey, this is getting done a lot faster than I thought it would," Paulette announced. "Let's call it a day here, and get a cold coke. Plus, we need to get you two acquainted around here."

"Oh sure, an ice cold coke here, in the middle of Hell, no complaint intended," Lindsey answered.

"Look at the three attached buildings just across the street from where we had coffee this morning?"

"We see them," both new recruits answered.

Jackie smiled as Paulette continued, "The building in the center with the Penny's sign, that's where we're going to get the cokes. It's close, so let's carry the shovels, brooms, and buckets. Don't want to set them in Old Nellie with what's been in and on them. We can wash the buckets and shovels off near the supply building, which is on the right front side of Penny's. We might just toss the brooms. Plus, we can wash off in the bathroom over there. Follow me." She smiled a bit.

"Can one of you carry my boots," Jackie asked.

"Sure, and maybe I can save the brooms! I am a doctor," Pam announced and picked the boots up.

Jackie drove Old Nellie and parked in front of Penny's. The rest walked the short distance down and across the street carrying everything around to the back of the three attached buildings. Paulette handed Lindsey the end of a hose connected to a huge water container which was near the center building. Then she took her boots off and walked in and back out of the end building to the right. She handed Pam one of the bottles of disinfectant she held and said, "Like I just told you, supplies are inside this end building. There's a bathroom in there, too. It'll be the schoolhouse bathroom. We'll show you more later." She poured disinfectant on her boots and in each bucket.

"Let's get this stuff washed off before Jackie comes back." The three started cleaning off their boots and tools.

A few minutes later Jackie stepped toward them and said, "Wow, you guys are speedy! We need to get our clothes off and washed. Follow me." They walked into a large bathroom that stretched from the back of Penny's partly to the opposite end building on the left side of the three buildings. "Does this look a bit familiar?"

"Here by the two sinks, it looks like the bathroom we used last night and this morning," Pam answered and added, "You're right about all of the bathrooms looking the same."

"Really? Well, get yourselves washed. There's two showers, see them?" Jackie pointed. "Get two towels from those plastic bags on that shelf, then give me your jeans and shirts, everything except your underwear. Take quick showers. The hot water doesn't last very long, so lather up the soap and hurry up. Put your underwear back on and wrap up in your towel when you're done showering."

Lindsey looked at Pam, then said to Jackie, "So we're going to Penny's for a coke and drive back to where we live wearing underwear and towels?"

Paulette grinned. "Just take your showers and hurry up. We want to get washed up, too. And, don't worry about it. Things here are very relaxed."

After they showered and wrapped themselves in their towels, they followed Jackie outside. They walked to the third attached building on the left where Paulette was waiting. She opened the door and along with Jackie began laughing.

Lindsey and Pam looked around the room seeing the beds they were pretty sure they'd slept in the night before. "I don't get it. How did we get back here," Pam asked.

"We wanted you to see the sights this morning, and we wanted to mess with you. So, we drove you around in a circle," Jackie grinned.

Lindsey and Pam looked at each other not grinning.

"Oh, come on, it's a little funny," Jackie kidded.

Pam smiled a bit, then Lindsey joined her, and in seconds the four of them were laughing.

"So we live across the street from the building we cleaned out all day, and we were this close to a bathroom we could have used?" Lindsey asked not laughing so much.

"Yep, we all live here, the guys, too. That bathroom is only used by us, volunteers, so always take your towel and robe with you into the shower room. Paulette and I will get cleaned up, now, then we'll show you the layout of this place and get those cokes. Put on some shorts. We're done with the tough stuff today," Jackie said and left with Paulette out the bedroom backdoor.

Pam looked at Lindsey, "For sure, I didn't think it would be like this." They got dressed, combed their hair, and put on a little makeup. "There, we look much better," Pam said looking at herself and Lindsey in the large mirror both were staring in. "Now what?"

Lindsey turned and looked around their room. "Well, let's open door number two and see what we find." They walked into a small main room that had a sitting area and a small kitchen. "Look at this. It's not bad." Seeing a couch, some chairs, end tables, a good size table with chairs, they also noticed board games and decks of cards. Lindsey walked to the small kitchen area and opened the refrigerator door finding orange juice, tomato juice, a pitcher of milk, cheese, lettuce, and other food. She closed it and walked to one of the chairs and sat down, "This is comfortable."

Both saw their open bedroom door and five more closed doors. One door was at the end of the kitchen area. Another was next to their bedroom door and two were directly across the room from those. Another larger door was in the middle of the wall facing the street. "Let's see where the big door gets us. It's gotta lead outside to the street. I feel a bit like Alice. Maybe we're in Wonderland," Pam joked.

"I never liked that story."

"Me either, that darn rabbit! I've heard a new song on the radio called 'White Rabbit." The song's cool. At first I just liked the sound of it, but listen to the lyrics when you hear it. Tell me what you think."

They turned around because the door next to their bedroom door opened, and Paulette walked out. "Isn't

Jackie here yet?" She looked across the room at Jackie's closed door. Then she said, "I'll show you around. Here's where I sleep. Jackie sleeps in the room directly across from yours. All of the bedrooms are similar. They looked in Paulette's room and saw that it was even smaller than theirs, but it looked much the same. "I have my own room. I got here first! Come on, let's go to Penny's."

Penny's, the middle building, looked like a bar because it had a bar with four stools in the back of the room and two lighted beer signs on the back wall. One sign spelled Pabst and the other had the letters, POC. The letters were lit and the signs had red, blue, and yellow lights giving the place warmth. Also behind the bar a shelf held glasses. They saw three small tables with checkered table cloths and chairs placed between the front door and the bar. Two fans hung from the ceiling. The room itself was not very large, and it had a cozy feel.

Lindsey looked at the beer signs thinking, *POC I know, Pride Of Cleveland. Pabst What's that jingle?* Then she glanced at the red coke machine.

Pam looked at the handsome guy who just walked in the back door. *Wow, is he a hunk,* she thought with a huge smile crossing her face.

"Well, look who's arrived," he said. "You two must be Lindsey and Pam. Hey, I've got some mail for you. I'll get it. Stan and I picked up the mail after we picked up our supplies today." Smiling he walked to a large wood cabinet and unlocked the upper doors. "There's mail for our own Mrs. Paulette Swanson from the good Dr. William Swanson." He handed that letter to Paulette along with another opened letter. "Here, he wrote to Stan and me, too. You may as well read it. He still warns us that he'll kick our butts if we aren't watching out for you. Sounds likes he's taking good care of the guys in Nam."

Still grinning he said, "Mrs. Lindsey Williams, don't you fret. You've already got mail, too. Looks like someone forwarded your mail from," he looked at the return address, "Bay Village, Ohio. Ohio, I believe that's POC land." He wondered which one would reach for the large envelope. A bigger smile crossed his dark handsome face when Lindsey reached her small hand.

She said, "My mom probably forwarded a few letters before I left so I'd have mail when I arrived here. Thanks." Opening the large envelope, she saw three letters one from Karen, her mom, and one from Bobby. She sat down at a table.

"By the way, Lindsey, I'm Ken Jones. That was nice of your mom. We're all glad you guys are here." He shook her small hand.

He looked at Pam. "And you must be the dazzling Dr. Pam Grady, Miss Dr. Pam, I truly hope." He shook hands holding Pam's hand a few seconds longer.

Pam smiled a giant smile back, taking in his big dimples and his clear brown eyes while flirting back, "Yes, it's Miss Doctor. I'm happy to meet you, the unattached Dr. Ken Jones?"

"Sweetie, if I wasn't, I am now!" With a big grin he handed her a letter.

"Ok, Casanova," Stan said as he came in from the storeroom. "How about giving me a chance to win these beautiful girls' hearts? They were too exhausted to give me a shot last night."

Jackie, who just walked in said, "Oh yes, I forgot to tell you last night, Lindsey and Pam, I'm Jackie Sutherland and Stan, here," she smiled and punched his arm, "is Stan Sutherland, my funny husband."

"Ouch!" He gave his wife a kiss and said, "We looked at the building you kids cleaned out today. You got a lot done, honey. Sorry we didn't get back in time to help you." He continued to explain, "All of the supplies were in the warehouse at the airport. Even a huge medical supply crate arrived. That's what took us so long. We needed to open the medical crate and catalog everything right there with the airport police watching. We got him to sign our catalog sheet, too. That was a great idea, honey," he kissed her cheek again. "Anyway, everything was good this time, no medical supplies missing. We picked up everything else, too. The paint, building supplies, all of that. A lot of school supplies arrived, all kinds of books, puzzles, a large blackboard, paper, pencils, crayons, and some furniture."

Ken called out, "What'll you have? We've got beer, coke, some chips, pretzels?"

Lindsey excitedly answered. "That's it," and sang, "What'll you have? Pabst Blue Ribbon. What'll you have? Pabst Blue Ribbon. What'll you have? Pabst Blue Ribbon, Pabst Blue Ribbon Beer! That's it!"

Ken answered, "So you'd like a beer?"

Lindsey walked to the bar and said, "No, no, I'd like a coke and chips sound great. It's the beer signs you have. I just couldn't get that tune out of my mind, but I couldn't remember the lyrics. Thanks."

Pam laughed, "I'd like a coke and chips, too."

"Comin right up." Ken got them, plus Paulette and Jackie, cokes and chips.

Stan resumed telling his wife, "Tomorrow we'll have to return the truck. Ken will need to follow me in Old Nellie. We'll go early, get back, and help you beautiful ladies."

"That sounds good." She looked over at Pam and Lindsey, who were reading their letters. "Those two are great. They literally dug right in and did everything we needed to do today. I'm going to show them the washing machine in a few minutes. I wonder if they've ever seen a wringer-washer. After we get our clothes hung, we'll have dinner. Sound good?"

"Sounds great. Ken and I will take care of dinner."

About twenty minutes later, Pam and Lindsey were shown the wringer-washing machine located just inside the storeroom. "My grandmother had a wringer-washer," Pam said. "I helped her wash clothes lots of times. I remember my granny was always worried I'd get my hair caught in the wringer. I used to have long hair."

"Wonderful, that makes things much easier." Jackie smiled, "I've rinsed our clothes and rung them. I wiped the basin with disinfectant, rinsed it, and put the clothes back in to wash them."

She looked at Lindsey and Pam. "So, we use the hose to fill the basin, and we use cold water. Add about one cup of detergent. This month we have Fab and Ivory Snow Detergents. Turn the washer on by pushing this button. Once the clothes have agitated around about twenty minutes, turn it off and empty the washer. There's a plug in the bottom basin. Pull it out. Another hose connected to the washer bottom empties the water about fifteen feet away. While it empties, wring out the clothes through the wringer and put them in one of these clean metal tubs. Rinse the washer with the hose and refill it when you're done wringing, and don't forget to push the plug back in. Add the clothes, and start the machine to rinse the soap from the clothes. This load may need two rinses fifteen minutes long. After the last rinse and wringing, empty the washer and hang the clothes up on the clothes line, outside, right there," Jackie pointed. "I'll do the washing today. You guys relax."

Lindsey looked at Pam and said, "We'll help with the laundry."

"I know how to hang clothes on a clothes-line. My granny didn't have a dryer." Pam stated. "I'm in."

"Me, too," Paulette said.

While their clothes were washing, Paulette and Jackie showed Pam and Lindsey a few more things. In the common room with their bedrooms on the sides, they learned   that they could get to the bathroom through the door at the end of the kitchen area. "We keep the outside bathroom door we used today and last night locked most of the time and always at night. Today, I unlocked it when I drove back. We keep the key in the big wood cabinet." Jackie showed them. "I thought it would be easier to use the outside door today. Plus, we wanted to mess with you. I bet you're relieved about being able to use the bathroom at night," Jackie laughed.

Pam looked at Lindsey and answered, "Very!"

Two hours later everyone was across the street sitting around a bonfire the guys had built. It was the same place the girls had coffee and Pop Tarts that morning. Stan and Ken had corn on the cob and hot dogs on the grill. They had a salad ready. Everything needed was on the picnic table, which was covered with a plastic table cloth. There were several lit candles on the table. Another small folding table held a metal tub filled with cold beers and some cokes.

They leisurely ate some food, talked and asked each other questions. It was easy for Pam and Lindsey and the other four to sit around the fire and begin their new friendships. Jackie and Stan told the new recruits how they met in college eight years earlier and about their fun wedding three years ago. Lindsey told everyone about

Bobby, that they met in fourth grade and that he's always made her feel perfect. She said they just got married and that Bobby hopes to have a career in politics. Pam happily talked about her wonderful family and how much fun they have together, telling them a few stories about two of her favorite cousins. Paulette talked about her brother and her husband, Bill, and said they behave like brothers. She told Lindsey and Pam that they are doctors helping on the battlefields in Vietnam. She said her husband and brother have humorous personalities and told a few family pranks they'd pulled off. She said that the two of them keep life fun.

Ken shared his story last. He told them that he'd never wanted to talk about this until now. He told everyone about the girlfriend he had in high school, who died from cancer during their senior year. Ken told everyone about many of the amazing things she accomplished during her seventeen years. He said that one of the last times he was with her, she told him to never stop having fun and enjoying life. And he laughed as he said, "She told me to never stop using my amazing mind. Wasn't that a wonderful thing for a beautiful, young, sweet, dying, girlfriend to say? Gosh, it's been over thirteen years, now."

Everyone was silent for a few seconds. Pam had tears in her eyes when she said, "Ken, what an amazing person you knew. I'm so happy she was not only your girlfriend but your very dear friend as well. I'm sorry she died."

They all looked at the glowing bonfire and stayed quiet for few minutes. Lindsey looked at the new friends she and Pam had known for only hours. "I want to tell you how much it means to me that you haven't questioned my capabilities because of my small arm and hand."

Paulette answered, "You are wonderful, Lindsey, more than you know, I bet."

"I second that," Jackie said.

"Ok," Ken spoke up, "I'm going to use my amazing mind." He asked Lindsey in Spanish if her grandmother had a pet.

She thought she answered perfectly that her grandmother had a cat that slept on her bed every night. Her Spanish was perfect except she confused goat for cat.

"I'd like to meet your grandmother," Ken kidded. He told her what she'd said.

"You know I've confused goat for cat before. I think it's wanting cat to begin with c in Spanish, too. I think I've got it now."

"There's a few Spanish language translation books at Penny's."

"Thanks, I'll check them out," she answered in perfect Spanish.

They continued speaking Spanish while drinking beer, and laughing at everyone's mistakes until close to midnight. That night they secured their new friendships.

The next morning Jackie rode with Stan in Old Nellie following Ken, who drove the truck. Paulette took care of some things that needed attention at Penny's. Pam and Lindsey slept in until close to noon. By one o'clock everyone was back working on the building they wanted to fix up for the children. They spent three weeks of long days getting the building ready. The little boy Lindsey saw the first day came by everyday to check their progress.

Finally the day came when the volunteers stood in the building they'd transformed. They looked around seeing the clean floor they'd painted royal blue and the very light shade of blue they'd painted the walls. The sunlight shined through the windows Ken and Stan installed. Smiles lit all of their faces as they looked around at their accomplishment. "Today's the day this becomes a school house. So much has been donated and sent here from the states. We've got the tables, chairs, and the blackboard put together. Let's get everything over here," Ken announced holding Pam's hand.

Everyone walked to the storeroom next to Penny's, carefully filled Old Nellie, then carried whatever they could over to the school house. Jackie and Paulette took turns driving Old Nellie. By late afternoon books, paper, and crayons set on two small tables and one larger table. A third small table had toy plates, cups, and a small basket full of plastic fruit, vegetables, and other food. Chairs surrounded each. A blackboard with erasers and chalk filled part of one wall. Colorful posters of the Spanish and English alphabets, the planets, and a food chart decorated the other upper walls along with a world map, a map of Bolivia, and a Bolivian Flag. One easel with a full tablet of paper clipped to the top set in a corner. Paint brushes, jars of paints, and extra supplies were in a cabinet. Shelves were at the bottom half of the walls and were filled with books, puzzles, blocks, trucks, little tea sets, play food, plastic dinosaurs, plastic farm animals, and dolls. And several red, green, and yellow sit-up-ons were stacked near the shelves.

In the middle of the afternoon, Lindsey saw the same little boy standing in the doorway watching them setting up the school room. He had the biggest smile on his face. She also had a huge smile and slowly walked toward him. She spread her small hand making a motion toward the tables inside the room. In perfect Spanish she said, "Come back in the morning. We're ready for you and the children."

His big brown eyes looked up at her, and his smile filled her heart as he shook his head letting her know he understood. Then he was running through the field.

The next morning the three teachers, Jackie, Paulette, and Lindsey, sat in the classroom talking about their plans for teaching the children. They heard some laughing and noticed about six children, including the same little boy, standing at the doorway. Jackie stood up, picked up a book, and motioned for them to come in.

More children came the next day and by the end of the week, the school house was full. They attached a tent, like a car port, to the building to include all of the children who came. They spent hours looking at books written in Spanish, working on puzzles, painting at the easel, playing with toys, and looking at the letters of the Spanish alphabet. A few of the children spoke another language, but all of them spoke with smiles. The first few days, tears appeared on some faces when it was time to leave. Once they understood the school was open everyday, except Sunday, the tears stopped.

Earning the children's trust was top priority. Many of these children had been terribly hurt. Jackie heard that the little boy with the big brown eyes, Tonk, watched while his parents were murdered. Several children lived with the loss of at least one parent or sibling who died from Illness, abuse, neglect, or some hideous action. Older children and sympathetic adults in their villages cared for some abandoned children. While things were calm in this area now; gang wars, thievery, ties to mafia, governing changes, all of these things and the terror they held had been the way of life for many children and adults.

With the help of the Care Core doctors, living conditions improved in near by villages. Stan, Ken, and Pam set up more vaccination sites and weekly health clinics. Together with the three teachers, they taught the children and adults updated hygiene practices and helped them improve their sanitary conditions. They helped plant more gardens and crops figuring out ways to irrigate the fields the villagers claimed. All of the volunteers set up gym classes for the children teaching them exercises, dances, and games. Some the children taught the volunteers dances and games native to Bolivia. They all worked together teaching the children and any interested adults how to read and write in Spanish. Jackie, Paulette, and Lindsey taught the Spanish and English alphabets, spelling, geography, arithmetic, and anything the children or adults wanted to learn. The biggest problem for the volunteers was helping the villagers without giving huge notice to the wrong people.

At the end of most days the three teachers and the three doctors ate dinner together. They played cards at Penny's or sat around the bonfire and talked. Sometimes a few of the adults they helped came by and sat with them. One thing was very apparent. Pam and Ken were falling in love.

1967

Lindsey loved working in Bolivia. Her small arm and hand didn't matter to the children or adults and, now, it didn't matter to her. The days were full. She wrote letters to Bobby and everyone at home about everything she and Pam were doing. She told them all about little Tonk and how amazing he was. The happiness she felt teaching the children and being with Pam and the other volunteers was clear in her letters.

But nothing could alleviate the ache in her heart missing Bobby. When she watched Ken and Pam or Jackie and Stan, the awful emptiness of not having him near broke her heart. She and Paulette talked with each other about missing their husbands. They shared their fear and wonder at what their husbands had gotten into. Bill, Paulette's husband, was indeed on the battlefields doing everything he could to take care of bullet ridden, wounded soldiers. Bobby's change of orders was still pending. The general he met on his flight, General Flagg, was still trying to get it done. He'd gotten two reassuring letters from the general stating that the new orders would happen soon.

The days, weeks, and months that included mid summer days, and most of the autumn season passed by. Many of the children and Tonk learned how to write words and sentences. They learned how to add and subtract. They could point out cities in Bolivia on the map and could locate countries on the world map. Some learned words and could speak sentences in English. They loved their time with the volunteers. Little Tonk loved being around Pam and Ken.

With these weeks and months passing, Lindsey could hardly comprehend all of the time still ahead with her and Bobby being apart. She was sitting in one of the comfortable chairs in the common room reading Bobby's latest letter, again. He wrote that the following week he would be in Saigon meeting with General Flagg. In the next hours, however, he and his squadron were leaving to help and support men pinned down in an area called the Central Highlands. He and his squad, plus several other squads from his platoon, were leaving in just a few hours.

Lindsey thought he seemed very confidant as he explained that he would be leading his squadron and that he and the men understood what they were to accomplish. He wrote her not to worry.

She read the rest of his letter reading that he missed her so much and loved her with all of his heart. Again, in this letter, he wrote how important it was that they were volunteering and doing much to help other people. He ended his letter the same way he always did, I love you always and forever. She carefully folded his letter, placed it in her letterbox, and tied the ribbon around the box securing the life they now shared.

She held her locket in her hand as Stan handed her a box. "Your mother-in-law sure seems like a sweet person sending you things so often. You're lucky!"

"I am," Lindsey said and smiled. She opened the box finding a bowl filled with dried hydrangea's. With a bigger smile, she opened Ann's letter.

1967

Bobby was ready. In ten minutes he and his squadron would be dropped off in a small clearing. They were to position themselves along a planned route behind the Viet Gong. For some of the men, this would be their first combat experience. Bobby patted his pocket to feel his compass.

There had been a lot of nervous talking earlier when their helicopter took off. As the flight continued forward, the men quieted. Lindsey filled Bobby's heart. He and some men placed letters that they quickly finished in a box next to the pilot. Bobby put his letter inside and shook the pilot's hand. He sat back down and a few minutes later the helicopter hovered on the ground in the clearing. "God Speed," the pilot shouted.

As Bobby and his squadron quickly leaped out he thought, *My gun is secure. Find cover.* "Find cover," he hollered over the noise from the helicopters. They quickly ran from the clearing into dense darkness. They could see the clearing they'd just run from and still hear the helicopters' fading sound. The jungle terrain, where they stayed hunched together for many minutes, was dense and dark in some places and dark with filtered light peaking through in other spots. They no longer heard the helicopters. It became strangely silent. No birds, no wind, nothing to hear but each other. They noticed the movement of the other squadrons. Bobby looked at his compass. His hands were shaking. As quietly as possible he said, "Check your compasses. Ready to move?" He motioned to move forward. They picked up and began walking and carefully looking around. *Stay alert, so far so good,* his mind reassured him. It was hot, quiet, eery. They moved ahead.

After some, many hours, they made it to a location near a platoon of American soldiers. At this point the squadrons were to remain scattered. Nightfall was upon them and Bobby was relieved to stop near other soldiers. His squadron and he sat down. They quietly talked and rested for about an hour. It had become very difficult to see anything. Suddenly the man next to Bobby slumped over as the sound of rapid machine gun fire filled the air. Very quickly everything was silent, again.

Bobby wasn't wounded. The man next to him was shot and bleeding. Some distance in front someone was yelling for everyone to stay down. In Bobby's squadron another man said he'd been hit in both legs and that the man next to him was down. "Ok," Bobby said, "I'm good. I'm going to get you to the men ahead of us. Stay still. I'll come back for you." To the others he said, "If you're able, move with me now. Stay low." Several men moved with Bobby as he and another man grabbed the bleeding man next to him and carried him to the platoon ahead. Thankfully, this platoon had a medic. Bobby went back to get the man shot in his legs. "We've got you. There's a medic ahead." The soldier who'd stayed with this man helped Bobby. Returning to get the third man, who had died minutes before, the darkness erupted with more machine guns killing the silence. Several bullets rammed into Bobby's chest. Then all was eerily still and silent once again.

1967

Bobby's mom, Ann, was in her front yard picking some hydrangeas that still held purple color. A few weeks ago she'd been getting ready for Thanksgiving buying everything non perishable she thought Bobby and Lindsey would like. She'd mailed each of them several boxes including one filled with dried purple hydrangeas. In her Thanksgiving letters she wrote that while everyone would not be at the same table this year, they'd all be sharing the same flowers. Now Thanksgiving had already passed, and Ann was amazed at how pretty the few remaining hydrangeas in her yard looked. As she clipped the last flowers she thought, *This will be the last hydrangea arrangement this year.*

The late November day was unusually warm and sunny. Actually the entire fall had been mild. She listened to the faint sound of a lawn mower and looked down the street seeing Art cutting his grass. Enjoying the warm breeze, she looked up at the blue sky. *It's just one of those days that seems dreamlike,* she thought. Then her life unraveled forever.

Slowly, the black car moved so slowly as it turned onto Ann's street. A warm breeze slipped past her face as she turned and noticed the car. Shiny and black it crept down her street, past her house, further to the next block. She stilled as she watched it deliberately creep toward Art's house, then intrude onto his driveway. The faint lawnmower sound quieted as two doors to the black car opened, and she saw the uniforms. Cut hydrangeas slipped out of her hands one by one onto the ground as she began running to Art's and Kate's house. Her legs picked up speed as she watched Art put his hands to his chest and then watched him crumble to the ground. She heard herself screaming, "No, Art!" and couldn't imagine the shrill sound she'd made. She ran to him kneeling on the grass, "No, Art, no." As one young man in uniform tried moving her from him and the other man pounded on Kate's front door, she saw the telegram on the freshly cut grass. Sobbing, she put her head on Art's chest, "No, no, no, no."

Kate ran outside to Art. Sammy ran to the phone and called for an ambulance, then called the rectory and Father Tom. She grabbed some afghan blankets and ran outside. She covered Art's legs, and Kate pulled it up to his shoulders. Ann had moved back a little but remained on the ground. Sammy put the other afghan across Ann's shoulders as Brice ran to the yard, lifted Ann to her feet, and held her as she continued to cry.

Kate stayed on the ground beside Art telling him, "Help is on the way. Hold on, Art". Her face was covered with tears. She kept rubbing his arm, crying, repeating, "I can hear the ambulance. They're coming, honey. Stay with us. We love you. I love you."

Sammy was crying. She held Ann tight, now, as Brice was kneeling beside Kate trying to help her. Holding on to Sammy, Ann said, "Just five minutes ago everything was fine. Please go back. Take us back. Take us back five minutes and let us be." She couldn't believe how quickly life had changed. She was sure Art was gone, and so was her precious son. Her legs began to buckle. Sammy tried to keep Ann from falling as Father Tom ran to them and kept them both from hitting the ground.

The two very young men in uniform were standing straight and still. They looked pale as one, determined to carry out their responsibility, began, "We regret,"

Ann said in a forceful voice, "He's my son. Please look at ME."

Both turned to look only at her. The young soldier started over changing the words, "It is with huge regret," His voice broke, and he swallowed, "we must inform you of the death of your dear son, Robert-"

Ann leaned into the side of Father Tom, and she felt his arm around her as he walked her to Kate's front step and sat down with her. Brice helped Kate stand up as the ambulance attendants began working on Art. Sammy walked to Kate's other side and held her hand as they both cried watching Art.

Bobby died instantly. He remembered non of it. It was just over. For moments or hours, he didn't know, everything around him was misty and very quiet. It could have been quickly, though, that the most wonderful warmth and brightening began surrounding and guiding him. He heard laughing, and he felt amazingly peaceful and curious. And, he felt something else that he'd known before but never at this devotion, or completeness. It was love, blissful love coming at him and through him from every direction.

Suddenly everything was bright and pristine. Seemingly a distance away, but then with no distance at all, two people were walking toward him. Although, maybe not people because he could see passed them, no, kind of through them. He wasn't a bit afraid. "Oh my God," Bobby cried in wonder.

Bobby could hear the answer, "Yes," coming from every direction as the two people, he decided they were people, were there with him.

"Oh my God!"

Again he heard, "Yes," gently echoing.

"Joan, Jack," he whispered, looking at them. "You're back."

"You're with us, now, Bobby," Joan reached for his hand and then hugged him.

"Where are we? What's this called? This wonderful happiness, love, and warmth, it feels so amazing. I've never felt anything like this." He looked at them. "Wow, you look great, just the same, kind of. Sammy will be so happy being all together, again. Wait until Lindsey knows, too. God, this is amazing."

And instantly the word, "Yes," filled in all around them. Bobby looked all around.

"You'll get used to that." Jack hugged him.

"Jack, Sammy's doing great. She and Jimmy are engaged. Jimmy loves her so much. Lindsey and I are married, now. And, Karen is happy and married, too. I have to see Lindsey and tell her about this. She'll be so happy."

"Lindsey has to stay with Kate and with our Samantha. She won't be with us, now, but you're coming with us." Resolutely he answered, "No, not without Lindsey. Come on, you must want to see Sammy. Let's go find them."

Joan took hold of his hand, "You must come with us, now, dear Bobby. We've come for you. We must go, now, right now."

"You mean, I'm, wait." He looked around. "I can't go with you, not without Lindsey. I can't leave her so soon. I have to see her. I can't just leave her, Joan. I promised her."

She and Jack stood smiling at him. Bobby felt such tranquility and warmth standing with them, but his mind filled with thoughts of Lindsey. "I have to remind Lindsey that she's not alone. Linds and I are 'always and forever.' That's right, isn't it? You know and understand. Our love is always and forever. I just can't go with you without making sure she knows. I need to make certain she knows and remembers."

Joan smiled. "Bobby, we will be meeting someone else so dear to us very soon. We all must be on our way, right now."

"I can't leave, Joan. I have to see my Lindsey just for a while. I have to remind her." Bobby tried to convince them. Without knowing how, he moved away with them.

Kate cried and cried. She whispered, "They're gone. Both are gone. This can't be happening." She kept repeating, "They're gone." She was kneeling on the pew staring at the Cross on the small altar in the hospital chapel. They'd arrived at Bay View Hospital just an hour ago. Twenty minutes after arriving in the emergency room, Art was pronounced dead. Ann Williams was admitted for the night. Bobby's dad, John, was with her, and his sister and brother-in-law were on their way from Columbus.

Father Tom prayed while kneeling beside Kate. He listened to her crying and whispering for a while. He said, "Now, listen to me, Kate. God is showing both, Bobby and Art, the glory of Heaven right now. Our hearts are breaking, but their hearts are full of spectacular warmth and glory that we can't imagine. Art and Bobby are together in Heaven, I know they are. The love they're experiencing is beyond our recognition. They have completed their journey. They are home with God."

"Thank you, Tom, thank you." She was quiet for minutes. "I can't imagine telling Lindsey." She put her head down and cried. "We have to get Lindsey home. Oh God, her Bobby and her daddy, both, how will we ever be able to tell her? I don't think she'll be able to handle losing them both."

Father Tom squeezed her hand and said, "We have to take care of you. Ann is being cared for. Bobby's dad is here and Bobby's sister is on the way. I'm going to stay with them for a while. Brice and Frank will take you to Grand's. You stay with her tonight. Samantha is there. We'll get Lindsey home. My dad will help us. I'll call him as soon as I can join you at Grand's house. Would you like to stay here until you see John and Bobby's sister?"

"Yes, and then I'll go with Brice and Frank. Sammy's so strong. She helped Ann and me. Sammy's lost her dad, again, and her dear friend. Oh God, Bobby is so young. I can't believe he's gone. He had so many plans, he and Linds. And Art's gone, too. I just walked passed the front window, and he was cutting the grass. Oh God, please, no." Tears covered her face.

Art couldn't believe what was happening. He noticed the black car just before it turned onto his driveway. He looked and thought, *God, no, don't do this. Please, don't do this.* The car stopped and two shiny doors resolutely opened. Two young men in uniform stepped out. *They're so young.* He saw the telegram in one hand. Intense pain filled his chest. His mind turned to the pain. He knew and whispered, "Dear God, forgive me my sins," and crumbled to the ground.

Everything was dark. He heard Ann Williams crying. And Kate, "Help is on the way. Hold on, Art. I can hear the ambulance. They're coming, honey. Stay with us. We love you. I love you."

The excruciating pain in Art's chest vanished. He felt warmth from the purest light surrounding him from every angle, and in this light Art saw him. He watched him moving near, then stopping right beside him. "Bobby, thank God you're all right!"

Both of them heard, "You're welcome," gently answering around them or inside them somehow.

"Did you hear that?" He felt so happy and excited, he didn't give Bobby the chance to answer. "You look fantastic! Army life is agreeing with you. It's just amazing here. I'll find Kate and Sammy. They'll be beyond happy that you're back." He looked around. "Joan, how did you get here? And Jack, oh my God, this is wonderful!"

Art and Bobby heard, "Yes, it is!" sounding everywhere as Joan hugged him.

"Wait, you mean, I think I understand. I'm, Bobby and I are, we're with you? We're dea,"

Radiant light surrounded them. Joan interjected, "Alive. We're here to take you and Bobby the rest of the way Home."

Art had never before felt such peace and complete devotion. He freely let go of everything and moved along with Joan and Jack.

Bobby used all of the substance left within him. "I have to see my Lindsey. I need to stay with her for just awhile. I can't just leave her without making sure she knows that she and I are always and forever. I can't let Lindsey stay sad for too long. I have to be with her, help her. Joan, please find me after Lindsey knows. Please."

"I don't know, Bobby. You're found, now." She smiled and blew him a kiss.

Instantly, he was alone.

Samantha was back in a hospital room after being transferred out of Intensive Care. Her temperature was finally normal and so far staying normal. The antibiotics worked. Dr. Jameson was shining a small light into her eyes as he lifted each eyelid. Jim and Father Tom were standing near the end of her bed.

Tom talked to her while she was examined. "Well, I can tell you, young lady, we're never going to get out of this hospital if you keep this up. We want you to wake up. You can do it. You just have to want to be with us. Open your eyes."

Jim spoke to her, "You have a beautiful home in Portland. I didn't see Rob or your daughter. Dr. Jameson, here, would like to hear from either one of them. I wish we could find your cell phone with their numbers. I looked for a personal phone book while at your house. I didn't find one. Sammy, are you and Rob separated, maybe?" Then in a stern tone, "You need to open your eyes and face it."

Dr. Jameson grimaced at Jim's last remark. "Maybe talk to her about less stressful things," he said and added, "When the nurse arrives, I'll finish examining her. I think she's out of the woods, now." The nurse walked in. The doctor looked at Jim, "Remember, no stress."

Father Tom gave Jim's shoulder a squeeze. "I agree, Jim, I think she's out of the forest. She'll wake soon." With a slight smile, he said, "Let's go get a coke."

Jim looked at him. "Out of the forest? Unbelievable! A coke sounds good."

About twenty-five minutes later, Jim returned to Samantha's room alone. Tom told him he'd be back a little after nine o'clock. Looking around the room and seeing the bags with the radio, pictures, and things, he began taking them out. He plugged in the radio, and it was still set at the oldie's station. Turning it on, he heard "Moon River."

Pulling out the pictures, he held one in his hand, "Gosh Sammy, I bet I'm looking at the last picture taken with Bobby and us. My God, look at him so young and so happy. He didn't have a clue how little time he had left. His and Art's funeral and Liz's have been the saddest for me. Remember how long it took Lindsey to leave the house? Seems like another lifetime now. We'd been so young and happy before everything happened. Sammy, life is what we make it. Happiness is always an option."

He set the picture down and placed others on the window sill. He covered her with one of the afghans, sat down, and gently rubbed her arm. "I didn't mean to startle you before. You still fill a place in my heart, Sammy," he whispered.

Tom walked into her room around ten o'clock. He smiled hearing the radio and noticing Jim had taken pictures and things out of the bags. "Nice job decorating the room," he whispered seeing Jim was also sleeping.

1967

Lindsey felt like screaming. Ken and Pam drove her to the airstrip in Old Nellie. "Shit," Lindsey said as she worked her way out of the jeep. She brushed the dust off her skirt and blouse, then looked up at her friends. "I'm sorry. It doesn't matter about the dust. Old Nellie's great, we'd be in deep shit without her, right?" A small smile crossed her face.

"Lindsey, it's ok, we understand," Pam answered.

"It's just that I don't know what's going on with my dad. I've been so worried since Father Tom called and left the message. Thank you, again Ken, for calling him back and helping me with everything. I didn't even know my dad had heart trouble. I never remember my dad being sick. I'm so worried." She walked with Pam and Ken over to the side of the airstrip to wait for the private jet Father Tom's dad had arranged. "I keep thinking, though, to need to get me home so fast," tears filled her eyes. She held her locket and gently smoothed it with her fingers. "You know, the funny part is, I just can't get Bobby out of my thoughts. Here my dad is sick, and I can't stop thinking about Bobby."

Pam turned away for a second and faked coughing. She knew the truth and knew she couldn't hold her tears back much longer. "Excuse me, that dust got to me, too." She pretended to clear her throat.

"I'm so glad you mentioned Bobby. Here, I have a letter. Stan picked it up earlier this morning." Getting it out of his pocket, Ken gave it to her.

"Thanks." Her face brightened a bit as she put it in her purse.

They heard the Caravelle jet approaching. "Wow, look at that!" They watched it land and come to a stop.

An unfamiliar airstrip mechanic / baggage handler / ticket agent rolled steps to the jet door as it opened and two stewards headed down. "Hi, I'm Steve and this is Jerry." Everyone smiled and exchanged names.

Steve shook hands with Lindsey and said, "If you're all set, let's get you on board and comfortable. We'll refuel, then be on our way." They noticed a fuel truck ready and waiting.

"Thank you. That sounds good." Lindsey turned to Pam and hugged her. "Love you, Pam. Take care of Tonk and the kids. I'll be back as soon as my dad is doing better." She hugged Ken, then Steve ushered her up the steps into the jet.

Ken and Jerry talked for a few minutes. Jerry said, "We'll be back for you when the decisions for the funerals are made. Call this number in forty-eight hours, the day after tomorrow, Ken. How many will be going to the funerals?"

"All of us, there will be five going. Thank you for making these arrangements."

"Mr. Brown, our boss, is a great man. He loves his son, Father Tom, and Father Tom loves Lindsey's family. So, we're here to help in any way we can. Lindsey will need her friends." Jerry asked another question, "She doesn't know anything more than her dad is in the hospital, right?"

"That's all she knows." Ken handed her suitcase to Jerry.

"We'll take special care of her. This will be her last chance to rest for a while, poor angel. We'll make her as comfortable as possible."

Jerry shook Ken's hand and said he'd see him in a few days. The refueling finished. Ken and Pam stood, waving, watching the jet take off. Then Pam turned into his arms and cried.

"I know, honey. I know."

"Her heart will break when she finds out. Ken, I need to go inside and call my parents. They'll want to attend the funerals. They love Lindsey."

Steve directed Lindsey into the lounge area of the jet where she sat down in the most comfortable chair. He left for a minute and returned with a tray holding hot tea, cream, sugar, and some lemon. "Thought this might be just the thing! Make yourself comfortable, Lindsey. We want you to have a relaxing flight. I'll let you get settled, and I'll be back after we're in the air. Press this button if you need anything in the meantime. It's a good idea to buckle your seat belt especially on take off and landing.

Would you like milk in your tea? Hold your cup during take off."

"How did you know that a cup of tea would be perfect. Thank you, Steve. Just this lemon for my tea, and I'll bucket up."

She looked out the window and saw Ken and Jerry talking. A few minutes later, she waved at Pam and Ken, who were waving to her as the jet picked up speed and took off.

Jerry checked on Lindsey when the jet leveled off. "How are you doing?"

"Fine, thanks," Lindsey answered.

"We'll be making two refueling stops, and we'll remain on board. Would you like to see the rest of the jet? Mr. Brown had it customized."

"I'd love to."

He showed her that the lounge she was in had a sleeping area and a bathroom with a shower. "Just pull this curtain closed if you want to sleep in one of the chairs. They recline, too. There's a movie screen I can pull down if you want to watch a movie in here. Then he walked her into a library/office complete with a bar and lounge sitting area. She noticed another movie screen, too. Next they walked to a galley kitchen. "We have a nice dinner planned for you whenever you're hungry. There's one more bathroom, and that's it. I'll take you back to the lounge."

"This jet is amazing," Lindsey said and smiled as she sat back down. "Thank you so much for everything you're doing. The tea was perfect, too."

"I see you have a letter to read. I'll bring you a hot pot of tea. I'll be right back." A minute later he came back with a pot of hot tea, sliced lemons, and a plate of warm pastries.

Lindsey got comfortable in the chair and opened the envelope she'd put on the table. She unfolded her letter and began reading.

Hi Sweetheart,

My squadron and others are on a mission to help a platoon on the ground. They've been pinned down for

355

days and are in desperate need of back up and supplies. We're on our way to help them right now.

Linds, I miss you more than I can say. You're in my mind and heart always. I know that what you and I are doing is worth it, but right now I would give anything to hold you and be with you. I miss your beautiful smile. I love you more each day. Our life together will be so wonderful, honey. I can't wait to start our family. Don't you ever worry about our babies, Lindsey. They'll be beautiful.

I heard from General Flagg. He has made arrangements for me to meet him in Saigon on Tuesday. I'll let you know what he says. He wants your Care Core address, so I'll give him it then. We're going to have a wonderful life. I have to go, now.

I love you always and forever,

Bobby

She folded his letter, put it back in the envelope, and in her purse. She closed her eyes as he filled her thoughts, and she smiled. She could feel herself wrapped in his arms.

1967

Jerry and Steve took great care of Lindsey, making sure she ate some delicious food and had opportunity to sleep during her flight. When they landed at Cleveland Burke Lakefront Airport, Steve walked her down the steps to Father Tom and Jimmy. Jerry followed with her suitcase. They shook hands with Tom, then quickly stepped back up the steps into the jet.

As soon as Lindsey saw Father Tom and Jimmy, tears filled her eyes. She hugged Jimmy, and he held her tight, gently rubbing her back. Father Tom hugged her and said, "Lindsey, honey, everything will be ok."

She looked over at Jimmy and then back at Father Tom. "Is my dad gone?"

His eyes filled, "Yes, Lindsey." He put his arms back around her as she hugged him and cried. Jimmy stood trying to hold back his tears and rubbed her shoulder. Feeling her trembling as she cried, Tom silently prayed, *Please, sweet Lord, help me find a way to tell her the rest.* Out loud he said, "My car is right over there. It's freezing here near the lake. Let's get you home. Everyone is with your mom."

There wasn't much traffic. They drove away from the airport on Memorial Shoreway toward the Main Avenue Bridge. Lindsey sat silently looking outside. Seeing Cleveland Municipal Stadium, she remembered her dad taking her to Indians games. She smiled a second remembering the times her dad, Jack, Father Tom, Brice, and Frank took all of the kids to some games, recalling how they argued over who was the best Indian's pitcher.

Tom drove along the Shoreway to Clifton Boulevard, and once in Lakewood he quickly passed through the series of green lights he was catching. Windshield wipers made the only sound keeping a continuous rhythm in the silence. She looked out at the houses, many with Christmas lights, watching snow flakes falling, quietly wishing someone could wake her from this terrible dream. Finally she spoke, "What happened? Had my dad been feeling sick for a while? Was he in the hospital when he died?Bobby's been on my mind so much, I wasn't worried about anyone else."

357

Father Tom asked, "Honey, would it be ok if we stop at the Chapel for a few minutes?"

She got a Kleenex from her purse and wiped her eyes. "I'd like that. My dad loves the Chapel. So does Bobby." She thought, *My dad loved the chapel.* Tears filled her eyes again.

1967

When they reached the small stone chapel and got out of the car, Jimmy hugged Lindsey and said, "I'll walk to Kate's from here and let everyone know you're home."

Father Tom and Lindsey stepped through the unlocked arched doors. He flipped the switch on softly lighting the chapel altar. They walked to the first pew, blessed themselves, and knelt down together. "This is such a sacred place. You can absolutely feel God's presence. You and Karen had beautiful weddings here."

In a soft voice she answered, "I feel Bobby's presence. I've felt him with me these past days so much. I can just feel his arms around me. Just a while ago in the plane, I read his recent letter, and I could just feel him with me. We've always had such a connection, but these last few days, it's been different." She looked at the crucifix of Jesus as she spoke.

He blessed himself, again. "You know your dad loved Bobby. He thought of him as," Tom's voice broke. A few seconds passed, "as his son, too."

She put her head down on the rail in front of her. Her locket touched the metal railing, and it softly chimed. She gently held it and slowly moved her fingers across it. "They're both gone," she whispered, "aren't they? Dear God, you have them both." She put her head back on the railing and cried.

"Yes, He has them both." Tom put his face in his hands and kneeling by her side, he cried, too.

After a while he got up and went into the sacristy. A few minutes later he came back with a glass of water and tissues for Lindsey. She'd stopped crying and was looking up at the crucifix. She whispered, "How can I breathe? How can I live without him? How can I lose my dad without having Bobby help me through it?" She looked at Jesus on the cross, "I trust you. I need you. Please help me. I love you."

"He hears you, honey," Father Tom assured her. "God is with you. He will help you, Kate, Bobby's mom, dad, all of us. You are precious to God that you trust Him, especially now, without question." Tom silently prayed his own prayer for Lindsey. He blessed himself and touched her arm. "Kate will be worried. We should go, now." He helped her up. They walked hand in hand to his car.

She looked out of the car window at everything so familiar on her street in Bay Village. *How can everything look the same when nothing is,* she wondered as they got out of the car. Her house was unusually quiet when they opened the front door. Bobby's mom, Ann, was the first one to hold her in her arms. "Oh, Lindsey, I'm so sorry. We love you, honey."

"I love you and John, too." She looked at Ann, "How are we going to live, now? I can't imagine anything without Bobby." Lindsey broke down in Ann's arms.

Bobby's mom suddenly realized that she was emotionally stronger than she'd ever imagined. She looked at Kate, who had tears streaming down her cheeks, sitting with Karen on one side and Sammy on her other. Ann knew Lindsey needed her. She held her tight and whispered, "Honey, we're going to be very strong and brave just as Bobby would want. We will figure life out, Lindsey. We will do everything to help you through this. Time, it will take time."

"Thank you. I love you. I know your heart is broken. Bobby loved you so much," She began crying again.

Grand, Brice, Frank, and Phillip stood near by. Ann gently said, "Everyone wants to see you."

Frank hugged Lindsey. He rubbed her back and let go of her. Then Brice, with huge tears falling, hugged her tight. Neither said one word. Grand's arms gently surrounded her. "My dear one, my dear girl, I'm so sorry. We love you." Then Phillip held her until her crying eased.

Lindsey and Bobby's dad hugged. He didn't, couldn't, speak. She could feel him shaking, and she whispered, "He thought you were the best dad ever." John gently kissed her cheek and let her go.

Finally Lindsey's and Kate's eyes locked. She knelt down and whispered, "Mom, how can this be true? My sweet Dad, I love him so much. I can't believe he's not going to walk in here any minute. We need him so much."

"Your dad loves you, and he's so proud of you. You, Sammy, and Karen made his life perfect. He loves Bobby as his son. They are together, Linds. I know they're together." Tears streamed down Kate's face. "I love you, honey."

Karen and Sammy wiped away tears, got up and went into the kitchen. Grand sat down and Kate slid over making room for Lindsey to sit between them. Linds sat, held her mom's hand, and lay her head on Grand's shoulder. Tears poured down their cheeks as they sat snuggled together.

A while later she kissed her mom, then kissed Grand. She stood up and hugged Bobby's sister and mom, again. Then she went into the kitchen to find Sammy and Karen.

They were standing near the sink staring out the window. Tears were flooding their eyes as they turned around. The three sisters reached out to one and other and held each other close as Lindsey finally let lose the pain and hurt she'd been holding inside. Huge gasps of crying filled the kitchen. They held each other tight and let their sadness echo through the house as they cried and cried.

Everyone in the living room could hear them. No one moved. "Our three, dear, precious daughters," Kate whispered to Grand. Ann and Bobby's sister held hands with tears streaming down their cheeks. John, Jimmy, Father Tom, Brice, Phillip, and Frank quietly stayed still. Each one of them listening to Lindsey, Sammy, and Karen releasing some grief that no one in Kate's house would ever fully rid.

1967

Both wakes took place a week later. They were
celebrated together, their coffins side by side at the funeral
home in Westlake. Acquaintances, friends, and family
members streamed, non stop, into the funeral home for
two days. Sammy and Karen met Lindsey's new friends
from Bolivia. They and Pam stayed near and helped
everyone. Many sounds of grief filled the atmosphere, but
blessed laughter also found it's way giving relief to broken
hearts.

Hubert and Roslyn came with Michael. They stayed at
Sammy's house. Hubert had dinners from restaurants
delivered to Kate's, and to Bobby's parents' houses many
nights. They also paid for the Holsten Inn rooms where
Lindsey's friends from Care Core stayed. Rosalyn helped
Grand and Kate with anything they needed each day.
Everyone felt a little respite spending time together.
Michael was wise for his age, fun, and engaging. His
sweet kindness and innocent happiness gave grieving
hearts pause and brought light to possibilities waiting
ahead.

After two days at the funeral home, St. Joseph Church
had never been so full. Flowers filled the altar and
candles softly danced as Jimmy, Phillip, two friends from
college, and two men in uniform walked Bobby's casket up
the aisle. Lindsey walked behind Bobby's casket with Ann,
John, Bobby's sister and family, then other family
members, and Father Tom. Once his casket was placed
near the altar, Lindsey turned to watch her dad's casket
while keeping her small hand on Bobby's. Jimmy, Phillip,
the pallbearers, and Father Tom walked back down the
aisle to Art's casket while Ann, John, and family went to
their front row pews and remained standing. Art's casket
was brought up the aisle with Kate, Sammy, Karen, Grand,
Brice, Frank, Aunt Cathy, her family, and Father Tom
walking behind. When his casket was placed next to
Bobby's, Jimmy helped Lindsey and Kate to their seats
while Phillip helped Karen and Sammy. "In the name of
the Father, and of the Son, and of the Holy Ghost, Amen,"
with those words that Art and Bobby had repeated
thousands of times, Father Tom began their funeral Mass.

362

At one o'clock everyone went to the Holsten Inn. Friends and family walked up the wide steps to the veranda seeing trees decorated for Christmas. Lindsey and Kate stepped past them and Kate smiled, just a little smile, "Lindsey, life around us is going to keep it's pace. Life isn't going to wait for us, honey."

Although the beautiful lobby was lavishly decorated for Christmas, Bette Lotis made sure the dining room held respectful grace. The Inn's owner had placed Bette in charge of many aspects concerning the inn, now. With Pam, Paulette, Jackie, Ken, and Stan staying at the Holsten, Bette accepted all of the help they offered. Following her lead, they had the dining room looking perfect. One large wreath hung over the six foot long fireplace. Several lit candles were on the mantle, and a generous fire warmed the room. Two white roses in crystal vases with four small red candles on white table cloths, gave every dining table life and light. The windows filling the back wall showed off a peaceful, light blue Lake Erie, an unusual lake site this time of year.

Ann, John, Bobby's sister, Kate, Lindsey, and Sammy did their best to walk around and talk with all of their friends and family. Karen and Phillip also took time to greet everyone. While they spent the afternoon at the Holsten Inn, precious Bobby and Art were on their way to Arlington National Cemetery.

Only immediate family members went to the military service two days later. Father Tom's dad had taken care of the arrangements. At this beautiful, serene, majestic cemetery; Bobby and Art were laid to rest side by side. Kate received one folded American flag and, at Lindsey's request, Ann and John received Bobby's. Taps played, and with tear streaked, proud faces they held those flags.

Getting close to two months since Art's and Bobby's funeral, Lindsey was still home. She wouldn't leave her room let alone leave the house to go anywhere. She kept her bedroom curtains closed all day and mostly slept. Care Core had sent two letters asking her to let them know when she'd be returning to Bolivia. Pam had called several times asking how she was doing.

The day finally came when I lost my temper with her. I began nicely, "Lindsey, you have got to eat more." I sat on her bed. "We're so worried about you. This has got to stop. All you're doing is sleeping." I rubbed her back while I spoke, but she didn't move or say one word. I tried a new approach, "Lindsey, aren't you worried about that little boy you wrote me about? You know, Tonk, the little boy with the big brown eyes. I bet he misses you."

She finally rolled over and gave me the same answer she'd been giving me for weeks, "Sammy, please go away. I need you to stop talking. I want to be alone. I need more time." Then, this time, she yelled, "Just get out of my room and leave me alone!"

Her yelling really got to me. "Fine," I yelled back. I slammed her door shut as I left and stormed into the kitchen to find Kate, Grand, and Karen.

1968

Lindsey jumped when the door slammed. She thought to herself, *Good, she's gone. How can I ever explain what's happening in here? Everyone would freak out. Even I thought I'd gone crazy that first time I saw Bobby, here, in my room, sitting on my pink chair.* A smile etched her face.

She looked at her chair. It was empty, and she knew it would be. At this point she knew when he was in her room. *He's probably not very happy with me yelling at Sammy,* she thought.

She remembered the first time all of this began. It happened a few days after the funeral. She'd been sleeping when she distinctly heard Bobby's voice. She abruptly woke up and looked around her room. Obviously, he wasn't in her room. She put her head back down on her pillow and cried. Her mind was consumed with him and the sound of his voice. Crying, she thought, *'Bobby, I need you.'*

She heard, very clearly, 'Lindsey, it's me.'

She sat up so quickly and said his name out loud, "Bobby?" Hearing no response, she realized she probably had fallen asleep and dreamed it. She put her head down and cried again, but this time she cried about her dad and how much she missed him. She cried that her mom was being so strong and that Sammy was being strong, and she wasn't. He slipped back into her thoughts. *'Bobby, I miss you so much. I need you. I just need you with me.'*

This time, absolutely, she heard, 'I miss you, too.'

She didn't move. She opened her eyes and didn't speak out loud. She kept her sentences in her mind, in her thoughts, *'Bobby, is that you?'*

'I'm not sure what's happening. It's me.'

'I hear you in my mind. I think.'

"My God, Thank you," Bobby whispered, and she didn't hear that.

'Honey, I've been hearing you when you think about me. I've been with you many times these past weeks. I wanted you to know I've been here, but never thought you could. I can hear your sweet voice. Lindsey, I'm here. I love you.'

'I love you! I hear you. I really do! It's your voice for me, too. I mean, I'm thinking about you all of the time, but now, I think, I can hear you talking in my mind.' She sat up, then was worried she shouldn't have moved. *'Bobby,'* she looked around, *'please, still be here.'*

'I'm here, honey.'

She thought, *'I can move around.'*

'Yes, I think you can.' He was full of joy having these moments with her.

'I can tell you're smiling. Please don't leave me.'

'I don't know what this is. I think God's answering my prayer. I can't control this. I mean, I leave sometimes.'

'Stay with me just like this.' Lindsey's mind didn't hear Bobby respond. *'Bobby, stay with me.'* Her mind was silent.

She sank back down on her bed as her bedroom door finished opening all of the way. Kate walked in carrying a tray holding toast and juice. "Lindsey, I want you to eat this, and later I want you to come sit in the living room. It's been days, honey."

And right then she understood! No one else could be in her room. She'd felt so angry that her mom walked in. "I need more time. Please, Mom, just leave me alone. I need more time."

Later that morning when she woke up, she was facing her pink chair. Bobby was sitting in her chair watching her. She could see him! Immediately she stood up to go to him. He vanished. She looked all around her room. *'Come back.'* She heard nothing. She flopped back in bed sobbing while thinking, *'Come back, stay with me.'*

Lindsey didn't hear Bobby in her mind, let alone see him, until two days later. That morning she woke up facing the pink chair. When her eyes opened, he was back sitting in that chair. She remained very still watching him smiling at her. *'It really is you, Bobby. I'm really seeing you. My eyes are open, and I'm not dreaming.'* She continued thinking, *'I won't move.'*

'Good idea,' he laughed.

'Do you think this is funny?'

'No, Linds, I think this is wonderful. We've been given this amazing gift. I think you can move around, but I don't think we can touch each other.'

366

'I figured that out!'

'Look who's being funny! It's wonderful to hear you kidding with me.'

Now after yelling at Sammy to get out of the bedroom, she remembered these first times hearing and seeing Bobby. She knew she'd been awful to Sam, but she couldn't lose this time with him.

She closed her eyes. *'Bobby, please, come back.'*

'I'm here, Lindsey.'

She looked at the chair and saw him. *'Stay with me,'* she thought.

'As long as I can. I love you, always and forever.'

She saw and talked with Bobby, in her thoughts, many times each day, and the days were approaching almost two months. They could reminisce things that they'd done together. She could tell him about Bolivia, her friends, and the children. She could tell him how much she missed her dad. She could tell Bobby that she would love him always and forever. This happened only through her thoughts. If she spoke out loud, he disappeared.

Bobby could listen and encourage her. He could reminisce with Lindsey their time together. As often as he wanted he could tell her that she must keep living her life and tell her that her future will be amazing. Whenever he wanted he could tell her that he will always and forever love her, that their love was endless.

He could not, however, tell her what had happened to him. He couldn't tell her where he went when he wasn't with her. He couldn't tell her who he'd seen and been with, or what death was like, or how he died. He had no recollection of any of these things when he was with Lindsey. And while he could clearly see everything in Lindsey's future, Bobby could not tell her. He simply could not.

367

I was so angry with Lindsey as I slammed her bedroom door shut. Kate, Grand, and Karen were sitting in the kitchen having a cup of hot tea when I stormed in. "That's it! We've got to do something! Lindsey can't go on like this. I think we've got to take Pam up on her offer to come back and help us."

"You're right, Sammy," Kate answered sounding very tired. "Everything is arranged. I told Father Tom I was going to buy a ticket for her to come back. Tom wouldn't hear it. He called his dad right here in the kitchen. His wonderful dad is sending his private jet back to Bolivia, and Pam will be here the day after tomorrow. I can take care of getting her and Lindsey back to Bolivia. Although, Mr. Brown said we'd discuss that when the time was right. I just don't know what else to do."

"Kate, that's wonderful," I got up and hugged her. "I love you."

"This behavior is so unlike Linds," Grand said. "I, also, think this has gone on too long. She's getting worse. Ann's very worried."

Karen stood up and said, "No, not again, I'm feeling sick." She quickly got to the bathroom.

Kate and Grand looked at one and other. Kate smiled and said, "I think, maybe, wonderful times are ahead."

I looked at them and asked, "Do you really think so?"

Grand ignored me and answered, "You know, with Pam coming in a few days, I think Karen could go home. As much as she wants to help Lindsey, she needs to go home to Columbus and stay put. No more driving back and forth for a while."

Karen came back into the kitchen, sat down, and said, "Kate, after Pam arrives, I think I'll drive home. I wouldn't ever leave Linds, but with the three of you and Pam, I think it will be all right."

"Honey, I bet your dad will drive you home," Grand answered.

Not figuring out what was happening with Karen, I said, "If anyone can help Lindsey, it'll be Pam. She won't let her get away with hiding in her bedroom. Even Father Tom can't be objective. Pam will get her out of her room."

No, this isn't right. My sweet daughter, my KJ, got me out of my room. She said, "Mom, this has gone on long enough. Dad's not coming back to you. Now, get out of bed and get dressed right now." Then she yelled, "Get your ass out of bed," and pulled my bedroom curtains and windows open.

I asked, "Young lady, what did you say to me?"

She determinedly glared at me and repeated, "Dad is not coming back to you."

"No, no, not that part, the other part," I said and smiled slightly.

"You mean, 'Get your ass out of bed?"

"Yep, that's the part!" And for a second looking at my KJ, I'd remembered Pam had yelled those very same words at Lindsey.

Then my KJ and I laughed as I sat up in bed, put my feet into my slippers, and for the first time in days put my arms out to hug my daughter.

KJ, I wish I could hug you right now.

Who's holding my hand? Jim? Yes, it's Jimmy. He's with me. Where's Father Tom? Ok, Father Tom, you're here. I hear you, now.

I remember. It was Lindsey who wouldn't leave her room, either, and Kate asked Pam to come back.

I hadn't stepped back into Lindsey's room since I'd slammed her door shut. Kate and Grand continued to take meals to her room. Karen looked in on her. I helped make food for her tray, but I stayed out of her room.

Blessings returned to us after Pam arrived. In just a few hours she got Lindsey out of bed. And a few days later, Karen and Phillip called to tell us Karen was expecting. For the first time since Bobby and Art died, joyful smiles appeared on our faces and happiness began seeping back into our hearts.

Father Tom walked in Samantha's hospital room hearing Johnny Mathis singing, "All the Time" and finding Jim sitting in the chair while holding Samantha's hand. He smiled seeing Jim's eyes were closed. "Nice job decorating the room," he whispered.

"That must be you," Jim opened his eyes and said. "I almost fell asleep."

"I can almost see that. I also see that you unpacked the pictures and things. Enjoying the radio?"

"As a matter of fact, I am." His phone buzzed, and he picked it up to look at the number. "I don't recognize this number. I'm going to the lobby."

"Hello, please hold on just a minute," he answered his phone as he walked toward the hallway. He heard an old voice answer that she would. At the same time he heard Samantha laugh and turned back to look at her.

Tom said, "Go to the floor lobby. Answer your phone call. I'm here."

He left and Father patted Sam's hand, "That's a girl, Sammy, laughing is always a good thing. We're right here waiting for you. Open those eyes. Come on, you need to get out of this bed."

With a slight smile on her face, her eyes stayed closed.

1968

Pam arrived in Cleveland on the private jet early in the morning. A short while after Jimmy picked her up at the airport, she and Kate were hugging each other and then sitting down in the kitchen. She listened while Kate tried to explain Lindsey's behavior. Then Sammy came in and a bit later she helped Pam carry her things to their room.

Pam took a nice bath, her first one in months. As she sat in the warm water she thought, *I could sit in this tub all day.* She soaked a little longer. *Ok, this has been heaven, but I need to find out what's going on here. I'll grab some aspirin to get rid of this headache.* She got out of the tub, got dressed, and forgot about the aspirin.

Walking into the living room she saw Grand and Karen sitting on the sofa and Sam sitting in a chair. Grand and Karen stood up to hug her. When they sat down Sammy didn't hesitate, "We've tried everything, Pam. She won't come out of her room. I went ape the other day and slammed her door shut."

They all could hear Kate trying to coax Lindsey out. They listened for over ten minutes. "Just come into the living room and say hi to Pam. Please, honey, come out for a few minutes. Lindsey, I'm worried about," Kate's voice broke. She hesitated some seconds, "I'm so worried about you, honey. If you come out, I'll"

"That's it!" Pam stood up. Her headache throbbed. She looked at Sammy, Karen, and Grand, "Sounds like 'little missy,' in there has been running this show long enough! I understand that Lindsey is devastated, but Kate's heart is broken, too. And Sammy, you lost a father, again, and a dear friend. Grand and Karen, you love everyone in this house. All of you have broken hearts, too. I can't listen to one more second of this." Pam walked straight into Lindsey's bedroom, and everyone followed. She saw Lindsey in bed with her back to Kate. Kate moved out of her way as Pam went directly to the window and pulled the shades up and opened the window. "Lindsey, it's me, Pam, and it's time for you to get your feet on the floor." She yanked Lindsey's quilt down.

"Pam, stop it. Why did you come back? Close my blinds, right now. Please, just leave me alone."

"If you think I came all the way back here to leave you alone, you have another thought coming. Now, get your lily, white ass out of bed, right now!"

Sammy actually laughed and Grand grabbed her hand and held it.

Pam looked at Sam, then back at Lindsey, and said in a calmer tone, "We're all worried about you. We love you. Now, I'm not going to let you stay like this. It's going on eight weeks. Come out, have a cup of tea with us, and then you can come back here and rest for a while. We'll go slowly with this. Lindsey, answer me."

"All right, I just need, I mean, in a few minutes, I'll come out. Pam, I'm sorry."

Calmly she answered, "Just take it slowly. We all love you. See you in a minute." She looked at Kate and around the room. "Come on everyone. Let's put the tea kettle on."

1968

Lindsey watched everyone leave her room. "God, how can I begin to move on," she prayed. "I know I'll lose what I have left with Bobby. I need him. Please let him stay with me. I can't let him go. I'll never let him go. God, help me."

She held onto her locket then wiped her eyes and sat up in bed a few seconds. Looking at her chair and around her room, she knew she wouldn't see him. She placed her feet in her slippers and got up. She walked into the bathroom.

During the past weeks she quietly used the bathroom and quickly got back to her room. The night light was all she needed. Sometimes late at night, she left her room to take quick baths when Bobby wasn't there. For the first time in weeks she took time to look in the mirror and couldn't believe how horrible she looked. The realization that for weeks she hadn't cared, hit hard. Her eyes were red and swollen, her skin was pale, and her hair looked awful. *What must Bobby think?* Yanking the shower curtain closed then turning on the shower, she waited until the water felt very warm on her hand. She got in, sat down, and with no intention her body relaxed responding to the soothing shower spray. After sitting for a few minutes and actually enjoying the warm water, she shampooed her hair, rinsed it, and rubbed in lilac scented cream rinse. Then she stood up, washed herself, and rinsed herself and her hair. Lindsey stood enjoying the warm shower until the water started getting too cool. She turned it off, toweled herself dry, and put lotion on her body. Toweling her hair as dry as she could, she brushed her hair into a pony tail. Then she put a little makeup under her eyes, added some blush to her cheeks, and just a touch of pink lipstick to her lips. She put her locket back on. Looking in the mirror she thought, *That's better. I'll have to pluck my eye brows sometime soon.*

We left Lindsey's room and walked into the kitchen. As Grand and Pam sat down, I turned on the stove putting the tea kettle on. Karen remained standing and said, "You guys, I'm going to Grand's to pack my things and see if my dad can leave now to drive me home. I told Linds I'm going home today. I think if I see her and hug her goodbye, I'll cry and stir things up. Grand, I'll call you after Dad leaves my house to come back here." She gave her, Kate, and me a hug. "Pam, would you walk me to Grand's." The two of them grabbed coats and went out the side door.

Kate smiled at Grand, "I really do think happy times are near." Her smile got bigger, "Do you hear that? Lindsey's taking her first shower in weeks! I've heard her take quick baths late at night, but as far as I know, this is the first shower since the funeral." She got up, turned the stove off, and opened her refrigerator taking food out. She put wine and beer glasses on the table. "I know it's early afternoon, but this," she looked toward the bathroom, "is cause for celebration!" She put some cheese and crackers on a plate, then quickly started spreading cream cheese on some rye bread slices, topping them with ham and a touch of mustard, cutting them into bite size pieces.

Grand helped and said, "I'll get a bottle of cabernet out of the cupboard." She got the cork screw, too.

Pam opened the side door into Kate's kitchen. I was just getting out of my chair and said to her, "Help me get some beer from the garage refrigerator. The tea kettle has been excused!" We returned, carrying several bottles, opened two, and sat back down at the table.

Kate raised her wine glass, and we followed, "God bless you, Pam, you did it."

I added, "You're a magic woman. We've been trying for weeks to get her to leave her room. She just wouldn't listen to us."

Still smiling Pam looked around the table, "You're quite the group! All of you are hurting very much, too. How are you doing?"

Grand answered, "You know, Pam, when you reach my age, things don't hurt the same way. Now, it's easier to accept life's pain and disappointments, remembering that love is always present. It's accepting life's circumstances. But I couldn't always do that, and I do ache for my young ones sitting here."

"Grand said, 'accepting life's circumstances.'" I forgot that.

~~~~~~~~~~~~

Father Tom straightened in his chair. "Samantha, did you say something?"

He heard her whisper, "Grand said, 'accepting life's circumstances."

He smiled and patted her hand, "Yes, we must accept life's circumstances. Dear, sweet, Grand was wonderful. We were so lucky to have those wonderful people for family. Come back to us, Sammy, open your eyes."

She turned her head away.

Kate smiled at Grand's answer to Pam's question about how they were doing. "I love you, Grand. You always include me with the young ones."

"Well, you are young compared to me!"

She patted my arm, "This is the one I admire so much. With all that's happened in your young life, you always find a way to keep smiling."

My eyes filled as I answered, "I'll always miss my mom, dad, Art, and Bobby. I'm so lucky to have each one of you. Grand, I've loved you forever. Karen and I were toddlers together. I can't remember life without you and Karen. You understood my mom, and you've been taking care of me forever. Kate, you've been telling me just the right thing, loving me, never criticizing, holding me together since the day we met. As long as I have you, I'll be fine."

It was silent a few seconds. Kate smiled and said to Pam, "We knew you'd get our Lindsey moving. Maybe not quite this fast, but we knew you'd do it."

"I hope I wasn't too bossy. To tell you the truth what I heard and saw this morning and what you told me on the phone about Lindsey, scared me too. I love that girl and all of you. You all are amazing. I didn't mean to be so nasty."

"Well, nasty worked," Grand laughed.

We all saw Lindsey as she walked into the kitchen looking at us. It got very quiet. We knew she'd heard us. "Is there a celebration going on in here that you forgot to tell me about?"

"Well, actually Linds, we're celebrating you taking a shower," I snapped, then added, "By the way, you look nice."

She smiled as her eyes filled, "I'm so sorry for the way I've been treating you. I'm not mad at you. I love you, Sam."

I got up and hugged her. Tears streamed down my cheeks, too, knowing the life she loved had vanished. None of us could fix her broken heart. Finally I got words out, "I love you, too, always. We've been so worried about you and didn't know how to help you."

377

Lindsey got some tissue and wiped my eyes and then hers. She whispered so softly, "I still have you." I hugged her tight, then walked to the counter for more Kleenex.

She said to Pam, "I'm sorry you had to come back here. I miss everyone in Bolivia. I'm letting all of you down. I just couldn't..."

"Hush. Everyone in Bolivia misses you very much, and they want you to feel better and come back. I wanted to be here." She looked at all of us. "I love these amazing ladies and you. Now, sit down with us."

"Mom, do you think I could have a small glass of wine?"

Kate hesitated, and Grand answered, "Absolutely you can. A glass of red wine will do your blood good!"

We could see Kate's happy, thankful expression as she looked around her kitchen table, "This day's turning out to be the best day in a long time. Grand, you're my dearest friend in the world. Pam, you're here, and that's such a blessing. Sammy, we're celebrating, again. Our Karen, I think she's happier than ever! Lindsey, you're in here with us, and honey, now each new day will help your heart heal." She got up, put her arms around her daughter, and I bet she silently thanked God for what we still had right here in her kitchen.

Then the back door opened. Father Tom hollered, "Kate?" He walked in and looked around. "What's going on in here? Lindsey, you're out, I mean, thank God, honey. And Pam, you've arrived. It looks like a party in here."

Grand was out of her chair getting him a beer, and I made more ham things and got more chips. Lindsey hugged him. "I'm doing much better." Then she whispered a little too loudly, "I need to talk with you."

"You let me know when."

With his phone at his ear to answer the person waiting to hear his voice again, Jim hurried to the lobby down the corridor from Samantha's room. The elderly Mrs. Green spoke again, "Hello, are you there?"

"Yes, I'm here."

"I don't know if you remember me. I live in Santa Barbara. You called me the other day looking for Robert Green. You are the person who called?"

"Yes, I'm Jim Peterson."

"I remember your name, now. Well, Mr. Peterson, I remembered something with the help of my daughter. I told her about your phone call, and she thinks you may be looking for my late husband's nephew. When you called me, you were looking for a Robert Green, who's wife was from Ohio. My daughter remembered my husband's nephew married a girl from Ohio, and she shortened his middle name and called him Rob. We knew my husband's nephew by the name, James. He was named James after his father and his middle name, Robert, was after my husband's name. We never called him Rob, and his parents never did either. His full name is James Robert Green. I couldn't, for the life of me, remember his wife's name. My daughter remembered her name. She was mentioned often in several news stories, and my daughter saw his wife's name in the articles. Seems silly, now, that I couldn't connect the dots when you called."

Jim asked, "Does the name, Samantha, sound familiar?"

"Yes, wait a second." He heard the elderly lady asking her daughter, he presumed, if Samantha sounded right for James' wife's name. "Why, yes, that's it," she answered and added, Why are you looking for him?"

"Samantha is very ill. She's in the hospital here in Cleveland, Ohio. She's too ill to reach him. I've been trying to call him and their daughter. I haven't been able to reach either one. Samantha's cell phone is missing. By the way, how did you get my number?"

"My daughter found it on my caller I D"

"Thank heaven for that."

"Yes, now, I have to tell you something. Are you alone, or are you with people right now?"

He smiled. "Right now I'm with my closest friend, who happens to be a priest. We're at the hospital with Samantha."

"Very good because I must tell you some bad news. First of all, I don't know why your friend, Samantha, never told you, but she and James divorced about a year ago."

"We haven't been in touch for years until very recently. I had a feeling they might have divorced," Jim explained her medical condition.

"I'm sorry she's doing poorly, but I'm not surprised. The divorce isn't the bad news, Mr. Peterson. I'm sorry to tell you that James, his fiancé, their baby daughter, and his daughter with Samantha were killed in a plain crash about six months ago."

Jim couldn't speak.

"Hello, are you all right?"

"Yes, yes, I'm fine. I wasn't expecting this. Everyone died?" *My God, she's lost everyone, again.* "Mrs. Green, her daughter died, too?"

"Now, you need to sit down and take a deep breath. Just breathe for a minute. You see, my daughter is mine from my first marriage. We really didn't know my Robert's brother or his nephew and family. My brother-n-law and nephew did come to my Robert's funeral. He died about the same time his nephew and Samantha were married, I bet. My daughter and I haven't seen any of them in many, many years."

She kept talking, "The plane crash was big news, and it was in the newspapers. My daughter and I read everything about it. You see, my husband's nephew, James (as we called him) or Rob (as you called him) was engaged to the only child of a wealthy, prominent family from Santa Barbara. My Robert's brother and wife are very wealthy, too, and this brother is a bigwig attorney. My Robert's late nephew was a bigwig attorney as well. They always have their pictures in the local paper's society pages. Well, the late nephew used to have his picture in the society pages. My daughter and I keep up on that! Mr. Peterson, I'm sorry. Are you still able to listen to me going on, I'm making this confusing, and I do ramble on."

380

"I'm grateful you called me back. Yes, I'm listening, and I think I'm following you."

"Well then, my daughter would like to speak with you."

"Hello, Mr. Peterson. I'm Dianne Blake."

"Hello, Dianne. Please call me Jim. Thank you for tracking me down. I just can't believe this."

"I'm very sorry for Samantha. I know this is terrible news. Months before this plane crash James Robert, his young pregnant fiancee, and Samantha were written about in all of the local newspapers' society pages. Their saga occasionally made local television news as well. The society news stories made Samantha the culprit for why her and James' divorce stalled. She was portrayed as the evil wife who wouldn't let go of her husband's money. There were many pictures in the paper of James Robert and his young pregnant fiancee looking very happy together, and there was always this one picture of Samantha looking angry. The truth was the divorce stalled because Samantha's lawyer wanted her to fight for a fair divorce settlement. Her lawyer advised her not to give in."

"There's more to tell you. Should I continue?"

"Yes, please, I'd like to know."

"Many years earlier, her lawyer and James Robert were friends, but their friendship ended. In one interview Samantha's lawyer stated that few people knew or saw the ruthless, ugly side of James Robert Green. He said that he had experienced his ugly side, and he knew Samantha had as well. After this interview, rumors circulated that she and her attorney had been having an affair for years. One newspaper printed a story stating that this affair was the reason James filed for divorce. Samantha and her attorney sued the newspaper and won. The settlement in this case was that the newspaper print a front page headline stating no affair between them ever occurred. The paper also had to state that although a large monetary settlement was offered to them, neither wanted financial reward."

"None of this made any difference. Most people still believed Samantha was vengeful and greedy. Terrible pictures of her remained in the newspapers and even on TV. Jim, you told my mother that she lives in Portland now. We didn't know her, but I'm sure all of the negative notoriety is the reason she left Santa Barbara. I'm going to airmail you all of the newspaper coverage right away." She repeated, "All of it is very sad. My mother wants to speak with you again."

"I'm back, Mr. Peterson," he heard the old voice.

Jim found his voice, "That bastard!"

"Well, yes, I think you're right. He is dead. He lost everything, didn't he? My Robert was a wonderful man. He was nothing like his nephew. We're very sorry to tell you all of this, Mr Peterson."

"It's Jim. Please, call me Jim. I'm sure your Robert was not like his nephew. You're very kind. You really are, Mrs. Green."

"Now you call me, Isabelle. We're going to send you the articles immediately. My husband's brother and nephew have not lived honest lives. My late husband's brother, James D. Green, the D stands for Douglas is known as JD. He is still alive and doing well, and I'm sure he and his late son had connections, if you know what I mean. And it isn't any of my business, Jim, but I hope Samantha's important to you. It was cruel what she went through. It would be wonderful to think that someone could make her happy again."

"Isabelle, I hope to make Samantha smile, again, more than I can tell you. I'm going to give you my address, and my home phone number, and phone number at St. Joseph School, too."

"Do you teach at St. Joseph's, Jim?"

"I'm the principal."

"Oh that's right, I think you told me that before. I taught history for many years, a long time ago. I'm ninety-one, now. Well, I want to keep in touch with you. Please, call me back after you read the articles. Take care of Samantha. We'll remember her in our prayers. My daughter will talk with you to get your address and phone numbers, goodbye for now." She handed the phone to her daughter.

Jim hung up with Dianne a few minutes later. He sat thinking about everything he just heard, the horrible divorce, Sammy's daughter's death, Rob's death and his being connected, the young pregnant girlfriend, and her baby's death all resinating his thoughts. He went back into

Samantha's room. "Tom, come with me to the cafeteria for a coke. I have some things to tell you."

After listening to him, Father Tom sadly answered, "My God, twice in her life, she lost her family. Maybe losing Kate 'tossed her over the edge.' She always knew she had Kate to hold her together. She really needs you and me."

"Let me stay with her tonight. I'm not going to get any sleep, anyway. At home I'll just toss and turn all night thinking about those news paper articles." Without warning, the messed up idiom got his attention. It's 'pushed her over the edge."

Father Tom sat with us in Kate's kitchen for a while. He had one beer and ate a few ham things. "Well, I'm going to let you ladies enjoy yourselves. Lindsey, this is a wonderful day. I'll see you tomorrow or sometime soon and Pam you, too." He left.

Everyone talked a while longer. Then Kate smiled at Linds, "Would you like to rest? I'd like you to join us for dinner later."

"I would, Mom. I'll see you at dinner." She smiled at me, "Sammy, would you come get me for dinner? No door slamming needed."

"No door slamming necessary, I'll be there."

Kate hugged her, "Honey, I know your dad is watching over all of us. I feel great peace in that. He's happy you're doing better. See you in a little while."

Lindsey left and Kate said, "Now, I really think we can get her back to Bolivia and back to living the rest of her life. I'm so lucky to have all of you."

Lindsey opened her bedroom door. Feeling chilled, she couldn't wait to settle under her soft quilt. Her mind was consumed with Bobby. She closed her eyes a minute and then opened them looking at her pink chair. Relief filled her heart. *'Each time you leave, I'm so frightened I'll never see you again. I do see you.'*

'I'm here. Honey, I love you so much. I wish I could change what's happened, but you're going to be all right, now.' He moved closer. 'You are my life, Linds. I'm most grateful for you. From the first moment I saw you, I knew, I just knew we'd be together. Do you understand? You and I are forever.'

'Yes,' filled her thoughts as her hand wrapped around her locket. *'I just can't live '*

'You can live without me, and you will.'

'No, Bobby, don't do this. I'm not ready to let go of you,' she pleaded.

'Sweetheart, you must go with Pam. Everything will be wonderful for you.'

'I don't think I can go back to Bolivia. I can't do it. I need to stay here, right here. I'll lose you completely if I leave.'

'You'll never lose us. Everything to this moment is ours for all time. You go with her. Your life will be amazing. I love you always and forever.'

She looked at him, and he had the brightest light surrounding him. *'You're changing. Please, Bobby, please make this stop. Don't leave me. I love'*

'I know you love me, honey. I'll always know your precious love. You go with Pam, and you complete your life. You have so much ahead. It'll be wonderful for you.' He was comprised with light.

She couldn't stop what was happening. It was too soon. She wasn't ready. *'No, please, not yet.'* She heard knocking on her bedroom door.

Kate came in saying, "Dinner will be ready in about fifteen minutes." She patted Lindsey's arm. "Oh, dear," she felt her forehead, "Honey, what's going on? You're too warm. Pam, come in here!"

Pam and Sammy ran into her room as Kate told them, "Her temperature's way up."

Pam felt Lindsey's forehead, arms, and took her pulse. "Sammy, get some aspirin, a glass of water, and some damp cool wash cloths. Then, could you get my black doctor's bag? It's in your room."

Lindsey was oblivious to the turmoil in her room as she was dreaming her reoccurring dream, the dream she'd been dreaming forever. Walking toward the beautiful golden castle, she saw the man.

"Hello, honey," the extraordinary man said. "What are you looking for? Tell me what you want."

She looked into the man's beautiful eyes and knew him. *"Bobby, it's you. It's always been you! I want to be with you in the castle. That's what I want, all I want."*

"No, honey, not yet, it's not your time. Happiness will find you. You have so much happiness ahead." His eyes were brilliantly bright.

She watched amazing, pristine light changing him and couldn't stop looking into his magnificent eyes. Complete understanding that their love would go on and on and never end encompassed her heart and mind. Although she wanted him to stay with her forever, she was seeing peaceful loving light shining in him and through him. Never had his smile looked so amazingly radiant and joyful.

She felt his hand on her cheek and then his lips kissing hers. She whispered, "I will love you always and forever."

Distinctly she heard him whisper back, "And I will always and forever love you." Even though he was leaving, her heart felt genuine Peace. He kept smiling at her as the distance between them grew. Then the golden castle faded away. The castle, Bobby, and such pure light were a wondrous moment; already a new memory she'd always have. She would never dream this dream again and never be able to exactly picture that pristine light.

About fifteen minutes passed since Pam lifted Lindsey's head, put the aspirin on the back of her tongue, and put her lips to the cool water in the glass. "That's the ticket, drink this water," Pam told her. She gently set her head back on her pillow.

Sammy continued squeezing water from the cloths in the bowl, then handing them to Pam. Pam kept pressing the wrung cloths on Lindsey's forehead, neck, wrists, and ankles.

Fifteen more minutes passed when she opened her eyes and saw Pam, her mom, and Sammy. Knowing Bobby wouldn't be there, her eyes still moved to see the empty pink chair. She knew she wouldn't see him again and was surprised how she felt. A bit of a smile formed on her lips as she thought, *Peaceful, I feel so peaceful.* She closed her eyes a few minutes. *'Dear God, Thank You. I know he's with You, now. Thank You.'* She kept her eyes closed and tried to remember what she'd just experienced. She knew Bobby was with God in Heaven and understood he'd been the person in her reoccurring dream. *Such amazing light and peace.* That was the new part that brightened her heart. Even though the brilliance of that light wouldn't ever again conjure as magnificently as it had just a while before, wonderful light filled her heart and mind.

She opened her eyes, again, looking at her night stand seeing aspirin and a bowl of water with wash cloths. "What's going on," she quietly asked.

"Well, I'm not sure," Pam answered.

"Some doctor!" Lindsey joked.

"Hey, you just had a very high temp. While I'm not sure why this happened, my magnificent doctoring got your temperature down in record breaking time, if I do say so myself."

"Um, Pam, I've used those magnificent skills a few times," Kate kidded.

"Oh sure, now everyone's a doctor! Linds, let me take your temperature." Pam opened her black doctor case.

Lindsey laughed and started to get out of bed. Pam put the thermometer under Lindsey's tongue. "Hey, you, I don't think so. Get back in bed." She waited several seconds and checked the thermometer. "Your temperature is normal, but I want you to stay in bed and rest."

387

"For crying out loud, will you people make up your minds?" She took a deep breath. "Do you want me out of this bed or in this bed?"

"For the rest of this day, I'm ordering you to rest in bed. Tomorrow we'll begin anew."

"Hey," Sammy said. "I've got an idea. Let's have dinner in here. I'll set up the card table in here for Grand, Kate, you, and I. Linds can sit up in bed, and we'll be together."

"Great idea," Kate patted her hand. "We'll party in here. Pam, what do you think?"

"Lindsey, how do you feel? Any headache, stomachache, dizziness? Is anything hurting?"

"Well, I do have to go to the bathroom, but I really feel wonderful." She looked around her room, at her empty pink chair, and back at them. "I think I feel like the luckiest person ever."

"Ok, go to the bathroom and come right back." A few minutes later Lindsey got back in bed and Pam said, "Let me use some of my big, important doctor stuff to check you out." She opened her doctor's bag. "First your throat, open your mouth, please."

Jim and Tom stood on the opposite sides of Samantha's bed. Both were thinking that it was unimaginable that she'd lost her immediate family, again. Father Tom kissed the top of her forehead and said, "Honey, I'm so sorry for everything that's happened to you. You are family to me, always have been. You, Lindsey, Karen, Phillip, their kids, and Jim are part of my family. You still have us. I'll see you tomorrow morning right after Mass."

He sadly smiled and said, "See you in the morning, Jim. Try to sleep." He left.

Jim looked down at Samantha thinking, she looks so fragile. He said, "Sammy, you've been through such sadness, again. No wonder you're exhausted, honey. I'm so sorry about everything." He moved the chair closer and sat down. "This has been a long day. Everything will be fine. I'll be right here all night if you need me." He sat thinking, *How could one person lose her family twice in her life? I can't believe this happened again.*

SLEEPING MEMORIES 1968

Brice and Grand arrived at Kate's with him carrying the picnic basket holding meatloaf, mashed potatoes, gravy, snap green beans, warm biscuits, and jello fruit salad. Everything, but the jello, was piping hot, and ready to eat.

I watched Brice kiss his mom's cheek after he set the basket down in Kate's kitchen. "I'm glad Lindsey's doing better. I'll see her soon. Hope you all have some fun. See you, Sammy." He hugged me and left.

Pam and I set up the card table, put a table cloth, four table settings, and flowers on it. We brought in a bed tray with a place setting and small vase of flowers for Lindsey and then got a folding table to put the food on. Back in the kitchen we watched Kate take a cake out of the oven, cover it to keep it warm, then pick up a bowl of fluffy frosting. Pam picked up a tray holding hot tea, cream, sugar, cups, and ice filled glasses. Grand picked up some ginger ale and cokes, and I got her picnic basket. All of us paraded into Lindsey's room.

We sat together enjoying dinner, reminiscing wonderful memories of Art and Bobby. Along with laughter, tears also easily fell but quickly gave way to more happy memories and smiles.

Pam talked about Ken and told everyone that she was in love with him, "I knew he was someone special the first second I saw him."

Lindsey laughed telling Pam that their friends in Bolivia knew she and Ken were crazy about one and other.

We ate warm cake and scooped up frosting we heaped on dessert plates. Grand told us about the first person she fell in love with. She met him in her high school English class. She looked so happy remembering, and we laughed with her as she told us about their first date and their last date. "Six weeks later," she said, "I'd fallen in love with someone else and within three years I married him, Brice's dad." We laughed more.

We stayed in Lindsey's room past eleven o'clock. Kate finally said, "I think we should call it a night." And we did, feeling so much happier than we had in a long time.

Pam and I carried everything to the kitchen. Kate and Grand said the dishes could wait until morning and put the

390

left over food in the refrigerator. Pam got ready for bed first and fell sound to sleep. Kate came in the back door after walking Grand home. She told me to let the dishes soak. She hugged me and said, "I love you, Sammy, very much. You're my dear girl." She went to her bedroom.

I sat at the kitchen table a minute, then washed the dishes.

On my way to bed, passing Lindsey's room, I heard music softly sounding from her radio. I opened her door just a little.

She smiled when she saw me. "I was hoping you'd come see me. Sit with me a while. I want to tell you something amazing." She made room for me to sit on her bed. "Sammy, Bobby's been here, in my room, with me these weeks since his funeral. I've seen him. I've heard his voice, and he could see me and hear me."

"Lindsey, are you ok? Do you want me to get mom or Pam?"

"Please, just listen to me."

I sat waiting to hear what she wanted to tell me, but she didn't say anything for several seconds. She just smiled, looked at me and at her pink chair. We heard the D.J. on the radio say, "This next song is a triple spin!" We listened to Andy Williams begin to sing, "Moon River."

Then she started telling me, "Bobby's been with me. He told me how much he loves me, and I told him how much I love him and how much I wish we could be together. He wants me to know that we will love each other, always and forever. Remember our reoccurring dreams, Sammy?"

"Yes."

"Do you remember that I used to dream about a castle and a man, who always asked me what was I looking for and what I wanted? I could never remember what I wanted to ask the man."

"Yes, you told Karen and me about him and about the castle."

"Sammy, that man has always been Bobby, and I finally know what I wanted so much. I wanted to go into the castle with him. All of the times I've dreamed that dream, it's been Bobby. Today I dreamed it, again. Only this time I understood that he's lived his earthly life, and now he's going into the castle, into Heaven. I watched him leave me, and I watched him go home to God. It was amazing! Sammy, he's home with God, now. He's safe. He's so happy." Lindsey wiped tears away while she smiled. She asked, "Sammy, you do believe me?"

"I believe you. It all makes so much sense, now. When my mom, dad, and I were in the car crash, I never told you or Karen that it was just like my dream. I heard a roaring sound, I was in the woods, alone and cold. Remember my dream ended with me in the woods?"

"Yes."

"After the car crash, my mom and dad were with me in the woods and took care of me until help came. And then I watched them walk into a magnificent light. I've never been able to picture that light, exactly the way it was, again. I just remember it was amazing."

We sat looking at each other for a minute. Then Lindsey said, "Sammy, I just saw that light surrounding Bobby, and I can't clearly remember how magnificent that light was, either.

I hugged her and looked at her sweet face. "This is so wonderful, Linds."

She wiped her tears and excitedly said, "I've been thinking about the people who were in our lives and everything that happened while we were growing up. Mrs. Lotis, Sister Gladiola, Brice and Frank, your mom and dad, Karen's and Phillip's frightening time, and me with my small arm and hand. It seems that you and I have always had each other and Jimmy and Bobby. We're so lucky! We've been given the opportunity to see how people handle things that happen in their lives and to their lives. How wonderful that we got to see the choices that were made. We've seen that how we choose to behave and live, makes all the difference. And, Sammy, our dreams, what a gift! We have to tell Karen how our dreams came to life. Remember Brice telling us that Karen's mom died a few months before Karen's and Phillip's accident? Maybe she helped Karen.

"Linds, maybe we should wait until she tells us about her dream. I think we should wait."

"I think you're right. We'll wait as long as we can."

392

"What a blessing, our dreams," I squeezed her hand. I decided not to mention that since my parents died, I've never dreamed my dream again. I decided to wait as long as I could to tell her that part.

"You and Karen are the best sisters, and my dearest friends, but Sammy, you have such a special place in my heart."

"And you have a special place in mine." I held her hand a few seconds.

"Now, you and I need to be off to see the world. There's a lot to see."

"Yes, Linds, we sure do, and there really is such a lot to see. My mom said that, too."

1968

Kate opened her eyes the next morning remembering everything that happened the day before. She smiled thinking about having dinner in Lindsey's room. Getting out of bed, she slipped on her pink robe and slippers. On her way to the kitchen, she peeked in on Lindsey and saw she was still sleeping. She arrived in her kitchen feeling happy, an emotion she hadn't felt for quite awhile.

The routine Kate followed every morning since she lived in this house with Art, Lindsey, and then Sammy came naturally. First, she turned on her radio. This morning she heard the Beatles singing, "All You Need Is Love." Next, she began making breakfast filling her coffee pot with cold water.

While she did these things, she spoke with God, *"Thank You, sweet Lord, for everything. Thank You for placing Pam in our lives and for keeping Lindsey in Your loving care these weeks. I was so frightened, yesterday, when her temperature shot up. It happened so quickly. Thank You for always keeping her in Your care. You've blessed Samantha with amazing strength. She is the dearest daughter. Keep Pam, Linds, Karen, and Sammy safe and happy. Karen will become a mom soon. Art thought it a true blessing that Phillip came into her life. Keep Phillip and his sweet family healthy. Bless Art and Bobby. I miss them so much. I'm grateful for all of the years of happiness Art and I shared. Thank you for placing Bobby with Lindsey. He always made her so happy.*

She stirred the frozen orange concentrate and water. Her prayer continued. *"Watch over sweet Grand, the dearest person. She holds us together. Take care of Brice and Frank. Their hearts are loving and so kind. Thank you for our new family members. The Avenstons and Father Tom's family have been wonderful and generous. I'm so grateful. Shine Your light on Bobby, Art, Joan, and Jack. My hope is they're all together in Heaven. Let Your Divine inspiration guide Father Tom. We're so blessed to have had Father Tom with us forever, it seems. Keep him safe and strong. In the name of the Father, and the Son, and the Holy Ghost, I mean, Holy Spirit. These changes aren't easy! Amen."*

Kate had the bacon sizzling hot when Lindsey walked into the kitchen. The unusual February sunshine shining through the windows matched her bright smile. "Good morning," she said hugging her mom.

"Look at you, Linds, you look rested and happy. You must be feeling much better."

"I am, much better. Mom, I'm so sorry for the way I've been behaving. I want to expla-"

"Stop. You don't owe me or anyone any explanations. What happened is beyond heartbreaking. We just have to know that God loves all of us. He'll help us figure out how to make each day happy, again. I believe that Bobby and your dad are together in Heaven, and that they're watching out for us. You've made it beyond your heartbreak, Linds. Each day will be easier, now. I was frightened for you, but I think your heart is mending. I love you so much. Pam, Grand, Karen, you, Sammy and I have each other to love, to lean on, to care for, and to laugh with."

Tears fell down her cheeks, but she was smiling at her mom. "I love you, Mom. We'll be happy, again." Kate blotted her daughter's tears, and her own, and handed Lindsey a glass of orange juice.

In the next hour Sammy, Pam, Grand, and Father Tom joined them at the kitchen table. Brice and Frank hurried in carrying Grand's just out of the oven doughnuts. Conversation, familiar warmth, and love reminiscent of the past filled Kate's kitchen once again.

Linds and I sat in Kate's kitchen the next morning with Kate, Pam, Grand, Frank, Brice and Father Tom. We were laughing, enjoying Grand's homemade doughnuts, and talking like old times. Linds told Father Tom that she was ready to return to Bolivia.

That changed.

The phone call for Pam came about noon. Kate answered the phone and quickly handed it to Pam, "It's Ken Jones calling for you.

Taking the receiver she answered, "Hi," and then, "You sound so close. This is a great connection. You're where? Why are you in Miami? What happened?"

Lindsey mouthed, "What's going on?" Pam shrugged her shoulders and stopped asking questions so Ken could tell her.

Kate, Linds, and I went into the living room to give her a little privacy, but we still could hear every word she said. Then we heard her scream, happy scream, "Yes, yes! I love you, too. Just tell me where and when. Ken, I'm so happy. You do? Is he ok? Is he still happy?"

Lindsey shot off the couch into the kitchen. "Can he come here? Get married here! That's it, isn't it? Ask him to come here."

Pam's smile was huge, as she shook her head, yes. "What do you think about getting married in Ohio?" She listened to him. "A week from Saturday? I have to tell my parents. I know, we'll keep it small. Ok, call me back. Two hours? Got it. Call back in two hours. Get married in two weeks. I'll be here. I love you, too!"

"I have to call my mom, she'll be so excited!"

After she talked with her mom, Lindsey asked, "Why is Ken in Miami, anyway?"

"I meant to tell you right away. One of the new officials from the airport told him that he needed to get himself and the rest of the Care Core Volunteers out, that all flights could be cancelled any minute. Apparently there's about to be a government change. People have already been killed. Did you notice that less children were coming to the schoolhouse, Lindsey?"

"I did notice that there were a few less children, but I didn't think there was reason to worry."

"There were a lot less recently. We noticed that many families picked up and moved to some other places. These people know the signs when things are about to erupt."

She excitedly added, "Lindsey, Ken has little Tom with him in Miami. We changed his name from Tonk to Tom! We're going to adopt him. Several times Ken and I fantasized about being a family. Tom understands Ken and I will be his mom and dad. He's beyond happy! Ken's parents are very excited about meeting me and their new grandson.

"I'm so happy for you. You guys will be great parents, and what a blessing for Tom." Then Lindsey said, "I wonder why Care Core sent me those letters. They must know what's happening. Well, I'll figure everything out after your wedding."

It took about half an hour for Pam to hear back from her mom that their family's church in Perrysburg, Ohio had three weddings scheduled a week from Saturday. Her aunt's church was booked as well.

"Pam, get married here, in Bay Village. Father Tom will do it. Come on, let's go ask him," Lindsey excitedly said. "He's already going to meet with me sometime today."

"That's a great idea, let me call my mom."

"Good, and I'll call the rectory."

Within the hour, Pam, Kate, Grand, Lindsey, and I were in the station wagon on our way to St. Joseph's to see our priest. He really didn't stand a chance telling Pam that St. Joseph's was booked. The Chapel had three weddings scheduled a week from Saturday, but St. Joseph's Church had one morning hour open: nine o'clock a.m.

Father Tom looked at us and said, "Pam, you're not a member of our Parish."

Grand gave Father Tom a look I'd never seen before and stated, "Thomas, one week from this Saturday there will be, with God's presence, a wedding for Pam and Ken either at your place or at Kate's place. What's it going to be?"

397

I thought Pam might faint as she looked at Grand. Lindsey and I bit the inside of our cheeks so we wouldn't laugh.

Father looked at Kate, who was right next to Grand looking every bit as determined. He smiled and said, "Let's make it God's place in church one week from Saturday, nine a.m. Pam, I'll need your baptism and confirmation certificates and Ken's as well. Also, I'll need to meet with you, both, as soon as possible. Are you, both, attending Church regularly and making weekly confessions?"

Pam answered truthfully that they, both, did their best to attend Mass each week. Grand cleared her throat, and now I saw that look for the second time. "These wonderful young doctors are helping people in remote places," she reminded him.

He looked at Grand, then answered, "Pam, I will need to meet with you and Ken as soon as possible." He smiled at Grand, then looked back at Pam, "He and you will need to go to the sacrament of confession before your Wedding Mass."

"By the way," he added, "my dad called an hour ago. He said his pilot heard that the airport where he picked Lindsey and Pam up is closed indefinitely."

One month later, Pam and Ken had been married for two weeks. Little Tom had a full name, Thomas Kenton Jones and a mom and dad.

With a few more weeks passing, the new family went to South Africa and joined other doctors caring for people in need. Jackie and Stan Sutherland and Lindsey met up with them. Everyone but Lindsey stayed for three years. She returned to Bay Village a year later.

Paulette Swanson went home to wait for her husband to come home from Vietnam. They hoped to start their family as soon as he returned. He didn't. Seven weeks later he was killed while helping a wounded soldier.

I broke up with Jim. I put my engagement ring and a letter in a box. I asked Kate to hand it to him. The night before I left, Kate and I talked for hours. She wasn't happy with me not talking with Jimmy in person, but she understood my reasons for leaving. Early the next morning a cap took me to Cleveland Hopkin's Airport.

Lindsey came back to Ohio, went on to graduate from medical school, and returned to Africa in 1976.

~~~~~~~~~~~~~

Three days after talking with Isabelle Green, Jim saw the airmail package on his front porch. Opening it, he saw the newspaper articles. He called Tom, "I'm going to be late returning to the hospital. The newspaper articles arrived."

"Make yourself some hot tea and read them. I'll be here. Samantha's fine."

Jim filled his Mr. Coffee and took a hot cup of coffee and the society newspaper pages into his home office. Isabelle was right. James or Rob, whichever name he went by, was not a good person. As he read further he realized James' parents weren't either.

There were a lot of pictures of James with his very young fiancee. Many articles were written about how in love they were and how much they wanted to be married. Every article portrayed Samantha as the vengeful, greedy wife, who wouldn't divorce her husband because she didn't want to lose the lavish lifestyle he provided her. There were pictures of Samantha looking very angry.

In several articles James' mother stated that she always felt Samantha trapped her son into marriage. His mother never thought James really loved his wife. She further stated that Samantha was a gold digger having come from a very poor family. She was quoted saying, "Samantha loved my son's money, not my son."

Annie Nichol Berkley was the love of James' life according to his mother and father. His parents stated that she was indeed younger than James, but her maturity, amazing wisdom, prestigious family background, and her love, commitment, and devotion for him had made their son fall completely in love. Several pictures of the happy couple surrounded these articles. There was one picture of Samantha. Looking at it even Jim thought she looked angry. There were many page filled articles that continued in this manner.

The series ended with a story about Annie and James. ANNIE NICHOL BERKLEY and JAMES ROBERT GREEN WILL STRIVE AHEAD This article was all about Annie and James, a beautiful, happy, engaged couple deciding to go on with their lives without being able to get married.

400

There were pictures of them at charity events, working together at James' company, and playing tennis. Near the end of this article, James stated, "As soon as Samantha gets a grip on reality and agrees to divorce me, Annie and I will immediately have a small wedding inviting family and a few dear friends. Later, we'll have an amazing celebration inviting hundreds of friends."

As he read Jim thought, *I hate this bastard!*

This article continued with Annie Nichol adding that their hearts were already married, anyhow. She stated, "No one can stop us from loving each other." Annie added that they were planning an exotic get away with both of James' children and themselves. This concluding article contained pictures of James with his happy, very young, very pregnant, non wife, Annie Nichol Berkley.

Dated several weeks later there was one article containing an interview with Samantha and her lawyer: JAMES ROBERT GREEN DIVORCE GRANTED. In this article, Samantha stated that for many years her and Rob's marriage was great. They had a beautiful daughter and their lives were happy. She stated that they'd been friends with Annie Nichol Berkley's parents and that Annie actually stayed with their daughter when the four adults went out together. She was blind sided when Rob and Annie Nichol, some years later, began their affair.

Jim read further about Samantha's divorce demands. She stated, "This is what I asked for in our divorce settlement. My requests remained the same from day one. I wanted him to pay for all of our daughter's expenses until she graduated from college and found employment; allowing six months after graduation for her to find employment. He would continue paying for our daughter's expenses and her education costs if she decided to attend graduate school. For myself, I wanted three hundred-fifty thousand dollars a year for life with inflation increases met. At Rob's expense, I wanted to purchase a new furnished and professionally decorated home in the eight hundred thousand dollar range, a new car every two years in the sixty to eighty-thousand dollar range, all insurances paid including health, and all taxes paid. And, I demanded he pay all of my attorney's fees."

For just a second, the word, *greedy,* slid into Jim's thoughts.

But then the word vanished!

"I stipulated that he could have the four million dollar house we lived in, all of the furnishings, the three luxury cars and the four vintage cars, the club memberships, our vacation homes, and everything else including his two million dollar plus yearly salary, his private jet, and any bonuses he acquired." She added, "Some gold digger, right? Rob wouldn't settle. After months my attorney took my settlement offer to Rob's father. Rather quickly, Rob settled. Much to his mother's chagrin, his father provided an income for our daughter and added that in the event of his son's death, our divorce settlement would remain binding throughout our daughter's and my lives. Rob and I signed this agreement forty-eight hours later. We are divorced. Have you noticed he hasn't remarried, yet? Obviously, those pesky church ethics and beliefs aren't at issue."

Jim read that sentence, laughed, and thought, *Maybe the father isn't all bad.*

He picked up the last of the newspaper pages and stared at: LUCAS ANTHONY BERKLEY'S DAUGHTER AND GRANDDAUGHTER KILLED IN PLANE CRASH. Jim's first thought was, *no mention of his son-n-law, James, in the headline.* He read that James' private plane had crashed in the vicinity of the Canary Islands shortly after taking off. There were several accounts from fishermen witnessing the crash. Some saw plane parts flying into the water first and some didn't. James' and Annie Nichol's bodies were found still buckled in their seats. The steward was, also, still buckled in his seat. Their baby daughter, Jessica Ann, and James' daughter, Katelyn Jamie, had been searched for but not found. However Katelyn's purse was recovered.

KJ is the name Sam called her daughter. He read further that the pilot's body had been recovered outside of the plane along with some luggage. The immediate cause of the crash hadn't been determined. Witnesses declared the private jet suddenly began heading for the water as though trying to make a water landing. It hit the water, flipped over and quickly sank. Fishing boats headed toward the crash and several fishermen dived into the water looking for survivors. They didn't find any. It was hours later that divers found the jet with the bodies inside.

The final newspaper clipping with the headline, PLANE CRASH SEARCH ENDS, stated that James' father, JD Green, and the coroner his father brought with him to the Island confirmed the bodies recovered were James', Annie Nichol's, his pilot's, and steward's. This final article confirmed that his granddaughters' bodies had not been recovered. The search was concluded and both granddaughters were listed dead as a result of the plane crash.

Jim stacked the newspapers, put them in his car, and headed for the hospital. Arriving in Sam's room, he found Father Tom with his eyes closed sitting in the chair beside her bed. "Read these articles." He set the newspaper pages on Father Tom's lap. "When you've finished, tell me your first thought."

"Whatever happened to saying hello, first? That's my first thought. You know, I might have been deep in prayerful meditation." As he held onto the papers, looked at Jim, and stood up; he regretted kidding around. "Let me take them to the cafeteria. I could use a coke. Do you want anything?"

"A coke sounds good, thanks. When you're finished reading, tell me your first thought. I'll be right here with Sammy."

He sat down in the same chair Tom just vacated. He smoothed Sam's hair back from her forehead. "Sammy," he softly said, "I'm going to find out what happened to KJ." She moved her legs. He picked up her hand. "Samantha, I want to help you. I will find out what happened. Open your beautiful eyes. You seem so close to waking. You have Father Tom and me. Come on." She stilled, and he adjusted her covers and sat back thinking all kinds of thoughts about the articles he just read.

A while later he heard Father Tom talking in the hallway. He quickly walked out of Samantha's room. Together they turned toward the floor lobby.

Father Tom said, "My first thought, why no body? They found the other adults buckled in their seats. KJ should have been buckled in. The baby, well, someone

403

was holding her and with the impact of the crash, they lost her. You need to find out more about the wreckage. Was the fuselage intact? My second thought was, maybe she wa-"

"Wasn't on the flight? That's what I thought. But, there are so many terrible possibilities of what might have happened to her. Maybe she-"

"Now, stop. You need more information."

"You're right. I'm going to call Isabelle, right now. Where was that flight headed? I need to get Rob's father's phone number and talk with him. One of the articles stated he and Jezebel-"

"Her name was Annie Nichol, Jim."

"One article said something about an exotic vacation. I need to find out where they were going, their flight plan, and the passenger list." Jim's mind was flooded with thoughts. He looked back at Samantha's room. "I've changed my mind. I'm going to get a flight to Santa Barbara. I want to meet and talk with Isabelle and her daughter. They'll help me. I need to get Rob's parents' Santa Barbara address and phone number. I want to get a look at them. They obviously have an unlisted phone number. And I didn't mention this to you the other day, Isabelle said something about Rob's parents being connected. I think she was talking about the mafia. That seemed silly to me the other day, but now I just want to get a look at these people and see their faces and reactions to my questions."

"I think that's a good idea. You've got to go."

~~~~~~~~~~~

Early the next morning, Jim got ready to leave for Cleveland Hopkins International Airport. About eight hours later he landed in Los Angeles International Airport and boarded a shuttle to Santa Barbara Municipal. He'd called Isabelle and gotten the only phone number and address she had for her late husband's brother. She wasn't sure about the private phone number but thought her brother-in-law and his wife still lived in the same house.

Late the following day, he was standing at Isabelle's front door ready to meet her in person and anxiously waiting to tell her about his visit with her late husband's brother and sister-in-law. She opened her front door smiling. "I'm so happy to meet you, Jim. Please come in."

He shook her wrinkled, yet, surprisingly strong hand and held it while she guided him to her couch in her front room. He noticed her beautiful Christmas decorations. "Isabelle," he said, "there's no way I could come to Santa Barbara and not see you. The advice you gave me, the first time we talked, gave me new purpose." He smiled as he noticed that her manicured nails were painted a soft shade of violet. Her silver/white styled hair and her kind face with a touch of lipstick and make-up held the decades of years she'd lived with kind dignity.

"Ah, Samantha is dear to you! I'm so happy you have someone special in your life. Tell me how she's doing."

"She's still sleeping. Dr. Jameson is optimistic that she'll wake soon. He has diagnosed her with anorexia, and it's taken a toll on her. I think I told you that she returned to Bay Village to attend her mother's funeral. Actually, Kate, was her second mom. Her parents died when she was in high school. With her daughter's death, and Kate's, this is the second time she's lost her family.

"I thought there was hope that her daughter might not have been on the plane that crashed," Isabelle said looking very concerned.

"Yes, well, I met with James' parents earlier today. Thank you, again, for giving me their private phone number and their address. By the way, they still have that phone number. Although, maybe they'll get it changed because of my call. They really are different, aren't they? I mean,"

"They're very cold people. That's the only way to put it," Isabelle interrupted.

"I definitely felt that they weren't happy with my discussing the possibility that their oldest granddaughter might still be alive. Mr. Green really didn't want to hear it. Neither did Mrs. Green."

Isabelle lit up, "And isn't that odd? You'd think they'd leap to that possibility. My goodness!"

"Well, they told me that there was no doubt about Katelyn being on the plane. She was on the plane, they insisted. Mr. Green let me read the factual report concerning the crash. I read that the private jet made two stops after leaving Miami. The crash occurred shortly after taking off from the second stop. Katelyn, KJ, is listed on the passenger list. The fueler/mechanic watched two women and one man, who was holding an infant, board the private jet along with one pilot and one steward. He has signed a sworn statement verifying this. There were no safety issues concerning the jet. The weather conditions were excellent. The sea was calm. So Isabelle, I still wonder why they didn't find KJ's body. All of the other adults were found."

"Actually Jim, the question is, if the flying conditions were so great and the plane checked out, why did it crash?"

"Exactly! And, one other thing, I just want to talk in person with that mechanic. I've got his name and the name of the Island and airport in the Canary Islands. I need to find out some things: Did this mechanic watch the plane until it took off? Could someone have gotten off, again? Maybe Katelyn got off the jet."

Isabelle was very excited. "That a boy, now you're talking! Go see him and find out for sure. I have a good feeling about this, Jim. This is great excitement. You're about to go on an adventure for the girl you love. This is wonderful for the soul." Isabelle squeezed his hand with amazing strength. He smiled at his new, old friend. Before he spoke again he heard, "My daughter will be here any minute. Stay a while longer, won't you? Dianne's bringing late afternoon supper, and she wants to

meet you. You said you'll be returning to Cleveland on the
night owl flight out of L. A., and you've got your connecting
reservation out of Municipal. So stay put a little longer
until you must leave for the airport. Let's call the cab
company, now, and tell them when to be here. Then I'll fill
you in on the gossip about my esteemed brother-n-law
and the mob."

"Isabelle, the mob, really?"

~~~~~~~~~~~

The next morning Father Tom sat with Samantha. Jim was in California. He sat holding her hand while watching her eyes moving under her closed eyelids. "Sammy, we've talked about many things that happened while you were growing up. We've reminisced the wonderful times, the sad things, the parties, the funeral's, the weddings, and I'm so hopeful you've heard me."

"Honey, I don't know very much about you, Rob, and KJ. I know you must have been a great mom, are a great mom. Honey, I'm so sorry."

Her eyes stayed closed, and she remained calm, but tears slipped down her cheeks.

"Sammy, honey, open your eyes." Tom watched her closely. She remained very still, and her eyes remained closed. "When you're ready to come back, I'll be here."

I broke off my engagement with Jimmy after Lindsey met up with Jackie and Stan Sutherland. I put my engagement ring in a box along with a letter and asked Kate to give it to him. She wanted me to do it in person. Why didn't I have the decency to tell him? I loved him, but that tiny thought in my mind, that he was stuck in a promise he'd made when we were seventeen, kept beat in my heart. My mom's words, "Go places, Sammy, go places," also echoed in my mind. I left for California.

I met Rob, and he took over. Six months later we were married. Kate came to visit me when KJ was born and two other times. My precious daughter and I visited Kate once.

My KJ, why did I let her go with them? Why didn't I stop her, make her stay home? Why didn't I? How could she die so young. If only I'd stopped her, kept her home. I needed Kate. I should have told Kate everything that happened. I was a good mom. I should have made KJ stay home.

Father Tom sat watching Samantha. He watched tears on the rims of her closed eyes slowly overflow and fall down her cheeks. She remained very still.

The buzz from his phone startled him, but not her. She didn't move. He looked at the number. "I'll be right back, honey. It's Jim calling. I'll be down the corridor lobby a few minutes."

"Hello, Jim. How's it going? Did you find out anything?"

"Well, yes and no. I met with Sammy's former in-laws, lovely people if you like cold blooded creatures. I want to go to the Island in the Atlantic where the plane took off and crashed. Mr. Green let me read the official report concerning the crash. There's a fueler/mechanic, who insists saw everyone board the jet. I just feel I need to find this guy. Everything hinges on what he saw."

"So you want to go see this man?"

"I don't know, Tom. Saying this out loud makes the idea seem crazy. What am I doing? The original investigators must have thoroughly questioned him. Mr. Green is KJ's grandfather, and he's convinced she got back on the plane. And yet, somehow, when I sat and talked with him and Mrs.Green, it was strange. I had the feeling they were hiding something."

"Jim, stop, don't question what's nagging you. I think you should go talk with the mechanic. Find out if there's any doubt at all that everyone got back on. You know what? I'm going to find out if my brother has a company jet available. He runs the company, now. I know he'll get me a jet from somewhere if I ask him. Every year when I stay with him and my sister-in-law, they tell me a thousand times to call them if I need anything."

"That would make everything so much easier, but what about expenses? I mean will they let me pay?"

"I doubt it, but I'll tell my brother you want to pay. He'll be more than happy to help us. You didn't say, are you at the airport?"

"Yes, I spent the afternoon with Isabelle Green and her daughter, Dianne. They're a trip! Wonderful people. You would never guess Isabelle is in her nineties. Got to the

410

airport about an hour ago. My flight is on schedule, although there isn't a plane at our gate, yet. I'll see you tomorrow afternoon at the hospital. Tom, if your brother can help us, please tell him how much I appreciate it."

"Will do." Father Tom hung up. He decided to go to the cafeteria to get a coke before checking back on Samantha and then calling his brother. Getting off the elevator and walking down the first floor corridor, the cafeteria appeared to be closed. He realized it was open when he saw the cashier.

She smiled at him after he asked for a coke, and she handed him a container holding two cokes with lids. "These are on the house, Father. Thought your friend might be thirsty, too."

He smiled back thinking, *She's seen me with Jim.* He looked at her name tag, "Thank-you, Joan."

As Tom got off of the elevator on Samantha's floor he saw Dr. Jameson grinning ear to ear looking toward the nurses station and at him. "She'd like a bath and a coke."

"What?"

Dr. Jameson happily continued, "While I was checking on Samantha, she opened her eyes and announced she'd like a bath and a coke. She's awake! She wants a coke."

He watched Tom quickly return to the elevator. "Hey, where are you going? She's awake!"

Father Tom anxiously pushed the button for the elevator. "Come on, Come on." He got in, then got out as the elevator doors reopened on the first floor. He rushed to the cafeteria. The lights were off, the cafeteria was empty, and according to the sign it had been closed for a little over an hour. He whispered, "Oh my God, Sammy, I just saw your mom." He set the cokes down and knelt. He blessed himself. "Glory be to God! God bless you, Joan." He'd never experienced such peaceful clarity. For several seconds the cafeteria glowed in shimmering light. Then it was dim once more. "Dear God, thank You." He wiped his tears, picked up the cokes, and rushed to Samantha's floor.

He walked into her room seeing her looking frail, yet siting up in bed with her eyes wide open. "Sammy," he set the cokes down, "you're awake. We were so worried."

411

"I'm thirsty. Is one of those cokes for me?" Her voice was clear but soft.

"Absolutely, you better believe it! One is for you." He looked at Dr. Jameson, "I think you can have one. Definitely she can, right, doctor?"

Dr. Jameson replied, "Samantha, have a few sips of water first. I'm going to check you over as soon as your nurse finishes with another patient. By the way, we met a few weeks ago. I'm Dr. Jameson."

"I remember."

Her doctor smiled noting she remembered as a nurse came in and placed a thermometer under Samantha's tongue. "I'll speak with you in the hall, Tom, as soon as we finish."

Twenty minutes later Dr. Jameson happily said, "I think she's doing great. She can have some of the cola. We'll start her on a soft diet tomorrow. I've ordered broth for her. Just give her a little pop."

"Could she go back into the coma again?"

"I'm sure she's passed that. We admitted her just before Thanksgiving, and now it's a few weeks until Christmas. If she seems confused, try not to alarm her. Tell her she's been resting for several days and that everything's fine. Catch her up as she asks questions. Therapists will meet with her tomorrow. Don't tell her anything that might upset her. Can you handle this?"

"Yes, we'll be fine. You know about the plane crash and about her daughter?"

"I do. Stay away from that topic. We don't want to upset her. Therapists will help her with these things. She does need to face the facts in her life, but not tonight. You're the best person she could have near. The nurse I called will be here any minute, and she's the next best person. She has a wonderful sense of humor. I'll check back before I leave the hospital. This is a good day. Will you be staying in her room all night?"

"Absolutely, I will. I need to make two phone calls. He explained what Jim was doing. Can she be alone for a few minutes?"

"Yes, but don't mention what Jim is up to, and let her sleep. I mean, don't try to keep her awake if she gets tired. I'll check back with you." He left for the nurses' station.

Father Tom opened the door to Samantha's room smiling, then he noticed the I.V. was still running.

She said as she held up her arm, "I should be rid of this, tomorrow, I hope."

"That's wonderful! Did you have any of your coke?"

"I have. It tastes perfect."

"I bet it does," he looked at the cross on the wall and thought, *Such a blessing.*

"Where's Jim," she asked.

She apparently doesn't want to talk about the last weeks. "Well, he certainly didn't want to leave right now, but he had some family business to settle, something to do with his sister," he fibbed. "When the nurse comes back, I'll go to the solarium and call him. I'll find out when he'll be back, and do you mind if I tell him you're doing so much better?"

"Sure, tell him. Do you, both, know everything? I tried, I really tried." She began crying.

"Don't cry, honey. Everything will be fine. You have Jim and me. We love you."

A nurse walked in the room certainly seeing the tears. "Hello, Samantha. I'm Jane. I'll be your nurse until midnight." She ignored the crying. "Would you like a little broth? Actually, I should just be honest. Dr. Jameson has decided you need to have some broth. I bet he didn't even ask you if you like it. Just like a man, you know? He decided you're going to have some broth whether you like it or not. Men!"

Sammy was wiping her eyes and somewhat smiling.

"Well, he didn't decide what kind. There's chicken, beef, or vegetable."

"Chicken, thank you, Jane."

"I'll be right back." She started to leave and turned back. "If I could smuggle in a glass of wine, I would! I'll get the chicken broth."

Samantha laughed and said, "I like her."

When she returned with two bowls of broth, one chicken and one vegetable, she asked Samantha if she could join her for dinner. "Taste the chicken broth. If you

413

don't like it, try the vegetable. I like both, and I'll have either one. There's lots of spoons."

Sammy noticed two pink roses in a small vase on the tray and smiled. She thought about Lindsey a second. "Thank you. I like the chicken broth."

Father Tom hurried to the solarium to make his phone calls.

Once in the Solarium, Tom called his brother, John, first. John ran the family company, now. Their parents died years ago. He explained Samantha's situation and what had happened to her daughter, KJ. He told John that he and Jim were questioning why KJ's body hadn't been recovered with the others. Explaining that Jim was in California now and had met with KJ's grandparents, he said that Jim wanted to go to the airport in the Canary Islands where the jet took off.

John asked a few questions, then told his brother he'd have a company jet at Cleveland Hopkins Airport the next morning along with Hal Thompson, one of the company's investigators. "Hal's in Chicago, along with a company jet, right now, He'll be on his way to Cleveland within two hours."

"You introduced me to Hal the last time I visited. He's just like I was when I became a priest: young for the job, but very qualified."

"No-one's more qualified than my brother, The Priest. At least that's what your sister-in-law tells everyone we know."

"Jen's my favorite! Thanks, John, I appreciate this. I'll have the name of the Island where the flight took off and who died within the hour. The crash happened about six months ago."

"Don't worry about it. Hal will quickly find out that information. He'll meet Jim at his landing gate tomorrow morning. He'll take good care of him. Get his passport and anything else he might need. I'll have a courier meet you at his house. Just call this number when you're ready, and he'll meet you at Jim's."

He wrote the number down. "Ok, John, I've got it."

"I'm glad you've come to your family for help. You so seldom ask us for anything. Jen's looking forward to seeing you this summer, if not sooner. It would be great if we could see you at Christmas. It's less than two weeks away. We know this is your busy season, well, one of them."

Tom smiled and answered, "Let's figure out a time to get together after the first of the year. Summer's too long

415

to wait. Back to the matter at hand. The names of those listed dead in the crash are James Robert Green, Katelyn Jamie Green, and Annie. Katelyn Jamie is called KJ. The pilot and steward also were killed. Oh, damn, I can't remember Annie's last name. I'll call you back. James' and Annie's baby died in the crash, also. The baby's body wasn't recovered either."

"Don't worry about anything, Tom. Hal will be at Jim's gate tomorrow when he lands. Do you know the home address?"

He gave his brother the address, hung up, and quickly called Jim's cell phone.

It was answered on the first ring. "Hi, Tom, we're just boarding the flight."

"She's awake, Jim! She's talking, and she's having some broth and a little coke a cola right now."

"Thank God! Did you tell her where I am?"

"No, I didn't. Listen, you should go, immediately, to the Island and talk with the mechanic. You shouldn't come to the hospital and tell her you're questioning what happened to her daughter. The doctor doesn't want anything upsetting her. She asked about you. I told her that you're with your sister for a few days helping with a family problem. I've already called my brother to see if he could help us. He's having a company investigator, Hal Thompson, meet you at your gate when you deplane tomorrow morning. He'll take you to a company jet, which will be at the airport as well. You'll have use of the jet and Hal as long as you need. Hal will help you find out everything about the doomed flight. Tell me where your passport is and what clothes you want. Like I said, Dr. Jameson doesn't want anything upsetting Sammy. If you still think there's a chance her daughter is alive after you check things out, we'll tell her."

"Doomed flight,' words a guy loves to hear as he's boarding a plane. Everything you've done is amazing. I appreciate your brother's help." He told Tom where to find his passport and what clothes. "They're about to shut the door without me. Thanks, Tom. We'll find out what happened. Take care of Sammy for me. Tell her I send my love, and I'm happy she's doing much better. Thank you, Tom." Jim got on his flight to Cleveland, and Father

416

Tom went back to Sam's room.

Tom and Samantha watched TV without talking very much. He noticed she kept nodding off to sleep, then quickly opening her eyes. "Sammy, sleep for a while. I need to leave, but I'll be back in an hour or so. Nurse Jane is here and will check in, too. I'll be back soon, and stay all night." He helped her get comfortable and watched her until she was sleeping. He said a prayer and quietly left the room.

"Jane, I'll be back in an hour. I'm glad you're here for Samantha tonight. She's sleeping. I left her TV on with the volume off."

"Father, Dr. Jameson and I are close. My husband died several years ago. He was a doctor here. Dave called and asked me to come in tonight. I have a Ph.D. in psychiatry as well as a nursing degree. I'm happy to be helping Mrs. Green. She's doing great."

"Thank you. I'll make a quick stop to check things at St. Joseph's, too. I'll be back soon."

417

A man dressed in casual clothes was standing at Jim's gate when he deplaned in Cleveland. Hal recognized Jim from the picture on his passport. He put his hand out to shake hands as he walked to him saying, "Jim Peterson, I'm Hal Thompson. Hope your first flight went well."

"Hal, it's great meeting you. I can't thank you enough for helping with this." Jim subconsciously assessed him, *Sharp young man, late twenties, early thirties.*

"I'm glad we can help, and I'm sorry to tell you that you'll be traveling another fifteen hours. I think you'll be more comfortable in our jet, though. We'll have three stops. We're set to leave as soon as we get you on board. I hear we have a young lady to find." Hal's last words lit Jim's face.

They immediately began walking through the terminal. "John Brown's brother means so much to him and his family. Most at the company have never met Father Tom, but I have. Everyone working for our company knows about him. John talks about him often. How long have you known him?"

"Most of my life, we're close friends. Father Tom's one of those people who makes everything around him better."

"Really, you appear considerably younger." They were outside the terminal now. He steered Jim to a waiting car, and they got in.

"I can't wait to tell him that you noticed I'm younger. It's harder to tell, now, at our ages." He thought, *You seem very young.* "He's been our parish priest since I was in fourth grade. Now, I'm his parish school's principal. We're contemporaries at this stage of our lives. He doesn't seem to age."

Hal, getting down to business, quickly answered, "Some people are lucky that way." He changed the subject. "I have quite a bit of information about Mr. James Robert Green, not such a respectable human being. I gather you know that much already. His family is quite the group. They have themselves some nasty, nasty friends."

"Actually, I don't know very much about Rob, I mean James. I only know him as Rob. I just know he was an attorney married to my, my friend, Samantha. I recently met his parents, and they were a trip."

Hal looked at Jim a second thinking, *By that look on your face, Samantha's more than a friend.*

The car pulled up along side a sharp looking jet. As they got out of the car Hal said, "We've tracked down the mechanic you want to talk with. We'll be meeting him at Tenerife Island's airport, Tenerife Norte, tomorrow. We've, also, gathered some information on Miss Green. In fact, we're learning more information from some of her former college classmates as we speak."

"This is amazing." Jim couldn't believe so much was happening so fast.

They were stepping up the steps into the private jet. "As soon as we level off, you'll be able to freshen up. Then I'll fill you in on everything we know about Miss Katelyn Jamie Green."

Jim looked around. He couldn't believe the elegance of the private jet. He sat down in a front facing chair and buckled his seat belt.

Hal sat facing him and said, "I'll show you around in a few minutes. Your suitcase is in back near the shower. Your clothes are hanging in the closet."

About forty-five minutes later, Jim had showered, shaved, and changed clothes. He walked through the jet past a compact library, and a bar finding Hal in the lounge area.

Hal smiled, "Sit down. Comfortable, aren't they?" He didn't give Jim the chance to agree. "Are you ready to hear what we know about K.J.?"

A steward carried in a tray filled with eggs, bacon, toast, sweet rolls, juices, and coffee. "Good morning, Mr. Peterson, we can add pancakes, waffles, anything you'd like."

"Thank you. This is perfect."

"May I pour you some coffee?"

"That would be great."

He poured Hal some coffee, too. "Hal, let me know if you need anything." He closed the door behind him as he left.

After they finished breakfast, Hal handed Jim a picture of a beautiful young woman and said, "Are you ready to

419

hear about Katelyn Green? Her friends call her KJ. Just before she graduated from college she legally changed her name to Kate J. Cole."

Looking at her picture slapped Jim's heart. "My God, she looks exactly how her mother looked at that age." He stared at the picture thinking, *That's just how Sammy looked when she bolted out of my life.* His eyes remained on the picture as he added, "Her mother's maiden name is Cole."

Hal noticed the sad expression on Jim's face and continued, "Katelyn graduated from USC with a dual degree in education and business finance. She'd planned on traveling to Africa with some college friends after her graduation. She'd gotten her shots, her updated passport, and everything. Apparently, she changed her mind and stayed home. Things had gotten nasty between her parents."

"She wanted to go to Africa? Kids usually graduate and travel to Europe, maybe, but Africa? Really?" Jim looked amazed. He thought about Lindsey, who'd been in Africa for years. "I read the accounts of Samantha's divorce in the newspapers. It was awful. That's when I read about the plane crash and got this feeling about KJ. It just seems so odd that her body wasn't found with the others, don't you think?"

Hal decided to level with him, kind of. "We think you're right about things seeming odd. Our findings indicate the plane crash, possibly, wasn't an accident."

Jim looked surprised.

"The report states that the plane went down and stayed intact. Some, who witnessed the crash, said it looked like the plane was intentionally landing on the water. A few witnesses saw plane parts in the air. Others didn't see any."

"Yes, I read that in the newspapers Isabelle sent me."

"Isabell?"

"It really doesn't matter. Isabelle is a dear, older lady, who happened to be married to Samantha's former father-in-law's brother. Her husband died many years ago."

Hal closed his eyes to figure out Jim's last sentence.

"She sent me the newspaper articles about Samantha's and Rob's divorce and about the plane crash.

Accounts in the newspaper said the plane looked like it was making a landing on the water and just disappeared beneath."

He studied Jim for several seconds and decided to tell him this much, "We think one of the fishing boats caused the plane to crash. The jet had been flying unusually close to the water. Possibly, the jet was shot down from one of the fishing boats. Possibly, there was collusion between the pilot and someone on board one of the fishing boats. Rob's, aka James', father, who is Isabelle's brother-in-law," Hal smiled, "pretty good, huh?" He continued, "had his private plane lifted out of the water onto a barge and disassembled immediately. It was back in his company's airplane hanger in the States very quickly."

"How did he get away with that?"

"You'd be surprised what people with the right connections and the right money can accomplish," Hal smugly stated.

"Oh."

"You bet your ass! Mr. James D. Green, James Robert's dad, is connected. What he wants done, gets done."

"Oh," Jim repeated in amazement.

"I have a feeling the mechanic you want to talk with knows a lot more than he's said. I think he'll find it in his best interest to level with us. We have our connections, too."

"We do?" Jim looked at him in disbelief, feeling like he was on an amusement park ride. He was tired and thought he was going to start laughing any second. *God, Tom, you should hear this stuff about your family being connected.* Then he considered, *Tom has never really said very much about his family's company.* Jim's smile faded.

"Hey, don't worry about it. We can get accurate information very quickly. Father Tom's family is very respectable. Their company and all business dealings are above board. I promise you." Hal changed the subject. "Would you like to relax and watch a movie? Let me show you the movie list. I have a few things to do, anyway."

Jim chose a James Bond movie. *Seems appropriate,* he thought. He watched the movie and fell asleep before it ended. He slept over three hours more.

Hal woke him up telling him they would be landing for refueling in ten minutes and that dinner would be ready an hour after they took off again. "How about a beer or something?

During dinner Jim heard about the times Father Tom's family had visited the White House. Father Tom's dad had become friends with Presidents Johnson, Nixon, Ford, and Carter. His brother, John, had been at White House events with the next three presidents.

"We've got about five more hours in the air," Hal said as they waited for dessert. "It'll be morning, with the time difference, when we arrive. A driver will meet us and take us to our hotel. We have rooms reserved. Hopefully, we'll get a little sleep. We're set to meet with the mechanic tomorrow at one. Sound ok?"

"Sounds great."

~~~~~~~~~~~~

Although Hal and Jim were tired, they spent a few morning hours in a restless sleep in their hotel rooms. By one o'clock they were face to face with the mechanic who serviced James Robert Green's, Rob's, jet.

Hal introduced himself and Jim to the mechanic. Although Hal already knew the mechanic's name, he let the man introduce himself. It was a ploy he used when he wanted to make the other person feel that he didn't have any information.

"Hi, I'm Mike. What can I do for you?"

Hal noticed that he didn't say his last name which he knew was Markum. *I'll go easy with this guy, for now.* "Well, we're trying to get some information about that flight that went down about six months ago."

"I've already told investigators everything."

"I'm sure you did, but we'd just like to pick your brain a minute or two."

Mike shifted his feet and looked over at a parked jet. "Look, I've got a lot to do. I'm the only mechanic here right now. I've said everything about Mr. Green's jet there is to say."

Hal thought, *So Mike seems to know the Green's.* "Humor us, look at this picture. Do you recognize her?" He handed Mike the picture of KJ.

Mike took a quick glance, "Yes, I watched her, another adult female, Mr. Green's son, and one infant come off the plane and I watched this one," he looked at her picture, "get back on ahead of the others. I also watched the pilot and one other male, a steward, deplane after the family."

He's rehearsed his answer, he's agitated, and he knows the older Mr. Green and the son. Maybe they've traveled here a few times. "She," Hal waved the picture he had back in his hand, "got back on before anyone else?"

"Yes."

"And you saw everyone else get back on board?"

"I saw the pilot and steward board after she did. The others boarded ten minutes or so later."

Hal glared at Mike. "You watched the others board?"

Mike shifted, again. "Look, obviously they got back on. They were the ones found later, after."

423

Jim remembered something Rob's father had told him. He said, "What a minute, I talked with Mr. Green, and read the factual report, and you swore you saw everyone get back on the plane. Did you?"

"I swore that two adult females, one adult male, one infant, one steward, and one pilot were listed on the flight manifest when it took off. I never swore I saw everyone board, again."

Jim couldn't remember the exact wording of what he'd read.

"I did see that one," he glanced at the picture Hal still held, "get back on the plane about twenty minutes after she got off. Like I said, we know the others were on board because they were found dead. Am I done, here?"

Hal grinned at him, "Yes. Thanks for talking with us."

Hal walked away with Jim and said, "Well, it sounds as though he saw KJ get back on the jet."

"Wait!" Jim hollered to Mike and jogged over to him. Hal jogged with him. "Before the plane took off again, could anyone have gotten off without you seeing them?"

"Look, this area of the airport isn't that busy. That day, I finished refueling and checking the plane, and believe me, it checked out perfectly. I began checking another smaller jet parked right beside the one in question. I was working between the two. I would have noticed a beautiful girl walking past me, trust me. Look around. You notice people moving around out here. I'm sure no-one got off, once they got back on."

"Thanks." Jim turned and walked away,

Mike turned away, closed his eyes a second, and exhaled as he walked toward the hanger. He thought about everything that he'd done that day, six months ago, and wiped the sweat now beading on his forehead. Once inside he waited until Hal and Jim were out of sight, then he got his phone and called someone.

Jim felt sick. He looked at Hal and said, "He does seem positive. She got back on, and the jet crashed. I guess that's all there is to say."

"What? You're giving up already? You better stick with your career in education because you'd make a lousy investigator! Come on. We need a beer and some lunch.

I've been told there's a great little place not far from the airport. There should be a car waiting for us."

Sure enough, when they got to the road a driver was waiting. He sped down the road to the popular bar and abruptly stopped. Hal spoke to the driver a second and paid him. Once inside, they saw a mix of happy vacationers and locals filling up much of the bar. Hal found a table with three chairs and they sat down. "Beer sound good," he asked.

"Great." Jim spat the word out. His emotions had run the gamut. He'd been hopeful about KJ, thrilled to hear Samantha was awake, impressed with Hal and the private jet, amazed to hear about Father Tom's family knowing US presidents, and bitterly sad and disappointed about KJ being on board the plane that crashed. All of this happening in about twenty-four non sleeping well hours. He felt wiped out.

"Hey, snap out of it." Hal slid a beer toward him. "Look, the mechanic said he didn't see the others board, again, right? He didn't see the others board, yet he's sure he would have noticed someone get off the plane. I mean, the line he just handed you is, horse shit! Mike's a jerk and maybe a liar as well. I've got a full list of every flight that landed and took off that day and the destinations. She may have gotten herself on another plane. There are three that seem the most interesting. One of the pilots from one of these flights is meeting us here in about an hour. Actually, his flight, six months ago, seems like the best bet."

"Ok, but I just keep wondering, why hasn't KJ's mom or anyone heard from her? That's the thing that wipes everything out, the more I think about it. If she's alive, she would have contacted her mom."

Hal looked at him a second thinking, *that bugs me, too.* He said, "We've talked with some of KJ's friends. According to them she wasn't thrilled with either one of her parents. "KJ's friends said she went along on her father's vacation for three reasons: First of all, she wanted to get away from her mom for a while because they'd been arguing so much. Reason number two, she wanted to spend time with her new baby sister. And the third reason, her dad and his girlfriend were getting married on this trip,

425

and he insisted both of his daughters be at the wedding ceremony. So here's what we have, Jim. We've got KJ maybe realizing she couldn't handle being on the trip with her father and his new woman. Difficult mother, new baby sister, demanding father; whatever made her go in the first place, maybe she wanted out of the trip. Maybe she hatched a plan to leave her dad's vacation when a plan became possible. You know, kind of moment by moment."

"You know what, Hal, that makes sense. And I can tell you from personal experience that kind of behavior, simply bolting out from a situation, runs in KJ's genes especially at her age." He felt optimistic, again.

"See that guy by the door? Doesn't he appear to be looking for someone? He's early, but I think that's the pilot we want to talk with." Hal waved him over to their table.

She could hardly stand it. They'd been traveling in her father's private jet less than a day, and this four week vacation with her father and his fiancé was already making her crazy. She looked at her baby sister nestled in Annie's arms, and smiled. She hadn't planned to like her father's new baby, but KJ loved her tiny sister as soon as she saw her. She asked Annie, "Can I hold her awhile?"

"Sure, honey."

KJ gently cradled Jessica while looking at her dear face. *You know,* she silently thought while gazing into her baby sister's blue eyes, *your mommy makes me crazy! She's just six years older than I am. Isn't that funny? You and I are sister's, and I'm twenty-two years older than you and six years younger than your mommy. Don't we have a special daddy? Your mommy and I, both, went to USC and we joined the same sorority; six years apart. Your mommy actually helped me fill out my applications.* KJ thought about that for a minute. She looked at her father, who was busy kissing the love of his life, as he called Annie Nichol. She softly swirled her finger across her sister's tiny cheek. *Sweet baby, they love you very much. So do I.*

She was amazed at the expressions on her baby sister's face as her thoughts rolled on. *I don't know how to do this vacation, sweet Jessica. I love you, baby girl, and we'll have so much time together. We've only been gone hours, and I'm already wanting to slap our daddy's and your mommy's happy faces. It's so hard for me to be around them.* She watched Jessica's bottom lip pout. KJ lifted her sister to her shoulder. *There, there, no need to worry. No slapping allowed!* She patted her little sister's back and felt her snuggle into place.

Her thoughts floated on as though quickly thinking it through would fix her anguish. *Our daddy used to be married to my mommy. He broke her heart because of your mommy. Our daddy insisted that I come on this vacation with the three of you. Well, my mommy wasn't thrilled about that! Our daddy put my mommy through a lot of humiliation. She begged me not to go on this trip, and argued with me, and told me I'd be miserable. So*

*basically I made one of my parent's happy, and I hurt the
other.*

KJ looked out the window at the perfect blue sky. She
moved Jessica from her shoulder back into her arms and
looked at her wide open blue eyes. She smiled and
thought, *Sweet baby sister, you're the only reason I came
on this trip. You are the amazing gift that has come from
all of this. Our daddy and your mommy love you with all of
their hearts. I do, too. You are precious. Yes, you're why
I came along. I do have to admit my mommy's behavior,
since everything began happening with your mommy,
hasn't been easy to handle. If I could just get away from
our daddy, your mommy, and my mommy for one week, let
alone four weeks, I would.*

James turned to look at both of his daughters.
"Katelyn, we'll be landing to refuel, again, in about twenty-
five minutes. Do you plan on getting off and walking
around for a bit? We'll be on the ground for fifty minutes."

He still calls me Katelyn. "Would you like me to stay
on board, Dad? I mean, do you want me to lay Jessica
down for her nap and stay with her?"

Annie glanced at James and answered, "I think we all
should get off, walk around, and get some fresh air. I'll
change Jessie, and, hopefully, she'll sleep when we take
off again."

Walking down the steps from the jet, KJ quickly got out ahead of her dad and Annie because she wanted to call her mom. She didn't want to use her cell phone chancing that her dad or Annie might notice the call. She found two pay phones across from the small snack bar. One was being used, so she walked to the other one.

The man on the other phone had a large sounding, jovial voice. She overheard him saying, "I have one more supply stop in Mali. Otherwise, I'm empty and on my way home. Tell the kids I love them. And you're feeling good, right?"

KJ smiled hearing his words and then noticed the other phone was out of order. She heard him ask, "You forgot to tell me what about Karlie? She made first chair in band? Lord! We've listened to her practice those ten minutes a week. The fifth/sixth grade band must be in band hell! No, don't tell her I said that," he laughed. "Tell her I'm very proud of her. Honey, I've got to go. There's a pretty young lady here waiting to use this phone. Nope, no-one is as pretty as you. See you late tomorrow. Glad all is good. I love you." He hung up.

"I'm sorry." K.J.'s face was bright red. "Excuse me, please," she said to the man who seemed to be in his late thirty's early forty's. "I didn't mean to make you hang up. I overheard you. You just looked so happy while you were talking. I wasn't trying to listen. I was just going to call my mom, but the other phone is out of order."

He gave her a big smile back and said, "Hey, don't worry about it."

She asked, "Are you a pilot?"

"I am that. My partner and I have a small fleet of planes that fly people, supplies, anything legal to just about anywhere." He handed her his card. She quickly read his name, Hank Kennedy.

"Where are you off to next?"

"Africa. There's a group of doctors we fly supplies to about every six weeks or so. Fun group, too, partied with them many times. We've become great friends. First time was when they found out I was getting married. That was a lot of years ago. They suspected they weren't invited to my bachelor's party back in the states, so they hauled me along with the medical supplies I'd just delivered to a weekend I'll never forget! We've partied a lot. Several parties later, two of them got married. That was the first party my wife attended. They're wonderful people."

KJ studied him as an idea shot through her mind. *Should I? Yes, she decided. Maybe I'm out of here.* "You know, I've always wanted to go to Africa. Are you flying to a city that has hotels?"

"What?" He looked at her as though she was crazy.

"Oh, I know you think I've lost it. I told my dear friend, see her over there," she pointed at Annie, while quickly fabricating her fib, "that I would go on this trip with her, her old husband," she pointed at her father, "their new baby, and the baby's nanny, who must be in the restroom, I guess." *Woow, I almost blew it adding the nanny,* she thought. "Well, let me tell you, this is the vacation from hell! They're all lovey, dovey. They need me around like a hole in the head, you know?"

Hank just looked at her with his mouth kind of open to speak, but he couldn't think of a thing to say.

She spoke more calmly as she added a few truthful sentences. "I was all set to go to Africa when I graduated from college. That trip was cancelled. Now, here you are, and here I am. I'm saved from the trip in hell and on my way to Africa, if I can hitch a ride with you. Believe me, they'll thank you, too."

Her words gained momentum, "I'm certain my friend wishes she hadn't asked me to come. She just wants to be alone with her husband. They'll never miss me. I can pay the amount you charge." She took a breath and stopped talking. Then as she and Hank looked over at Annie and her old husband, her dad planted a long kiss on Annie's lips as if on cue. "See what I mean?" For the first time ever, she silently thanked her dad for slobbering all over Annie.

Hank wasn't exactly smiling as he looked back at KJ, but he did look amazed.

"Listen, look," she fumbled through her purse and handed him her immunization card and her passport. *One last ploy,* she thought. "I know this seems crazy. But you know, you're only young and free to do crazy things maybe once or twice in life. I'm educated, I've got my bachelor's degree in education and business finance, I haven't gotten a job, yet, and I'm unattached. I have my parents, who I will let know my change of plans. Please! My friend and her little family will never miss me. I'll go tell them right now. You can watch me. Are you flying to a city where I could fly back to the states if I want?"

Hank studied her passport and immunization card, then looked at her. He thought about all of the adventures he'd had and his wife had before they married each other. He smiled at KJ and said, "You know, I could be a mass murderer or someone even worse!"

She knew she had him. "No, not you, I heard you say you love your kids and your wife."

He smiled and looked at his watch. "Ok, you're on! Meet me outside of that," he pointed, "orange door in twenty minutes. Is that enough time? And, yes, there are hotels and points of interest in Bamako, the city in Mali where I'm flying supplies. I'll make sure you get into a safe cab that will take you to a good hotel. After that you'll be on your own. I have to add your name to my flight manifest. I'll need your passport. Make sure I give it back to you. See you in twenty minutes by the orange door."

"Thank you! Thank you so much!" Her name on her passport read, Kate J. Cole. She hadn't ever really liked the name Katelyn Jamie Green. She'd had her sir name legally changed from Green to her mom's maiden name, Cole. She made the change just before she graduated. She knew this change would really irritate her father and that gave her vengeful satisfaction. "I'll go tell my friend my change of plans. They'll be so happy. I need to get my bag off of their plane. I'll see you outside of that orange door in less than twenty minutes." She quickly looked at his card in her hand and said, "Thanks, Mr. Kennedy."

"Call me, Hank," he said as she started walking toward her dad and Annie. He watched her hug the older man and then her friend. Hank shook his head as he walked out the orange door.

KJ was making it up as she was standing in front of Annie and her dad. "Annie, Dad, I just want to tell you, both, that I'm sorry for the way I've been acting." She gave a her dad a hug, "I love you, Dad." She was

431

surprised those words slipped out. She'd been angry with him for so long. She hadn't told him she loved him in two years. She hugged Annie. She opened her purse, so they would see it, and took out a Kleenex. "Dad, I'm going back in the plane to lie down. Would you wake me in an hour if I'm still sleeping?"

James hugged his oldest daughter, again, while thinking, *Maybe she's finally coming around and accepting things.* He said, "We'll get you off, I mean, up."

KJ walked quickly passed her baby sister. Jessica with her sweet blue eyes and precious face was the only one who could make her reconsider her escape. She hurried away with her own eyes on the exit door.

Once inside her dad's private plane, she emptied all essentials from her purse into her suitcase leaving a few items in it including her cell phone. She left her purse where her dad would see it knowing he'd think she was sleeping in the back cabin. Just in case he checked, she made the bed look like she was in it arranging the pillows in a body shape and pulling up the comforter. She buckled the seat belt around the covers and pulled the blind so it was almost closed, making the body shape more convincing. Looking at it she thought, *Looks real.* She swiftly changed clothes putting on her grey running pants and black jacket, putting what she took off into her suitcase.

She wrote her dad a note telling him not to worry that she needed time to herself. Quickly she added that she'd call her mom in a few days and that she'd stay safe. After sliding the note near the pillow and under the top of the cover, she shoved hair under her red baseball cap. KJ looked out a small window to see if the mechanic, who watched her board, was still around. She didn't see him and realized it didn't matter anyway and immediately picked up her suitcase, stepped down the steps, and walked toward the orange door. Just seconds before she saw Hank walking toward her, she pulled her cap off and fluffed her hair. He took hold of her suitcase and walked with her to his plane.

After they took off and reached altitude, KJ asked Hank about his family. He happily told her how he met his wife, Peg, and all about their two daughters. Everything

he said had a funny side. KJ found herself laughing at the stories he told about himself and his family.

Hank was making her laugh one minute and lecturing her the next. "I know you'll want to see the sights." He wrote the name of a hotel on a note card and handed it to her. "Stay in this hotel, and use this hotel's concierge only. Make sure the concierge knows where you're going and when you'll need a car to return. This is important, young lady. Do not go anywhere alone at night. Do you understand me? It isn't safe for a young lady to go anyplace alone at night. My doctor friends stay here. It's a very good and safe hotel."

He pulled cards out of his pocket. "Look through these cards and take the travel agent card. Take two if you want. This is a good agency. They'll know about other groups traveling with people your age. Also, they'll get you back home. If you decide to travel elsewhere in Africa, use this agency, and tell them if you want to travel with people your age." He smiled at her and shook his head. He said, "I'm telling you, if my daughters ever pull a stunt like this, I'll kill them myself!"

"Now, don't forget, you're their father and you had fun times. And it sounds like Peg had her own adventures. Thanks Hank, you're a very special person." She relaxed feeling positively calm and carefree. She hadn't experienced this feeling for a long, long time.

He wouldn't take any money for the flight. He walked her to the cab driver he knew, paid her fare, and told him which hotel

433

SIX MONTHS EARLIER

She was tired when she walked into the lobby. At the front desk she paid for three nights stay in cash and did what Hank told her: used the hotel safe to keep most of her money and her credit cards. Feeling so tired while she waited for the elevator, she closed her eyes not noticing the elevator door opened.

A lady stepping out into the lobby, noticed and said. You must be tired, long day?"

KJ opened her eyes, smiled, and answered, "Yes, to both."

The lady stayed in front of her and stared at her for a few moments. "Excuse me, I'm sorry," she moved aside. "It's just that, wow! Never mind. Enjoy your stay."

"I will, thank you." KJ stepped past her and got off on the fifth floor, found her room with her suitcase inside, and put the Do Not Disturb sign outside her door. Minutes later she showered and got into bed. She slept for the rest of the evening, all night, and didn't leave her room until late the next morning.

Feeling very hungry when she woke up, she decided to have breakfast or lunch in the hotel dining room. Her brunch set in front of her twenty minutes later. KJ told the waiter, "Just looking at my food arranged on this plate is wonderful. It looks so pretty."

He smiled, "We hope you enjoy eating it, too, Miss."

She sure enjoyed eating it, thinking, *This is delicious. I love it.* Without realizing that someone was standing near her table, she finally looked up and saw the same lady she'd seen at the elevator the night before.

"Excuse me, again," the lady said. "I just can't believe how much you look like my sister. She and I haven't seen each other for years. Well, actually, we became sisters." She laughed, "I sound crazier now than I did yesterday. You look like a twin version of her when she was your age."

"I do?" KJ asked and smiled while looking into her kind eyes.

"Yes, you really do. Her name is Samantha Cole, I mean Samantha Green."

KJ's fork slipped from her fingers onto the floor, and then she noticed this lady's arm. She remembered. She looked back up at the smiling face and said, "That's my mom."

Talking for hours and listening to stories about her mom's, Karen's, and Lindsey's sweet relationship filled KJ's heart. Pieces of her own childhood, that she hadn't remembered for a long time, came to life. Looking at Lindsey's kind eyes, and hearing about Kate, she remembered Kate and spending time with her twice. Lindsey opened her to a side of her mom she hadn't ever known.

After spending several hours together, Lindsey laughed and said, "You realize you're my niece! It would be wonderful if you could stay for a while, live with us, and help us. Alex, your uncle, is an amazing person, and you must meet him. Let's call Sammy and see what she thinks. You'll need to stay for several months, however. KJ, you'll experience and see parts of Africa you'll otherwise miss."

"Staying with you is just what I want to do. You're going to have to help me talk my mom," she hugged Lindsey, "your sister, into this. Aunt Lindsey, this is crazy! My mom thinks I'm with my dad, and she wasn't happy about that. I'll explain that later. I have no idea what her reaction will be to my bolting out of my dad's vacation."

Lindsey laughed, "I think she just may understand how you could do that!"

They tried calling Sammy's number and a message said it wasn't a working number. They had the number checked to no avail. "I forgot. We were getting a ton of annoying phone calls. My mom wanted to get a private phone number. She knows we have cell phones. I bet she already got a private number. The only problem is, I left my cell phone on my dad's jet, and I don't know her cell phone number." Her face lit up. "Wait, I wrote it down! It's in my wallet. I'll get it." Minutes later KJ tried her mom's cell phone number and nothing happened, no ringing, no way to leave a message, nothing! "You know, she did keep forgetting to charge her phone."

435

Before leaving the hotel the next day to join Alex, Lindsey tried calling Samantha's cell phone. She had the same result. She looked at her niece, "We'll write her everything as soon as we're settled. We'll send pictures. Honey, we'll be gone for months, though. What do you think? You know what, KJ? If Sam wants you back home or if you want to leave, Alex will figure out how to get you back to Portland. Let's do this!"

"Yes, let's! I really want to do this, Aunt Lindsey.

KJ and her Aunt Lindsey spent the better part of the next six months together. During these months they had some relaxing breaks, but not at the hotel where they met. She worked with her aunt and her Uncle Alex, Dr. Alex Jefferson, doing anything she could to help them. She loved living with them, seeing how wonderful a happy marriage could be.

Hank stood by the door of the crowded bar thinking, *How in the hell am I going to find these two guys?* He continued to look around at everyone. Finally, he saw a man waving him to his table. *I hope this isn't some lunatic.* He walked toward the table and put his hand out to the young man who'd waved him over. "Hi, I'm Hank Kennedy." He shook his hand. "I understand you want to talk with me."

"I'm Hal Thompson and this is Jim Peterson. Thanks for meeting us here. How about a beer?"

"Looks like I'm weathered in for the night. All flights are cancelled. Won't be flying anyone or anything anywhere until morning. A beer sounds great."

Hal went to the bar and asked for three beers and paid for them. He sat back down at the table. "It's jammed in here." He looked at Hank. "You know, I think you may be our man."

"What do you mean?"

Hal handed him a picture of KJ. "Have you ever seen this young lady, Katelyn Jamie Green?" Not wanting to give this guy too much information, he used her original name for now.

Hank's smile faded. "Who are you guys? You know, the man who called me about meeting with you really didn't give me a choice. I'd like a little information about who in the hell you are."

Jim spoke up. "Look Hank, I just met Hal yesterday. He grows on you." He tried to lighten the moment, then added, "Long story short, her mother, Samantha Green, has been ill in a hospital in Ohio. We've been trying to get in touch with Samantha's family, and we weren't able to contact any family member. A few days ago, I learned that Samantha's ex husband, who is Katelyn's dad, and his new family were killed in a plane crash about six months ago. The crash occurred shortly after taking off from the airport here. Katelyn was traveling with her father, his girlfriend, and their baby. All of the bodies were recovered except the baby's and KJ's. That's Katelyn's nickname."

"Yes, I heard about a plane going down. It was a while back. I don't focus on those things. This is my first trip back this way. My partners have been flying this route."

Hal was a bit mad and thought, *Oh good, now we've told this guy everything.* He handed Hank the picture, again. "Do you know her?"

Looking at it he answered, "Yes, I know her, only the name on her passport was Kate J. Cole. She said she liked to be called KJ. I had no idea the downed plane was the plane she'd been on. I've been flying routes closer to home. My wife has been ill, but she's doing fine now." Hank looked at the picture, again. "She wasn't exactly truthful with me. She told me she was traveling with her girlfriend, her girlfriend's older husband, and their baby. I think she said something about a nanny, too." He handed the picture back to Hal and told them about meeting her and flying her to Bamako, Mali. "I made sure she got into a safe cab, paid her fare, and had the driver take her to a good hotel in Bamako. I didn't charge her anything for her flight. I was flying supplies there.

Jim was elated. He patted Hank's shoulder. "Thank God. You saved her life, KJ's alive. I can't imagine how happy this will make her mom. Her mom thinks she died. I've got to call Father Tom."

Hal looked at Jim and said, "Slow down. We haven't found her. Just hold on. Don't make any phone calls, yet. We need to check everything out. We need to find her before you make any phone calls. I'll be right back." He walked out the front door.

Hank wasn't smiling at all. Everything was beginning to sink in. He said, "Let me get this straight. In all of these months, she never contacted her mom? No-one's had any idea where she's been all of this time? That little devil. Had I known she wasn't going to let anyone know where she was, I never would have helped her. She's quite the actress. I actually believed her story about her girlfriend, her friend's older husband, and their baby. The older man was actually her father? I watched her walk over to tell them she wanted to change her plans so they'd have some privacy. At least, that's what I thought she was telling them. And all of these months her mother thought she was dead? My God, why would she put her mother through such agony?"

Hank was getting angrier by the second. "I've got two daughters. If either one of them ever pulls a stunt like this. You know, I'd like to have a few minutes with Miss Cole when we find her." He looked at Jim, "Sorry. God, KJ's lost her father and her baby sister, and she doesn't even know. Her heart will be broken, too. This is a mess." Then he remembered something. "I heard rumors that the plane that crashed might have been sabotaged or something. Some of the fishermen thought they heard a gun shot or something. I don't think that was reported. Just rumors, I guess. Thank God she was with me. But for crying out loud, look what she's put her poor mother through." He shook his head.

Hal came back to the table. "We can't fly out of here until morning, either. Hank, I'd like you to join us, if you can. We could use your help. Do you know the name of the cab driver who took KJ to the hotel? We have to make sure she made it that far."

Jim glared at Hal. "Oh no, you don't. Don't you even try to make it sound like KJ's not alive. Don't do it!"

"Jim, no-one has heard from her for months, no-one. Not her mom, grandparents, not one friend; she hasn't contacted anyone in months. Hopefully, she just wanted time away. We still have to find her. Africa is one huge place to find someone."

Hank, still in disbelief at how she'd lied to him, said, "Look, she didn't talk with me about her family. She just wanted one great adventure before she settled in on the rest of her life. She did tell me she'd graduated from USC with a dual degree in education, and I can't remember what. Anyway, she mentioned she'd missed out on a trip to Africa that most of her college friends took. She thought it was destiny that she met me."

"I still want to call Tom. You know, she probably had a cell phone, not to mention conventional phones. Why hasn't she called her mom even once?" He looked pale, again.

"She was waiting to use a pay phone when she first spoke to me." He decided not to tell them she was going to call her mother. "Maybe she didn't have a cell phone.

Maybe she lost it. Truth is, the phone systems in parts of Africa are pretty bad." Hank decided he really liked these two men. He wasn't sure in the beginning, but now he was. "I'd like to do anything I can to help you. I can definitely be a few days late flying the supplies. I have nothing perishable on board and no medical supplies. I just need to make a few calls." He stood up, "Let's get out of here. I know of a great place to eat just down the street. Look, Jim, I personally put KJ in a cab with a driver I know in Bamako. I told him to drive her to the same hotel where my doctor friends stay. This driver is a good man. I asked him to keep an eye on her, too. She's alive. That little devil is alive, I just feel it."

"Really? You think so? That's what I think, too," Jim said as the color returned to his face.

Hal asked, "Hank, what's this cab driver's name?"

He didn't answer as they piled into the same car Hal had arranged for Jim and himself earlier. It was ready and waiting at the curb. Hank directed the driver to the restaurant, and it was a good one. They ordered their food, and more beers, and talked about KJ.

Jim said, "You know Hank, a very close friend from my childhood is a doctor somewhere in Africa. Actually, KJ's mom and Lindsey, my doctor friend, are very close, like sisters, although they haven't seen each other for many, many years. Lindsey's lived and worked in Africa for most of her adult life. She isn't married and obviously doesn't have children. She just stayed in Africa. "

Hal looked at Jim and said, "You didn't mention the sister to me."

"Well, why would I?"

"No reason you should have, I guess. What's Lindsey's last name?"

"Her name is Lindsey Williams."

He wrote the name down, then asked Hank again, "Hank what's the name of that cab driver who drove KJ to the hotel in Bamako?"

Hank was lost in thought.

"Hank, what's the cab driver's name?"

"I'm sorry, I was thinking about something. There's no way. Never mind. You asked me the cab driver's name? It's Timmy."

"Timmy, what?"

"I don't know his last name. Everyone just calls him Timmy."

"Ok," Hal slid a pen and paper to Hank, "Write down the name of the hotel where he drove her." Hal was mulling over a few things. *Could there be a connection here.* "Did you have a chance to get a place to stay tonight? There's rooms available in our hotel. I'd like you to join us flying to Bamako tomorrow. Hopefully we can leave in the morning. We can stop and pick up anything you need when we leave here."

"Thanks, I'm all set. Here's where I'm staying." He gave Hal a card. "Call me and let me know when we're leaving tomorrow, and I'll be at the airport." Hank swallowed the rest of his beer and got up to leave thinking, *Lindsey is the name of one of my doctor friends. Her last name isn't Williams and the Lindsey I know is married. It's just coincidence.* "See you tomorrow morning," he smiled and left.

Early the next morning they met at the airport in Tenerife for their flight to Bamako in the company jet. Two hours after they landed, Hank caught up with Timmy, the cab driver. They learned that Katelyn Jamie Green, who now is known as Kate J. Cole, stayed in the same hotel Hank told her to use. It didn't take Hal long to find out the rest. He showed the hotel concierge KJ's picture. He further explained that her mother was ill and that they needed to find her. Seconds later he, Jim, and Hank knew for certain that she'd stayed in this hotel for a few nights about six months earlier. The concierge told them, that to his amazement, Miss Cole knew Dr. Lindsey Jefferson, who many on the hotel staff hold in high esteem. The concierge excitedly said, "Dr. Lindsey was so happy that she saw Miss Kate eating in the dining room. She told me and others that Miss Kate was her niece and was grateful Miss Kate had not arrived a few days later because they never would have met one and other."

The concierge waved for another employee to take over for him, and he walked Hal, Jim, and Hank to the front desk. He continued, "The next thing we knew, Dr. Lindsey asked her niece to go with her to spend the next several months helping them in villages deep within Mali. Miss Kate was happy and wanted to go. We have her suitcase in storage here along with mail and other things we keep for the doctors who stay with us. The doctors use our hotel's mail service. We hold mail and send mail at their request. Miss Kate asked me if we could mail a letter for her, but she must have forgotten because when they left ,she didn't leave any mail." He looked something up in a file drawer, took out a file, and wrote down the name of the village where Dr. Lindsey, Dr. Alex Jefferson, and other doctors stay at times. "Here, if they aren't in this village, perhaps the doctors who are there will know Dr. Lindsey's and Miss Kate's current location."

"Thank you," Hal said.

Jim was elated, "I just can't imagine the chances of this happening. Lindsey found KJ. He looked at Hal, "Lindsey's who I told you about. I didn't know that she'd gotten married." He stopped talking and thought, *I wonder if Kate and Father Tom knew?*

Hank said, "You aren't going to believe this, but Lindsey and Alex are my doctor friends. My wife and I attended their wedding many years ago. It really is a small world."

They spent the night at the hotel and left for the airport early the next morning. Hal arranged for a flight and a guide to land them as close as possible to the village the concierge had written down.

Once they landed, several children ran toward them happily calling, "Hello! Hello!"

Their guide spoke to the children and the three men only understood one word he said, "English."

One little boy happily answered, "Me!"

Hal smiled at this little boy and called out, "Hello, I'm Hal. What's your name?"

The little boy, about five or six years old, happily answered, "I'm Pete! We hear you coming. We like candy. You have candy?"

"Sure, we have candy." He looked at Hank understanding, now, why he had a bag of candy with him. "We need you to help us. Have you seen doctors from America? We need to find them, before we have candy. Do you know where the doctors are?"

The little boy's smile grew even bigger, "Yes, I know. I show you." He began walking very quickly. The rest of the children, Jim, Hank, Hal, and their guide quickly followed.

About twenty minutes later, Lindsey and Jim were looking at each other in complete amazement. Lindsey had spent time with him when she'd visited her mom in Bay Village almost a year ago and was shocked seeing him, here, in this remote African village. In absolute disbelief she said, "Oh my God, Jim, what are you doing here," and hugged him. "I can't believe I'm looking at you!" They hugged again.

Then her arms were around Hank. "We haven't seen you for months. How's Peg doing? I hear she's doing much better now."

"Peg's doing great, thanks. I've missed you guys."

Alex walked near his wife with a big smile and shook Hank's hand, then gave him a hug. "Great to see you, man."

Lindsey introduced Jim, "Alex, this is Jim Peterson, my dear friend I've told you so much about. I just can't believe he's here!"

"Jim, this is my husband, Alex." She immediately thought, *Opps!*

They shook hands as Alex thought, *I'm pretty sure you haven't heard about me!* He said, "Jim, I feel as though I know you."

Jim couldn't believe Lindsey hadn't ever mentioned in letters or when she was home recently that she was married. He looked at her a second or two and then at Alex, thinking, *I haven't heard a thing about you!* "Glad meeting you, Alex."

Then he realized no-one knew Hal. "Everyone, this is Hal Thompson, the great man who found you here."

Lindsey, still thinking about the fact that no-one from home knew she was married, took hold of Jim's hand. "I've gotten word that my mom died. She didn't want me returning home for her funeral. You, of all people, must know that. I hope you haven't come all this way to tell me about my mom."

As she heard her Aunt speaking, KJ walked out of the permanent camp tent thinking, *I have a feeling this is all about me.* She put her arm around her aunt and looked at Hank.

He smiled at KJ as she stood beside Lindsey, but he didn't speak. Neither did Jim.

Lindsey said, "Oh my God, Jim, you'll never believe! Do you recognize this face? Isn't she amazing? This is Sammy's daughter, KJ."

A small smile crossed his face, and he quietly said, "Hi, KJ. You sure look just like your mom." He gently shook her hand. Then he said, "Hal helped me find you, honey. Is there a place we could all go and sit down?"

Their guide and all of the children except Pete were someplace enjoying the candy Hank gave them. Pete was holding his candy and Jim noticed he seemed glued to Alex's side. Alex led them into the large tent where everyone found a place to sit. Lindsey silently wondered, *What's going on?*

Jim's face looked serious as he looked at Lindsey and then only at KJ. "I have some sad things to tell you, KJ." He told her about the plane that crashed six months earlier. "I'm so sorry."

KJ stood up and Lindsey did, too. Lindsey wrapped her arms around her. Alex remained sitting looking down at the ground and little Pete mimicked him. It was quiet.

Jim decided he should tell KJ and Lindsey the rest. "KJ, your mom is in the hospital. She's doing much, much better, now. She's been in the hospital since Kate's funeral, but very recently she's really doing better. We've been trying to find you and your father to tell you about your mom and to get her medical history. She wouldn't give the doctor that information and then she couldn't. Honey, I'm telling you the truth. Your mom is going to be fine. She'll be the happiest person on earth when she sees you."

Only several seconds passed, but it seemed much longer. KJ wasn't crying. She looked at Jim and repeated everything he'd told her, "So, you're telling me that my dad and baby sister died in a plane crash about six months ago and so did, and so did Annie. And my mom thinks I was in that plane and died, too. And my mom has been very ill in the hospital in the same town where all of you grew up?"

"Your mom was taken to the hospital the same day as Kate's funeral."

"And she's recently doing better, but for months my mom thought that I was dead, too. Oh God, I can't imagine. We love each other so much." Her legs gave way.

Alex stood up and caught her. He put his arms around her as she began crying. He held her tight until her legs supported her less, and they both sat down next to Pete. Lindsey stood silently. No-one spoke.

It seemed longer, but a few minutes later KJ asked, "Could you and I go outside, Uncle Alex? I need air."

They walked out as she leaned against him, and he secured her steps. Little Pete followed them. Jim got up, hugged Lindsey, "We miss your mom." Then told her more about Sammy's health. He didn't ask about her marriage. They stayed in the tent.

After about ten minutes, Alex, KJ, and Pete came back. KJ's eyes and nose were red from crying. She looked at Jim and quietly said, "Jim, I've written my mom a ton of letters. I've told her all about Aunt Lindsey finding me. I've told her what we're doing here and that I'll be home within a year. I'm so happy here, helping Lindsey and Alex."

446

Lindsey spoke up, "We haven't gotten any letters here. Our mail is being held at our hotel in Bamako. I've written Sammy and my mom, too. I've told them to write us, but that we probably wouldn't be reading their letters until we return to the hotel."

KJ looked at Lindsey, "My mom would have figured out some way to get word to me that my dad and my baby sister," tears rolled down her cheeks, and she wiped them away, "were killed in a crash, if she'd gotten letters from me. I mean just like your priest, Father Tom, got word to you about your mom."

"Honey, I think it was pure luck that his telegram made it to us. We've been setting up camps and taking them down in so many different remote locations these last months. With other small groups of doctors doing the same, I really don't know how that telegram found us."

Lindsey looked at Hal, Hank, and Jim, "We only returned here a day ago. This is a place to take a break, and we've been here with KJ several times these past months. Over the years, Alex and I have stayed here many times, but there are other places set up just like this. In two days we'll be leaving and other doctors will rest here. It's lucky that you came here looking for us today." She took hold of KJ's hand. "A few days earlier or later, we wouldn't have been here."

Jim answered, "We really lucked out, thank God. KJ, your mom's doing better now, but a few weeks ago we were very worried, and the doctor needed her medical history. I went to Portland to her house to find your dad and you. I looked for phone books trying to find your and your dad's cellular phone numbers. I kind of thought after I looked around your house that your parents might be separated." He paused a second, "Anyway, I didn't see any mail from you at your house in Portland, no letters at all. I did find some phone books, and I called every R and Robert Green listed. Eventually, days after I returned home, an older lady from Santa Barbara, who used to be married to your dad's uncle, returned my phone call. She told me she knew your dad as James not Rob. I'll tell you about her later."

KJ shook her head understanding, "Yes, only my mom calls him Rob. Everyone else calls him James." She

447

looked down, "I mean called." In a stronger voice she asked, "But at my mom's house in Portland, you didn't find any letters from us?"

"No, I didn't."

KJ and Lindsey looked at little Pete and Lindsey said, "We've given you lots of letters to mail." He moved a little behind Alex and leaned against him. "We told you to take good care of them. We're not mad at you. You took them to a mail drop, right? You told us you'd take good care of them. What did you do with the letters?"

Alex picked Pete up. "Now, hold on, honey. We can't pin this whole thing on this little guy."

KJ looked at him, "Pete, where are our letters, our papers that we give you to mail?"

He put his hands on Alex' shoulders and looked at him. "I show you, Dr. Alex. I take good care, like you tell me." Pete wiggled out of Alex' strong arms, took hold of his hand, and pulled him toward the tent doorway.

"We'll be back soon, I hope," Alex turned and said.

KJ finally spoke to Hank. "I'm sorry I lied to you. I just needed to get away from both of my parents for a while. I didn't know I'd find Aunt Lindsey in Africa. I wasn't planning on staying away long. I can't imagine that my dad has died and my baby sister, Jessica, I can't. Even Annie, I didn't really want her dead. I guess I said I did a few times." Tears started forming in her eyes. "I didn't mean it. My dad was a good dad. He could be very, very difficult and," she couldn't find the right word and changed her thought, "He was a good dad, though. He and I still had so much to work through. Everything was such a mess. My sweet baby sister," She began crying, again. This time she was shaking. "Aunt Linds, I'm freezing."

Lindsey felt her forehead. "Honey, lay down for a few minutes." Hank helped her and Lindsey covered her and gave her some Advil and water. "Just rest a little while."

"Lying down is good, but stay with me. Hank, is Peg really ok?"

"Yes, she really is doing fine, now," Hank answered. "Honey, I believe you wrote to your mom. I understand that you were really in the middle of your mom's and dad's problems. I can't imagine what that was like. I'm so sorry about your dad and sister. I wish we could change what

448

happened, but we can't. Thank God we talked at the airport, and you came with me. KJ, think of your mom's happiness when she learns you're alive."

Jim spoke up, "Sammy will be the happiest person on earth when she sees you."

"You, my mother, Aunt Lindsey, Aunt Karen, and Lindsey's first husband, Bobby, grew up together, right? My mom hasn't told me a lot about her life in Ohio, but my aunt's been telling me. My mom's said how much she loves Kate, Aunt Karen, Aunt Lindsey and Father Tom. She's told me things, just not," *Oh gosh, stop talking,* she thought.

"Just not much about me," Jim said with a slight smile. "Honey, that's understandable, don't you think?"

"I need to get to Ohio to be with my mom."

"I'd like to go home now, too," Lindsey unexpectedly announced. "I want to be with Sammy. Karen, Sammy, and I haven't been together for years. Considering all of the people we've helped in Africa, my sister needs us, now. KJ, I want to be a part of your life. It's a miracle we found each other here. You've become precious to Alex and me. Your Uncle is ready to leave. We've been talking about it. He wants time with his family, too." She watched Alex and Pete duck down as they returned. Alex had Pete up on his shoulders and Pete was holding a box. She smiled and continued, "Alex has missed so many family reunions, births of nieces and nephews, and now some of his nieces and nephews are going to be parents. He wants to be there. He wants to spend time with his parents and family. Time is getting more precious." She smiled a second, "I'm so glad I was with my mom earlier in the year. I should have been home with her these last few years. And Alex should have come home with me. I've been so foolish. My mom and Alex would've loved each other. I don't know what I was thinking."

Alex interrupted, "Until Pete helped us with our mail, your mom received letters from me. Honey, I did know and love your mom. My mother contacted Kate shortly before our marriage." He put Pete down, pulled his duffle bag from under their bed, got out his mother's string-secured stack of letters, and handed them to her. "We wrote to each other through my mom. Your mom wrote to

449

me," he smiled, "sending her letters to my mom. Mom put my letters in another envelope and addressed them to me at our hotel in Bamako. I did the same thing. I sent letters from Bamako to my mom that I wrote to Kate, and she forwarded them. Honey, our parents knew and loved one and other, too. They visited each other and stayed in each other's homes. Your mom saw pictures of our wedding, of us working, places we've traveled. I sent the pictures home to my parents, and they made sure Kate saw them, too. I bet my mom and dad were at Kate's funeral. I figured when the time was right, I'd tell you. This sure seems like the right time."

Lindsey stood there with tears streaming from her eyes, "Thank you, Alex."

He said, "Now Pete, give Dr. Lindsey and Miss KJ your box."

Lindsey and KJ opened the box, looked through it, and saw every letter they and Alex had written home since KJ was with them.

Pete beamed at both of them saying, "See? I do what you say. I take care of papers. See? When you tell me you never come back, I give you back papers. You never tell me you never come back. So I keep them safe."

Alex added, "His mother told me he looked in this box every day. He kept our letters safe and made sure no one took them. She proudly told me, 'He take good care of doctor's papers." He smiled at him and said, "Apparently, as simple as it is to us, Pete and his family don't know about mail drops. This little guy kept his promise. He took good care, great care, actually."

KJ smiled at Pete as she thought, *Such a simple thing.* She gave him a big hug.

A few hours later Jim, Hank, the guide, and Hal returned to Bamako.

Alex, Lindsey, and KJ spent the rest of this day and most of the next day organizing things. The two doctors gave notice that they were immediately returning to the states. When everything was done, Alex and KJ took Pete and his mother to a mail drop and explained what it was. They told them that they and other friends from the United States would be mailing them packages telling Pete to begin looking, after ten days, at this location for mail. KJ gave him thirty envelopes with correct postage that already had Kate's home address. She told him to take the envelopes home and put them in the box where he kept their letters, doctor's papers. She said, "Pete, when you get mail from us, go home and draw us a picture or write us, put your drawing in one of these envelopes, and mail it to us from this mail drop. This way we'll stay friends! We'll send you more envelopes, too."

Late the next day Alex, Lindsey, and KJ boarded the plane Hal arranged to fly them to Bamako. Arriving, they saw Hal's crew members waiting to transfer their duffle bags and other belongings to the company jet that would take them to Cleveland, Ohio. One crew member told them, "We have the things you stored at the hotel already on board, too. I'll walk you to the car that's waiting to take you to the hotel." When the opportunity came, he quietly told KJ that a farewell for the doctors had gathered at the hotel.

Stepping into the lobby, Lindsey and Alex were surprised by many of their friends from the hotel and few shops and restaurants they'd frequented over the years. Jim, Hal, Hank, and KJ were standing and clapping with them. The hotel concierge happily arranged this small celebration serving drinks and appetizers. It was a happy send off.

After Lindsey, Alex, KJ, Jim, and Hal were on the company jet for about an hour, Jim called Father Tom again. "We have KJ and a surprise on board, and we're heading home. We'll see you tomorrow afternoon. Tom, thanks for letting me be the one to tell Sammy about KJ. I'm glad you suggested it when we talked yesterday. See you soon."

KJ sat looking through the jet window. *I can't comprehend all that has happened. I'm so excited to see my mom, and I can't imagine she thought I was gone. I can't imagine that sweet Jessica won't grow up and that I'll never see her or my father again. It seems wrong to feel happy about my mom. I can't seem to feel the pain in losing my baby sister and father.* She continued to look out. *This sky is so beautiful, so endless, so peaceful. I think I really understand the idea of taking one day at a time. Right now I should consider my mom. She'll be so happy.* Tears spilled down her cheeks.

Jim sat down beside her and said, "I'll do anything to help you."

She leaned against his shoulder. "Thank you for finding me."

I looked around my hospital room and couldn't stop looking at the seasonal flower arrangements. Feeling a little happy that Christmas was near, surprised me. Way before hearing about Kate, I couldn't even imagine Thanksgiving or this Christmas. I couldn't imagine anything. But, now, with the doctors and Father Tom helping me face things that broke my heart, the burden's beginning to lift. My heart and mind are appreciating precious moments in front of me. Weeks ago I didn't have any hope for the future. Now, things are seemingly better. Looking around, again, at the beautiful holiday flowers I thought about the kind, sweet love that Christmas brings forth and the wonderful hope.

Hearing Father Tom's and Jim's voices, I sat up straighter in my chair and quickly fluffed my hair with my hands. They walked in and Father Tom cheerfully said, "Here he is!"

Jim took hold of my hand a few seconds. "I'm so glad you're doing much better."

"Before he could say anything more, I said, "I am doing better." I tried kidding around, "It's a good thing it was your sister you needed to be with, or I might be slightly mad at you for bolting out on me this time!" Immediately I thought, *I wish I could take that sentence back. Stupid, stupid!*

He looked at me a second, then smiled and said, "Yes, we probably never need to mention the word 'bolt' again. Ugly word!"

"Your flowers are beautiful, thank you." Jim looked a little surprised as I changed the subject, and we both looked at the flowers. His eyes met Father's and I saw Father Tom wink. I asked, "Is your sister ok?"

"Sammy, I have a beautiful story to tell you." As he spoke, Father Tom walked out into the corridor. "You are the most precious person, and it's time you feel the most perfect joy. Your heart has been broken more than once, but as sad as you've ever been, the moment just ahead will fill your heart with happiness you will hold forever."

And then I saw the most amazing sight. My beautiful daughter was standing in the doorway. I looked around a second. I thought maybe I was dreaming, still, or again.

Jim took hold of my hand and kissed it. "Honey, this is real." He went to KJ, walked with her toward me, and put her hand in mine.

I heard, "Mom? Mom, I'm here safe and sound."

And instantly those words jumped in my heart. I could see my mom and dad walking away in the woods toward that amazing light and hearing my mom, *"Way ahead, can you see it, Jack? She'll be safe and sound."*

Tears filled my eyes. "KJ?" I could feel her hand holding mine tight, and we were standing. Then I was hugging her and looking into her beautiful eyes making so sure I was holding my daughter. "KJ, I thought you were gone," I whispered and began crying the happiest tears. I couldn't stop looking at her sweet face, just to be absolutely sure. I held her tight. I hugged her and her arms held and hugged me. "Thank You, God, thank You," The words quietly spilled out, and I looked at her again.

At the doorway I saw that several nurses, Jane, and Dr. Jameson were wiping away tears as they all were watching and smiling. Immediately my eyes found my daughter's sweet face, again, and I asked, "KJ, are you all right? Have you been hurt or sick? Honey, where have you been all of these months? Let me just look at you. You're here, you're back. You're really here with me." I hugged her, again. "Honey, where have you been?"

"Mom, I'm so sorry about all of this. I thought you knew. I've been in Africa. I couldn't stay on that vacation with them. Just like you told me, I didn't want to be there. I had an opportunity to leave their vacation, and I took it. I made dad think I was still on his plane. I left my phone behind. I snuck off and got on a plane going to Mali. I left dad a note telling him I'd stay safe and let you know where I was. I wrote you lots of letters. My letters were never mailed. I'll tell you everything, Mom, later. I love you. I'm so sorry about everything." Tears filled her eyes.

"Honey, everything is good, now. Everything is wonderful, now. You're here and you're safe. Did Jim find you?" I looked at him.

"Mom, you'll never guess who found me. She's here, too."

KJ slipped out of my arms and walked into the hallway. With the biggest smiles, Lindsey and KJ walked in together with a handsome, smiling man walking behind them.

"Oh my gosh, Lindsey!" I hurried to hug her. "Lindsey, you're back, too." KJ, Linds, and I were hugging and crying and laughing. I saw and heard Jim, Father Tom, and the man who came in with Lindsey laughing and talking, too, as though they knew one and other.

I heard Father Tom, "Alex, it's wonderful to meet you in person. This is truly a day of days."

"Sammy," Lindsey said, "meet my husband, Dr. Alex Jefferson. We've been married for years and years."

Questions flooded me, but I held them inside. "Alex, I'm so happy to meet you." I hugged him.

He gently hugged me. "We took great care of your beautiful daughter these past six or so months. She's an amazing person. I couldn't have a sweeter niece."

"Yes, you're KJ's uncle." I was glad Alex was right there because I felt a little dizzy, and he steadied me in his strong arms.

"Maybe we should have you sit down." He walked me to the chair.

Dr. Jameson walked in. He smiled at everyone while saying, "I'm just going to do my daily check. Could you all go to the solarium for just a few minutes?"

I told Dr. Jameson, "This is my precious daughter, KJ Cole, and she is staying in here with me."

"KJ, I've never been happier to meet someone." He looked at her and then back at me, "Of course she's staying in here!" He put the thermometer in my mouth. "I think your mom will be leaving here as soon as tomorrow."

In short minutes KJ and I walked to the solarium. Lots of balloons, and snacks, and smiling nurses greeted us. KJ, Lindsey, and Alex talked with me non-stop. Father Tom, Jim, and I listened and laughed at their stories.

And just like that, I was surrounded with everyone and everything I'd ever loved and hoped to have.

Two days later Jim took me home to Kate's. As we drove through Bay Village passed the schools, Cahoon Park, city hall, the shopping center; I realized I still loved this place. When we opened the front door, a lighted Christmas tree with Kate's gleaming ornaments, warmth from the fire in the fireplace, and the aroma of sugary, buttery, baking cookies welcomed us. "Jim, this is perfect."

My KJ greeted us with hugs and Lindsey was right behind her. Alex happily took our coats while Jim carried my suitcase to the bedroom Kate and Art had made mine. I walked with Linds and KJ to the kitchen and saw Karen and Phillip sitting at the table smiling huge smiles. In a split second Karen was hugging me, and I began crying more happy tears.

"We had a bit of trouble getting a flight out of Italy, or we'd have been here sooner. Sammy, I've missed you so much," Karen hugged me so tight. "I'm so glad we're all together. This will be a wonderful Christmas. It's been wonderful seeing KJ. She's perfect and looks just like you. We love her, Sam." Then she whispered, "I had no idea what was going on." Tears formed in her eyes.

"It's all much better, now, much better. Everything is perfect, now," I told her, and Lindsey joined in our hug.

Karen happily stated, "Our kids and grand kids are coming here for Christmas. You'll love them, you guys. They're full of energy."

Lindsey laughed, "Can't wait to see them!"

"Phillip hugged me and said, "Hey, the rest of these sugar cookies aren't going to bake themselves." Seeing a bowl of cookie dough waiting to be tasted and rolled flat for the cookie cutters, I thought, *Home, this is everything that matters. Dear God, thank You.*

It seemed as though Alex had lived in this house forever. He made sure everyone had drinks, hot, cold, whatever. Soon Father Tom was walking in the side door just like old times, only now he hollered, "Lindsey, Linds." Before we knew it, Father Tom, Jim, Phillip, and Alex were heading down the basement for a game of pool. Kate's wonderful house was full of happy conversation and love, still. And, instead of feeling that I'd missed so many years, I felt pure happiness for this very day.

Alex came upstairs asking if he could use the oven yet. "I've just told Father Tom, Phillip, and Jim that they are about to experience the best pizza ever."

Linds backed him up, "It's true. Hands down, the best pizza I've ever eaten. Then she added, "Guess who'll be here soon to have dinner with us? Bette and her husband, Ron. I ran into her when we picked up your things from the Holsten Inn, Sammy."

"That's wonderful," I smiled

We made a big salad and sat around the dining room table, indeed, eating the best pizza ever. There were beers, and bottles of wine, and coke a cola, and Christmas cookies. Lindsey and Alex announced that they'd decided to stay and live in Bay Village in this very house. They happily told us about some renovations they hoped to do. Alex said, "I know my dad and mom have stayed here while visiting Kate, so my dad might have some ideas. He's remodeled a lot of homes in Georgia."

I looked at the two of them and thought how beautiful life is. Karen and Phillip joined in with remodeling ideas. And I smiled knowing that I wanted to live in Bay Village, again, too, very near my sister, Lindsey.

Later that night after Lindsey and Alex went to bed in Lindsey's old bedroom, KJ went to bed in Kate's bedroom, and Phillip and Karen left for the Holsten Inn; I sat alone at Kate's kitchen table. I turned the volume low on Kate's radio and heard the oldies station playing The Dixie Cups "Chapel of Love." I listened, aware of the music, and closed my eyes picturing the very first time my mom, Kate, Grand, Karen, Linds, and I sat here at our tea party. I thought how special that day was, and tears filled my eyes.

There was a soft knock at the back door. I got up and saw Jim's smiling face through one of the four windows in the door. He walked in and said, "Sammy, why are you crying? What's wrong?" He hugged me and gently rubbed my back.

"If God told me I could have my childhood back, I'd grow up with every one of you again. I loved growing up here. I loved you. I don't know what I was thinking when I left. My life never got messed up until I left here." Words poured out of me, "When I was in the hospital, I remembered many things that happened while we were growing up, and I remembered wonderful things I learned from Kate and Grand. I was ready to face that I'd lost KJ. But she was alive, you brought her back to me. You found her and gave me everything again. When we were growing up, we were so lucky. Why didn't I realize that? All of these years, why didn't I appreciate how special our childhood was? Why did I run away? Why did I leave you?"

"You and I loved each other, but the timing was off. Don't question any of it. I loved you, and then I loved Liz. You have your beautiful daughter because of Rob. Honey, I'm so glad we found KJ with Lindsey, but she would have come home eventually."

"Well, maybe not. Look how long Linds stayed in Africa."

"You got me there." He took hold of my hands. "Sammy, everything that's happening, now, is just right. A very special person recently told me that you're as young as you act. I guess I'm, let's call it mature, but I feel damn young. I love you with all of my heart. Marry me, Sammy. We're right for each other now."

I threw my arms around him. "I thought you'd probably given up on that idea. Yes, with all of my heart, yes!"

Jim gently removed my arms from around his neck. He took a small box out of his jacket pocket and opened it up for me to see. The ring in the box was gorgeous, yet I know my smile slipped a little.

"What's wrong?"

"Nothing, it's beautiful," I looked up at him.

He put his hand in his pocket, and he held the ring that once belonged to his grandmother. "Would you rather have this one?"

"Yes, this one! This is the ring I love and want." He slipped it on my finger. "I love you. I've never stopped loving you." I hugged him so close. Then, very quietly, I was moving him toward and into my bedroom, very quietly closing the door.

"What would Kate say about this?" Jim whispered and laughed.

I whispered back, "She'd say, 'Do it already, with my blessing!"

On the Saturday before New Year's Eve, our closest friends and family gathered in St. Joseph Chapel for Lindsey's and my double Wedding Mass. Alex and Linds told Jim and I that they wanted to be married within the Church. "Let's all get married at the same time! Our family is all here, and we can ask KJ and Karen to be our maid and matron of honors," I said. Lindsey loved the idea.

Bette was so happy about our weddings. We asked her if we could rent the private dining room for our reception. "Absolutely! Your timing couldn't be better. A party just cancelled that room yesterday. Tell me everything you want, and I'll make it happen."

Alex' mom, Virginia, arrived two days ahead of his dad and their family, and Karen's in-laws also came. Virginia, her husband, and the Avenston's, all were near or over eighty years old, and had more energy than us. We had so much fun with them. Virginia and Roslyn became fast friends and helped Karen, KJ, and Bette. Then they told Lindsey and me what to do.

The early morning of our wedding day, John surprised his brother, Father Tom, by ringing the rectory doorbell at five-thirty a.m. and handing him his newspaper. He and Jen had flown in on the private jet bringing Hal, Isabelle Green, and Dianne with them.   Jimmy and I had asked Hal to be our best man and KJ our maid of honor. Lindsey and Alex asked Karen and Phillip.

After the chapel filled with family and friends, the eight of us walked two by two from the side chapel door to the altar steps. Hal and KJ separated for KJ to be next to me and for Hal to stand beside Jim. Karen and Phillip did the same with Lindsey and Alex. As we looked at the pews, we couldn't stop smiling and chatting. We were amazed so many, given very short notice, were able to be with us on our wedding day. With so much joy, we looked at the pews whispering about who we were seeing. I pointed, "Look you guys, Pam and Ken Jones are here. Karen, look, that must be little Tom, with his wife and children, Pam's grandchildren. Pam's granddaughter just climbed on her lap."

Linds whispered, "KJ, there's Hank and Peg with their two daughters. Sammy, I can't wait for you guys to meet Hank. KJ, do you see him?"

We tried not to laugh as we watched Virginia, sitting in the front pew next to Alex' dad, trying to get Alex' nieces and nephews, who were sitting behind her, to sit still. She reached her arms to one of her grandsons, and he happily put his arms out to sit on her lap. He waved at Alex.

Jim squeezed my hand and whispered, "See that older lady, silver hair and blue dress with the red print scarf? That's Isabelle, and her daughter, Dianne, is here, too. I can't wait for Isabelle to meet you. See her? She's waving to us."

I smiled and waved back saying, "Yes, and there's Dr. Jameson with Jane, my favorite nurse. They're sitting near them."

We saw Father Tom smiling, standing near the arched doors with two altar girls waiting to walk the aisle to the altar. I whispered to Linds and Karen, "We couldn't help Father Tom serve Mass when we were kids."

"That's probably a good thing," Alex, Jim, and Phillip answered at the same time.

Father said the most perfect Mass for the four of us. He remembered Kate. "Our dear Kate is throwing a party in Heaven celebrating this day. She loves her girls and granddaughter," he smiled at KJ, "with all of her heart." His eyes met Lindsey's, mine, and Karen's. "She, Grand, and Joan lovingly raised you to live and celebrate your own lives and to come home and have this very day. Yes, they're preparing a feast with the glory of God. Art, Jack, Brice, and Frank are following their orders, and Heaven's going to party tonight!" Everyone laughed and then began clapping. "And now, with the grace of God, I present Lindsey and Alex Jefferson and Samantha and Jim Peterson. Two couples married in the name of the Father and of the Son and of the Holy Spirit, AMEN!"

The nine of us stepped from the altar, down the aisle to waiting cars that took us to the Holsten Inn. Bette arranged a great dinner party celebration at her beautiful Inn. She and Jimmy watched me, making sure I wasn't over doing it. I rested for a while, then we laughed and danced until the wee hours. Bette surprised everyone with a buffet breakfast at two am. Then almost everyone who attended our celebration went to their rooms.

Late in this night that was becoming a new day, Lindsey sat alone at her mom's kitchen table. She was certain about what she was experiencing, although she hadn't experienced it since her precious dream vanished. Her house was so quiet as she let the words slip through her mind. *'Bobby, are you here? This is the very first time since so many, many years ago. Bobby, I have felt you with me every minute of this day. Please, are you here?'* She slowly turned her head toward her mom's back door and saw Bobby standing on the steps smiling his beautiful smile. She picked up her locket gently resting on her chest and held it. *'I love you always and forever,'* she thought.

'Always and forever, I love you, too.'

'You were right. I had so much ahead.'

'You still do, Dr. Lindsey, you still do. I'm happy for you, Linds. Always and forever, honey.' Bobby's smile encompassed her soul.

Alex walked into the kitchen. "Here you are, sweetheart. Everything all right?"

"Yes, everything's perfect." She stood up and hugged her husband. She looked toward the back door and saw her Bobby smiling, and then he slowly faded from her eyes.

"Alex, I love you so much. We're about to celebrate our first New Year's Eve in Bay Village. Bette has invited all of us to her and Ron's party at the Inn."

In this very late December night or very early morning, Lindsey stood in her mom's wonderful kitchen with her husband's strong arms holding her tight. Samantha slept soundly in her old bedroom wrapped in her Jimmy's arms. In the rec room Art made down in his basement so many years ago, KJ and Hal sat side by side eating popcorn while watching *Sleepless in Seattle*. Karen and Phillip along with their sons, and daughter-in-laws, and their grandchildren; were in their beds in three attached suites at the Holsten Inn where lots of whispering and giggling filled their rooms.

In this very late night, Father Thomas Patrick Brown knelt down beside his bed and thanked God for everyone in his family and for all of their blessings.

Gifts are always near.

Hal had his arm around KJ as she rested her head on his shoulder. He'd tuned out of *Sleepless in Seattle*. An uneasy feeling he'd been trying hard to dismiss filled his thoughts again. He reached for more popcorn thinking, *None of it seems right, none of it: The older Green's, KJ's grandparents, lacking emotion concerning the deaths of their family members and now denying KJ is alive. Lucas Burkley's emotional reaction concerning his daughter's, Anne Nichol's, and his granddaughter's deaths. The quick investigation concerning the jet crash. The Green's organized crime connection. There's so much more to all of this.*

KJ looked at him, "What's wrong?"

The Million Star Hotel in this story is fictional.

The Holsten Inn in Bay Village is fictional. It does not exist. Although, there was a hotel on the lake in Bay Village at one time.

St. Joseph Church, Chapel, school, and cemetery in this story are made up. They do not exist.

Sacred Heart Hospital in this story is made up. It does not exist.

This story and all characters are from my imagination. Names used were popular in the nineteen-fifties and nineteen-sixties. They do not represent any person living or dead. The characters in this book do not and have not existed.

This story is fiction.

Made in the USA
Middletown, DE
24 May 2021